THE
KILLING
GROUNDS

JACK FORD

ONE PLACE. MANY STORIES

This novel is entirely a work of fiction. The names, characters and incidents portrayed in it are the work of the author's imagination. Any resemblance to actual persons, living or dead, events or localities is entirely coincidental.

HQ
An imprint of HarperCollins*Publishers* Ltd.
1 London Bridge Street
London SE1 9GF

This edition 2017

1
First published in Great Britain by
HQ, an imprint of HarperCollins*Publishers* Ltd. 2017

ISBN: 978-0-00-820307-8

Printed and bound by
CPI Group, Croydon CR0 4YY

For Darley Anderson, my hero – the Alex Ferguson
of the literary world.
Forever love, Jx

'It is estimated that between 26.4 million and 36 million people abuse opioids worldwide, with an estimated 2.5 million people in the United States abusing prescription opioids'

- US Centers for Disease Control and Prevention

'You said I killed you – haunt me then. The murdered do haunt their murderers. I believe I know that ghosts have wandered the earth. Be with me always, take any form, drive me mad. Only do not leave me in this abyss, where I cannot find you!'

- Emily Brontë – Wuthering Heights

Seven years ago

Kenya's northern coast – 30 miles south of
the Somali border

How long does it take a man to realize his life is going to change forever? For Thomas J. Cooper it was barely a moment. Just a flicker of a stare to trace the angles of dark stretching shadows against the oak cabin walls. The slightest of turns towards the fluctuating sounds of the lapping waves. And that was all. Yet it told him everything he needed to know… They were in trouble.

'Jackson…! Jackson…! What the hell…!'

Knocking over the glass of iced lemonade, Cooper scrambled up from the cream leather recliner he'd been asleep on. Took the yacht's wood and chrome stairs three at a time. Charging along the highly polished deck of the sleek, white vessel. Cursing to himself as he slipped on the wet.

Bolting forward, he spotted the tall, sun-drenched figure of Jackson leaning against the bow rails. A bottle of whiskey in hand. A grin on his face. And a half cut look in his eye.

'Hey Coop, is this the life or what? Nothing but open waters. Reckon I should get myself a job on the high seas…'

Cooper could see he was drunk. And God knows, it was the last thing he needed.

He watched Jackson step on to the top rails of the yacht.

Take the last slug of whiskey.

Throw the bottle casually into the sea.

Stretched out his arms shouting loudly. Forcing his slurred

words to rise high above the sound of the sea. 'Name the film, Coop… But I'll give you a clue… *I'm king of the world*!'

But Cooper said nothing. Instead, he instinctively squinted up at the African skies.

Slipped off his watch to lie it flat on his palm.

Lined up the hour hand to point at the sun.

Giving him a crude idea of the direction they were sailing in.

And the knot in his stomach told him it was as he'd feared. North. They were heading north.

Swaying precariously on the bow rails, Jackson didn't sense or notice or care or see or feel Cooper's alarm. 'Oh come on man, you gotta know. Coop, it's easy… *Titanic*. Even my dog could've got that one. Maybe I make a better Rose though. What do you think? Can you see me playing opposite DiCaprio…? *I love you Jack. I love you. Never let me go!*'

'*Get* the hell down! Now!'

Cooper yanked on Jackson's arm. Hard. Real hard. Dragging him to the safety of the deck. And with the smell of alcohol heavy on his breath and a look of indignation he said, 'Hey! What's got up your nose Coop? All that… '

'Listen to me… ' Cooper stopped suddenly as a cold uneasiness came over him like a sudden temperature drop. His eyes darting across the cerulean sea. 'Jackson, I need you to start turning the boat round. We're going to have to jibe her, but we gotta to do it fast.'

Jackson stared at him in astonishment. 'Jibe? You're crazy. The crosswind's too strong to try to turn downwind. You'll capsize her for sure.'

'What's going on?' Ellie Granger, Cooper's long-term girlfriend, stood bleary eyed behind them. She asked the same question which was on Jackson's lips.

Cooper turned to her. And although his words were quickly spoken, he made sure they held warmth. He said, 'Hey baby, look there's no need to panic, but we're going to have to turn the boat round. We've got to get back to Lamu as quickly as we can.'

She pushed her blond hair out of her big blue eyes and looked around puzzled and said, 'I don't get it. How long have I been asleep, Tom? I thought we were anchored up?'

Giving a side-glance to Jackson, Cooper spoke more to himself than her. 'So did I, honey, so did I.'

Upon which his attention snapped back to Jackson. He barked out orders. Short. Sharp and precise. 'Start pulling in the main sheet, I'll come and help you but I've got to go and radio in our position.'

A veil of fear crossed Ellie's face. She'd known Cooper since high school. Childhood sweethearts. Inseparable from the very first day. Fifteen years ago. Give or take a month. Yet in all that time she'd never seen him look the way he did now.

Her voice edged with anxiety. With unease. 'Tom, you're still not making sense. Why do you need to radio in? Is something wrong with the engine?'

Taking her hands, Cooper stared into her eyes intently. Locked into her gaze. And gave her a reassurance which he didn't feel. 'It's just a precaution baby, okay.'

'Tom, *please*. You're making me nervous.'

'Trust me honey, it'll be okay. I promise.'

Jackson, beginning to sober up, grabbed Cooper's arm. 'Listen man, I didn't mean anything by it. You guys were asleep so I thought it'd be fun to sail her. No harm done. Right?'

Shaking himself free from Jackson' grip and not wanting to spend any more time explaining or talking or reassuring,

Cooper began to hurry back below decks to where the mounted chart table was. His reply to Jackson was lost in the wind.

*

At the chart table, Cooper quickly scrutinized the radar screen. Watched the sweeping beam detect the flashing targets approaching their yacht at speed. And without hesitation, he picked up the radio. Selected the emergency maritime frequency.

'Mayday, mayday, mayday! This is the *Yankee Girl* requesting urgent assistance from any US naval vessel. I repeat, this is *Yankee Girl* requesting urgent assistance. We are at 0-2 degrees, 21 north, 26-41 west. Mayday, mayday.'

There was a brief interval of silence before the radio crackled loudly. 'Affirmative. I understand the vessel's name is *Yankee Girl*. Break. Break. Vessel *Yankee Girl*. Vessel *Yankee Girl*, this is USS *Abraham Lincoln*. Request to know if you are in need of assistance. Over.'

'Roger. In need of urgent military assistance.'

Cooper paused. Glanced at the target approaching on screen, adding. 'Potential piracy situation. Over.'

'Pirates? Oh my God, Tom, is that why we have to get back to Lamu?'

Ellie stood on the stairs. Her face drained of the softness of color as the voice on the radio cut through the air.

'*Yankee Girl*, please identify yourself. Over.'

'Ellie, please. Just go back to Jackson. I promise, I'll explain everything. Let me just sort this out.'

Her voice trembled and she said, 'Not until you tell me exactly what's going on.'

'*Yankee Girl*, I repeat. Identify yourself.'

'I'm sorry baby, I got to do this.'

He turned his back on her. Not wanting. Not being able to deal with the hurt. The fear in her eyes. He raised the handset to his mouth. 'This is Lieutenant Thomas J. Cooper of the US Naval Special Forces. Over.'

He heard a hint of surprise in the voice on the other end of the radio.

'Lieutenant Cooper? This is Petty Officer Monroe, you are aware that this is an open radio channel and contrary to naval protocol for military personnel. Over.'

Cooper clenched his jaw as well as his fist. Tried to keep his composure. But it was tough. And he heard the strain in his own voice. 'Affirmative, Officer Monroe, I *am* fully aware of protocol, but I *repeat,* urgent assistance required. Over.'

'Lieut...'

Cooper cut him off as he heard Ellie walk away. The authority of rank speeding into his voice.

'I repeat! This is a mayday call and as such, Monroe, you just need to listen and do your job... Over.'

'Sir, yes sir! Please stand by, *Yankee Girl.*'

Placing the radio handset on the table, Cooper grabbed the binoculars before running back up the stairs to the deck. Two at a time.

He could see Ellie had now joined Jackson, who was pulling on the ropes. Struggling. Hauling in the main sheet as it billowed in the oceanic winds.

Pointing at the flapping sail, Cooper yelled, 'Pull her tight! Jackson. Keep pulling her tight!'

Then through his binoculars, he scanned the horizon whilst listening to the desperate cries of Jackson.

'Cooper…! Cooper! I need your help! She's going to capsize!'

'Hold her down Jackson. Just try to keep her steady… Ellie, take the slack up from behind him. I'll come and take over in a minute… Whatever you do, just hold on.'

Chasing back down below decks, Cooper picked up the radio again to a different, but familiar sounding voice. A voice he could've done without.

'Come in *Yankee Girl*. I repeat, this is Captain Neill. Do you copy? Over.'

'Copy, sir. Requesting urgent assistance.'

'Lieutenant Cooper, I understand you're at 02 degrees, 21 north, 26-41 west, though presumably, Lieutenant, you're aware it's a high risk area with a code two situational alert.'

Cooper glanced at the flashing targets on the navigational screen moving closer. So close. Too close to the yacht. And the strangling panic wrung tighter and his words singed with anger. 'With respect *sir*, both of us know it's my business to be aware of *all* situational alerts, and therefore I understand the likelihood of a pirate attack is real, *and* most likely imminent.'

'Have you had visual?'

'Negative sir, but radar shows targets – likely to be pirates – heading straight for us at around 35 knots. ETA, just under ten minutes. Over.'

The captain's voice was closed. Hostile. And it took every bit of restraint inside Cooper not to rip out the radio from the wall.

'Cooper, let me get this straight. You've had no visual, yet you're expecting me to send out my men on the *likelihood*.'

That was it. The wall invited him to punch it. And he accepted. Gratefully.

Frustrated, his tone still held discipline. He said, 'That's correct, *sir.*'

A pause.

A hush.

A silence which sounded like a ticking clock.

And eventually. Tightly. Captain Beau Neill said, 'Lieutenant, request understood... and approved. I'm passing you back over to Petty Officer Monroe... But Cooper, don't think I won't speak to you about this when you get back on the ship.'

A couple of drawn, long seconds, followed by the voice of Officer Monroe. 'Yankee Girl, have you had visual yet, sir? Over.'

'Negative, but targets nearing.'

'Are you on your own?'

'Negative Monroe, two adult civilians on board. One male, one female.'

'Are you armed, Lieutenant?'

'Affirmative.'

Then the words Thomas J. Cooper had been waiting for.

'Air support on its way. ETA twelve minutes. In the meantime, I advise you to get the civilians below decks... And Lieutenant, good luck.'

*

'Ellie...! Ellie...! I want you to go downstairs to the cabin, lock the door, hide in the closet. Anywhere you'll be out of sight.'

Charging towards her, Cooper watched as she shook her head, terror sketched and engraved into her features. She stood portside behind Jackson and, taking up the slack of the rope, she raised her voice to compete with the wind,

'No, Tom! No way, I'm staying up here to help.'

Before he had time to argue, Jackson began to jibe the boat. Forcing the yacht to make the hazardous one-eighty turn. It tilted dangerously. Rolling treacherously in the waves. Cutting sharply through the water like a blade on silk as he expertly coaxed in the mainsail. Fighting. Battling the surging wind.

And the noise of the thick canvas sail, thunderous as it snapped through the air.

The boom swung across the decks. Shaking violently. Threatening to come lose from her tacks. And with the wind becoming increasingly stronger, harder to defeat, Jackson yelled frantically. 'Coop! I can't hold her! Coop! Please!'

Cooper hurried to help. But as he did the crosswind caught under the mainsail. Filling it out and causing the boom to swing back at speed across the deck towards Jackson.

'Look out!'

The rapidity of the vessel's boom hurtling sideways made it impossible for Jackson to get out of the way.

It hit him hard.

Split open his forehead from the bridge of his nose to the base of his hairline.

A large skin flap exposed an inch-wide wound as a fountain of blood first patterned then soaked his top. Pooling down onto the deck. He jerked backwards. His body going into seizure. Caused him to slump hard into Ellie as his legs gave way. Sending her staggering back towards the rails.

'No! ...'

Cooper's cry stretched further than his reach. His fingertips only managing to brush Ellie's hands. Too far to catch her but not too far to miss the terror, the panic, frozen in her eyes as she mouthed his name. Screaming out for him to help as she buckled under Jackson's weight. Losing balance as both she and Jackson plunged overboard.

Racing over the chain rigging, steadying himself as the yacht bobbed fiercely up and down, Cooper grabbed the lifebuoy. Stole a quick glimpse round.

The wind had begun to blow the sails straight on. Denying them any lift. Leaving them to flutter passively like flags at half-mast. And he knew the combination of the dying sails and the boom crashing freely from side to side would stall the vessel to an eventual stop, allowing him to attempt to rescue Jackson and Ellie without fear of the yacht drifting away.

Dashing over to the rails, Cooper leant over.

Ellie had always teased him about the concern he'd shown over her not being able to swim, but she was now floundering and struggling and battling and terrified as the force of the ocean pounded her into the side of the yacht, her hands sliding down the fiberglass side as she desperately scrabbled for some kind of hold.

With water rushing over her face and into her mouth, Ellie's words were punctuated with the sounds of wild gasping.

'Help… me… Tom…! Tom…! Help… me… please…'

Throwing the buoy to her, Cooper's eyes once again darted along the surface of the ocean. But this time he was looking for Jackson. 'Ellie, hang on to that…Whatever you do, keep hold of it.'

'Pull me up!'

'I have to get Jackson… just hold on.'

'Tom…! No, wait! …'

He turned away and Ellie continued to scream his name. The draw for him to look back was hypnotic. But he couldn't. Shouldn't. Wouldn't. In truth, he didn't dare. His composure was already beginning to crack. Peeling away. Exposing his vulnerability which he knew would serve only to distract. Costing time. Costing lives.

There… He could see Jackson to the left of the boat. Unconscious. Floating face down.

And without a breath of hesitation, Thomas J. Cooper dived in.

'I'm here… It's okay, I'm here… Stay with me Jackson, stay with me!'

Treading water, Cooper turned Jackson over carefully. Real slowly. And the sea turned red with blood.

'Jackson…! Jackson!'

There was no response, but that didn't surprise Cooper. He could see the injuries to Jackson's head were worse than he'd initially thought. The gash so deep he could see skull. His eyes so swollen, if he'd been conscious, Cooper doubted Jackson would've been able to open them anyway. But at least he was alive. Barely. But alive all the same, and whatever happened, he was determined to keep it that way.

Using an extended arm tow with his hand under Jackson's chin, Cooper swam, heading for the yacht's ladder. He could hear Ellie still screaming. Screaming strong. But that was good. Real good. It told him what he wanted to know… She was still there.

Unexpected swells of rolling waves suddenly carried Cooper and Jackson sideward. And the sound of roaring and chugging and racing engines and a glance to his left confirmed his fears. Old battered white skiffs. And in them, Somalian pirates. Heavily armed and sporting t-shirts bearing American logos and wearing Bedouin scarfs showing only their eyes.

They hadn't seen him. Though he knew it was only a

matter of time. His only chance, however slim, was to get to the stern box on the other side of the yacht which held his gun. In desperation, Cooper dived under the water, dragging an unconscious Jackson with him.

Under the surface the sounds were distorted. The vision blurred, made harder from the dark billowing clouds of Jackson's blood. And Cooper counted down, calculating how long it'd be safe to keep an unconscious Jackson under water.

Four seconds.

Three.

Two.

Re-surfacing, and hoping he was near enough to the yacht, Cooper was met by an onslaught of bullets and a firing of guns and a fusion of sounds and a discord of chaos and Cooper's breathing was hard and his chest was tight and his energy was slowly draining away.

Chopping waves and whirling blades hovering above sent a downdraft of stinging ocean spray. And to the soundtrack of machine guns and through a gusting wind, Cooper squinted up.

And there in the sun drenched sky, reflecting light like armored angels waging war with dragons, were two US Navy helicopters.

As the skiffs turned and retreated the aerial rescue basket was lowered into the water and Cooper kissed Jackson on the side of his head. He whispered, 'It's goin' to be alright. You hear me, Jackson? It's going to be alright.'

*

'Lieutenant, we're going to take you both back to the ship,' the US navy officer shouted above the blare of the rotating blades as the air crewmen hoisted Jackson and Cooper into the Seahawk helicopter.

And with the helicopter beginning to rise and veer away from the yacht, Cooper shook his head. Gesturing desperately to the crewmen as he watched them tend to an unconscious Jackson.

'Lower me back down… Now!'

'Sorry sir, we have orders to get you straight back to the ship.'

Cooper's voice was barely heard but he had no doubt his face conveyed the lost sound of anger. 'I don't give a damn about orders, Officer. Just lower me the hell down. There's one other civilian still in the water.'

'Sir, the other helicopter will have it covered. I'm sorry sir, there's nothing I can do.'

*

'Where's Ellie? Answer me, Officer, when I'm talking to you.'

Struggling to hold down his sense of panic, Cooper stood on the landing pad of the USS *Abraham Lincoln*, as the air crewmen from the second Seahawk helicopter made their way from the chopper.

His panic. His fear. Emotions which held familiar echoes of his childhood. Feelings he'd refused to allow to penetrate as an adult began to engulf him. Overwhelm him.

'You heard me, Daniels, where's Ellie?'

The tall. Sinewy. Bald-headed seaman who Cooper could see was now regretting being first out of the helicopter, paled. Muttering the fewest of words.

'I'm… I'm sorry, Lieutenant.'

The mix of bewilderment and shock and disbelief and

confusion acted as a catalyst for Cooper's anger. He lunged at the new recruit. Grabbed him by his oversized flight suit and shook the hell out of him.

'What are you talking about? Answer the goddamn question!'

Daniels looked behind him, hoping his colleagues would come to help – not to his physical rescue, but to his verbal one. 'I… I am, sir… I did.'

The pain of the migraine behind Cooper's eyes began to blur his vision. The pain of it shooting down his nose. But he didn't care. He didn't give a damn. All he wanted was answers. 'Then tell it to me again, Daniels. Tell me *again*… Where *is* Ellie?'

'She's gone. I'm sorry.'

Hysteria channelled Cooper's words. He shook his head in disbelief. His voice a cocktail of laughter and pain and dread rose louder and louder. 'Gone? Gone where, Officer? Where is it you think she's gone? To the mall? To a baby shower? To a goddamn Yankees game?'

'Sir, no sir. When I say gone, I mean missing, lost at sea… presumed… presumed dead… sir.'

Letting go, he pushed Daniels hard away. Knocked him to the floor. But Cooper's rage engulfed him. Driving him on to crouch down to where the officer had fallen. Leaning over him and squeezing and pressing the officer's throat. Feeling the man's trachea moving about on his palm.

Daniels rasped.

'I know what you mean officer, but you see, that's not possible. Shall I tell you why it isn't? Because she was *there*, you son of a bitch. I heard her… Do you understand what I'm saying? She was still there!'

'That's enough, Cooper.'

Captain Beau Neill stood slightly to the side of Cooper, kneading the base of his back with his knuckles as shock-waves of pain darted through his body. Sciatica. It was the damnedest of things. He'd experienced the battle of Huê, Vietnam, in the late February of '68. Been on more tours of duty than he could easily recall without referring to naval records. Yet it was the sciatica which was beating him. Slowly. Painfully. Relentlessly. Forcing him to give up his career, which was tantamount to giving up life.

Through gritted teeth, Neill directed his conversation to Officer Daniels. 'Go ahead, explain to Lieutenant Cooper what happened, he needs to hear it.'

Daniels stood up. Held his throat. Looked hesitant. Wasn't able to hold eye contact, though he articulated the course of events confidently. 'I was in the second helicopter sir, and once the lieutenant and the male civilian had been rescued safely, and due to civilian one being…'

Cooper snapped. 'His name's Jackson. Jackson Woods.'

'Sir. Due to… due to *Mr. Woods's* severe injury, Seahawk one headed back to the ship. Seahawk two's main objective was then to pick up the second civilian… I'm sorry, Lieutenant, I don't know her name.'

Staring at Daniels, Cooper's eyes were void of emotion. Listlessly he uttered,

'Just carry on.'

'From the air we couldn't see the second civilian, and as we were able to establish the present threat had left the area, as well as alerting the Kenyan coast guards, two divers began a search and rescue.'

Knowing the answer already but for due diligence, Captain Neill probed. 'Were you one of the divers, Officer?'

'No sir, I continued in the helicopter which located the

skiffs, eight miles north. By then we also had assistance from the counter piracy control unit. After warning shots, the two skiffs conceded and the PC unit searched the vessels. It was clear, sir, they'd discarded their weapons overboard because the only items found were fuel barrels, long ladders and grappling hooks. The PC unit then commenced to confiscate the property to ensure the suspects had no means to conduct any attacks. We then transferred them all into the one skiff, destroying and sinking the other one, prior to escorting the suspects back to the Somali shoreline. On our way back to assist the divers, we were informed by the appropriate authorities they were changing the MO from search and rescue to search and recover… I'm really sorry, Lieutenant Cooper.'

Captain Neill, visibly tormented by the pain hitting the top of his legs with unyielding brutality, and opposed to any sort of sentiment in the line of duty, snarled at Daniels.

'Now get the hell out of here.'

'Wait…! I said wait.'

Cooper strode up to Daniels. He was finding it hard to focus. Thoughts chaotically crossing from Ellie to Jackson, who'd earlier been flown on to Nairobi.

'Yes, sir?'

'You said two.'

'Excuse me?'

'You said there were two skiffs.'

'Yes sir.'

'There were three… *Three* skiffs.'

Daniels shook his head. 'With respect, sir, there were just the two.'

Cooper pressed his palm into his eye, feeling the pulsating throb. 'Are you trying to tell me I don't know the difference between two and goddamn three?'

'No sir, of course not. But in this case there were only two skiffs.'

The bellow from Cooper made the crew on the far side of the landing pad turn round curiously. 'Three! *One, two, three*. Which means, she's on the third.'

A puzzled crease formed on Daniels's forehead. 'Who... who sir?'

'Ellie. Who the hell do you think I mean? I...' Cooper stopped to ride on a wave of nausea as sweet saliva rushed into his mouth like a fountain. He swallowed hard. 'She can't have drowned, so there's no *point* in search and recover. There *isn't* a body to find.'

Turing to Captain Neill. The strain. The urgency in Cooper's voice was palpable.

'We have to deploy two, perhaps three units to the shore and contact the naval land base in Lamu, then...'

Neill cut through Cooper's animation with tangible disdain. 'Get yourself under control, Lieutenant, you've got a position to keep. Your subordinates are watching.'

'My *only* concern here is with Ellie and sending an operations team to get her.'

'Maybe you should've thought about that before.'

Captain Beau Neill pivoted on his heel and walked away. He nodded to Daniels to do the same which he gratefully did.

'Don't walk away from me, *Beau*. You hear me? Don't you walk away.'

The captain jerked to a standstill. The words acting like the slamming of brakes. He spoke to Cooper with his back turned. His tenor a quiet menace. 'Who the hell do you think you're speaking to, Lieutenant?'

'I don't know, *Captain*, I've often wondered that myself.'

'Be very careful, Cooper.'

'Careful, careful of what? How the hell do you expect me to behave, when every minute we stand here Ellie gets further away from my reach? From our help. They'll take her God knows where and do God knows what. And maybe they'll ask for a ransom or maybe like others before her she'll just disappear without a trace.'

Neill swiveled round. Flexing and relaxing his mouth. 'Now you've finished lecturing me, I'll tell you what I expect. I expect you to conduct yourself with the appropriate decorum, Lieutenant, as is your duty.'

Cooper tasted the bitterness coating his reply. 'Decorum. Conduct. Goddamn duty. Those words read like a handbook from my childhood, *Captain*.'

Neill stepped in closer. Inches away. 'I also expect you to see the truth when it's in front of you… There was no third skiff. Ellie's dead. Drowned, Lieutenant.'

'No… no, you've all got it wrong. She was *there*. Moments before, she was *there*.'

'You're embarrassing yourself, Lieutenant… Answer me this. Was Ellie wearing a harness? A lifejacket?'

Blinking, Cooper stared for a minute. Introvertedly he said, 'No,'

'And so correct me if I'm wrong, Cooper; you knew Ellie had no idea how to swim, yet you didn't insist on her wearing a jacket on the yacht? Do the math.'

Cooper grabbed him. And grabbed him hard. 'You son of a bitch, you're enjoying this aren't you, Beau?'

Neill stared coldly. 'Get your hands off me, Lieutenant.'

There was silence between the two men before Cooper, awash with a sense of defeat, dropped his hold. His hope.

'I'm asking for your help, Captain. I've never asked you for anything. Not when I was a kid. Not as an adult. But I'm asking you now. *Please*. Please, Beau, I beg you. Send a unit to look for Ellie. Help me bring her back.'

For a moment Captain Neill held Cooper's gaze. His mouth moved as if about to say something but instead, he turned and walked away without saying another word.

*

'Lieutenant. Governor Woods has arrived en route from Lamu, he's asking to speak to you, sir, before we fly him on to see his son in Nairobi.'

Cooper stood in a catatonic state by the ship's railings as the slightly overweight 3rd petty officer informed him of the arrival. He nodded, too consumed with grief to speak.

'Thomas, it's good to see you.' Woods stopped, realizing his voice seemed too loud. His composure too contrived. Then quietly he tried again. 'Your Uncle Beau's just filled me in on everything. I'm sorry about Ellie. It's devastating. I liked her a lot.'

Continuing to stare out to sea as the night's sky merged with the darkness of the ocean, Cooper answered. Barely. 'And if you hadn't, you wouldn't be sorry?'

John Woods, the newly elected Governor of Illinois, pulled gently on his arm. Turning Cooper round to face him. 'Hey, you know I didn't mean that. Come on, Coop, don't make me your enemy. I'm on your side.'

Cooper's tone was flat. He sighed. Noticed the painful sunburn on Woods's nose. Then a memory came to mind of how proud Jackson had been of him when he was elected Governor. 'She's alive. I know it. I can feel it... What? You're going to tell me I didn't see three skiffs as well?'

'No... No. I just...' The Governor trailed off before

continuing a moment later. 'What the hell happened out there anyway?'

Cooper said nothing. His thoughts trailed away. It'd only been this morning that he'd been laughing with Ellie. So pleased. So delighted. So happy she'd decided to come and see him.

The trip to Kenya had been a last minute, spur of the moment kind of holiday for Ellie, Jackson and John. The one time everyone's diaries had coincided, but the driving force had definitely been Ellie.

Having been deployed to the naval base in Lamu – setting up and heading a new counter piracy taskforce in the area – Ellie had missed Cooper, and although his military training and experience had taught him to dissociate, damn, he'd missed her too.

Finding out he'd had a week off, Ellie had decided to fly out and visit, and when she'd mentioned it to Jackson – who she'd known almost fifteen years – he'd decided to come too. And then there was John, who, having always wanted to go on safari, and having a rare few days off, had taken the opportunity to join them as well. It'd been perfect. But like the petals of a rose, *perfect* never lasted.

Woods interrupted Cooper's thoughts. Gently encouraging him, pushing him to talk.

'Coop...? Tell me what happened.'

'Okay. Alright... So you'd already left to go on safari. Ellie thought it'd be cool for us to all sail up the coast on the yacht we hired and have a picnic. I didn't see a problem and Jackson was up for it. When we got there I anchored up. Had something to eat. And that was it really.'

'Coop, come on, you guys were found just a few miles off the coast of Somalia. There's no way you of all people would've sailed into danger and put anyone, especially Ellie or Jackson, at risk.'

'Look, I was in charge of the yacht, so there's no-one else to blame…'

'Just tell me what happened. I want to hear it.'

'It was hot. She was tired. So Ellie and I went downstairs for a sleep. I dunno, maybe I shouldn't have done… Anyway, when I woke up… I knew we were in trouble.'

'So it was Jackson.'

'But he didn't know the dangers. He's a great yachtsman so I guess he wouldn't have seen the harm in it.'

'Jesus.'

Governor Woods leant on the railings.

Cooper spoke matter-of-factly. 'I'm going to say it was me.'

The shock in the Governor's voice was as clear as it was in his eyes. 'What the hell for?'

'Jackson. He'd been drinking.'

'Oh, Christ.'

'If I say it was me, it should really be the end of it.'

'Not sure if the Navy will see it like that.'

Cooper shrugged his shoulders. 'So I get disciplined. You know something, John? I really don't care anymore.'

Woods shook his head. 'No, I can't let you do that.'

'What's the alternative? They find out Jackson was drinking, and then what? You really think the Kenyan authorities will just give him a slap on the wrist when he was drunk in charge of a vessel and caused…' Cooper stopped, unable *and* unwilling to finish the sentence.

'I don't know, Coop.'

'Well, I do. And I also know what a hell-hole a Kenyan jail will be. We both know Jackson couldn't cope for a day in somewhere like that, let alone serve a long prison sentence.

I won't do that to him. Or to you. There's your job to think about.'

'Look, this isn't about my job.'

'Oh yeah? Try telling the opposing party that. You know what's it like, they'll want to destroy you, John. They look for anything. And even though this has nothing to do with you, it'll affect your political career... Jackson's so proud of what you've achieved. Let him continue being proud.'

'Governor Woods, excuse me, sir...' The 3rd petty officer walked towards Cooper and Woods, slightly hesitant after what he'd seen happen to his colleague earlier.

He said, 'Sorry to disturb you sir, but your helicopter is ready to take you to the hospital.'

'Thank you, officer, just give me a minute.'

Woods turned to Cooper. Face taut with stress. Mirroring each other. 'Okay. Do what you have to do... But Tom, this conversation never happened.'

He began to walk away but stopped. Quietly said,

'I really am sorry about Ellie. Maybe you should go and see the Medic. He can give you something. You've had a shock.'

Cooper didn't mean to sound so bitter, but he knew he did. 'Pop a pill to make it alright? Make it all go away, John?'

'That's not what I'm saying.'

'Thanks but no thanks. I've never been a believer in medicating myself and I'm not about to start now.'

'Well okay, it was just a thought... And I'm here for you. If you need to talk, you know where I am.'

Cooper nodded slowly. Tried to smile. Gave up. 'I appreciate that. Keep me informed about Jackson... And hey, put some cream on that nose, it looks sore.'

Absentmindedly, Woods touched the sunburn on his face, wincing slightly. 'You know, Cooper, the hardest thing to do is to let someone we love go. But you have to, Tom. You have to let her go.'

Present Day

Eritrea – Horn of Africa
Mai Edaga detention center

1

Thomas J. Cooper knew there were moments in life when you only had one chance. One shot. One opportunity to get it right. And he also knew such moments were often lost. Often wasted. Went unseen. But as he stood in the solidity of darkness, in his tomb-like cell, unshod and ankle deep in human waste, Cooper trusted his moment would come soon. And when it did, hell, there was no way he was going to lose it.

His tomb – part prison cell, part grave – was a hole in the ground. The place he'd been lowered into when he'd first been brought to the detention center, however many days ago that'd been.

The bodies of the unknown decomposing dead surrounded him; the ones who were still alive thinking their nameless brothers were the lucky ones. For the uncharged, untried prisoners of Mai Edaga, death would be their only salvation. A deliverance from the near ritualistic daily torture and the searing, crippling heat from the sheet of corrugated metal covering the hole, which acted like a furnace in the Eritrean sun.

The scraping sound of the cover being dragged off the hole had Cooper, along with the other men, protecting their eyes from the burning light.

'Out.' The guard – rich black skin, dressed in a knee-length shirt over heavy cotton pants – wiped away the veil of sweat forming on his upper lip. He sniffed contemptuously. Gestured his head to the prisoners.

Whilst the rest of the detainees fought to scrabble out of the hole, using the rotting corpses as a step to reach the edge and pull themselves out, Cooper waited patiently for an elderly man to climb up at the only point which didn't require such extreme measures.

Once out, the guard sneered and jeered and jabbed the steel muzzle of his gun aggressively into Cooper's stomach.

It took more than a minute before Cooper shifted his gaze from the gun to the guard. Lifting his eyes slowly. Staring with cutting derision. Then a wry smile spread across his face.

The guard's broken English was deep. Guttural. He said, 'What so funny James Dean?'

It was an anomalous reference from a bygone era as if somehow the guard, like the wild barren landscape Cooper found himself standing in, was frozen in time.

In stark contrast to the guard's voice was the lilt of Cooper's soft Missouri accent, scornful in its gentle defiance. 'I don't have to explain anything to anybody.'

The guard's hostility darkened. Angered. Aware that he was somehow being mocked, though ignorant of the fact the reply had been a line from an old James Dean movie.

The butt of the guard's gun smashed into the side of Cooper's face.

'What do you say now Americano?'

He stumbled back and it took a moment for him to recover. Longer than he wanted. But it hurt. Real bad. Shot pain waves through his entire body, setting his jawline on fire. But he was damned if he was going to show it… Never did.

Wiping his mouth and tasting the salty blood trickling from his lips, he locked his stare with the guard's. Stepped forward. Pushed his stomach onto the muzzle of the gun.

'Haven't they ever told you?'

'Told me what?'

Cooper winked. Whispered. 'Never take on a crazy guy who's got nothing left to lose.'

The guard, unnerved and taken aback by Cooper's apparent fearlessness, took a few seconds to regain his composure. 'Less of your mouth Americano… Now, move it!'

He pushed Cooper towards the line of barefoot prisoners waiting to walk the scorching six kilometre trek through the rough, hard, brutal terrain, to bring back heavy hessian sacks full of rice which tore mercilessly at the men's hands, leaving them with painful open sores.

And the sun beat down. Ruthless and fierce and unrelenting, and the guard shouted and fired his gun giving the men no choice but to set off.

*

Ten minutes into the journey and the ground was unforgiving. Sharp stones cut into Cooper's feet but he knew better than to stop, the guards being crueller than any barren land.

Vehicles made their way dangerously fast down the unmarked rocky track. Like giant clouds of powdered cinnamon, the sands swirled densely, high above the road. A battered truck sped along towards them as Cooper and his fellow prisoners approached a huddled figure clad in a full blue chadri, sat beside the road. Their face was entirely covered with dense material, save the small section around the eyes which was laced with a net grille.

As the empty sheep truck slowed down, coming to a noisy stop, Cooper stared at the driver. Locking eyes. Holding his gaze. And then he knew. This was the moment. The one chance he'd been waiting for.

With arresting speed and a quick glance round, he rotated his body and a caught the gun which was thrown to him by the huddled figure in blue, who now stood up, revealing the weapon concealed underneath their chadri. Cooper aimed the gun at the guard.

To the chants and cries and calls and yells of the other inmates of Mai Edaga, Cooper fired warning shots towards the guard, as his disguised associate jumped in the waiting truck. He fired a few more shots for caution. For himself. For every dead man who never made it… For every dead man that was still there.

'Cooper…! Come on…! Come on…! Jump in!'

Thomas J. Cooper did just that.

2

'What kept you?'

Cooper was wired. And he could feel his eyes were wild with adrenalin as the truck sped and raced along the rough sand terrain. He broke into a smile which made him flinch as his parched, inflamed lips cracked further. He licked them in the hope of some relief. There wasn't any. But damn, it tasted good. Freedom always did.

Levi Walker, a small stocky black man from Connecticut, with a cynical outlook on life, kept his eyes on the road as he spoke. 'Oh, I don't know, Coop, maybe a few thousand miles of sand. That, and the tiny matter of the Eritrean government.'

A woman's voice came from the back. 'More like deciding whether or not to bother getting your ass out of trouble… Again.' Cooper swivelled round in the vehicle's hard front seat, watching as she busily took off the chadri she'd been wearing. Grinned. Leant his well-built but battered body across the seat. Stretched over to the back where she was sitting. And landed a large kiss on her cheek.

Soft.

Warm.

Everything he hadn't had for the past few weeks.

He said, 'It's good to see you too, Maddie… and you should keep that chadri, it's a good look on you.'

Levi Walker burst into laughter. 'Maybe I should take one

home for Mrs. Walker. Save me having to look at her sour face across the breakfast table in the mornings.'

Cooper shook his head. He liked Levi. Always did. Always had. And he knew he couldn't say that about a lot of guys. 'Who wouldn't have a sour face if they'd been married to you for the last twenty years? Beats me why Dorothy hasn't thrown you out a long time ago... Oh shit, we've got company.'

Maddie span round and watched as a sheep lorry, driven by the prison guards, drove up behind them on the narrow mountain road, ramming into their tailgate and bucking them forward. She glanced quickly to her left; nothing but a crumbling sheer drop down to the hillside below. 'Won't this thing go any faster?'

'I've got my foot right down on the gas! Our only hope is that their truck turns out to be slower than ours.'

Grabbing hold of the Heckler & Koch UMP 40 on the seat next to him, Cooper pulled back the folding stock. Leant his body out of the window. Began to fire at the truck as it continued to ram into them.

He shouted at Levi, 'Keep it straight!'

'I can't! The road's too bumpy. Too many potholes and any closer to the side, we're going over!'

Without saying another word, and holding onto the truck's roof handle, Cooper leant out of the window and began to fire at the truck behind as they veered precariously close to the edge.

The forty calibre shots ricocheted off the hood as Cooper struggled to get a good aim, as his hand shook and the truck bounced around.

'Give it to me, Tom...! Now!' Climbing over her seat, Maddie snatched the closed bolt weapon out of Cooper's hands and pushed across the selector switch to fully automatic. 'Hold on to me!' she shouted at him over the sound of the racing engine. 'And make it tight!'

Without waiting she pushed open the passenger door which swung out over the three hundred foot drop, and as Cooper held onto her waist she leant out over the deadly drop and expertly aimed and held her hand steady and cut out everything around her and closed one eye and aimed at the truck's tyre…

Bullseye.

The front left wheel exploded into a mix of sound and shreds of rubber, and Maddie watched as the driver of the vehicle fought with the steering wheel as if he were driving a herd of wild horses. And as she pumped a last hail of bullets into the other tyre, the guards' truck came to a screeching halt, millimetres from going over the edge.

Closing her eyes for a moment and breathing deeply, Maddie gave a last glance to the drop below and, helped by Cooper, carefully sidled back into her seat. Put on the safety lock of the submachine gun. Threw it down on the floor. Turned to Cooper and said, 'You're a total jackass.'

'But you, Maddison, you're something else and the best shot around and that's why we all love you.' He winked. Caught the look of incredulity on her face. And he knew her well enough to know she was pissed. Well and truly.

'You think this is funny do you, Tom? None of this is funny. Not even close. I told you a long time ago that I'm not going through this crap again, you hear me? You could've been killed in that place and *we* could've all been killed just now. I thought you'd finished with all this. Remember? Remember your promises to stop this crap? But oh no. Suddenly you're playing action hero again, whilst Levi and I put our jobs on the line – not to mention our necks – and it's not over yet. We still have to get over the border. You really need to start growing up, because there's a lot of people who rely on you.'

Levi swerved the truck, only narrowly avoiding hitting the carcass of a large goat lying in the middle of the road. 'Seriously Maddie,' he said. 'Do this some other time. He'll be wishing he's back in Mai Edaga.'

Watching a fly hitch a ride on the truck as they weaved up the mountain trail, Cooper rubbed his head. Felt the tiredness beginning to hit. He'd barely slept for the past few days, partly because of the cramped conditions in Mai Edaga, but mainly because he hadn't wanted to let down his guard.

'No, it's cool,' he said. 'Maddie's right. It isn't funny, but honey, you know it's just our way to get through stuff. I'm sorry though, okay?'

Maddie, not interested in being appeased – not interested in anything Cooper had to say – snapped angrily. 'That's bullshit, Tom. Bullshit! You're not sorry. You never are. But like I said before, I won't be part of it anymore.'

'Maddie, come on, I…'

'No, Tom, I don't want to hear it. I've heard it, too many times. But the worst thing is, I've fallen for it too many times, but you can bet your ass not this time.'

Cooper turned to appeal to Levi, who was driving hard up the mountainside, wanting to get to the Ethiopian border before night fall. 'Levi, help me out here.'

'Bro, you know I love you man but on this one, Maddie's right. You know that. It's some crazy stuff you got yourself into back there. We all know you're good at what you do. The best. But… hell, I dunno, recently it feels like you're always looking for the edge and you wouldn't care if you fell off. I don't know what's happened. It's like we're back in the past. And they were bad days, bro. Real bad days. And I'll tell you something else for free, I'm not looking forward to the crap we'll get when Granger realizes we took off to come and find you...'

Levi ended his sentence with a whistle to emphasis his words, as was his habit.

Resigned, Cooper said, 'Leave Granger to me.'

Changing gears and grinding the gear box, Levi shook his head. 'Listen Coop, I know you've pulled me out of some near misses. Jeez, I probably wouldn't be here today if it wasn't for you, but those days are over and I thought they were for you as well. We all did. I left the Navy to have a peaceful life, man, and apart from Mrs. Walker bitching every day, that's what I get. I'm not looking for excitement, I'm looking to earn money and go fishing. Fishing and money. The only two things that matter. Everything else, especially women – sorry Maddie – is too much of a headache. But you and whatever's going on, well it's some kind of crazy.'

Maddie sighed, 'I don't get it, Tom, why make everything harder? Why do this after all this time?'

Cooper opened the tepid bottle of water Levi had passed him earlier. Drank it down. Didn't seem to quench his thirst. Sighed. Knew he should have some patience. Because he got it. God knows he got what she was trying to say. Problem was, he didn't want to hear it. Not now. Not ever. He said, 'Christ, Maddie, can't you just leave it? I'm just doing my job. That's all.'

Red with anger and frustration and pain at not being able to get her words out properly, Maddie spluttered. 'No. No you're not. This has nothing to do with the job. We both know that. And we both know who it's about.'

Levi took his eyes off the road to shoot her a hard stare.

A stare which Cooper had no doubt he'd been practising for Mrs Walker. 'Leave it, Maddie... She don't mean nothing by it, Coop. We're all upset.' ━━

Tying back her long corkscrew brown hair in a tight pony-tail, Maddie's face was flushed. Red like a fever. 'Yes I do mean something by it. Don't tell me I don't, Levi, and what's more, don't get into my business.'

Levi Walker, always hoping he and confrontation had parted company a long time ago, tried to smooth down the situation, though he couldn't help thinking how scarily like his wife Maddie was when she had something bugging her.

'Hey guys, listen. Let's not get into a fight. It's been a tough day and Cooper, you look beat. And although I know he'll never say it, Maddie, I bet he had one helluva tough time in that detention center. We've still got a long-ass drive in front of us, but the sooner we get to the border, the better. The plane we chartered from Addis Ababa is thirty miles west from there. We'll fly it back to the airport and then tomorrow there are three tickets with our names on. So it'll be goodbye Africa, hello USA.'

Levi's attempt at peace-making fell short of the mark for Maddie. Always did. Never got close.

'Shut the hell up, Levi. I want Tom to admit it that the whole thing in Eritrea, it wasn't about the job.'

'Maddie,' said Cooper. 'Enough.'

'You don't get off that easily. It's started again, hasn't it? But what I don't know is why... Come on Tom, I want you to admit this is about Ell... '

Cooper's voice raised. Shouted. Shot her down as he inter-rupted. 'Don't say it...! You hear me? Just don't.' He paused. Clenched his fist to stop the past pouring in. Turned away to watch the unfamiliar countryside speed by. But even after a minute, all Thomas J. Cooper could manage was a whisper. 'Just don't say it, Maddie… Levi, wake me up when we get there.'

Cooper closed his eyes. Goddamn it the woman drove him mad. But he supposed that was part of her job. It was what women did.

Like Levi, he'd known Maddie for over twenty years and all that time she'd never changed. Tough and strong and loyal and caring and intelligent as hell. Put most men he knew to shame. But that didn't mean she didn't get under his skin.

He'd met her on the first day of Aviation Officer Candidate School at the beginning of his military career. The three of them were all tight friends. Been through tough times, and looking back he knew it'd made them stronger.

Even when he'd left the military they'd kept in touch. Or rather, Levi and Maddie had kept in touch with him. But he hadn't appreciated it. After the accident he wanted to be allowed to hide away from the world, so he could be consumed by his own grief. His own loss. His own guilt. But they hadn't let him. Not even for a moment.

The job they were now in, that had been Maddie's idea, when she and Levi's commissions in the Navy had come to an end. They'd both joined Onyx, an aviation and marine asset recovery company, specializing in tracking down high value commercial and private boats and planes for banks, leasing companies and, on occasion, the US government. Stolen, involved in a crime, or left with payments outstanding, it was their job as investigators to find them and bring them back. From wherever. However. And from whoever.

He had known Dax Granger, the owner of the firm, even before the others had, and being an experienced pilot as well as having a SEAL background, he'd been ideal for the job.

It had taken a while for Maddie to persuade him to leave fixing up his ranch in Colorado, which never seemed to get fixed, and five years ago he had succumbed to the pressure. Joined the firm. Got his investigator license, thinking it was all a bit of a joke.

But quickly he'd learnt there was nothing funny about it at all. The first job he'd investigated had been to track down a Learjet 60XR, the purchaser not having kept up with the repayments. It was a beautifully crafted plane. But what he'd found inside had been at odds with both the plane and the quiet splendour of the Tahitian island he'd traced it to. Inside were the bodies of three women. Raped and killed. The owner of the plane? Whereabouts unknown.

The local police closed the case before it had really opened. But the vision of the women had sat inside his head, and much to Levi's and Maddie's dismay and protestations and objections, he'd tracked down the women's families to let them know what'd happened to their mothers, sisters, daughters. Because to him it was the not knowing which killed you.

The job paid well. But it wasn't about the money. Not for him. Especially not at the beginning. For the first year of working for Onyx he'd found himself most interested in the investigations which took him to Africa. And he knew why. And eventually everyone else did too… It had given him the permission. The reason. The opportunity to keep looking. To keep searching for *her*.

God knows he wasn't good at remembering the past. Or maybe it was more a case of not wanting to. Too many shadows. Too many memories hiding round corners, things not even a loaded gun could protect him from. So he kept on pushing forward. Not stopping. Not caring, but always hoping and wanting and needing to know he'd been right all those years ago when he'd believed *she* was still alive. Somewhere in this beautiful, dark yet dangerous sprawling mistress called Africa.

But then things had changed. He'd stopped looking for her. Not because he'd wanted to, but because it'd been the right thing to do. Or that's what they'd told him. That's what his therapist had told him. And he'd made promises. Vows. And he'd kept to them. Until now. Because now was different.

The days he'd spent in the hole in Mai Edaga, that was stupid. A mistake. Nobody's fault but his own. He knew that. The rule was if you had no papers, or if international relations with the country were volatile, just find the plane and fly it the hell out without being seen.

Eritrea had ticked both boxes. No papers, and no international relations with America to speak of. But instead of leaving when he should have done, for the first time since he'd made the promise to stop looking, just over four years ago, he'd taken the opportunity. Broken his promises and headed south, hoping to speak to a tribe of the Rashaida, a nomadic Arabic-speaking people, living predominantly in scattered areas of western Eritrea, wanting to know if they knew anything. Seen anything. Heard anything… about *her*.

But he'd been spotted by authorities. Accused of being a political spy and thrown into the detention center with no access to anything even slightly resembling an American consul. But then taking such stupid risks came with consequences. Danger. He of all people knew that. And at times he thought he lived for that. It was one of the few things which made him feel.

He also knew that was part of his problem.

Although he hadn't known how and when, he knew Maddie and Levi would track him down and come. As they'd always done in the past. And he owed them. Both of them. But especially Maddie, for more reasons than one.

Abruptly. Cutting through the silence of his thoughts, Maddie spoke, in the high-pitched tone which made it impossible for him to ignore no matter how much he tried. 'You know what I don't understand is why you want to go that little bit further? What are you trying to prove? You wanna see if it breaks? Well it does, Tom. It has. We all do eventually and you of all people should know that.'

Opening his eyes. Slowly. Cooper looked at her. Sighed real heavy. 'Listen, I made a mistake, deciding to travel through Eritrea. Don't make this about us, Maddie.'

Maddie shook her head. Her look of disappointment hitting him like an ice cold shower.

'Don't do that Tom. Don't try to get me to back off. You're right, I am making it about *us* because it *is* about us. About you. More to the point it's about *her*… You know what Tom. Forget it. Just forget the whole goddamn thing.'

Eight miles outside
Buziba, Sud-Kivu

Democratic Republic of Congo

3

It was only the sound of the heavy rain which hid the screams. The blood flowed from the palm leaf roofed hut into the red dirt track like a tributary feeding into a river. Inside only an oil light flickered, barely disturbing the darkness. The carcass of a rotted goat writhed and wriggled as maggots fed and moved inside it. The sickly sweet smell of putrefying mounds of blood-covered feathers filled the air.

The villagers sat on the floor, dressed in vibrantly colored cloths with batik print and bold patterns – a stark contrast to the bleak. Taut. Tense atmosphere.

Papa Bemba nodded. Stood on the home made dais next to his folding wooden altar. His face disfigured, mutilated by his own hands. Scarred raised flesh filling the sockets where his eyes should be. It had been the souls of the undead, the spirits of those greater, who'd directed him to gouge out his own eyes. A gift bestowed on him to drive out the evil, allowing him to be the conveyer of all that is pure, and to rid those amongst them of the sorcery within. The darkness of blindness had given him the power along with the vision of the possessed. For now he saw better. Clearer.

His fingers expertly guided him along the body of the naked man lying on the altar. He stopped. Thoughtful for a moment as he felt a lump on the man's neck, before his furrowed swollen hands moved on, down to the area where his liver lay.

It was there. The evil. The Kindoki spirit. The force of wrong which had taken over this man's being. Making him defiant. Making him question.

And then Papa Bemba cried out. Flamboyancy lacing his tone as he pressed down on the man's ribs, rubbing his skin with berries.

'I have found it. It rises. Pushes out towards the living to harm those gathered. To harm those with child. To harm those who seek a better life. Let us deliver your brother, Emmanuel Mutombo.'

Mutterings of Amen sounded through the hut as Bemba leant over Emmanuel again, pushing his ear down on the man's face. He could hear the shallow rasps coming from him which told him the spirits were there.

He spoke to those assembled. His voice, trance like. 'Pray for him. Pray for your brother, Mutombo… Vous êtes le médecin de mon âme. Vous êtes le salut de ceux qui se tournent vers vous. Je vous exhorte à bannir et chasser tous les maux et les esprits des ténèbres.'

He swayed rhythmically and the humming and moaning and chanting became louder.

Yes… yes, he could feel it now. It was time…

And with a sudden movement, Papa Bemba drove his thumbs deep into Emmanuel's eyes, saving him from the sight of evil in the next life.

Helped by one of the assembled, Bemba, leaving behind Emmanuel, descended from the dais. Moved outside into the pouring Congolese rain and spoke once more to those gathered.

'Il est temps,' he said. 'It is time.'

Kneeling down in the mud, where the wet red clay earth mixed with blood and stained his white and gold dashiki, he took out a piece of charcoal from his pocket. Placed it on the ground near where the other villagers had placed theirs. And shouted out once more.

'Deliver him...! Deliver him!'

The hut having already being doused with petrol, and the twisted branches of the banana tree piled around, even in the humid, wet rain it took only a single match. A single moment for it to be greedily swallowed up by dancing orange flames.

And as Papa Bemba stood outside, he could feel the heat of the fire. Hear the smothered rasps. The terrified cries of Emmanuel Mutombo amid the crackling and sizzling and splintering noise of the blaze. He smiled. The screams were the sound of the possessed burning. Defeated. Overcome by the righteous. By the chosen one and he, like the other villagers, was satisfied.

*

As the night drew in and darkness set, cementing its rule over the day, a solitary figure, shadowed and blotted out by the night, moved quickly across the mud-logged ground. The noise of breaking branches over the sound of the heavy rain made the man crouch down, hiding behind the tangled foliage of the sprawling forest.

After a while, and deciding it was probably only the sound of the nocturnal animals who roamed and hunted for prey and, like him, didn't want to be seen, he moved on, hurrying towards the partially burnt down hut – now doused by the heavy rain.

Drawing himself up against it, he looked round, making sure he hadn't been followed. And it took a moment for him to be assured that darkness had been his advocate; letting him come here without being seen.

Inside the hut he called out. Moving towards the dais. 'Emmanuel…? Emmanuel? C'est moi.'

The putrid smell from the burnt flesh of Emmanuel Mutombo was overpowering, but a groan – a sign of life – made him speak once more.

'Emmanuel, I'm here to help you.'

Then picking up Emmanuel, he carried him out into the night, before both of them disappeared into the darkness and sanctuary of the forest.

4

At the Scottsdale airport, Arizona, which served as the home for many of the area's corporate aircraft, Levi Walker wiped the sweat from his forehead.

'Man, I'm hot. I got to get me a cold drink. I can almost taste the beer on my lips.'

Joining Levi by the side of the airstrip, Cooper leant on the hood of Maddie's truck. His six foot three frame towering over both Maddie and Walker. He gave a crooked smile to his friend, relieved to be on US soil. He'd thought about this moment since Eritrea, and it sure as hell didn't disappoint.

'Anyone would think *you'd* spent the last week in a hot penitentiary, the way you're talking.'

'Not me, Coop, no way. I'll leave that to the crazy folk... Oh crap. Is that who I think it is, Maddie?'

Levi pointed up to the sky. Shielded his eyes from the dazzling sun. Watched as a beautiful Diamond DA62 aircraft with turbocharged Austro AE330 jet fuel piston engines came into view. Soaring down gracefully.

'I'm afraid so.'

Levi raised his eyebrows. Scratched his newly cornrowed afro and admired the expert landing of the plane. He walked towards it but stopped. Turned back. 'You know, Coop, I never told you earlier, but it's good to have you back.'

And in the glaring sun a few hundred meters back from the plane, the warm winds caressed Cooper's handsome face and the light bounced off the white body of the aircraft, making it difficult for him to see.

The jet's door opened and casually he sauntered forward. Greeted the pilot with warm words and a gesture of his hand.

'Hey! Good to see you, Granger.'

The punch to Cooper's jaw was quick. Hard. Knocked his head sideward. He touched his lip with his tongue and tasted the spring of blood. He stared back at Granger. Said nothing.

'If you ever. *Ever*, do anything like this again, you're out. You got that Cooper? You want to play Superman, maybe you should've done that when it mattered.'

Cooper lunged forward, but although he was angry he let Maddie grab him, letting the familiarity of her touch calm him down.

'Don't like the truth Cooper? Neither do I.'

Granger rubbed his face, red from stress. He turned to Maddie and Levi. 'I expected better from you Maddison, thought you were the one who was supposed to have a sensible head on. And as for you, Levi, *never, ever* try to pull a fast one on me again.'

And with that he stomped back to the plane, stamping his feet into the dust, followed by Levi.

Cooper watched on, unable to move. Resentment had a funny way of doing that to him. Granger had a funny way of doing that to him. He felt Maddie touch his arm gently.

'It's only because he cares, Tom. We were all worried. I don't know what you expected. You can't just go around doing what you want and think it won't hurt others. Because it does… It really does.'

Without bothering to say anything, Cooper lit a cigarette before walking over to join the others. Something told him this was going to be one helluva day.

5

Cooper wasn't sure what had woken him up. Knowing it could have been one of many things he decided not to dwell on it. Even though the Colorado night was cool . Chill. Both he and the white linen sheets which Levi, or rather Levi's wife Dorothy, had bought him last year for Thanksgiving were drenched in sweat. He kicked them off. Sighed away the images of the past which had awoken and were playing in his head like a movie reel.

Reaching across he grabbed one of the many bottles of pills by the side of his bed. It didn't matter which. As long as they worked. How many he took, it didn't matter to him either, though tonight it happened to be three. Two OxyContin and a Xanax always seemed to do the trick.

Rubbing his face and feeling the hurried job he'd done with shaving the night before, Cooper wearily got out of bed to get some water. Just to do something, rather than just lying there. Thinking. Anything was better than that.

He didn't bother to look at the clock. It was dark. He was tired, which could only mean it was late. Any other information seemed irrelevant. He wasn't going anywhere, not even to sleep, it seemed.

The sanded wooden stairs felt smooth under foot. It'd taken him the whole of last year's 4th July holiday weekend to complete them. Unlike the unfinished kitchen of the ranch. Seven years untouched. Semi-masked up, with unopened paint tins with names such as *Ancient Map* and *Cottage Leaf* and *Proud Peacock*, colors he couldn't even guess without opening the tins, yet colors he and Ellie had argued about when they'd bought them… just before he'd been deployed to Lamu.

He hadn't seen the point of finishing the kitchen. Not now. He never cooked anyway. At a push he used the microwave to heat up the meals Maddie or Dorothy Walker made for him. Because it was Ellie who'd wanted the big, open plan room with a Sully seven burner stove and a view out over the acres of meadow which ran up to the aspen covered hills and on to the mountain ridges beyond. She'd wanted it. Not him. But like the ranch, which she'd fallen in love with when the realtor had simply shown them photos of it, he'd been happy to give it to her. He'd have given her anything.

So now he was stuck with the ranch along with the paint and the unused brushes and the stove which he'd always thought too big and the view of the goddamn meadow. And the only way he could see round the problem was for her to come back. Come back to him. Just so he could give it to her all over again. Because he needed her to remind him of what the colors were, to prove to him why the hell, when there were just the two of them, they needed seven burners instead of four, but this time, this time, he wouldn't care if she painted the whole of the goddamn place bright green.

He shook his head. This was bullshit. He wasn't thinking straight. Didn't know if it was the pills beginning to work or just him. He snorted with audible self-contempt. Jesus, he couldn't recall the last time he'd managed to spend more than a few days at the ranch. Hell, nor did he have any desire to try. He wasn't good at quiet. Give him a crowded prison cell any day. What the hell had he been thinking coming here? He never learnt. He thought each time it would be different.

Already he could feel the tightness in his chest. And it wasn't just the opiates. It was his warning sign. The sign telling him he had to stop. Get away. Because any minute now it was going to hurt. Hurt real bad. Memories hypoxic. Stopping him breathing. Depriving him of air.

Turning to leave the kitchen to grab his clothes, he stopped, not wanting to, but unable to force himself to walk past without looking. To his right, where he and Ellie had planned to build a row of cream wooden cupboards, was a map. A map of Africa adorned with multi colored pins and criss-cross patterns of nylon red string, depicting the towns, the routes and ultimately the dead ends. Illustrating all the days and weeks and months which had translated to years he'd spent searching for Ellie.

His thoughts spilled aloud. 'Come on, Ellie. Where did you get to baby? Where the hell are you?'

'Tom?'

'Ellie?'

Maddie threw down her car keys on the side as she walked into the kitchen.

'What did you say…? What did you just say to me?'

Confused, Cooper said, 'I didn't say anything.'

She brushed past Cooper, her face sketched with tiredness and stress. Looking around and shaking her head she picked up a photo of Ellie and Cooper before resting her eyes on him.

'Seriously? Jesus, Tom, this place is like a shrine to her. Why the hell did you get all this stuff out of the attic? Could you push me away anymore?'

'What are you doing here?'

'You really did skip charm school didn't you?'

'I didn't mean it like that.'

'No?'

'No.'

Maddie's gaze drifted from Cooper to the large table in the corner of the room. Her voice accusatory. Her manner tense. She said, 'What are they?'

Cooper followed Maddie's stare. He shrugged. Never met her eye. 'Nothing.'

'You're back on those pills aren't you?'

'Maddie… look…'

'Don't, Tom. I don't want to hear any bullshit. No more than you've told me already.'

Cooper walked across to the table. Scooped the bottle of pills up. Quickly threw them in the khaki canvas bag on the floor. 'I'm not. They're old pills. Stuff from before. I was just having a clear out, okay? Anyway, you didn't answer my question. How come you're here?'

Hands on hip and a shake of the head. 'Well if you do turn off your phone for two days what do you expect? And you know what, Tom, some people might think a wife coming to see her husband was kind of a normal thing to do, but not you, Tom? Not you, hey? You want to just disappear whenever you feel like it and don't give a damn how anyone else feels.'

It was Cooper's turn to shake his head. He licked his lips. Tried to conjure up saliva from his dry mouth. A side effect of the pills. 'You came all this way to tell me what a hopeless husband I am? Well you wasted your time. I already know… but believe it or not, I'm sorry.'

Her beautiful brown face flushed red. Flushed anger. 'No, Tom, I didn't come here to tell you how bad you are as a husband. I came to tell you our daughter wouldn't blow out her candles at her party until her daddy came. And you know

52

we waited. Me and her friends, Levi and Granger, and my parents all waiting for you. But guess what...'

'Maddison, I'm so sorry. Is Cora okay?'

'Oh she will be, once she's put her heart back together. No little girl should have their heart broken at four years old. Especially not by her daddy.'

'I don't know what happened, I was going to come. I got her a present.'

Maddie's voice was loud and broken. 'She doesn't want a present, she wants you. That's all, Tom. You!' Her tone softened. 'A bit like the rest of us.'

'Please, Maddie...'

'*Don't* say you're sorry, Tom because you're not. No, I'm wrong, you *are* sorry but only sorry for yourself. I came to get you from Eritrea, Tom, and you couldn't even come home to us. That hurt.'

'I thought you might want some time on your own.'

'No you didn't, because you never even asked me! You came here so you could be close to *her*. Let me ask you something. Why did you marry me?'

'What?'

'Just answer me.'

'Maddie, do we really need to do this?'

Maddie cocked her head to one side. 'Is it that hard to tell me?'

'No... I just...'

'Let me guess, Tom... You're not in the mood to do emotion.'

Cooper sighed. Hard. Heavy. Long. Real long. 'Okay... I married you because I loved you... *love* you, I mean. Happy?'

'Happy? Are you serious? How could I ever be happy when

53

there are three people in this marriage? Though in our case the third one happens to be a goddamn ghost.'

Cooper clenched his jaw. Felt the pulse on his temples. Decided to focus on something else. 'I know I didn't turn up to Cora's party and I'm so sorry, but I know you, Maddie, and I know this isn't just about that.'

Bitter and angry and hurt and sad and trying her damnedest not to cry, she spoke evenly. 'You're right. You promised me, Tom. You told me no more searching. No more disappearing. Remember?'

'And I didn't... I haven't.'

'Oh come on. I'm not stupid.'

'Jesus, Maddie. If this is about Eritrea, I was just doing my job. Don't make something out of nothing.'

'Sounds a bit like our marriage.'

Cooper rubbed his face. Tried not to be drawn in. Felt irritated as hell. 'Look, you need to get some sleep. Why don't we go check into a motel? We can talk in the morning on our way home.'

Maddie picked up her keys from the side. 'You know something, Tom? When we got together five and a half years ago, my daddy warned me about you. He told me not to do it. Told me you were going to hurt me.'

Iced. 'Oh come on, Maddie, Marvin's never liked me. I was never good enough for his precious daughter.'

'That's not true.'

'It is and you know it.'

'What I know is I've become one of those women I never thought I'd become.'

'What are you talking about?'

'The woman who thinks they can change the guy. Tries to save him but ends up drowning themselves. But you

54

know what, no more... ' She paused to sweep the mass of brown curls out of her face. She glanced down at nothing in particular. A faraway look in her eyes. 'I'm leaving you, Tom.'

'What? Oh come on, Maddie, don't make this a big deal.'

'You still don't get it. There really isn't any other way. And you know what? It hurts so bad because I love you so much, but I can't go under with you. Not anymore. Not this time. I gotta think of Cora. The irony is I was always so afraid to lose you. But then, I don't think I ever had you in the first place, did I?'

With the pills making it difficult to concentrate, Cooper said, 'Maddie... come on. You're looking into things too deeply. You don't have to be like this.'

'I do and you know I do. Remember the first two years of us being together? You were gone. Never there. Too busy looking for *her*. Have you any idea how that felt? Do you?'

'What did you want me to do? Leave her? Let her rot in some godforsaken place? You knew her, and you also knew how I felt about her. I loved her.'

Maddie stepped towards Cooper. Her body weary from the pain which lay heavy. 'Yeah, I know, but she wasn't here and I was. And I loved you, Tom.'

'You make it sound so simple. You knew how I felt about Ellie when we got together, but you still went ahead with our relationship.'

'I knew how you felt about Ellie when she was *alive*, and I also knew about the guilt you felt surrounding the accident. But Jesus Christ, Tom, not for one moment did I think we'd have a ghost in our marriage.'

'Why do you have to say stupid things like that?'

Maddie stared at him blankly. 'It's really never occurred to you that she could've drowned that day has it?'

'You know it has. That's why I stopped looking for her.'

'No, you stopped looking for her because everybody told you to. Told you to let it go.'

'And that's what I did. I let it go.'

'No you didn't, you just hid it well… I'm right, aren't I?'

'For God's sake Maddie, you're the one who needs to let things go.'

There was a heavy silence before Maddie eventually spoke. 'I do. At least we agree on something. So that's why I'm going to go now. But tell me one thing. Why now? If you really did let it go. *Her* go. Why all of a sudden can I see it in your eyes that you still think she's alive? Why after all this time start searching for her again?'

'I don't know what you're talking about.'

Maddie turned and walked towards the door.

'Goodbye, Tom.'

6

Ten minutes later, on a deserted stretch of dirt road, Maddie pulled up the '54 Chevy truck Cooper had bought her last Christmas, and stepped out into the cool of the Colorado night and, looking up to the starry sky and to the silver moon, her legs gave way under her and she fell to the soft earth and cried. Weeping. Hurting. Anguish cutting into her shredded heart. Deep and painful cries and howls coming from her very soul.

Managing. Just. To go into her pocket, she pulled out her cell and dialled.

'Daddy, it's me. I need you to come and get me.'

7

The sunset, a blended color wheel of powder pinks and eggplant purples, splashed with intensity across the Congolese sky, seemed to go unnoticed by the elderly man resting on the isolated red clay shores of the Congo river. The heated mounds of rotting, stinking rubbish now cooled down by the evening air gave the man a place to sit, alongside the raw sewage which flowed down the bank as if from a mountain spring. It was the only place of solace, a sanctuary of quiet away from the squalid living conditions of the Kitchanga refugee camp, home to the displaced, the desperate, where diseases ran through like the east winds.

The old battered truck pulling alongside, its load covered with blue tarpaulin, went similarly unnoticed by the man, untroubled by its presence. It was nothing to do with him. It certainly wasn't unusual for the locals to park their vehicles, to take the rest of the narrow road on foot, rather than risk the hazards of the crumbling tracks, risk being another casualty of the snaking and twisting river.

Unperturbed, and grateful for the peace, the elderly man continued to relax, not bothering to turn round at the sound of the men walking towards the water. It was only when he felt the coarseness of the thick rope, pulling and dragging him backwards, tightening his airways, dragging him through the clay that he tried to turn. Escape.

He heard a gruff voice, words fused by putrid-smelling breath.

'Stay still. Do not struggle, my brother, it won't do you any good. It's too late... Arrête de lutter. Stop fighting.'

A hood placed over his face began to burn as the cotton, transfused with chilli, irritated and blistered his skin. He squirmed in pain whilst a noise made him jolt. He heard it again. Then again. Only this time it was nearer. Closer. Much closer.

He swivelled round, panicked, unable to see through the hood, but he suddenly froze. He felt the breath on his back. Warm. A different voice. A gentle voice. Which said,

'Bonjour monsieur...'

A pain he didn't think imaginable sped through his body as his eyes were driven down into his skull. He felt the pressure and then the pull and the digging and the gouging and blood streamed down his face. He retched with agony, choking on his own vomit as more quiet words were spoken.

'C'est bon, vomis le diable... Vomit up the devil... That's it, you did well my brother, you did well.'

He felt a soothing hand on his head, mixed in with his pain as he was carried. Lifted. Thrown. Hitting a hard surface with force.

Feeling something next to him, he realized there were others there. And too terrified to speak, too raked with pain to cry for help, he heard the voices of several men followed by the sound of an engine, driving him away, taking him somewhere he didn't want to go, somewhere he didn't know. A place he was sure he was never coming back from.

8

Throwing the empty pill bottle into the glove compartment of his classic Chevrolet truck, Cooper saw the small airstrip of the Onyx Asset Recovery Company come into view as he drove up the dusty, cactus-lined road whilst swallowing, with some difficulty, the two pills in his mouth.

The office he'd been working out of for the past five years was built in the middle of four hundred acres of wilderness. Hot. Remote. Dry desert land, based just outside North Scottsdale, Arizona, with panoramic views of the Granite Mountain. It was one helluva place.

It was mainly himself, Granger, Levi and Maddie, along with a scattering of aircraft engineers who worked out of the Scottsdale office. Granger had other investigators out in the field on an ad hoc basis, but his core staff rarely changed. Partly due to trust and partly due to Granger believing he already had the best team in the business.

There were huge risks involved with every job, with all of them feeling like legal heists. Granger's motto was, *No job is too big or too much trouble*, though at times Cooper doubted that was true. Many times. Especially when the jobs he'd been sent on involved trying to recover Russian-bought military jets from a remote, perilous location in Belize, in the middle of a multi-million dollar dispute with an Austrian import-export company. Or when a court order had been acquired to impound a sixty-million-dollar plane from the middle of Ecuador, and the owners happened to be a drugs cartel who were after his butt to the point he'd found himself hiding out in a derelict house in the city of Guayaquil for four days without food or water. Or when he was facing the irate owner of a helicopter who hadn't kept up with the repayments, in the heart of Mexico, who greeted him with a smile and an Uzi Pro 9mm which could blow his head off in an instant. It was then that Granger's motto, *No job is too big or too much trouble*, made him want to stick those words right up his ass and ask Granger, too much trouble for who?

With Onyx being one of the most successful high asset recovery firms worldwide, with a hit rate of just over ninety-seven percent, several of the companies and banks they dealt with wanted the business to expand, encouraging Granger with monetary incentives to open other branches in major cities, as well as wanting him to take the head office to New York. But Granger, being Granger, refused point blank. Not wanting to risk weakening the firm by expansion. Believing that by keeping it small but strong it would hold onto its powerful reputation for reliability and results. But ultimately not wanting to leave the isolated, yet picturesque part of Arizona that Granger called *God's country*.

Cooper sighed. Pushing the thought of Maddie out of his head. Hell, he was going to see her soon enough and he hoped by then she would have calmed down and realized he hadn't meant any harm. Never did.

Putting his foot down on the gas, he was surprised how good it felt to see the place again. Even broke a smile. The past couple of weeks he'd rather forget. They'd been tough. Real tough. Tougher than he wanted to admit, and strangely he'd spent a lot of the time thinking about his Uncle Beau, and his days in Missouri, something he rarely let himself do. He and the past just didn't go.

Levi waved as Cooper pulled up.

'Hey, Coop, thought you'd be at the ranch for another few days. How you feeling? I bet you never thought you'd see this place again.'

It was a good sight. A friendly face. Something he needed right now.

Leaning out of the driver's window, Cooper's smile turned into a grin. His strawberry blonde hair, in dire need of a cut, fell over his eyes. 'I hope you've been practising your pool, Levi, you owe me a game. What is it now? Eight-one down?'

'Eight-two. And it would've been three if it wasn't for the fact you decided to call it a night.'

Cooper's deeply tanned face lit up. 'Levi, don't push it. If I remember rightly, it was actually *you* who called it a night… or was it Dorothy, when she found out where you were hiding your butt?'

Levi laughed. Couldn't deny it. Knew what Cooper was saying held more than a ring of truth. Though his laugh was quickly replaced by concern. 'I've spoken to Maddie. She told me. I'm sorry, but I guess it was a long time coming.'

'What are you talking about?'

Levi screwed up his face, beads of sweat pushing out between the creases. 'You and her. You do know she's left you?'

Cooper closed his eyes then slowly opened them enough to squint at Levi through the rays of the Arizona sun. And the OxyContin began to hit and he rolled his tongue round his dry mouth. 'Yeah, she came over to the ranch. She said a lot of stuff but I don't think she was being serious. You know how she get sometimes when I mess up. She just needs a couple of days to calm down.'

Levi let out a long whistle. 'Coop, I love you man but get real, you've just pushed her too far this time. It's like from nowhere you've stepped back to how it was a few years ago. Gone all crazy on our ass. You can't expect her to go through all what she did before.'

Cooper rested his head on the steering wheel. 'I know she's hurting but I got things going on, Levi.'

'Like what, Coop? Whatever it is it's in your head, because from where I'm standing, you got it made, bro. A great job. A great daughter and a great wife. Maddie, she's one of the best... Look, why don't you come across to stay with Dorothy and I? She'd like that. She worries about you like the rest of us.'

'I appreciate the offer but I'll just find a motel. Give me time to think and try to sort things out with her.'

'And what about the job?'

Rubbing his chin and watching specs of sand be blown on and off the car window, Cooper said, 'What about it?'

'You and Maddie. Won't it be awkward the two of you working together?'

'Levi, you're taking all this too far but to answer your question, no it won't. Why would it? Nothing's changed. But if it's really a case of her taking some time out from me, which I don't think it is, well we're both grown-ups. Both trained in the military just to get on with the job at hand. We still care for each other. Still respect each other. Want the best for each other and our daughter... I can't see there'd be a problem.'

'You're serious aren't you...? Coop, let me tell you something, brother... You've got a hell of a lot to learn about women.'

And with that, Levi's laughter soared once more, cutting through the Arizona air.

'All this is funny to you, isn't it?' Granger's voice broke through the banter. Silenced the moment as he stalked towards them. 'It's all one big joke to you, Cooper. Maybe I should've punched you harder. Knock some sense into you.'

Cooper stared at Granger. He hadn't seen him since the airport in Scottsdale. After that he'd headed out, taking the five-hundred-mile journey back to the ranch just outside Telluride, Colorado.

He felt the vein in his temple throbbing as he clenched his jaw. A habit. Not a particularly bad one as his habits went. Absentmindedly, he rubbed the side of his head as he got out of the truck. Without bothering or wanting or needing to look at Granger, Cooper said, 'I can think of a lot of things to call the last couple of weeks, but a joke sure isn't one of them.'

'And that's my fault, is it? You're a mess, Cooper. A total bag of mess. But like always you expect the rest of us to clear up. Look at your eyes… I see you're back popping those pills.'

Cooper shot him a stare. 'I don't know what you're talking about. So let's just drop it, hey?'

'You'd like that wouldn't you, Cooper? Drop everything. That should be your middle name.'

Cooper shook his head and kicked up the bleached white gravel with his desert boots and felt the warm Arizona winds whip up the dusty ground and maybe it was just tiredness and maybe it was his own shame but he was pissed. Real pissed with what Granger had just said.

'I don't want *anyone* to clear up my mess. I never have done, never will do, and you of all people know that.'

'Really? Try telling that to Levi and Maddie. They clear

up your mess that often, sometimes I get them mixed up with the garbage men.'

'Real funny, Granger. Look…'

'Save it, Cooper, it'll just turn out to be bull anyway. Oh, and Maddie told me the news about you two. I should say I'm sorry, but I'm not. She deserves better.'

'I know that, but I'd appreciate it if you'd keep out of my business.'

Granger sniffed loudly, emphasizing the words he was about to say. 'I know you would but when it's going to affect *my* business then it becomes *my* business.'

'Nothing's going to affect anything. What is it with everyone, huh? Just because Maddie and I are having… I don't know… *difficulties*, that doesn't mean it's going to alter anything.'

Granger's blue eyes cut Cooper a stare. 'I wouldn't call leaving somebody *difficulties*. And if you think it's going to be a bed of roses, you clearly don't know women.'

'So everyone likes to tell me, and maybe you guys are right, I don't know women. But I do know Maddie, and I know she and I are going to be fine with it all. I'll sort it out.'

'You think you've got it all sewn up don't you Cooper? The sun always shines out of your ass.'

Cooper chewed the inside of his cheek. Even before Eritrea, he and Granger had been at loggerheads. Seemed like nothing had changed. Hell, he doubted it ever would. And he knew it wasn't just because he'd screwed up with the last assignment. No, Granger's problem was with him and him alone.

There'd always been the snipes, and until recently he'd left it. Letting it ride. Always. Usually. Not this time. 'What's your goddamn problem, Granger? The fact that you didn't get the plane back from Eritrea, or the fact that it was *me* that didn't get the plane back?'

'You know what my problem is, Cooper, so why don't you do us all a favor and grow up.'

Maddie, who'd now come outside into Onyx's parking lot, stood back and watched. Listened.

Cooper could feel the anger rising up. Something he felt a lot these days. He said, 'You want me gone, Granger? Just say the word, and you won't see me again.'

Granger, at five foot three, stood a foot shorter than Cooper, though his height had never hindered him in any way; taking on one or three men at a time, if justified, was all the same to him. His face was gnarled and ruddy. And Cooper thought he was doing a good impression of a man who hated him.

'What I *want*, Cooper, is for you to take responsibility. Be accountable.'

'Like you, Granger?'

'Hey, I can live with the decisions I've made. Question is, can you?'

'Why don't you say what's really bugging you, Granger. Let's clear the air once and for all.'

Maddie cut in. 'Hey guys, this is stupid. We're all on the same side here… Tom, leave it.'

Although once, a long time ago, he'd had the ability not to be goaded into arguments, that was no longer the case. She knew it. He knew it. Hell, and so did Granger. 'No, Maddie, I want to hear what Granger has to say.'

Not backing down either, Granger stepped forward. Real close. 'You can't deal with what I've got to say.'

'Guys! Come on! Stop this… Tom, for God's sake, come on! *Please*.' Maddie signalled to Levi to do something other than just stand there. Cooper ignored anything other than what Granger was saying to him.

'Try me. Come on.'

The bitterness was entrenched in Granger's words. Shovelled on like tar on a highway. 'Try you? Yeah? Is that what you want? Well let's see. You want to talk about responsibility, then why don't we talk about just that. Let's talk about my daughter, Ellie, and let's talk about why you *actually* went to Eritrea and how it's connected. And why when I'd given someone else the job, and I'd *specifically* told you not to go there, you still did.'

Cooper crashed into silence. Span there fast. Stared ahead, not seeing Levi's concerned expression. Not seeing Maddie's unease. All he could see was the moment. All he could hear was Ellie shouting his name. All he...

Jesus... No... No... He shook himself both physically and mentally out of the mesmeric memory. He wasn't going to go there for anyone. *Couldn't* go there. He stared at Granger, then looked at Levi and felt the strain in his chest. He touched his back pocket of his blue jeans feeling the blister packet of pills. Somehow comforting.

'Granger, what are you talking about?'

Dax Granger swung round. 'Hasn't he told you Maddison?'

'Tom, what's he talking about?'

Granger pushed. And hard. 'Tell them, Cooper. Tell them what this is all about.'

'It's not about anything. I just thought I'd be better doing the job than the other guy.'

'Without consulting me?'

Cooper said, 'Yeah.'

Granger, not intrinsically cruel but beyond angry, pushed again. Tone bitter. 'Oh come on, Cooper, don't give me that.

That's not how things work. You and I both know why this is happening again, why you've decided to throw away everything you've built over the past few years. Come on, tell your wife why. Surely she deserves to know doesn't she?'

'Shut up, Granger.'

'Why can't you be like the rest of us, hey? Having to deal with things even though we don't want to. You don't see me reaching for the funny pills or running amok or putting my wife and friend in jeopardy! But then, you know what I think. I think it's all just one big excuse to be that prize jackass which is always bursting to get out of you… Go on, tell them. Tell them why you've begun to search again.'

Cooper knew he sounded like a broken man. '*Please*, Granger, don't do this.'

Maddie's face was a picture of anguish and pain and hurt. 'Will someone tell me what the hell this is about?'

'You want to tell her?'

Cooper spoke in a controlled whisper. A mixture of pain and steely resolve.

'Leave it. Okay…? Just leave it. You don't know what you're talking about. I'll give you anything, Granger. But I can't give you that… So yeah, you're right. I can't deal with it. I can't talk about your daughter.'

9

Going straight across to the cooler in the kitchen of Onyx, Cooper took out a small carton of juice which he drank down thirstily. Threw a non-alc beer to Levi.

He felt as refreshed as he could after taking an ice cold shower which, after the showdown with Granger, was much needed. He'd put on clean clothes. His usual attire of jeans and a gray marl long sleeved top. Splashed some of Granger's aftershave on and combed his hair and brushed his teeth and checked his hair again and then finally took a pill. Xanax. Just to get him through. Then he'd taken another one. Just to make sure.

'You okay?' asked Levi.

'Yep.'

'You wanna talk?'

'Nope.'

'Was Granger right? You been having to take some pills again?'

Cooper didn't bother answering. Wondered if it was because he didn't want to lie.

'You were bad on them before, Coop... Have the flashbacks come back? You not sleeping again? Is the old injury playing up? You think you need to go and see that shrink again? I mean, I could come with you and all. And if...'

'If what?'

'Well, if you need me, I'm here.'

Cooper shrugged. 'I'm fine. But thanks.'

Levi gave him that look. The look that said he didn't quite believe him, but he carried on talking anyway. 'Dorothy wants to see you. She wants you to come to dinner on Sunday… maybe you could bring somebody…' He paused, before twisting his hands like a kid does. Innocence was sure as hell being feigned. '… Maybe Maddie? Maybe it would be good for you two just to sit down and talk? You know, on neutral ground.'

Cooper raised his eyebrows, shooting Levi a warning glance not to go there. He grabbed another juice. Headed to the office he shared with the others without saying another word.

10

Walking out into the familiar cream and orange hallway filled with photos of various planes and boats always made Cooper feel he'd stepped back into the seventies. It got him every time. He didn't mind, hell he could live with anything, but Maddie, she'd whined like a tomcat. She'd campaigned to Granger to get it changed, even bringing in samples and color charts. But each time it came to the place being re-decorated, Granger would select the same old colors and same old photos and Maddie's complaints would start all over again.

'Tom.'

Cooper turned round. Readying himself for the show-down. Justified. Inevitable.

'Whatever it is you're going to say, Maddie, you're right and I'm sorry but everyone now thinks you've left me, so it's kind of a bit awkward explaining you haven't.'

'What are you talking about? You think I didn't mean it? What is wrong with you? Are you really that arrogant, or is it you just don't care enough to see and believe how I feel?'

'Look, I'll take Cora out for some ice-cream, make up for missing her birthday party.'

It was a mix between a laugh and a snort but he got it. The derision was coming hard and fast. Straight his way.

'You really don't get it do you? It's over. I'm not coming back. I can't.'

A punch in the stomach would've been preferable. 'And

Cora? How do you think it's going to affect her me not being around?'

'Tom, you're never around anyway... You don't deserve that little girl, but for some unknown reason she idolizes you. Only thing she talks about. Well, you and Mr. Crawley.'

'Mr. Crawley?'

'Her caterpillar. I think it's dead but you know Cora, she's insisting on keeping it in a cookie jar... Anyway, look, I don't want to talk about Mr. Crawley. I just want to know in what universe do you think a scoop of Rocky Road is going to make up for letting her down on her birthday?'

The pounding throb above Cooper's eyes sent pain waves down the bridge of his nose. Like a jackhammer breaking through granite stone. He knew what it was. Good old fashioned stress. 'She can be the judge of that.'

'She's just a little girl, Tom.'

'I know what she is... Listen, I was wrong, I should've showed up.'

'Yes you should, but there's nothing you can do about that now. But you can tell me about Granger. What was he talking about? What was he trying to get you to say?'

Partly to stall for time and find some plausibility, because Maddie was like kryptonite when it came to annihilating his bullshit, and partly because he had a damn crick at the base of his neck, he shrugged. 'Who knows, Granger makes his own rules up as he goes along.'

'Don't lie to me Tom. I'm not stupid.'

Cornered, Cooper did what he was certain felt like second nature to most men: changed the subject. Spun it the hell round. Put the heat on her instead.

'Look, Maddie, do you think this is going to work? Us.

72

Here. Together like this. Is this how it's going to be from now on?'

By Cooper's reckoning it was at least twenty-five seconds before Maddie spoke, give or take the last three seconds which she spent cutting her eyes at him.

'Seriously? You of all people ask me that? In case it escaped your notice I'm not just a wife. I'm a mom. I'm a damn good pilot and investigator. I've got over fifteen years of military experience behind me, and I work hard at my job. So if you think for one moment that just because you and I aren't together any longer I'll suddenly fall apart, become neurotic, unreliable and unprofessional, and bring my home life to work... If that's what you think, Tom, then you don't know women at all.'

11

Grateful to get away from any more conversation, Cooper headed to the office, musing and bitching and ruminating on how, in hindsight, life inside the Eritrean prison seemed so much less stressful than coming back home. He stopped short of the doorway.

'Well, I'll be damned. If it ain't Thomas J. Cooper!' Austin Rosedale Young sat back in the brown leather chair, his feet clad in a pair of garish blue cowboy boots to match his sky blue suit and shirt and tie. His strong Texan accent and over-tanned skin, along with his visibly dyed black hair, gave out an inaccurate, foppish impression. The truth, though, was that Austin Rosedale Young was at one time America's top sniper. A natural born killer. A man who'd earned almost mythical status amongst his fellow SEALS.

Cooper spoke. Just. Not really wanting to hear the answer from his one-time nemesis. Not really wanting to hear anything from the man at all. 'What the hell are you doing here?'

Young, or Rosedale as he liked to be called, opened his arms in an exuberant manner. Chewed on the oversized, unlit cigar as he delighted in telling him exactly that.

'I thought they would've told you, Thomas. I work here now. Retirement just doesn't suit me.'

Cooper said nothing. He'd known Rosedale for a long time. Too long. Their paths had met on several occasions, working together several years ago.

When Rosedale had left the Navy, he'd gone to work in the Central Intelligence Agency, employed in their Clandestine Service. It was the front-line source of clandestine information on critical international developments, working on everything from terrorism, weapons of mass destruction, to military and political issues which challenged the deepest resources of personal intelligence, self-reliance and responsibility. And Austin Rosedale Young had been what they called *the perfect candidate*.

Cooper blew out his cheeks and moved over to the far side of the office. Threw his empty juice carton with an overhead shot in the bin. Hole in one. Turned to look at Rosedale. And even though the guy's elaborate and crazy screwball ways covered the fact he was a highly intelligent, highly skilled, ruthless individual, Cooper had no intention of working with him again. Ever. He also had no intention of letting him sit at his desk. 'That's my desk, Rosedale... Move.'

'Not any more it isn't, sugar.'

Cooper moved nearer. Much nearer. So near he could feel the heat rising from Rosedale's skin and smell the mix of cigar and toothpaste and a cologne which should've been left on the shelf. 'I repeat, *that's my desk.*'

Rosedale picked up the brass name plate from the desk. He read it out, his Texan drawl flavoring the mockery. 'Thomas J. Cooper... Now tell me, Thomas, I've forgotten, what does the *J* stand for?'

'Put that the hell down... *Now.*'

Rosedale swept his feet off the desk and leant forward, his face lighting up. 'Hell no, Thomas, I'm sensing something here... Tell me what the J stands for.'

The scorn for the man, Cooper felt it right to the heart

of him. 'You're not sensing anything Rosedale, you're just being a jackass. So I'll tell you again. Leave it.'

'And what if I don't, Thomas J? What exactly are you going to do about it?'

'You sound like a kid, Rosedale. Why don't you just leave it like he asked you to?'

Maddie, who'd just come in to the office, walked up to Rosedale, snatching the brass name plate out of his hands.

Rosedale grinned. 'Now that ain't a nice thing to do, Miss Maddison.'

Maddie looked at him with disdain. 'Grow up.'

Winking at her, Rosedale sprang his six foot five body from the chair, standing tall on another two inches of cowboy boot. He smiled down at Cooper who didn't bother meeting his stare.

'I'm one of the few men you gotta look up to hey, Thomas?'

'Go to hell.'

'Not until you tell me what the J is for.'

'Drop it Rosedale. Just let it go.'

'Oh, you mean like you let things go? There's a funny thing. You of all people telling me to let something go.'

Cooper breathed deeply. Stared down at the floor. Watched the tiny spider disappear under the door. Let the seconds tick by. Then eventually he lifted his head. Locked eyes with Rosedale and said,

'Don't cross that line with me, Rosedale.'

'You know in Texas they've got a saying, big hat and no cattle. And that's exactly what I think you are, Thomas, all talk and no action.'

Rosedale poked Cooper. Jabbed his finger right into his chest. Mistake. Big one.

'You've just crossed the line.'

With rapid speed, channelling his anger from Granger and Maddie, Cooper threw a double punch. Caught Rosedale tight on his mouth and followed it through with a body shot to the ribs. He quickly ducked, curving his body out of the way to avoid Rosedale's counter attack, before he powered a left scissor punch right to his jaw.

'What the hell is the matter with you?' Granger dragged Cooper off Rosedale, who grinned, licking the blood from his mouth as he spoke.

'Can't remember the last time a man split my lip. I have to give it to you, Thomas, you still have it. Shame for everyone, you didn't have it when it mattered.'

It was one helluva roar from Granger. 'Shut it Rosedale…! I want you both in my office. *Now!*'

12

Gazing out of the large window overlooking the dusty, cactus-filled flatlands leading up to the Granite Mountain, Dax Granger sat back in his hard wooden chair. He was tired. Real tired. Tired enough for the doctor to tell him he had to rest and take it easy. Unfit enough for the doctor to be throwing numbers at him like he was carving up the batter in a baseball game. Blood pressure one sixty over a hundred. Cholesterol level one ninety. Goddamn doctors, only thing they were good at was scaring the life out of people, triggering his wife to start looking for a retirement condo down in South Florida. If that's what old age and ill health had in store for him, let God take him now. Irritated, he pointed at Rosedale and Cooper with the chewed blue biro top he held in his hand.

'Is this the way it's going to be, huh guys? You two at each other's throats like a pair of Coyotes? I thought it was Maddie and Cooper I had to worry about, but oh no, you always like to prove me wrong.'

Rosedale yawned, adjusting the angle of his large cream cowboy hat whilst looking down at his watch.

'You got some place else you need to be, Rosedale?'

Rosedale smirked, lighting his cigar. 'Hell no, I'm staying around for the entertainment.'

Not having said anything so far, Cooper kept his words to

a minimum. He took a drag from his cigarette. 'You should've told me.'

Granger pulled a face. 'I don't need to discuss my staffing policies with anyone, least of all you. You're here to do a job, nothing else.'

Cooper had a feeling the man was enjoying this. But he tried not to focus on that. Pills had a way of making a man feel paranoid. 'Then tell me why.'

Rosedale cut in. Grinned widely. 'I think that's plain obvious, don't you, Thomas?'

'What's he talking about?'

Granger had never been a man who liked to be questioned and today was no different. He snapped and barked and growled. 'You were away where you shouldn't have even been. I was a man down.' He shrugged his shoulders to mark the end of his sentence.

'And that's it?'

'That's it, Cooper. Nothing more than a short tale.'

Rosedale said, 'Oh, I wouldn't say that.'

Granger stared hard at him. 'Cut it out.'

Cooper turned to Granger. He wanted answers. But more than that he didn't want anyone to be making him their fool. 'I'm missing something here, aren't I…? What's going on?'

Drinking the coffee Maddie hadn't bothered sugaring – orders from his wife – Granger sighed, not wanting to say anything more.

At which Rosedale was clearly amused. He winked. 'Somebody thinks you need your hand holding, Thomas. So who better? Here I am. You've got yourself a babysitter.'

'I don't get it… Granger… I'm talking to you.'

Cooper could see Granger was uncomfortable. Forced into a corner. And he wasn't about to let him out.

'Okay, I got a call, but Cooper, you've got to understand…'

Cooper put his hand up to stop Granger saying anymore. 'Oh I understand alright, and you can bet your life I'm going to go and sort it out.'

13

'Hey Jackson, it's Coop.' Exhaustion threatened to overwhelm Cooper, but nothing could stop the strength of his feelings coming through in his voice. And in return he received the same warmth and love back. It felt good.

'Coop! Hey Coop! Levi told me you were back. Thank God you're okay. I was worried. I thought… hey, it's good to hear your voice. I tried to call you at the ranch, got the answer machine… I missed you, man… Anyway, when you coming across?'

Hearing Jackson's voice gave Cooper the first real sense of relief since he'd been back. And even though he knew it was only a fleeting moment, when he spoke to Jackson it always felt like everything was going to be just fine. Real fine.

'I've got a couple of days off, thought I'd fly over tonight, but I've got something I need to do first so I'm not sure what time. I've got Cora with me. I know she'd like to see you and I'm trying to make up for being a deadbeat dad.'

'Well let her know I'm looking forward to seeing her too. You flying yourself?'

'No, I thought I'd catch the red eye.'

Jackson laughed. 'Shatters my illusion Coop. You on a red eye. Can't quite see it, man.'

'Stranger things have happened Jackson, just you believe it. And besides, I'm tired and I don't think Maddie would thank me if I flew solo with Cora.'

'She's got a point. Which reminds me, Levi told me about you and Maddie. I'm sorry. If there's anything I can do.'

'News travels fast,' said Cooper. 'But thanks, it's cool. I guess it'll sort itself one way or another.'

'You okay with it?'

'I dunno.'

'Which translates into you don't want to talk about it, right?'

'You got it in one.'

'Okay, well, I'll see you in the morning, and maybe you could try to get here in one piece.'

'No-one wants that more than me... Oh hey, will your dad be about?'

'Yeah, I think so. You wanna say hi to him? He'll be pleased to catch up with you.'

'Cool. I'll see you later... and Jackson? I missed you too.'

*

'You ready, honey?' Cooper clicked off his cell. Looked back at Cora who was sitting quietly in the back seat, seemingly oblivious to the rental car's overpowering smell of cheap plastic and *X-tra Strength* wild cherry which oozed out in menacing waves from the innocuous-looking pink cardboard tree dangling from the driver's mirror. He said, 'What you got in your hands, baby?'

'Mr. Crawley.'

'Can I see it?'

'*Him*, Daddy. Can you see *him*.'

'Sorry. Can I see him?'

Cora Cooper raised her eyebrows just like she'd seen her mom do when she was asked something important. She looked at her dad with caution and a deep frown befitting someone far older than her four years.

Thinking hard, she decided there were a lot of things she knew. She knew how to do her math in Mrs. Bradbury's class without crossing out. She knew how to do her shoelaces, though not on her new red sneakers she got last week; *those* laces were too long. She also knew really big things… *Secrets*. Like her mommy sometimes cried at night when she put on her music, and her daddy hid his red and blue and white candy in lots of bottles in the horse barn. Oh yes, she knew all those things and a whole lot more, but she didn't know this. She didn't know if she should let her daddy see Mr. Crawley because she didn't know if Mr. Crawley would *want* to see her daddy. But then, *she* always enjoyed being with her daddy, so perhaps Mr. Crawley would.

Cora Cooper gave a long sigh and screwed up her nose and, just to be on the safe side, cupped her hands, brought them close to her face and asked, 'Mr. Crawley, what do you think?'

'What did he say?'

'Sshhhh, Daddy! I can't hear him…'

'Sorry.' Cooper glanced at his watch. Tried not to let impatience show. And hoped to God the clearly deceased Mr. Crawley would make up his mind one way or another. And fast. It was 3.34. Fifteen minutes late. Shit.

'Well baby? What did he say? Can I see him?'

Cora opened her blue eyes. Wide. Gave Cooper an incredulous stare. 'I don't know yet Daddy, he hasn't told me.'

Cooper rubbed his face. Pinched the bridge of his nose. The smell from the car freshener burning into his nostrils like a bad case of sinusitis. 'Okay, well listen, honey, maybe you tell Mr. Crawley I'll see him some other time. I'm meant to be somewhere and if I don't get there soon, Daddy will be in trouble.'

'With who?'

'With a man.'

'Which man?'

'With a man who Daddy has to see.'

'Why?'

'Why what?'

'Why do you have to see him?'

'Has anyone told you, you ask a lot of questions?'

'That's what you say to Mommy.'

Cooper smiled and chuckled and laughed. Hard and loud. 'Cora. I love you. Never forget that.'

'And Mr. Crawley?'

'Yeah, and Mr. Crawley.'

'Daddy?'

'Yes?

'Do you think this man wants to see Mr. Crawley?'

'He probably does. Problem is, honey, I don't think Mr. Crawley would want to see this man.'

14

'It really isn't appropriate bringing a child to session, but I suppose now she's here there's nothing we can do about it. You can put her out in the hall.'

To which Cooper said, 'She's not a damn cat. She'll be fine just there in the corner. She can play with her bug and read her book. She won't be any trouble.'

'I'm not happy about this, Mr. Cooper. And that's even without wanting to mention you're twenty minutes late.'

'So why did you?'

'Why did I what?'

'Mention it. If you didn't want to do something, why do it?'

'Is that what happens to you? If you don't want to do something you don't bother?'

'You tell me,' said Cooper. 'That's why I'm here, isn't it?'

'No, Mr. Cooper. You're here for court-ordered psychological sessions. Two years of monthly sessions extended to three years due to non-compliance, as you probably recall. It was either that or a residential psychiatric facility treatment center, but I recollect your attorney was vigorously opposed to that suggestion... You seem to be in denial about the truth about why you're here.'

Cooper stared at the doctor, with the overly gelled hair and brown mule shoes looking like they pinched a little too tight, and he noticed the doctor staring back, which wasn't a good thing because he was certain the doctor with the over gelled hair and too small shoes would read something into it and write it down and show it to his colleagues and send it to the court probation officer and finally to the judge who would never know the whole situation could've been avoided with the right size shoes. 'Jesus. I was joking, Doc. I know why I'm here.'

'I wouldn't call it a joke. Do you often try to cover feelings with jokes – however unfunny?'

'You gotta stop this.'

'Stop what Mr. Cooper?'

'Every time I say something you see a different meaning.'

'Does that trouble you?'

'Too damn right it does.'

'Would you say you have feelings of paranoia?'

'No.'

'You seem agitated.'

'Wouldn't you?'

'That all depends.'

Cooper said, 'On what?'

'I think you're trying to deflect. This session is about you. Do you often try to avoid conversations about yourself?'

'Jesus Christ.'

'Do you feel yourself getting angry?'

'No… It's just… it's difficult.'

'What is?'

'This… you… Maddie… the whole situation.'

'Now I feel we're getting somewhere. Tell me about Maddie.'

'She left me.'

'And how does that make you feel?'

'I want to say I feel bad, but I can't feel anything. For a

moment I did but now not a damn thing. It's like I've rubbed a tube of Lidocaine on my insides. There's nothing there.'

'And what about your daughter?'

Cooper gave a side glance to Cora, who was busy examining Mr. Crawley. He lowered his voice. 'You mean do I feel anything about her? I do, but only when I'm with her. When I'm not, it's like I'm locked off, she doesn't exist anymore.'

'That's common amongst people with PTSD, especially people with combat trauma... You don't like me saying that do you?'

'Come on, Doc, you sound like a broken record. I haven't got that and besides, it was a long time ago... I've moved on.'

'I don't believe that any more than you do.'

'Like I say, it was a long time ago.'

'Seven years.'

'I know,' said Cooper. 'You don't have to tell me that.'

'The brain is very complex, Mr. Cooper, it can either be your best friend or your worst enemy and these things, especially trauma-based mental health issues, can last a very long time. May be there for the rest of your life. It also has a way of lying dormant, it doesn't always hit the person straight away. And there'll always be triggers. And as we've discussed before it's not so much about *curing* the problem – if it were only that simple – it's about the management of it. And let me tell you this: the more you try avoid your issues, the less control you'll have over them, and before you know what's happened they'll grow to the point where they take on a life of their own.'

'I'm not saying it's always easy. At times it feels like I've a monster living inside me. Destroying everything I touch and those around me, and when it's done creating havoc, that

87

monster turns on me, pushing me to the edge and there's nothing I can do to get away from it. It just devours me whole....' Cooper trailed off, feeling like he'd said too much. He shrugged his shoulders, adding, 'But hey, we've all got our demons, haven't we? It's no big deal.'

'Why is it so hard for you to accept what I'm saying? Why are you always so adamant on rejecting my diagnosis and lessening your problems?'

'Doc, you know I'm proud of having served and fought for my country, but here's the thing: I'm okay, I got through it all, but I know some guys don't and I won't have you comparing my situation with my brothers – those military vets who really do suffer in silence, whose voices aren't heard until it's too late, and they put a gun to their head and blow themselves away. They're the ones who end up losing everything after giving everything to their country. I won't disrespect them like that. My problems, if I have any, don't even compare. Jesus, I was on a yacht when it happened, not on the goddamn front line.'

'You don't have to be in a combat situation to be traumatized, *however* in your case I think you were. Look at the facts, Mr. Cooper: you were a serving officer at the time and although you were taking a couple of days' vacation, you still came under attack. As a consequence of this attack your life and others were in danger. You had no control and felt there was no-one there to help you. You were injured and so was the other person with you.'

'My injuries were nothing. Hurt my back, that's all.'

'Yet you take medication for it.'

Cooper was evasive. 'Maybe. Sometimes… I dunno.'

'Look, my point is your behaviour has got all the hallmarks of combat-related PTSD. All the hallmarks. And furthermore, you lost Ellie, and I don't believe you've dealt with the guilt.'

'I'd appreciate it if we didn't go down that road.'

The hair-gelled doctor stared hard at Cooper. 'Let me ask you this. You get flashbacks?'

'Yes.'

'Do you feel disconnected from emotions?'

'Yes.'

'Heightened alert?'

'Yes.'

'Nightmares?'

'Yes.'

'Unable to sleep?'

'Yes.'

'… You still sleep with your knife?'

'Yes, if Maddie or Cora aren't about. Maddie was never keen on it. Made her feel uneasy. Worried I'd jump out of my sleep and not know who they were. Fill in the rest.'

'Feel unable to relate to family or friends?'

'Yes.'

'Do you alter your reality with the abuse of narcotics or alcohol?'

'No, but whilst we're on that subject, I'd appreciate it if you could write me another prescription for those pills.'

*

Cooper opened the car door for Cora. 'Sorry it took so long but now we can go and get on a plane tonight and have some real fun.'

'Daddy?'

'Yes?'

'Do you still love her?'

'Of course I do. Listen, I don't want you to worry about that. I'll never stop loving Mommy.'

'I don't mean Mommy, I mean Ellie.'

15

The long cream hallway, adorned with family photographs, on the second floor of the Executive Residence, 1600 Pennsylvania Avenue, is a section of the White House only the first family, and those closet to them, get to see. And it was here in the quiet hush of the early morning that Cooper found himself.

'Coop!' Jackson stuck his head round the door of the east bedroom, his face conveying delight.

'Hey buddy!' Cooper gave a wink and a smile and watched as Jackson walked towards him with a wide grin on his face.

Even from part-way down the hall, Cooper could see the thick raised scar running down Jackson's forehead; the result, as well a constant reminder, of what happened on the boat with Ellie that day.

For a while no-one – least of all Cooper – had thought Jackson would recover from his head injury, but he'd been flown to the Mayo Clinic in Rochester, Minnesota, an eminent neurological hospital, and slowly things had begun to turn around.

Rehabilitation had been long and painful and frustrating for Jackson, but he was a fighter. And he'd battled. Battled hard. And eventually after sixteen arduous months, that fight had paid off and he'd been discharged – though he certainly hadn't been left unscathed.

His head injury from the boom had been of sufficient force

to twist and turn Jackson's brain on its axis. Interrupting the normal nerve pathways. Tearing and damaging its surface and leaving him with a left-side partial paralysis. A direct corollary of his injuries.

And the large, disfiguring scar ran visibly but the deeper, unseen ones ran right to the heart of Jackson, triggering him on occasion to be lost, unreachable in the dark, debilitating days of depression.

Cooper grabbed hold of Jackson before he was really near enough to do so. Embracing him and making it last long enough to let Jackson know he cared. Damn, it seemed easier than words.

'Can anyone join in?'

John Woods stood a few feet from Cooper and Jackson, immaculately dressed in a tailored blue suit, a starched white open shirt and a pair of mismatched socks. His warm smile reflecting in his green eyes. 'Coop, it's really good to see you. We were worried… Hey Cora, it's good to see you. Don't you look beautiful? I like your dress. How about a hello hug?'

'No.'

'Please?'

'No.'

'Just a small one.'

'No.'

Cooper put his hand on her shoulder. 'You want to show him Mr. Crawley, honey?'

'No.'

Jackson smiled. 'Maybe she knows you're a democrat, Dad.'

Cooper returned the smile John was giving him. But he knew his was more guarded. 'Good to see you too, sir.'

John Woods shook his head. 'Do we have to go through this every time? Coop, come on, it's me.'

Cooper said nothing.

With a sigh and still with his eyes on Cooper, Woods said, 'Okay, guys, I gotta get out of here.'

'Hold on,' said Jackson. 'Let me go and get that book you wanted to read… Oh and Dad, change those socks… Cora, why don't you come with me? I've got something for you.'

'A flamingo?'

'I'm afraid not. Is that what you want?'

'No.'

'Has anyone told you, you're a funny little girl?'

'No.'

'Well hurry up, Jackson,' said Woods. 'I'm on the clock.'

*

Cooper followed President Woods into the West Sitting Hall, an informal yet elegant living room, classically decorated in creams and quilted gold. They stood by the large lunette window looking out onto the West Wing.

'Jackson looks happy. Is it for real?'

Woods shrugged. 'Who knows? He hasn't been good recently. Sometimes I don't know how to reach him, Coop, he's like you in that respect. Maybe that's why you understand him so well. Each time I think I've got him back, a few months later, like a wave it hits him, and I lose him all over again.'

Cooper stayed silent. Watched the Secret Service through the window doing their morning sweep of the White House grounds. Then after a time, he drew his attention away.

Turned to Woods. Made sure his manner was biting. 'Is Rosedale something to do with you?'

'What?'

'Rosedale. Is he something to do with you?'

Woods shook his head. 'Come on, Coop.'

Cooper's poise stayed hostile. He knew when somebody was trying to be a wiseguy. 'Is he or not?'

'What do you want me to do?'

'Stay out of my life when it comes to my work.'

'You want me to stop caring? Is that what you want Coop?' Woods's tone appealed, but he was wasting his time.

'I don't need babysitting, and especially not from Rosedale. I want you to stop thinking you can make it alright.'

'Then tell me what you want.'

'I want you to tell me the truth about Rosedale. Is that so hard?'

Woods poured himself some water from the glass decanter sitting on the French antique silver tray. Tried to ignore his toothache. Gestured to Cooper who shook his head at the unspoken offer of a drink.

'Look, okay. All I did was make a few calls. Granger and I go back a long way, you know that, so it wasn't a big deal. It wasn't like I was calling up a stranger. And Granger was happy to give Rosedale a job.'

Exasperated, as Cooper often was by Woods, he said, 'Of all people. Rosedale?'

'Relax. Rosedale's a good guy. He'll look out for you. Okay, he has his oddball ways but he's one of the best. He owed me a favor, plus the man was bored. God knows why he thought retirement would suit him... Look, I know you're pissed, but Granger's been keeping me in the loop.

Coop, there's been too many near-misses in the past and now, according to Granger, it's started again.'

'The hell it has, and Granger should keep his goddamn nose out of my business.'

'It has, Coop, and I know why and so do you.'

'You don't know what you're talking about.'

'Oh I think I do. It's about why you went back to Africa, when you said you wouldn't. Breaking your promise to Maddie.'

'What do you know about Maddie? You've never even met her.'

'And is that my fault? You've kept her away, Coop. God knows what you tell her.'

'I don't tell her anything. Might surprise you but you're not the conversation of the day.'

'Why is it that every time I see you there's so much hostility?'

'Listen John, I don't want to talk about that. Let's just stick to the point shall we?'

'Which is?'

'That I just want everyone to understand that they need to keep out of my business and realize I was just doing my job.'

'No, that doesn't cut it... Granger told me about Ellie's death certificate finally coming through... I'm so sorry.'

The heat behind Cooper's eyes began to blur his vision. He pressed his palms into them. 'It didn't just magically come through. Granger couldn't send off for it fast enough, could he? Almost as the clock struck seven years, he was applying to court for a notice of legal presumption of death.'

'Coop, it's only right. You know as well as I do, if the accident had happened in US waters, the death certificate would've been issued years ago because the element of peril would've accelerated the presumption of death. It's only because it happened in international waters that things were different.'

'I don't need a legal lecture. I know how it works.'

'Then you know it's the first time Granger has been able to get some kind of proper closure. Maybe now this is the time for you to get it too.'

'Closure? Because of a piece of paper saying she's..... so we're all supposed to just shut it away and pretend it never happened?'

'You know I don't mean that.'

'Then what do you mean, John?'

'What I mean is, it's there. Written down. It's like an anchor to hold onto. It's tragic, but maybe now it'll help you accept it. Accept what we've been saying for years, rather than it send you spinning.'

'So this is about you being right, is it? And now you want me to just get on with my life?'

'Yes, because you were doing good with Maddie and with Cora. You'd moved on. I could see it. We all could.'

'Had I? Or is that what you all wanted to believe, so that's all you saw?'

'Jesus, listen, Coop. Do *not* throw your life away over this. Nothing's changed. Not since yesterday or last week, or last month or even last year. Everything's still the same. You're just struggling to see it now the death certificate's come through. But you need to accept this... It's finally over.'

'And what if it's not? Think about... No... no, just hear me out. So let's say I accept it because there it is on that damn piece of paper. The date stamps her death... But what if she's alive and the day after the date stamp there's no-one there to keep on looking for her? Don't you see, John? If the truth dies, I'll kill her all over again!'

'Goddamn it, Cooper. The truth is she's dead! The best thing you can do is try to get things sorted with Maddie.'

Cooper shook his head and eyes wide he counted on his fingers.

'One… Two… Three. Three skiffs that day. Three, not two. I know how many there were. I'm not crazy. I wasn't then and I'm not now.'

John Woods strained towards Cooper. 'There were witnesses Coop. And they all say there were only *two* skiffs.'

'You don't know what you're talking about.'

'Jesus. I can see it. That look in your eye. I haven't seen it for a long time, but it's come back and it scares me Coop. No-one wants to lose you… Think about Jackson. How do you think he'd cope if anything happened to you? Please, just tell me you'll accept it. Accept it's over.'

Cooper's eyes darted manically round the room. His breathing. Shallow. Short. Teeth grinding down. Biting hard. Panting, he rested his gaze back on John. 'Whatever you say… I accept it.'

'Coop…? You okay?'

'Fine.'

'Your mouth's bleeding.'

Cooper touched his lips with his fingers. Saw the blood. 'I'll be damned, must've bitten my tongue.'

'You sound real strange. Coop, are you on something?'

'No.'

'You know you can trust me, right? I don't want to see you going down that road again.'

'It wasn't that bad.'

'Come off it. You were doctor shopping with the best of

them. What was it? About twenty, twenty-five different doctors, all writing prescriptions for you in different aliases for painkillers, benzos and opiates, and God knows what else. The way you were and what you did, it's amazing the court only sentenced you to psychological sessions.'

Cooper shifted uncomfortably. He said, 'It's not like that anymore. It's all good.'

'I hope so Coop, because you don't realize how much your behavior affects everyone around you. I'm not laying the blame here but when you just took off to Eritrea and then fell off the radar, Jackson was in a real dark place. I wasn't sure what I'd find from one morning to another when I went into his room…'

The president stopped. Embarrassed. Overwhelmed. Cooper decided it was probably a bit of both. But whatever it was, he wasn't going to push it, he could see John was unprepared for his emotions taking such a stranglehold.

After a minute or so, and regaining his composure, Woods continued. 'Jackson needs you, Coop… he values your friendship above anything else.'

'And that's why I lie to him is it? Because my friendship's so valuable…? It's all based on a house of cards, John.'

President Woods stared at Cooper in disbelief. 'You want me to tell him the truth? Is that it? Is this what this is all about?'

Cooper tried his best to mirror Woods's look of incredulity, but the pills were making his face feel strange. Kinda numb. 'The truth?' he said with scorn. 'Don't make me laugh, John. Everything's secrets and lies. So no, that's not what I'm saying. I just want you to keep the hell out of my work and my business. So you don't have to worry, I'll continue being part of your lies. Though, on reflection, I guess it also makes it convenient for you to keep Jackson in the dark because we both know it sure as hell would destroy *you* if it got out.'

'Wait a goddamn minute, you really think…'

'Hey guys…' Jackson, burst exuberantly into the room with Cora piggybacking. He stopped by the door. Frowned. Glanced at Cooper. Glanced at his father. 'What's going on?'

'I was just telling Coop about last month's Redskins game.'

Jackson pulled a face. 'Why does everyone say they're talking about football when they don't want to say what they were really talking about?'

President Woods winked at his son as he popped a peanut in his mouth. 'Okay, I was actually telling Cooper he needs to look after himself.'

'He's right, Coop.'

Not wanting to get into it with Jackson, Cooper picked up a small framed photo of the president standing next to Captain Beau Neill. 'I haven't seen this before.'

Woods moved round to look at which of the numerous photographs sitting on the mahogany cabinet Cooper had picked up. He gave a small laugh. 'That's the day your Uncle Beau became Captain. He had to go and see the promotion board, but he'd been staying with me and he'd left his jacket at the base. My car wouldn't start, so I had to get my next door neighbor to give him a lift on the back of his Harley to get there in time, and you know how much Beau hates bikes… They were good times.'

There was a knock on the door.

'Yes?'

A young woman, with a quiet demeanour and hair scraped back too tight, entered. Said,

'Mr. President, they're waiting for you downstairs. Senator Walmsley's call is due in seven minutes.'

'Thanks, I'll be with you in a moment.'

John Woods waited for the woman to leave the room, always liking to create a discernible divide between his private and public life. 'Jackson, I'll see you tonight. Coop, will you still be around later?'

Cooper gave a small nod. 'I don't think so, *sir,* so I'll see you around.'

16

In the wet steaming air, near where the muddy brown waters of the Congo River ran deep, Papa Bemba stood over the mounds of unmarked red clay graves. It was best this way. Best for the possessed to remain without a name. To die alone. Unmourned. Unseen. Far away from the living.

Emmanuel had started to ask questions, when there should have been none to ask. Shown concern where there was no place for his scrutiny. And though he'd been warned, his asinine tongue had plagued his words. Voicing his opinion against what he'd learned. Then driven on by an injudicious spirit, and demons which had taken over his mind, Emmanuel had tried to direct others to his way of thinking.

When the illness had struck Emmanuel he'd known it was just. Unlike the others, his illness had been one where repentance and payment were not enough. He'd needed to be an example, to show the villagers how unwise it had been to question Papa Bemba.

Then afterwards, Emmanuel's family had come to speak to him, asking him the whereabouts of their son. The whereabouts of his body. Wanting to give him a burial he didn't deserve. But Papa Bemba hadn't told them because he hadn't known. Though once he'd thought about it, it seemed so clear. Emmanuel was obviously walking amongst them. Part of the living dead. Because how else had his body disappeared from the hut? Emmanuel had gone. Risen up to walk again. And it was obvious to him that with the power of wicked prayer, Emmanuel's family had brought him back from the dead – getting him to walk with evil once more. But his family had paid the price. A heavy price. And the sorcery had been burnt out from them just like the others.

'Papa Bemba are you ready to go?'

He nodded, turning towards the voice of Lumumba, a worthy man, who'd worked for him for six years.

'I am. What time is it?'

'Nearly four o clock. Shall I take you to them?'

Papa Bemba stayed silent for a moment. Although his certainty in his calling was irrefutable, and he would continue to follow the path set out before him, there was a lot of work to be done.

Smiling and using Lumumba's arm to guide him across the uneven ground, Papa Bemba spoke. 'No, I want to rest, I need to think more about Emmanuel. The others can wait.'

Lumumba sounded uneasy, something Papa Bemba picked up on.

'Are you sure?'

Papa Bemba laughed, tapping the man on his arm. 'Quite. But do not trouble yourself my friend, for their time amongst us is at a close. My mission is to subjugate sorcerers, and those who wish to block my path. I realize the only way to overcome the darkness is by the blood of the suffering, and with your help, I will pick them off one by one.'

17

'Goddamn it…! Goddamn it…! Is this how it's going to be?'

John Woods swept the phone off the Resolute desk in the Oval Office, taking with it the gold rimmed white china cup half filled with bad tasting coffee. Landed on the cream foot-rug left over from the Obama administration.

'I thought Senator Walmsley was on board?'

'He was.'

Woods, ignoring his tension headache, stared at Edward 'Teddy' Adleman, his chief of staff and a trusted friend who'd been part of the last administration.

'Then if he was,' replied Woods, 'why the hell isn't he now? He knows we were going to give him what he wanted on the main immigration bill, as well as on some of the smaller points. Jesus, short of blood, I'm giving him everything he asked for. Now all of a sudden he's backing out on our reforms.'

'Mr. President, it's not just Senator Walmsley.'

'What are the numbers now?'

'Nothing's changed since yesterday.'

'Bullshit. Shall I tell you exactly what's changed since yesterday…? Around about three hundred people in this country including kids have been shot in murders or assaults, suicides and suicide attempts, as well shooting accidents, all since we had our last conversation. So don't give me the line about nothing having changed, Teddy... Now give me the numbers.'

'Okay like we discussed yesterday two thirds of Republicans are aiming to block, as well as a number of moderate democrats. We gotta face it: there's no way we're going to gather up enough bipartisan support on these new measures.'

'Jesus Christ, what is wrong with these people?'

Adleman, a tall, dignified Afro-American, shook his head solemnly. 'Come on, John, you know how it is.'

'I do, but every day I keep having hope that someone up on Capitol Hill will eventually decide to do the right god-damn thing. That they'll wake up and realize they have a responsibility to the country. What about any of the senators who backed health care? Have you tried them? There must be some of them who are open to negotiation on this?'

'You got to face it John, they're not happy with you. You got a hostile senate and you know what you're offering on immigration won't even *tempt* them to read the new gun control proposals. They're not interested. A lot of people see your immigration policies as too liberal. They want less immigrants, not more. You're not going to be able to bargain for these gun reform unless you completely change your ethos on the Immigration and Naturalization Act. Right now we have one of the biggest divides in this country that's been seen for a long time.'

Woods shook his head. 'I won't accept there's nothing that can be done.'

'It might be different if we were talking about Homeland issues, but the way things are you haven't really got anything to give them. Nothing that they want. They're not going to budge. And the pressure they're getting from the NRA, along with other pro-gun groups... Well, I'd say that's the main reason you're not going to get the votes. You know as well as I do there's a climate of fear in this country, people want to hold on to what they know and that includes the second amendment... John, I'm sorry but you know these groups spend millions of dollars on campaign contributions, particularly during the election cycle, as well as millions of dollars on lobbying. And every time there's a shooting tragedy...'

Woods interrupted. Annoyance bouncing on his words. 'That's every day, don't forget that. Every day there's a shooting tragedy, not just the ones that are in the press, Teddy.'

'Apologies, Mr. President, I should've worded that better. The problem we've got is when we call for stricter controls what happens, as you know, are the pro-gun groups rally their members to fight against new restrictions. They spread fear and uncertainty and donations go up. There are a hell of a lot of senators falling out of these groups' pockets. The gun groups have bankrolled their campaigns. They've got a vice-like grip on half of Capitol Hill.'

Frustrated, Woods said, 'Yeah, I know all that, but Walmsley knew all this and he was okay about it before. What's changed?'

'Pressure, John. That's what's changed. He's even got a few anonymous threats. Those senators don't have the balls when it comes to standing up to special interest groups. They get intimidated and as a consequence our reforms get undermined.'

'Oh come on, don't give me that Teddy. You say this every time.'

'You know how high passions run on gun control. This goes right to the heart of our constitution. As a nation, we want to preserve that.'

'And what about preserving lives? And the American

people tend to agree. What did the last polls come in at? 85 percent backed our reforms?'

'Oh come on, we haven't believed what polls have said in a long time. And anyway, even if they were right, you could have a hundred polls saying we got a hundred percent backing. That's not the problem, Mr. President, and you know that. The problem is the overwhelming sense coming down from Capitol Hill is that you're trying to overstep your legal authority on these reforms. Plus, the gun control campaign we've been running hasn't helped. Seems like a lot of the Republican senators feel like we've demonized them along with the pro-gun groups. It's a mess. They think the social media campaigns we've run have made them look like the criminals. No-one's going to like that, especially when it looks like it comes from the White House.'

'I don't get how the hell they can talk about us and our campaign? Have you seen what the lobbyists are doing? They're blatantly spreading lies about our reforms. Making out that it'll be a kind of Big Brother atmosphere for gun owners. You talk about a climate of fear? Jesus, nobody's trying to take away the second amendment here, we're just trying to stop our children being killed.'

'I know, but when it's time to vote, they're going to vote against, and they'll say they're just protecting the rule of law and the constitution.'

'Bullshit! I'm trying to protect the American people and they know it, it's an excuse. This issue totally exemplifies the dysfunctional nature of Congress. Every goddamn time restrictions are proposed, the pro-gun groups tells everyone it'll make no difference to the number of shootings and massacres and the perpetrator would've committed these crimes anyway... But try telling that to the families who've lost loved ones. Senator Walmsley needs to get his head out of his ass and see what's really important.'

Woods stopped to take a deep breath. It took all of his resolve not to put the Smith and Watson Georgian-style chair through one of the eleven foot high oval windows. Though in truth, he knew he might have a tough time trying – bullet resistant glass had a way of stopping things.

His temper and this job, sometimes they just didn't match. Hell, it didn't even get close. Damn problem was he cared too much. And it wasn't lost on him that this was something he told Cooper not to do. He actually thought he'd got his temper on something of an even keel, though whether he'd achieved that was an entirely different matter. The *Post* certainly didn't think so. As of late, most of the cartoon captions had some kind of reference to his legendary outbursts. Exaggerated, yes. But not altogether untrue. Though he would rather call it passion.

He pointed his finger at Adleman. Jaw so tight from stress it damn near felt it'd locked. He rubbed the side of his face. 'You need to give Congress a goddamn message from me. They need to stop fighting me on these gun reforms and start thinking about the families and their communities. And you can also send Walmsley the photos.'

'You can't do that. It's not going to help. If anything, it's going to make it worse.'

'I said, send him the photos… Joan…! Joan! Can you come in here a minute?'

Woods's secretary hurried in. Calm. Unruffled. Two qualities that explained why he'd hired her. And two qualities, at moments like this, he wished he had. 'I want you to send Senator Walmsley the pictures of the kids who were killed at Liberbush Elementary. He needs to see what backing out of the reform means.'

The side glance from Joan to Alderman didn't get missed. Woods chewed on the skin of his thumb nail. 'You got a problem with that, Joan?'

'No, sir.'

'I think you have.'

'No.'

'Tell me honestly. You know I value your opinion.'

Joan tucked her almost-too-short dyed black hair behind her ear. She glanced at Teddy Adleman who nodded encouragingly.

'Okay, well, I think it's the wrong thing to do, Mr. President. The rationale rests on the supposition that it's not the gun that kills a person, it's the person. And I agree with that sentiment and so do a lot of other people. So sending photos to Senator Walmsley of the babies who were shot and killed, however hideous the injuries, won't serve any purpose apart from alienating yourself more from the Senate.'

'But I need to show Walmsley and a few other senators *exactly* what happened on this latest massacre.'

'Mr. President, with due respect they're intelligent men and I have no doubt they know *exactly* what happened and how. Seeing the photos won't make a difference to getting votes for your reform. The people who are going to vote against are pro-gun, not pro-violence. That's a big difference right there.'

'Then how come the rest of the world are looking at America in bewilderment and wondering why the hell we don't do something about our gun laws and our predilection for guns?'

'We're unique in that we have our constitution to uphold.'

'Bullshit… sorry, Joan, but bullshit.'

'There are a lot people who are worried your reforms aren't going to uphold the second amendment.'

'The second amendment was written in 1791, for God's sake! People quite rightly were defending their land and their cattle, but they did it with muskets and Kentucky long rifles, not a 516 multicaliber semiautomatic which blows a hole in you the size of a grapefruit. America has to change with the times. Let me give you a couple of figures.'

Joan looked exasperated, but Woods carried on: 'Over seventeen thousand children and teens are shot each year. Over three thousand of them die. And if you include adults in that figure then we have a goddamn grand total of over *one hundred and ten thousand* people shot in this country on average *each year*. And nearly thirty-three thousand of them die. So come on, Joan, tell me about your precious second amendment now.'

Joan, red faced and needing the bathroom, held her ground. 'I could point out that gun ownership in places like Finland and Switzerland are high but they don't have a problem with their crime rates. And the states here in America with the strongest gun control laws, like California, are the ones with the highest gun-homicide rates. Then conversely you've got places like Utah, who have very few gun control laws, but they also have a very low number of gun crime homicides. So truly, I don't see these reforms will have any bearing.'

'I'm not trying to stop people having guns, but there's got to be more we can do. More reforms on assault and high caliber weapons, more criminal and mental health background checks, and the ability to close the loopholes which allow guns to be sold to the wrong people.'

Joan sniffed. Pulled down the hem of her spotted cardigan.

'My point still stands, Mr. President. It's not the gun, it's the person.'

'And my point is if we don't try these restrictions then America won't know if they work. But I appreciate you telling me your view… Now send him the goddamn photos. And Teddy, you need to find those votes and I don't care how we do it, just get them.'

18

It had been two days since Cooper had returned from Washington and even though there was a lot to think about, he'd been trying to do anything but. Work was his escape as well as his self-imposed imprisonment. A license to avoid anything other than the job he was doing. A place where the task in hand was a substitute for his reality.

He remembered back to how his Uncle Beau had been just before he'd left the Navy, unable to contemplate anything other than the life he'd built around it. Unable to see any future in the midst of his own fear of leaving everything he'd ever known. Everything he'd relied on after a lifetime of avoiding his own conflicts. His own internal war, which seemed worse than facing any adversary out on the field. But unlike his Uncle, who'd found his peace through God, giving him the courage and strength to think, allowing him just to be, he knew he didn't have that. He had no God. No peace. And no matter how unafraid of his fellow man he was, how many perilous situations he found himself in, he didn't have the courage just to be. For that, he envied his Uncle.

He stood in Granger's office next to Maddie and Rosedale, impatient to know what was on offer. He had to get out. Feel like he was doing something worthwhile. And maybe it'd be a good thing to put some distance between himself and Maddie. Not that there'd been a problem. They'd been cordial, hell, almost friendly, when he'd dropped Cora off.

He'd had the feeling Maddie had wanted to talk. But that was women! He didn't have anything to say. Nothing to give her even if he wanted to. He couldn't feel a goddamn thing. So why make things harder and disappoint her more by talking? It was better for Maddie to think him an uncommunicative jackass than let her know that her husband, estranged or not, felt absolutely nothing at all.

'There's a job for you if you want it, Cooper. Came in from one of the international banks.' Granger unapologetically threw some papers at Cooper, but it was Maddie who bent down to pick them up. After skim reading the details she stared at Granger in disbelief.

'Are you serious? You can't send him there.'

Granger leant forward, clearly annoyed but somewhat curious to hear Maddie's rationale. He swivelled round in his chair letting her talk. 'Go on.'

'I thought we'd decided we were going to send that job back to the bank. It's too dangerous. Let them sign it off.'

'And why would I do that if I've got Cooper here to do it?'

Maddie's face flushed. A flash of anger crossed her eyes. She chewed on her lip – something she did when she was trying not to show her true feelings. But she didn't have to say anything. Cooper knew she was worried about him.

He said, 'Listen, Maddie, it's cool, okay?'

She stared at Granger. God, she hated that she felt like this. In fact, she hated that she felt anything at all. She wanted to be free of it. But how could she? How do you just turn off loving someone? She'd loved him from the beginning.

But he'd been in love with Ellie. As obsessed with Ellie as Ellie had been with him. So there was nothing to be done apart from try to get on with things. And that had been fine, or rather she'd had to make it fine. But, after the accident, she'd reached out to him. She could see he'd needed someone to help and love him, as his obsession over his search for Ellie had grown, and he'd spiralled. Helter-skeltering into bottles of pills. Getting further and further away from reality. Out of control. Out of his mind.

When things had got really dark, really bleak, she'd almost lost faith. Almost. But then in one session at the veteran's psychiatric medical facility, promoted by his therapist, he'd asked her to marry him and – maybe foolishly – she'd said yes. Hoping her love for him would help him begin to live again.

Initially there was no glimmer of anything nearing hope. But when Cora had been born, he'd stopped searching. Fought his addiction. Fought his demons. Given up the ghost… literally. And they'd been happy… or so she'd thought.

But now, like a haunting, the ghost had come back. She could see it in his eyes. But now it was different because they had Cora. She couldn't stay and disappear down the tunnel with him. Drowning alongside. And even though it had hurt to leave. Did hurt. Still hurt. Couldn't breathe. It was the right thing to do. Happy or not.

Keeping a level voice, she spoke to Granger. 'If you care about him at all, you wouldn't let him go. Not there.'

Cooper looked embarrassed by the care Maddie still showed him, even after everything; it made him feel uncomfortable. He decided to take over the conversation. It was the easiest way out.

'Can someone just tell me what we're talking about rather than talk around me? If it's escaped anyone's notice, I'm a grown man.'

With his slow Texas drawl like a lazy summer's day, Rosedale winked. 'The jury's still out on that one, Thomas.'

Cooper gave him a cold stare, but avoided being drawn in. 'Granger, what's this job?'

Granger rubbed the middle of his chest, the eggs over easy his wife had made him for breakfast repeating on him. 'Guy's fallen behind on his payments for a plane.' He stopped to study the paperwork before continuing to talk. 'Looks like he hasn't paid for six months. The usual deal. The banks and the like have tried to get in touch with him but he seems to have gone underground, so now of course they're looking to get the plane back. It's a nice little number, a Daher-Socata TBM-900, six seater with up to 330 knot cruise speed and a G1000 Avionics Suite. The whole thing is worth in the region of 3 to 4 mill. Less than a year old, so it's worth the bank pursuing it for a resale. The problem is the place they have to go to get it.'

'Which is?' asked Cooper.

Maddie butted in. 'Which is the Democratic Republic of the Congo. Go figure.'

Granger spoke dryly to her. 'I think I can manage this conversation on my own, Maddison. But she's right, that's where it is, and it's also why they asked us… *No job is too big or too much trouble.*'

'Seriously, Granger,' said Cooper, 'you need to change that tag line.'

Rosedale, flicking the flame of his silver lighter on and off, grinned. 'Hell, Thomas, if you'd rather go home and drink your milk, I'm sure we can handle it. Me and Miss Maddison here. I'd rather take my chances on her.'

Maddie, who also seemed to want to ignore Rosedale, seethed, her cheeks turning even redder than before.

Cooper was glad she refused to rise to the obvious bait. The man was a schmuck. Maddie had confided in him that

Rosedale had annoyed her from the very first day they'd met, and she and Levi had apparently had various discussions as to why Granger had employed him. She'd thought his employment was strange, mainly because Granger was usually so transparent in his business and staffing policies.

He knew Maddie had picked up an air of secrecy over the hiring of Rosedale, and he also knew, women being women, she'd wanted to get to the bottom of it. She'd asked him what he thought, but he hadn't said anything. Just shrugged as she'd carried on surmising, with her concluding that although she didn't care for Rosedale, and she was sure Granger was hiding something, she could understand why he'd asked him to join the firm; he was probably one of the best. But being one of the best didn't mean she was ever going to like him.

'You can't do this, Granger.'

Granger, already irritated by the invasion of his office, snapped. 'Maddison, you're part of the team which means you're part of the family. I appreciate what you're saying, but don't tell me what I should do.'

Maddie bristled but kept her composure. Despair colored her voice. 'This is crazy guys. Granger, he's just come back from Africa. I don't know why he went but you do, and you're willing to send him again? Tell me what's going on.'

'That's down to Cooper to tell you, not me. And anyway, him going to Africa got me thinking. If I can't beat them, join them.'

'What's that supposed to mean?'

'What it's supposed to mean Maddison, is that Cooper here seems insistent, no matter what I say, on turning into the next Livingstone. And as that's the case I might as well use it to my advantage. Give him the jobs nobody else wants. Earn some money from the bug up his ass.'

'Don't do this, Granger. Tom, you're not really going to go. Why don't you take some time out? Even back at the ranch for a couple of weeks? I'll come across at the weekend and drop off Cora. You can go riding with her. Fishing. She'd love that. What do you say?'

Rosedale winked. 'Should do as the little lady says.'

Cooper gave Maddie a small smile, but his mind was elsewhere. Taking the job in the Congo would mean he needn't stay. He could get away from all the questions and the probing and the issues and the problems.

'I'll take one of the helicopters to go and get my things from the ranch. I left some of my equipment there. I could take Cora for the ride. What do you think, Maddie?'

Maddie shook her head. 'I can't believe you're going to do this. *Please,* Tom. It's crazy. Granger, *please.*'

'This is getting good! There's nothing like the Midwest for melodrama.'

Cooper snarled. Thought about punching Rosedale. Would leave it for another time. 'Put a sock in it, Rosedale… Listen, Maddie, I really…'

'You know what Tom, I don't want to hear it. I don't want to hear you telling me you've got to do it, because we both know that's not true. If you take this job there's nothing I can do… other than what Granger just said… *If I can't beat them, join them.* So that's what I'm going to do! Get on with it, and join you.'

Cooper had no doubt he looked shocked. 'What?'

'You heard me. If you go, I'm going too. We've always worked together as a team. So what's the problem? You were the one who said being separated wouldn't be an issue when it came to working together. I quote, *it'll be cool, business as usual*. And us working together on an investigation, well that's normal, wouldn't you say?'

Cooper spun round to Granger. 'No way. No way is she coming.'

'For God's sake if she says she wants to go, then she can go. We're not in fifth grade.'

'She can't!'

'What d'ya mean she can't? She's a better shot than you. Keeps her head. And knows her way around a plane and a boat as well as the two of you do. I'm not in the business of employing people who aren't up to the job. So there should be no problem. Should there?'

'What if something happened to her?'

Granger rubbed his head, drawing his hand down his face in weary exasperation. 'I don't know what to tell you, Coop.'

Cooper turned to Maddie. 'Listen, it's not happening. Maddie, I'm sorry there's no way you're going.'

'Excuse me? I'm not quite sure if I heard right. I thought for a moment you were trying to tell me what I could or couldn't do.'

Cooper glared back at her. 'And what about Cora? Who's going to look after her? You need to be at home with her.'

'Oh my God, tell me you just didn't say that.'

'Listen to me…'

'No, stop! Don't go there. Cora will be fine as she always is when we go on a job. She'll stay with my parents *as usual*. She'll love it *as usual*. The only person who doesn't seem to be able to do *usual* is you. Now if suddenly you've got a problem with the child care arrangements why don't *you* stay and look after Cora, and Rosedale and I will go.'

Rosedale tipped his hat and winked at Maddie. He grinned. 'There's a word in Texas for strong women like you.'

'Shut up, Rosedale, I don't want to hear it.'

Wanting to defuse the situation, Cooper tried to sound deliberately casual. 'Maddie, look. It's no big deal for me to go to the DRC. But for you? Come on, it's crazy.'

Maddie raised her voice. Her suppressed emotions twisting and transferring, channelling her feelings into hurt, hostile words.

'Don't you dare, Tom! Don't try to manipulate this situation and make out you're worried about me. You just want, for whatever reason, to go out there on your own. Next thing we know you'll have disappeared, like so many times before. Admit it. You know I'm right.'

Cooper clenched his jaw. Tightened his fist. Unclenched his jaw. Untightened his fist. He said. 'You're not right. It's just work.'

'Then if this is purely professional, if it's not really a big deal to go to the DRC, then hell, I've got bills to pay as well. In fact, why don't we make this a party? Why don't we all go...? Levi, you coming?'

Levi, who'd walked into Granger's office just moments before, stared at Maddie wide eyed. 'You lost your mind, Maddie? No. *No* way. You can count me out of this one.'

Maddie, continuing her emotional outburst, leant across Granger's desk. 'Then how about you, Granger? What do you say? You want to join us? Seeing as going to the Congo isn't a big deal... Come on, how about it? Being as you're so keen to send Tom. What do you say?'

Granger turned three shades of red. Stood up. Surpassed himself by slamming both fists down. 'I say you need to go and calm down, Maddison. Go and drink some camomile tea or whatever it is that you women do at this time of the month.'

'Are you freaking kidding me? What cave have you just stepped out of? And if anybody should go there it's me. I know that place better than anybody here. It's part of who I am.'

'Maddie,' said Cooper, 'you were born here. It's only your daddy who comes from there and he left when he was twenty. And as for your Mom, she's an all American girl from Wyoming.'

'It's still a place I know well. I visited my grandma a lot when I was a little girl, until...' She trailed off. A flicker of pain crossing her face. 'Anyway, enough... I've got things to do. But I'll be ready to go with Cooper and Rosedale. I'll call you later for the details.'

'Maddie!' Cooper called after her as she slammed out of Granger's office.

Rosedale, who at this point was polishing his cowboy boots with the edge of the drapes, broke the silence.

'Looks like someone's upset. Hands up if y'all reckon the worst decision this great country ever made was to give women their rights and let them out of the kitchen and into the workforce?' He gazed round at the solemn faces of the other three then grinned. 'Or is that just me?'

Cooper didn't bite. Wasn't going to give him that. Instead, he turned to Granger.

'How soon can we leave?'

'If admin can sort out the paperwork, we can have you all ready to roll by Wednesday. And Cooper, just find the plane this time and fly it back to the international BLC office in Nairobi. We'll go over details later. Keep your mind on the job. No distractions, otherwise someone may get hurt. You understand what I'm saying?'

Cooper regarded Granger. Like with Rosedale, he wasn't going to get into anything with him. 'Who's the plane registered to?'

Putting on his glasses, Granger glanced again at the pile of papers in front of him, scanning them for a name. He peered at one of the plane documents, trying to read the signature. Gave up, and grumbled aloud. 'What the hell sort of writing is this? That looks like a three.'

Gazing at the document, Cooper turned it round towards him, staring at the signature in question.

'That's not a three, Granger, that's an E… Look.'

'Who the hell writes an E backwards? Are you sure?'

'Yeah look. Emmanuel.' He held up the document for the others to see.

3mmanuel Mutombo

'The plane's registered to someone called Mutombo. Emmanuel Mutombo.'

19

'No way Maddison, you've lost your mind.' Marvin Menga stared and despaired and appealed to his daughter as they stood in the large pretty bedroom of the Arizona house she and Cooper had bought after they'd got married. 'Put that stuff down and listen… Maddie, I'm talking to you.'

Maddie turned to her father. 'I've got to pack… Cora! Hey, Cora, are you coming to help me put my clothes in?'

Like a whirlwind, Cora Cooper ran through. Went straight up to Maddie's open suitcase. Dropped in what she held in her hands. 'Here you are, I thought they could keep you company.'

'Baby they're worms!'

'Don't be silly. They're not worms, Mommy, they're magic. Shall I go and get some more?'

'No, it's fine honey, I think I've got enough magic there don't you?' Maddie paused looked at her father. 'Actually, Cora, why don't you go and get Grandpappy some magic. I think he needs some to make him smile.'

With a nod and a skip, Cora bounced out of the bedroom.

'I don't want you going. Not to there. There's no way you're going.'

'Daddy, that's the second time somebody's said that to me today. The first time it didn't make any difference and it's not going to this time.'

Patting down his neatly cut afro, Marvin sat on the bed

harder than he'd intended to. Knocked the pile of clothes right off. 'What can I say to stop you?'

'There isn't anything you can say.'

'What if I told you that I won't look after Cora if you go?'

'Then I know that wouldn't be really you speaking. I've got to do this. Don't make it harder.'

Marvin sighed. 'Why?'

'Tom can't go on his own. He's not in a good place.'

Those words were all that was needed for Marvin to lose his cool.

'*He's* not in a good place? Can I remind you Maddison it was less than a week ago when I had to come and pick you up from the floor in the middle of nowhere? And why did I? Because of that man. Yet it's *him* who's not in a good place. I bet he hasn't even noticed how cut up you are. Was this his idea, for you to go along and hold his hand?'

'No. In fact he didn't want me to go.'

'Doesn't surprise me. He probably wants to go and disappear like he always does. To hell with responsibilities.'

Quiet, real quiet, Maddie said, 'Daddy, he can't do anything right in your eyes, can he? He said as much.'

'Well at least he and I agree on something. I don't know why you had to pick a man like him.'

'Don't start this again.'

'You could've stayed in Mississippi and caught yourself a decent man. A church-going man.'

'You make it sound like a fishing trip. And I would've been happy staying back at home?'

'Well you made it clear enough by running off and getting some unsuitable job.'

It was Maddie's turn to sigh. 'I didn't run off, you know that, and joining the Navy was hardly unsuitable.'

'It is for a woman.'

'What is wrong with you Daddy?'

'Me? I'm not the one trying to prove something. You're a mother, Maddison, you need to remember that.'

'Sorry, have I just suddenly time-travelled to a different century? Why is it when men want to do certain things or certain jobs it's accepted or maybe they're even admired for it, but when women do these things it suddenly becomes a question of us wanting to prove ourselves? You need to get it into your head that I'm just good at my job – better than a lot of men I know. Plus I enjoy it. Period. I don't need to prove anything.'

'Maddie, I'm not talking about proving yourself with your job. I'm talking about proving to yourself you can go back to the DRC after what happened to you.'

Maddie froze. Dead still. Closed her eyes. 'That was a long time ago and it's got nothing to do with it.'

'I think it has, I think…'

'Just stop, Daddy. I love you but you don't know every-thing.'

'I do know you don't have to do this.'

'I do, and I'm going to, and nothing you say will change my mind. Now let's just leave it at that.'

20

'Hey.'

'Look, if you've come here for a fight, don't bother. Oh, and don't bother trying to change my mind about coming either.'

Cooper tilted his head as he stood at the kitchen door of Maddie's house. *Their house*. 'No, I come in peace. Here, I even brought you a donut from Mac's diner… Thought I'd come to see how you were getting on with the research. Sorry, I left it for you. Had a few things to sort out.'

Looking up from her computer screen, Maddie gave a half smile. Ignored the way her tummy had butterflies when she looked at him. 'It's as I thought, I can't get any kind of information from the authorities over there. They're notoriously secretive, and pretty paranoid. The contacts we've got over there have drawn a blank. Not that it really matters, because the likelihood of them having a record of a small plane is zero to none. And from what I hear, their aviation department has troubles of their own. It's not looking good for them.'

'What do you mean?'

'Well for a start, the Democratic Republic of Congo has one of the world's *worst* aviation safety records. Did you know the majority of their airlines are banned from entering any EU airspace because of failing to meet regulatory standards? Also, one of the main DRC airlines – connected to the government, incidentally – have had a couple of planes impounded for non-payment themselves. They've been impounded over in South Africa after a court order. To release them, they're looking at well over thirty mill. So it looks like they're in the same boat as our Emmanuel Mutombo. So getting any sort of help from them just isn't about to happen.'

Taking a bite from one of the sugared donuts, Cooper sat down. 'What about international data records? See if it's been flown out of the country.'

'Usual story. Like trying to find a pin in the ocean. You know the score. It's one thing tracking down a commercial airliner – though that's not altogether easy – but when someone's flying a private plane, the ability to track it has so many variables. It'll depend on location and the routing of their flight, and of course if the flight has been filed by the pilot, which in this case it won't have. My guess is, if this Emmanuel guy *did* fly it he would've blocked the aircraft tail number.'

'In other words, impossible to trace.'

'Totally. Here in the States the Federal Aviation Administration requires all aircraft to have a visible registered tail number… but that's certainly not the case for a lot of countries. The problem is, if by some kind of miracle they *hadn't* blocked out the tail number, and they had filed a flight out of the country, the accuracy level of tracing the plane is mainly based on which technology is available in that particular geographical area, which won't be a lot in the DRC and surrounding countries. It's only been in the past few years that N'Djili Airport in Kinshasa has had a radar system, so we don't have the luxury of the vast sources of data from receivers that track ADS-B or aircraft equipped with Mode S, like we do here. So it looks like we'll be looking for this plane the old school way… Knocking on doors. But you know all this anyway.'

Cooper grinned. 'I know, but I didn't want to stop you in full flow. I know how much you like your research.'

'No. I know how much you *don't* like yours and hey, someone has to do it.'

He winked. 'And you're great at it. You see, you'd be wasted just in the kitchen.'

Maddie picked up the pen next to her and threw it at Cooper. 'You're starting to sound like Rosedale.'

'Difference is, I don't mean it... Hey baby.' Cooper's face lit up as Cora walked into the kitchen, clad in a pair of pink fluffy teddy bear pyjamas.

'What have you got there, honey?'

'A picture.'

'Can I see it?'

'No.'

'Why not?'

'Because you haven't said please.'

Cooper laughed. 'You're right, Cora, I should know better and mind my manners... *Please* can I see your picture?'

'No.'

'Why not?'

'Because it's a secret.'

'A secret?'

Cora nodded furiously, making her chestnut curly hair bounce over her face. 'You said it was a secret.'

'I said that?'

'You said when we went to see John, it was a secret.'

Cooper stiffened as he felt Maddie's gaze on him. 'Can Mommy see it, honey?'

'No.'

'*Please.*'

'No. Daddy said it was a secret.'

To which Cooper grinned. 'Well then you better go and hide it.'

Maddie frowned. 'Who's John, Cora?'

'Daddy's friend.'

Cooper shrugged his shoulders. Bit his lip. Pulled a face. 'I think she means James. I took her to see him when we were looking to buy a pony for her.'

Cora giggled. 'Not James, Daddy. *John*. John in the big white house.'

Quietly, Maddie pressed on. 'Tell me about John, honey.'

'Jesus, Maddie, stop questioning her.'

Maddie stopped. Stared. Narrowed her eyes. 'Why is that such a problem to you?'

'Because she's a kid, and all she's done is draw a picture and you're going in at her like the CIA. Leave her alone... Cora, why don't you get back into bed and I'll come and tuck you up in a minute.'

Cora looked at Mommy and then at Daddy, and something told her maybe what she'd said had made them cross. 'Have I done something wrong?'

Cooper shook his head and gently pulled Cora in towards him. 'Listen to me, baby. You have done nothing wrong. You understand that?'

'You're not mad at me?'

'Oh honey, I couldn't be mad at you if I tried. I love you.'

'I love you too, Daddy.'

'Go on, go to bed. I'll be through in a minute.'

Cooper watched Cora skip out of the room. He stood up in an atmosphere which was so heavy he would've sworn you could've knocked it with a hammer. As he got to the door, Maddie's words hooked him and tried to reel him in. 'Don't do that again.'

'What?'

'Well apart from making me look like the bad guy, don't get our daughter to keep secrets.'

'I'm not.'

'Tom, I know you, and I know Cora would do anything you asked her to. Don't abuse her trust.'

Cooper rubbed his head. 'Jesus Christ, Maddie, have you heard yourself? You know what Cora's like. She loves pretending she's got secrets.'

'I know what you're like. I know how you love *having* secrets.'

'Well thanks for that vote of confidence, Maddison. I didn't come here for this… Look, I'll speak to you tomorrow.'

'Tom, who's John?'

'Maddie, leave it okay. There is *no* John. Cora's just a kid, she's got it wrong.'

21

Wednesday turned into Thursday which turned into Friday, before the trio finally arrived in the oppressive humidity of the towered chaos of the capital city, Kinshasa, which spread and sprawled out from the shoreline of the Congo River.

It had been a long trip, with the heat hitting them like they'd just opened a stove door. The twenty-mile taxi ride from the airport hadn't helped either. The driver hadn't seemed as if he'd known what he was doing; swerving precariously and speeding, weaving along the city's half-built tarmac roads like he was the emergency services.

The city was a mass of contrasts; high-rise luxury apartment blocks and offices stood centrally, surrounded by eroded housing with bad sanitation, and crumbling roadways. Kinshasa was home to more than six million people. Homeless young children hid amongst the rubble of derelict buildings and the displaced sat alongside the roads as the disorder of the traffic mirrored so many people's lives, and poverty roamed the streets like a predatory beast.

And as Cooper stood contemplating all this in the hotel lobby, dressed inconspicuously in casual blue jeans and t-shirt, he stared at Rosedale, dressed in a gaudy canary yellow suit.

'Do you have to wear that?' It was Rosedale who spoke.

'Me?' Cooper looked at him incredulously. Said nothing else. Took a drink from his water bottle to help the two pills he had under his tongue to go down easier, and walked across to Maddie.

'You okay?'

'Yeah, I'm cool, Tom. Why wouldn't I be?'

'You just seem quiet. How does it feel to be back?'

'I'm fine and it feels fine.'

'You don't have to pretend.'

Snapping, Maddie said, 'Well you'd be the expert on that wouldn't you? It's a bit late to start worrying about me now… God, where did that come from? Sorry. I'm just tired. Listen, why don't we go straight to the address we've got once Tweety Pie over there finishes checking in.'

Cooper grinned. 'I know, right. But as long as I've known Rosedale, he's dressed like that. But don't ever be fooled by him, when he wants to be he's one of the most dangerous…'

'Okay, guys, you want the good news or the bad?' Rosedale's voice boomed across the lobby, interrupting the rest of Cooper's sentence. Then Maddie, with zero tolerance of Rosedale, sighed.

'Just tell us already.'

'Well the bad news is the booking's been messed up and they've only got one room. But the good news is, it means you, little lady, will be sharing a bed with me, and maybe if you're lucky, I'll show you what a real Texan cowboy can do with his lasso.'

22

'If you go left down the Avenue du Kasai for about three miles, we should be close to where we want to be.' Absent-mindedly, Maddie directed Rosedale as they drove the battered white Toyota they'd been overcharged to hire.

The place looked exactly the same as it had been when she'd visited years ago. And the tight knot in her stomach told her what she'd refused to think… Maybe she shouldn't have come. Maybe she just wouldn't ever be ready to come back here. A place where anarchy and the chase for survival was part of the daily life. And the overwhelming pain in the street children's eyes rushed out of them like an unexpected snow storm. But it was a place, a country which was part of her soul and one she'd once loved. Sighing, as an overwhelming sense of sadness descended on her, she closed her eyes.

In the backseat of the SUV, Cooper was having similar thoughts. Doubting the wisdom of coming. The last time he'd been here, he'd been looking for Ellie, after watching a news report talking about a group of long-forgotten foreign hostages who'd originally been kidnapped in Somalia, but who had been found enslaved by the M23 movement – a Congolese revolutionary army, based mainly in the eastern areas of the Democratic Republic of Congo and operating on the whole in the province of North Kivu. A violent, militia rebel force, known for their use of torture and rape as weapons of war, with forced recruitment of both men and boys.

Of course the search for Ellie had been futile. But it was probably the first time he'd prayed for her to be dead. The idea that somewhere, somehow, she was caught up in the tragic legacy of the relentless scrabble and pursuit of violence and power, along with the merciless use of sexual torture, was beyond contemplation.

Rosedale broke his reverie. 'Down here?' he asked, but turned left anyhow as the road they were driving on turned into a risky obstacle course of potholes. Maddie nodded but didn't say anything. Turned round to look at Cooper. 'Okay?'

He stared out of the window. 'It's not great, is it?'

Giving a half smile, Maddie replied with a hint of wistfulness. 'No. Sadly, this country seems to have just been forgotten by the rest of the world. The DRC has got so much potential, and okay I know I'm biased, but I just don't get why the US isn't doing more work in partnership with this government. President Woods seems to be at a hiatus over Africa. His foreign policy has just been focused in the Middle East. There's a lot of catch up to do in sub-Saharan Africa in general. And when I think about it, every time Woods speaks about Africa, this country hardly gets a mention. The man's a real disappointment.'

Cooper bristled. He couldn't help it. And he had to work hard to ignore Rosedale's quick, sly, sideward glance. 'It's complicated.'

'Complicated! Tom, look around you. There's nothing complicated about homeless, starving children. On this journey alone, how many kids have we seen? Twenty? Thirty? The *Post* and *New York Times* need to come and spend a week here. This should be splashed across the front pages. And it's not just because my daddy's side of the family come from here. It makes me so mad that Woods gave us all the *one world, one people* speech, talking about helping to make strong nations, because that's what we want. No-one's looking for pity, and a Band-Aid record with a group of over privileged westerners looking to come to help the *underprivileged* is not going to help. This isn't about poverty porn. This is about helping to develop and grow a strong and sustainable economic market and future for the next generation. It's always the same thing, everyone thinking the next president is going to be better than the last. They said Woods was going to be something special, Kennedy-esqe. But it's bull, he clearly doesn't care.'

Cooper mumbled quietly. Shifted in his seat. 'I'm sure he does, Maddie, but like I say, it's complicated. I guess to understand the place you have to understand the history. The colonialism, the dictatorial rule, the plundering of the country's wealth by the government and other nations, and of course the wars which left the people scarred and trau-matized. And now there's a complete lack of state rule, with militia and rebel forces running amok. It's a mess, and there aren't any simple solutions.'

Maddie stared at Cooper. Her face reddening, she spoke in a high pitch tone, which always sent Cooper crazy. 'Don't. Don't you dare tell me about the country I spent a lot of my childhood in, Tom. The place my daddy was born in and eventually had to leave. I understand it all too well. This place is in me. And it breaks my heart to see it how it is, to see those children back there without any hope. And I know only too well why it is how it is. So I don't need you to give me facts out of a history book, when what I know, and what my family have been through is real.'

Cooper looked at her evenly. 'Have you finished now? You're getting yourself upset.'

'Don't patronize me.'

'Me? Patronize you?'

'What's that supposed to mean?'

Cooper shrugged. 'Nothing. Forget it. We're all tired.'

'You can be so arrogant at times, Tom. That's one of the things that always annoyed me about you. Why did I think it'd be any different now we're not together?'

It was an audible groan from Cooper. 'Maddie, *please.*'

To which Rosedale whistled. Grinned. Turned his head to wink at Maddie. 'You are some kind of woman, Miss Maddison. I think I'm getting to like you. What do they say? Never mix politics with affairs of the heart. But you, honey, you are just throwing that goddamn rule book away. Lord only knows I can feel this is going to be one helluva trip.'

The trio fell silent and Cooper glanced round as Rosedale continued driving at speed downtown. He felt ridiculous, being so defensive over Woods.

What was it with him? He could see exactly what Maddie was saying. He could see it all. He'd travelled extensively throughout the place. And even watching out of the window, as he was now, it was there. Staring at him in the face. All there, yet he could never just sit back and let anyone say anything about Woods or his politics. And it pissed him off.

Hell, it wasn't as if he even agreed with all of Woods's policies either. There'd been many a time he and Jackson had had heated, midnight discussions with John about home and international issues. Often ending with John or Cooper knocking off a couple of plates from the table. But when it came to anyone *else* saying something, relative or otherwise, he was ready to endorse every goddamn one of John's decisions.

It was another reason for him to keep people at a distance.

The less people knew he had any sort of relationship with Jackson, never mind Woods, the better. Even Maddie.

Sometimes he felt bad for not telling her, but even after she had his child, he'd never mentioned he knew Jackson, and neither had anyone else. He guessed Maddie knew better than to ask where he was going. She'd just come to accept that was him. That was how it was. So it'd been easy to go and visit Jackson and John when he wanted to. And so far it'd been fine to take Cora – well it had been, until she'd drawn the picture of John. He guessed he needed to rethink it all, especially as Cora's favorite pastime now was to convey in great detail the events of her day and tell everyone about her *secrets*.

And as for Granger, he'd been friends with John and Beau, growing up together in Hannibal, Missouri, so of course Granger knew of his connection with Woods, as did Rosedale. The other person who'd known, apart from Levi and Dorothy Walker, who he'd confided in a long time ago, was Ellie. He'd told her everything. Everything. There wasn't anything she hadn't known about him. But then, Ellie had been perfect… *was* perfect.

So there it was. Beau, Granger, Levi, Dorothy and Rosedale. Five people who knew some or all of his business. Five people all keeping a secret from Maddie. Secrets and lies. Always secrets and lies.

'What the…' Rosedale began to speak but trailed off, as an erratically driven minibus, for no apparent reason, slammed on its brakes, causing him to do the same.

A stream of street vendors wandered between the lines of cars carrying everything from household objects to an array of pungent smelling foods, adding to the already stifling air.

Cooper leant across from the back to try to get a better view. 'Can you see what's happening?'

'No, but it looks like this line goes down quite a way.'

For the next ten minutes, sweating and stifling, they sat alongside one of the many markets in the heart of Kinshasa. It teemed with energy as sellers sold everything from live chickens to live tortoises piled high, one on top of the other, and delicacies of grasshoppers and goats heads swapped hands.

'Toilet seat?' A young boy no more than eight, covered in dust, nails full of grime, banged with enthusiasm on the window, waving a seventies-style aquamarine toilet seat.

Rosedale rolled down the window, letting in the heat. 'Hell, why not. It probably beats the one back at the hotel… Thank you.'

Having given the boy ten times the asking price, which equated to the entire contents of his wallet, Rosedale threw the toilet seat into the back. Watched a throng of people casually walk into the road as if on some kind of procession. Lit a cigar. 'Maybe it's best to ditch the car here. Walk the rest of the way and stretch these little ol' legs of mine.'

Maddie glanced about. There were people coming in every direction. But looking at it now there was no way of even turning the car around. They were totally blocked in by a human wall. 'Okay,' she said. 'Sounds like a good idea. It's not far from here. We can cut through the alleyways.'

Cooper grinned. 'And the good thing is, Rosedale, if we do get split up, there's no missing you in that suit.'

And with the cigar hanging out of the corner of his mouth, and the smoke in his eyes, Rosedale squinted. Rubbed his hands eagerly. 'Well let's go then, ladies and gentlemen. Let's go and see if we can find the elusive Mr. Mutombo.'

23

'They're asking for comments on what the VP supposedly said in private about the new Iran deal. It's all over the dailies, they even did a call in on C-span this morning. How do you want us to shut it down? We can do a press briefing.'

John Woods sat back in the soft black seats of Cadillac 1, being driven to the latest in what seemed to be a never ending circuit of fundraising dinners. The last couple of days had been difficult and the last thing he needed was his vice president speaking and then being taken out of context by the Washington muckrakers. 'No, send out a tweet, something along the lines of *the White House does not comment on private conversations between individuals*. What else? Any updates on the Nashville shooting?'

Woods's senior advisor, Mattie Brown, ginger haired and on the unhealthy side of slim, sat opposite the president and Teddy Adleman. 'We're keeping in constant contact with the hospital. The three students who were critical last night, well I'm afraid it's not looking good, sir.'

'Jesus.'

'You're scheduled to fly out to see the families at thirteen hundred hours tomorrow, but I think we could manage to create an earlier window by changing the morning visit from the North American Baptist Women's Union, though we probably won't be able to reschedule them for another three months.'

'Teddy what d'ya think?'

Adleman adjusted the gold plated cufflink on his some-what over-starched white shirt and noticed a stain on his blue suit. Tried to wipe it off. Failed. Then tried to ignore the tight, burning sensation on his scalp from where he'd left the hair relaxer on too long the night before. Eventually he spoke. 'I think it'd be worth keeping the meeting with the NABWU. They're big advocates for gun control, and there's a lot of support for this administration. It's important to keep the women's vote. Their influence amongst their families and communities is pretty powerful. You don't want them to be pissed with you.'

Woods nodded. 'Hell hath no fury like a Baptist Women's Union scorned.'

'Unless of course it's a drop in the polls,' said Mattie.

The men sat in silence for a moment until the president spoke. 'Teddy, have we been able to contact Senator Walmsley?'

'No, sir. I think he's running scared. He's not returning any calls, but there's a possibility he might be at the fundraising dinner.'

John stared at his senior advisor. Who the hell did Walmsley think he was? The man was an A-class jerk. And if all things were equal, knocking a bit of sense into him in a downtown bar would be the most gratifying option to sort this out. As it stood, he was going to have to act the circus dog and roll over and hope and beg and plead with the senator to reconsider his support on the reforms.

Walmsley was playing games. Games with the welfare of the American people while sitting on his fat ass up at the Hill where the air of dysfunction and paralysis was at an all-time high. America was losing faith, and the only comfort he had was that in a recent poll, Congress came out lower than he did in the approval ratings.

He got that the pro-gun groups were putting pressure on certain senators, but they had to grow some. Think about others, like he had to. These gun control reforms weren't about him. Hell yes, he had an ego like any other red blooded male, but contrary to what the double page spread in the *Wall Street Journal* last week had reported, his mission was *not* to be put on the presidential map because of his own narcissism.

The truth was a cliché. One which no-one seemed to believe, and which echoed a beauty pageant finalist. But he'd worked hard. Been ambitious. Been determined, all to make a difference. And God, how simple did that sound? Yet if any word should have a semantic shift, it was that one. Simple. Because simple seemed nothing short of goddamn impossible.

24

'Well I think we've found our address, but look…' Rosedale pointed at a small, single storey concrete house. A group of around fifty people stood jeering. Shouting and heckling as a man, dressed in a gray tattered t-shirt, held a semi-filled glass bottle with a soaking, hanging rag wrapped round it.

Maddie ran forward. Sprinted down the partly laid tarmac road, followed by Cooper, with Rosedale fractionally in front. Recognizing the bottle for what it was. A crude incendiary bomb. She shouted, 'He's going to light it! Quick!'

'Move…! Move!' Cooper pushed through the crowd, barging the congregated group out of the way to get to the front. He could see Rosedale and Maddie doing the same, but he was nearer, almost within touching distance of the man.

He heard Maddie shout. 'Drop it! Now!'

Instruction ignored.

The home-made petrol bomb was lit, aimed and thrown. Perfect shot. It shattered on impact and engulfed the front door along with the wooden roof in a fireball of flames. A loud cacophony of applause rose up along with the heat of the fire and the fervour of the people. Cooper grabbed one of the perpetrators, disarmed him and pulled him quickly down. He stopped the man from reaching for yet another makeshift firebomb, as the now-angry crowd began to close in.

From the corner of his eye Cooper could see Rosedale taking on three other men with ease, they being no match for the skilful, highly trained, CIA veteran. And Maddie, helping to hold off the rest of the crowd – a mix of women, men and a scattering of young children – although vocal, seemed hesitant to fully take them on.

Cooper stared at the crowd… Wired.

'Can someone tell me what the hell is going on…? Ce qui se passe?'

A sinewy, dark skinned man stepped forward, the whites of his eyes distinctly yellow with vessels of red marbling through them. Pulled down the sleeve of his pinstripe blue suit monogrammed in gold with the letters, *NRC.* He looked first at Rosedale, a hint of ridicule in his eyes, then at Maddie and finally Cooper, who he directed his speech towards.

'This has nothing to do with you. I think you better leave.'

Cooper stood his ground. Observed the authority this man seemed to carry within the group. 'We need to try to get this fire under control.'

A small smile spread across the man's face, which turned into a mocking grin. 'This fire *is* under control. There's nothing to be done here, and, as I said before, this has nothing to do with you.'

Before Cooper could answer, Maddie shouted. 'There's people inside!'

Both Rosedale and Cooper spun round. And Cooper was just able to make out, through the curtain of fire, the figures of two people at the tiny window of the house.

Glancing at the wooden front door, he saw it was still engulfed in flames.

'Maddie, you stay and make sure nobody moves, and Rosedale, go round the other side, see if there's another exit.'

He turned to the crowd, looking at no-one in particular. 'Somebody, I need your jacket. Anyone…? Come on!'

The group stood motionless. Staring blankly.

'Come on! I need a jacket… Anything!… What's wrong with you?'

An expanse of faces gazing ahead as if they saw as one. As if what was in front of them was not the billowing, burning inferno of flames, but a vision of calm and tranquillity.

The man in the well-tailored suit spoke in a quiet of cool. 'You would do well to leave now.'

The helpless cries of those inside cloaked the man's words as Cooper noticed a threadbare drape hanging in the cemented rectangle window of the house opposite. He charged across the road, into the building.

Storming into the one room home, Cooper automatically smiled at the two startled children clad in sagging nappies, playing happily on the soiled mattress on the floor. An old lady scowled and stood up from her chair. Speaking in Lingala she launched into a tirade, and raged and hit Cooper hard with a rusting soup bowl, as he dragged and pulled down her drape, before apologizing and running back out to the burning house across the road.

Cooper could see Rosedale, who'd come from around the back of the building. He shook his head. 'Nothing there, Thomas. There's no way out.'

Cooper acknowledged the information with a small nod, but he was now entirely focussed on the burning door. There wasn't time to go and find water to soak the drape in, though by his reckoning the drape could only give about five seconds of protection before it caught alight.

The one thing they had on their side was if the house he'd just been in was similar to this one, it was just one single concrete room. And with concrete's inherent material properties, its built-in resistance to fire and slow rate of heat transfer, the majority of the internal section would be fire free. Smoke and the falling burning roof would be his biggest hazards.

'Rosedale, I'll go inside and get them, you and Maddie be ready to take over when I come out.'

Noticing the right hand side of the door was almost burnt through, Cooper covered his face and arms with the drape. Charged towards the weakened side. Shoulder first.

The force he used had the desired effect. Part of the door crashed in. Sent him falling forward, head first into the room.

Immediately abandoning the burning drape, he was greeted by a dense cloud of black smoke. An opaque, thick haze. Obscuring vision. Burning eyes. He covered his mouth with his t-shirt. Sucked onto the material. Tried to keep the strangling smoke from drying out his mouth, to stop it filling and cutting and spreading into his lungs like linguoid ripples on sand.

Crouching down, Cooper crawled on his hands and knees, where the air was less hazardous and easier to see through. A few feet in front of him he could just make out the two people lying unconscious on the floor, wedged next to a large piece of burning debris from the fallen roof.

He kicked the blazing timber away. Instinctively felt for a pulse. Faint but still there. Carefully he pulled the man up, shocked to feel how light he was. Even more shocked to realize that he, like the woman, were somewhere in their eighties.

It was easy for Cooper to hike them both up. Propelling the man with ease over his right shoulder before squatting down to scoop up the old lady.

Rushing out the door, Cooper was met by Rosedale. Helped by Maddie. They grabbed hold of the couple, turning them onto the floor and banging out what little flames were present on their clothes.

Maddie turned to the crowd. 'Quickly! We need help…! Please!'

Again, her plea was met with no response, not even mild curiosity.

Coughing hoarsely, and bent over with his hands on his knees, Cooper quickly glanced up at Maddie. 'We need to get them to the medical center ourselves. Rosedale, you take the old man, I'll carry the woman. Maddie, stay close, and watch our backs.'

As the three of them moved off carrying the elderly couple, the well-dressed man in the blue pinstriped suit, complete with the gold monogrammed initials, stepped forward.

'You don't know what you've just done.'

25

John Woods had a strong urge to sit down. Hell, he'd had that urge for the past forty-five minutes. And with the fundraising dinner due to go on for another hour and a half he knew that urge wasn't going to be met any time soon.

His tux was tight and his black shoes tighter, and the soles of his feet were on fire. With a smile on his face, he shifted his weight first to his right foot and then to his left foot and then decided it didn't make a goddamn bit of difference, as he thought about the cushioned insoles he'd left back at the house. 'Have you seen Walmsley?'

Teddy Adleman stood in the middle of the grand marbled hall in the home of Senator Bush – who happened not to be related to the forty-third president of the United States, though the name did come in useful when booking a table at *The Monocle* up at Capitol Hill.

The fundraising was for a joint committee set up for congressional candidates. Notable people present:

House Minority Leader.

Senate Minority Leader.

Senate Minority Whip.

Governor of Rhode Island.

Those donating $53,400 or more, and listed as sponsors: one hundred and three.

Those donating $75,800 or more, and listed as hosts: forty eight.

Adleman said, 'Yeah, we exchanged a couple of words right before your speech. Which was pretty good, by the way. I think he wants to speak to you after we finish the meet and VIP clutch, and going by the line of people that should be anywhere between thirty-five and fifty minutes. We scheduled sixty minutes so you'll have a small window before Senator Bush's speech of thanks.'

'Did he give you any clue whether he's open to any more negotiation?'

'No, but I doubt it.'

'So he wants me to sit up and beg, just for him to say no.'

Teddy said, 'Probably.'

*

Fifty-three minutes later. 'Come on, Walmsley, don't give me that. You were biting my hand off for further amendments to shield immigrants from deportation. What do I have to do? Give me a break here. At least see if you can meet me half way.'

Senator Walmsley, a man who enjoyed a late night brandy as much as he did a late night cigar, tucked the ringed roll of fat hanging over of the top of his winged collar shirt back in.

'Mr. President, I don't know how much clearer I need to make this for you, or for your staff, who've persisted on calling my office at *every* available opportunity. I have not changed my stance when it comes to giving you my support on the reforms. I have a family to consider and my support stops when I begin to get anonymous threats.'

'Walmsley…'

The senator cut in. 'No. I've told you my answer.'

'There must be something which will change your mind?'

'You've got nothing to give me.'

John Woods bent down to whisper in Walmsley's ear. 'Whose pocket are you in, Jerry?'

Walmsley pulled back his head. His hair brushing against Woods's cheek to leave a smear of Brylcreem on it. 'Probably the same one you're in, John.'

Woods rubbed his face. Wiped away the sticky residue. Tried to wipe away his anger. Only the former was managed. 'Who the hell do you think you are?'

Teddy Adleman touched Woods's arm very lightly. 'Mr. President, people are looking. Maybe it'd be more appropriate to schedule a telephone meeting to have this discussion. There's a window at 23.00.'

To which Woods said, 'It's fine, Teddy. I just want Jerry to understand I won't let the American people be held to ransom by him or any of the pro-gun groups.'

Walmsley shook his head. Supercilious written in bold. 'Come off it. There's no-one being held to ransom over these gun reforms. If anyone is guilty of that, I'd say it was you, Mr. President. Those photos of the kids killed at the Liberbush Elementary. What the hell did you think they were going to do? I grieved with rest of America when it happened and so did groups like the NRA. Just because we support the right to bear arms does not mean we support crime in anyway. So, no. I'm not going to cry over a bunch of emotive pictures.'

Wood's stepped in closer. 'You bastard. They were kids. *Kids*, Jerry. Five, six, seven year olds. Gunned down. Massacred whilst in class. Helpless. Completely vulnerable. Their future wiped out, along with the future of their families who'll have a lifetime of pain. What happened to politicians having a conscience, hey?'

'What happened is that we got into politics... What's

wrong with you? You think a few reforms will make a difference?'

'If it won't, what's the big deal then in giving me your support? Look, let's make the reforms. Let's make a *difference* to the America of tomorrow.'

'I love my country,' said Walmsley. 'And I'm also a man of God, and all that that stands for. And I believe that people are driven by one of two things. Reason or force. Most of us manage to make the correct choice. But those that don't, well, it won't make a difference to them *what* laws you bring in. Meanwhile good people, law abiding people, have their constitutional rights infringed. People are worried, Mr. President, that once you start playing about with the constitution, re-writing the amendments – the soul of this country – then who's to say the same won't happen to the other ones? What about the sixth amendment? *The accused shall enjoy the right to a speedy and public trial, by an impartial jury.* Shall we change people's right to justice? Hell, why not? And whilst we're about it, what about the Fifteenth? Shall we play about with that one too? *The right of citizens of the United States to vote shall not be denied or abridged on account of race, or color…* Mr. President, guns have always been a part of who we are as a nation.'

'But that doesn't mean it isn't time for change.'

'Without the will to harm, the gun for most people is nothing more than security or a sporting weapon. Maybe before we start to look at gun control we need to look at why it's happening. We need to look at the health care system, *especially* mental health. Poverty and the disenfranchised, disenchanted youth. Education, employment, communities, the long history and divide of black people and white people. And mostly we have to understand why the world as a whole has become desensitized to violence. Make a change on all of that. Find me the answers to solve *those* things and then, Mr. President, you'll have my support.'

'You're talking crap, Jerry. It's bullshit and you know it. All I'm trying to do is make a safer America by addressing the issue of gun-related crimes, by making sure the *whole* of the US, and not just a few states, have better background checks before people can buy assault rifles. That all larger capacity magazines are completely banned, which will help to make mass-shootings less easy. As well as ensuring that people with known affiliations and sympathies to terrorist activities and organizations have a lifetime ban from purchasing any kind of weapon. Doesn't it worry you that we might be complicit – by refusing to make a political choice, by being afraid of change – in allowing influential interest groups with big bucks to buy votes in Congress with election funding…? So I'll ask you again, whose pocket are you in? Who's paying you to say no?'

Walmsley's face reddened. 'I'd be careful what you say. You've got enough enemies up at the Hill without making new ones… Oh, and John, I'd do something about that temper of yours, before it gets you into real trouble.'

And Walmsley turned on his heel and walked away.

'Teddy, don't even tell me how badly I handled that.'

'…Everything alright, Mr. President?'

Woods turned to look at Senator Bush standing with a tall, gray haired man with a deep tan and a wide smile. 'It is, thank you, Senator. And I appreciate you opening your home like this for the fundraiser.'

Picking a piece of buttered lobster out of his back right wisdom tooth, Bush replied. 'My honour, Mr. President… And may I introduce you to Donald Parker? He's a great supporter of your administration.'

Donald Parker put out his hand for the presidential hand-shake.

Woods smiled.

Asked the go-to meet and greet questions.

How are you?

What line of business are you in?

To which Donald Parker said. 'I'm good. Mainly electronics. I've a very large company here in the States, but also several in the Democratic Republic of the Congo.'

26

In the early hours of the next morning, when the sunrise was tinting the sky and the oppressive heat had already begun to strangle the day, Cooper stood with Maddie and Rosedale by the burnt-out house in the heart of the Kinshasa's rambling slums. Nearby a man cycled past, towing a rusty trailer of water bottles. Power lines sagged overhead, their connections overloaded and jerry-rigged.

'So what do you think it was all about?' asked Maddie.

Cooper shrugged, feeling sluggish. He was tired, and could do with anything that had a bit of caffeine in it right now. But for once, his sleepless night and irritable fatigue hadn't been due to the lack of pills. He had plenty of those. Xanax and OxyContin were like old friends. And neither was his lethargy due to his dreams nor the thoughts which ran uncontrollably in his head. Though on reflection those things might've been preferable to what did keep him wide awake, and leave him to stare mindlessly at a line of bugs marching decisively along the chipped walls.

Rosedale patted Cooper on his back, slightly too hard for his liking. 'You look tired, Thomas, didn't you sleep well? Me and Maddison here slept like the dead.'

'Well maybe I look tired because I *am* tired, Rosedale. Not to put too fine a point on it, the combination of the noise of the traffic and your snoring, which can only be described as... *thunderous*, really isn't conducive to a good night's rest.

And what is it with you and the in *and* out breath snore? Jeez. You need to go and check that out, Rosedale. How the hell did you sleep through it, Maddie?'

Maddie smiled sympathetically. And Cooper appreciated that.

'You know me, Tom, I can sleep through anything. Besides, Rosedale has nothing on my daddy. You must remember how crazy his snoring was.'

'All I know is I'd happily pay a thousand bucks for my own room.'

Rosedale laughed. 'If that's the case, Thomas, we need to find Emmanuel and the plane as soon as possible, so we can get you back to Colorado for your beauty sleep.'

Maddie said, 'Then I guess we need to find out if this is, well *was*, Emmanuel's house and if the attack is in anyway related to him. Easiest way to do that is to go and speak to the couple from yesterday. Hopefully they'll talk to us.'

'I'm going to take a look around the back.'

Cooper watched Rosedale wander off towards the side of the house along the red clay sidewalks, leaving just him and Maddie. A frown cut deep into her forehead. 'What about the guy who warned us off? Any thoughts?'

Kicking through the wreckage with his boot, Cooper threw her an answer, not really wanting to get into a conversation. Sometimes women and him just didn't mix. Especially when he was tired. Especially when he knew he was probably going to be a jackass.

'Perhaps it was nothing. Maybe just a dispute with neighbors.'

'Don't give me that.'

'Different places, different rules.'

'Right there.'

Quickly Cooper looked around. 'What?'

She shook her head. Hands placed on her hips. And Cooper instinctively knew she was pissed.

'No, I mean right there, what you just said about there being different rules. Like it sums it all up. But you couldn't be more wrong. This may be a different place, Tom, but Jesus, that doesn't mean it's the norm here to go around burning down houses. Frankly, I find it offensive that you think it is. This place is unique. There's been a lot of darkness here. This country has been damaged by its history but there's also a lot of beauty in it.'

Cooper sighed. 'Look, I'm sorry if it comes across that way, Maddie, of course I didn't mean that...'

Crouching down, Maddie got distracted from what Cooper was saying. His reply to her like a distant hum.

By the path she noticed some charcoal perfectly piled, built up like a pyramid with a circle of large black glossy berries around it. She picked one up and rolled it between her fingers and encouraged the scent to develop. She inhaled a sweet, almost vanilla fragrance. She stared. Her heart racing and beating and pounding, her head began to spin and she was only slightly aware of Cooper kneeling down next to her to pick up one of the berries and drop it into his small evidence collecting bag, something he often did.

Rosedale sauntered back. 'I'm surprised you're not wearing blue gloves and a white suit. Ain't you gonna tape off the area? He thinks he's in CSI, don't you Thomas? Anything he sees, he puts in that damn bag of his. I'd say there were kleptomaniac qualities about him... Miss Maddison, are you okay...? Maddison?'

'I'm fine.'

'You don't look it... What are you thinking?'

With a slight hesitation and a deep breath she said, 'Okay, I may be way off here but this berry comes from the Macrocarpa tree. It's found mainly in the east of the country, up towards Kivu where a lot of my family came from. The berry is used to treat a lot of things like tuberculosis, tooth problems, abdominal pain and…'

Maddie paused.

'Go on,' said Cooper.

'No, it's nothing.'

'Maddie?'

'I said it's nothing.'

'What's wrong with you?'

'For God's sake, Tom, there's nothing wrong. So stop, okay.'

Cooper tilted his head. 'I know there's something wrong.'

'Enough already.'

'Then say what you were going to say.'

'Fine, if it'll shut you up… The berries are also sometimes used in rituals and ceremonies. Just part of everyday life, and it certainly isn't a bad thing… well, not usually. These ceremonies are often held for the most routine stuff. Like if you wanted your kid to get good grades at school, or want a family member to do well, you might ask someone to take a service for you, whether it be just a spiritual one, kind of like a normal prayer service, or perhaps it might be an exchange.'

'Exchange?' asked Rosedale.

Feeling uncomfortable and knowing it showed, Maddie said, 'It's an exchange because by giving the spirits or ancestors something, you'll get something back too. So you kill your chicken and Tommy gets good grades.'

'And if he doesn't?'

'Then that's to do with the spirits too. All causation is spiritual, which means…'

Rosedale interrupted. 'Means no-one's ever to blame, sugar pie. So if after the exchange, Tommy's grades are still low, then it's not down to him or the exchange going wrong, it's about another spirit, a *stronger* spirit influencing it.'

Maddie nodded. Said nothing. Felt something she didn't want to.

Contemplating what Maddie had said. Spirits. Exchanges. Cooper lit up his first cigarette of the day. He looked at Rosedale. Although he hadn't travelled extensively through Africa, the man had spent a lot of his clandestine career immersed in other cultures and accepted the world was made up by differences. Stifling a yawn, Cooper asked, 'So how do the berries come into this?'

Putting her head down and not holding Cooper's gaze, Maddie quietly said, 'It's not just the berries, it's the charcoal as well… listen, I'm not the best person to speak to about this. Why don't we go back to the hotel and Skype my daddy, if we can get through? He'll be able to tell you better than I can.'

Rosedale said, 'Skype Marvin? That sounds great.'

And with a very tight smile, Cooper nodded, 'Yeah great. Real great.'

27

After a lot of trouble and a moving of the bed, along with the moving of the heavy wooden chest of drawers which they discovered covered a large hole in the hotel room floor, the trio managed to get a signal by standing at the window where the bed had been.

'Hey Daddy! How are you? How's Cora?' Maddie grinned at the blurred image of Marvin on the laptop screen.

'I'm fine. We all are honey. She's gone to the mall with your mom. They've gone to get some stuff to make a house for that caterpillar of hers, though I'd say a coffin would be more fitting.'

Maddie grinned. 'Daddy, I've got a couple of questions for you. Oh, but say hey first to Rosedale.'

Rosedale looked at the monitor. Tipped his hat said, 'Hey Mr. Menga.'

'Call me, Marvin, Rosedale… I hope you're looking after my daughter.'

'I think it's actually her who's looking after us, Marvin.'

'And say hello to Tom, Daddy.' Marvin sat motionless in his chair. 'Damn, I think it's frozen… Daddy?'

'Oh no baby, there's nothing wrong with the picture, well not this one anyway… Why don't you ask me what you wanted to?'

'Okay, well did you get my email with the photograph?'

Marvin's face turned serious. Real serious. 'I did, but Maddie I think you should be careful. Are you sure this is wise? I think you should be careful baby and you know what I mean.'

Conscious of Cooper staring at her, Maddie felt herself blush. 'That hasn't got anything to do with this, and it certainly isn't the time to talk about it… *Please.*'

'Okay, but I'm not happy.'

'I know… So that photograph I sent you was of the charcoal and the berries we found outside the house which they tried to burn down. I was hoping you'd know exactly what it meant, or what you think it might mean.'

Marvin took a moment to find his words. 'You see how the charcoal was built up in a high pyramid? Well I think that's supposed to depict a person. Sometimes it can be leaves or grass, a piece of stone, but it's never some random object. Everything has a meaning. And if I'm right, the charcoal means someone thinks the person in this house was bad. Or, if you like, had bad spirits within them. In a way it's more about the color. Charcoal and the circle of berries around it are a representation. And when used together it becomes more powerful. So the color black, along with charcoal and the berries, symbolizes that someone thinks the person was possessed by Kindoki… Are you okay, Maddison?'

'I'm fine. Just carry on, Daddy.'

'Well, as you know, Kindoki is like witchcraft, and the berry and charcoal are a sign the person has a black liver.'

'Liver?'

'Yes, that's where it's believed the evil lives. The whole world is filled with signs and symbols, this is just another kind of one. Signs are relative to the people, the culture, and there's an understanding and an acceptance to them. When was the last time you questioned the symbol of a red heart with a pierced arrow through it on a Valentine's card?'

Maddie pulled a face. 'You mean the ones which were never sent me…? Never, I guess.'

Cooper ignored Maddie's slight, and Rosedale's grin – focused instead on the conversation. Not that it hadn't irritated the hell out of him.

'Exactly,' continued Marvin. 'You just accepted it when really the physiology of a heart in actuality has nothing to do with love, but like some Congolese believe evil lives in the liver, here in the States they believe love lives in the heart.'

'So what exactly do the berries mean, Daddy?'

'The berries were in a circle around the charcoal, which I'm sure represents a person who's been so overtaken and possessed by the sorcery or witchcraft they've now become a danger to the community. Capable of killing someone. Therefore, it's down to the neighborhood or village to get rid of them before he or she gets their bad spirit to do harm.'

'How?'

'It could be as extreme as killing them. Nobody wants to live next to a witch who's going to do harm. And that's how the charcoal and berries come about. There're placed outside the house to warn others as well as acting as a frightener, you know, to scare the people who've been accused of witchcraft away. Then its job is done. The people pack up and go off on their own accord, and no-one has to get hurt.'

'So you think it's what happened here? They thought those two old people were possessed?'

'Perhaps... Honey, I don't know all the answers. But I do know the belief system of Kindoki is real, as you know only too well, whether you agree with it or not, or whether you think it's right or wrong. That is part of the culture there, for better or worse, which means nobody wants outsiders coming in to judge or mess with it. So my advice to all of you is to come home, and come home *now*.'

28

'You sure we're in the right place, Rosedale?' Cooper looked uncertain as they walked along the narrow mud paths on the outskirts of Kinshasa where a group of young boys wearing faded soccer shorts and worn down flip-flops played in the sludge by an open sewer.

Rosedale stood in front of Maddie and Cooper, glancing around the alleyways.

'It'd help if this place had street signs. It seems like we've already been along here. A person could lose their way.'

Cooper laughed. 'That's not very reassuring, Rosedale, coming from a guy who's spent a big part of his life working in the CIA.'

Rosedale leaned on the white crumbling wall and lit the cigar he'd had in his mouth for the past hour. He smirked. And it got right under Cooper's skin.

'The same could be said about you, Thomas, a highly decorated ex-military man such as yourself, who needs to keep his wits about him at all times – especially as you feel it was your wits which let you down when it mattered the most. And as such you barely sleep in case you miss another moment. You pop your pills as if they were candy, hoping no-one will notice. But you can't give them up because they're the only way you can sleep, and they're the only way you can keep awake. But you don't care, do you, Thomas?

Because the only thing that matters to you is you don't miss another chance to get it right.'

Cooper visibly stiffened at the unexpected but accurate analysis.

'So it surprises me, Thomas, you failed to notice I used the words, *seems* and *could*. It *seems* like we've already been here. A person *could* lose their way. Which is not the same as saying, *we are lost*. Quite the contrary, Thomas, if you look to your right, the run-down building at the end of the path is, in fact, the place we're looking for.'

Maddie hissed at Rosedale, not wanting Cooper to hear.

'Don't you ever get tired of playing these games no-one's interested in?'

'You feeling left out, Maddison? Well let's see now, shall we? You joined the military because you needed to prove to yourself and to show Daddy, who never loved you enough, that you weren't a victim. But when you joined it wasn't for you and you felt more like a victim than ever. You've got average pilot skills but that doesn't matter, because Onyx needed to employ a woman. It's an unspoken secret you got pregnant to get Thomas to marry you. He may be a lot of things but he's a gentleman, so you knew it'd work. If you had a choice you'd leave, but you can't, because that'd mean you couldn't look after Thomas, and even though you're no longer together, you're hoping someday he'll give up his ghost and you'll be a family again.'

The slap to Rosedale's face created an angry sound, along with an angry mark. He rubbed his face. Tilted his head. Broke into a smile. 'Well I'll be damned, there's me thinking we were only playing games.'

Maddie stepped back, hands on her hips. 'Oh we are, and you were wrong. I'm damn good at my job and my Daddy couldn't give me any more love if he tried. But hey, now it's my turn… Let's see, shall we? You joined the Navy because you had nowhere else to go. Nobody to care and the nearest you got to love was when your daddy dropped you off at a children's home and said goodbye. You couldn't cut it in the SEALs because you didn't know how to relate to other people so you joined the Clandestine Service in the CIA so you could spend your life pretending you were someone else, because the real you is a neglected little boy from Texas. You would cry but you don't know how to, just like you don't know how to love… How did I do? Did I win?'

Rosedale stared at Maddie and as he turned to walk away he quietly said, 'Yeah, Miss Maddison, you did. You won.'

29

With Maddie feeling awful at what she'd said, she walked along in silence with Cooper who was feeling just as bad, but for entirely different reasons, as he tried to distract his thoughts from Ellie.

'You know if you want to go back home, we can go to the airport anytime. Don't think you have to stay.'

'You'd like that wouldn't you, Tom?'

Before Cooper had time to answer, Rosedale butted in as he caught up with them.

'What and have Miss Maddison miss out on all the fun and games? We can't have that, can we? She's already one-zero up.'

Looking at him softly, she smiled gratefully. 'No, we can't, and I'd say we were even… Come on.'

Leading the way down the dark alleyway towards the house, Cooper thought about how easy it'd been to get the details of where the elderly couple were staying from the nurse in the medical center, who'd looked as tired and weary as her patients. It had just been a question of asking, and she'd freely told him, along with additional information about the smoke inhalation the couple had suffered. And as much as it'd been a clear breach of confidentiality – a hell of a big one – it'd done them a favor. So who was he to knock it?

They arrived at the door of the house. 'I've no idea how much they'll tell us, if anything,' said Cooper. 'Main thing we need to rule out is the address. We want to find out if Emmanuel lives or has ever lived here. If they knew anything about him. But we need to go easy. No heavy handed stuff, alright?'

'I think that's directed at you, Maddison.'

Maddie rolled her eyes at Rosedale. 'What about the fire though, Tom? Shall we mention anything about the Kindoki?'

'Well, if Emmanuel has nothing to do with these people, then I don't think we should get involved. Just move right on.'

She looked surprised. 'You? Seriously? Not get involved? You're kidding me.'

Cooper pulled a play face. 'Yeah, well, perhaps I've learnt my lesson or at least I'm trying to. Like Granger said, several times, and I mean *several* times, all I have to do is bring back the plane.' He paused, clearing his throat before imitating Granger. 'You got that Coop? Just bring back the goddamn plane, unless of course you want me to kick your ass. We don't need another hero, Hollywood's got enough of those.'

Maddie laughed. Cooper thought it was good to see. It'd been a long time since they'd both goofed around together. He hoped it'd stay like this. For him. For her. And of course, for Cora.

Maddie joined in, giving a good impression of their boss. 'I can see it's that time of month again Maddie, maybe you should get yourself home and come back in a week when your women's problems are over.'

Rosedale's slow drawl broke into the good humor. 'When y'all have finished your *Saturday Night Live* routine, I'd like to get on.'

And without another word, Rosedale banged on the door. Hard. Hammering and beating and knocking and pounding unremittingly until, eventually, a diminutive woman in her forties with tight braids answered.

Oozing charm, Rosedale took off his cowboy hat. Rested it on his chest. 'Howdy Ma'am, my friends and I are wondering if we could have a word with you.'

The woman stayed silent. Her eyes darting around nervously. Cooper could see the deep root of fear within them as Rosedale continued to talk. 'It was my friends here who saved the old couple from the fire. We just want to see how they're doing.'

A young man in his early twenties came from within the house and stood silently next to the woman, whose words were hurried as she wrapped a scarf tightly around her shoulders.

'Non… No, I'm sorry, you can't come in. Please, it would be better if you left.'

The frightened woman quickly tried to shut the door but her attempt was blocked by Rosedale's large, white pointed boot. His tone dropped. A hint of menace.

'Now that's not very polite and I've never been keen on bad manners, says a lot about a person don't you think? And seeing as we saved their lives n'all, it wouldn't be right not to let us in.'

Rosedale pushed the woman out of the way, and knowing she was powerless to stop him she didn't object, letting Maddie follow through, but as Cooper began to walk in, the woman stood in front of him, obstructing his way.

It looked to Cooper like a train load of anxiety had passed over her. Making her tremble. Making small beads of sweat prickle her forehead and push through her skin, looking like dew drops on grass. She leaned back against the door, her hands shaking as she tried to push him away.

Rosedale looked annoyed at what was going on. 'I thought I said it was bad manners not to let us in. That means all of us in. So I reckon you need to let my friend here pass.'

The woman searched Rosedale's face. Puzzled. Turning fearfully to stare at Maddie, her voice muted. Terrified. Desperate.

'No… no. Son yeux. Le signe du diable. Laisse maintenant…Maintenant!'

Maddie looked back at the woman. She nodded, and spoke with a gentle lull of reassurance. 'Ne vous inquiétez pas. Je suis désolé. Désolé.'

Rosedale looked puzzled. 'What's going on Maddie? I get what she just said but what the hell is she talking about his eyes for? Let's just get inside so we can sort this mess out and find out where the plane is. I just want go home.'

Maddie shook her head. 'She's got a problem with them.'

Rosedale snarled. 'What?'

'Tom's eyes.'

'What the hell's wrong with them?'

'The color.'

Rosedale looked at Cooper blankly.

'Haven't you noticed his left eye's blue and his right one's brown?'

'Miss Maddison, you do me a disservice. Of course I've noticed, I just don't know what the problem is. It just makes ol' blue eyes here, not so blue.'

'Well that's the point. Heterochromia is viewed very differently here. A lot of people think, as she does, it's the sign of the devil. Sorcery. People with different colored eyes are thought to be witches. And I'm guessing she thinks if he goes into her house he'll be bringing those bad spirits with him… Listen, Tom, you go and have a wander around and Rosedale and I will see what we can find out. We'll meet you here in half an hour.'

30

The alleyway Cooper found himself walking along was a reeking sludge of red mud and raw sewage, whilst the shadows of people huddled in corners seeking shelter from the rain journeyed across his path.

Trying to avoid the worst of the mud, Cooper walked to the side. Scraped his worn Khaki jacket against the walls of the buildings. The night sky seemed darker than usual and as the rain began to fall harder he found himself trying to find relief from the torrential downpour.

He huddled in the doorway of a building. Tried to convince himself that having a cigarette because there was nothing else to do but wait for the rain to ease up, wasn't the same as just having a cigarette for a cigarette's sake. Deciding his reasoning was the kind of bull he'd hear coming from Rosedale, he lit one anyway.

With the cigarette hanging out from the side of his mouth, he went in his pocket. Pulled out a wrap of tissue. And his hands shook as he unfolded it. Three blue pills. Three yellow pills. And he stared at them, wanting there to be a hesitation. There wasn't. By the time there was, he'd already swallowed them.

*

Ten minutes passed and the rain still fell and Cooper was still enjoying the smoke going down into his lungs as the beginnings of the tablets began to take effect.

But then a sound behind him. Coming from the darkness of the derelict building. Instincts propelled him to high alert and, not wanting to have his back to whatever it was, he spun round. Listened again. But hearing anything above the noise of the rain as it ricocheted off the ground proved difficult.

He peered through the broken, jagged wooden door. Felt the rush of a passing wind cross his feet which began to encircle him with a blanket of warmth, before leaving him chilled. He listened again, and yes, there it was. Like a bristle brush against a hard concrete floor.

He glanced around.

Waited a moment.

Used the toe of his boot to force the door.

Creaked open with ease. Though Cooper could have done without it falling off one of its hinges to swing down noisily on one side.

He stood in the entrance opposite a row of broken windows. Observed the stark emptiness of the place. Abandoned like so many other buildings in Kinshasa.

He watched curiously. Speculating how it was that the few scattered leaves in the middle of the floor which had found their way inside, still blew. Still twisted. Still circled.

An odd sensation crept over Cooper, causing him to rub his chest, and he could feel a tightness begin to grow and it made it hard to breathe and it was if the air was draining of oxygen, and he wondered and it crossed his mind and he refused to panic at the thought that this time it really was the pills and this time he'd really pushed it too far.

His skin became clammy. Then a steam train of a

headache. It pierced through the backs of his eyes making the pain bulge against his sinuses. He leant forward and reached out and felt for the wall to steady himself. He flinched as his touch hit ice cold wet. Freezing on his hand in a painful burn.

Pulling away, Cooper locked his armpit over his hand in an attempt to warm it up.

'You're here to see Emmanuel aren't you?'

The voice from the darkness, although a whisper, made him jump. Something he rarely did. But his instinct to run wasn't there. A lifetime of training had eliminated that.

'I am. You know where he is?'

'No.'

Cooper cleared his throat, then spoke slightly louder than necessary to assert himself. 'Well, we need to speak to him, need to get a matter sorted... Sorry, can you come nearer? I can't see you and I'm not too keen on talking to somebody I can't see.'

The man stepped forward into the light. And Cooper recognized him as the young man who'd stood at the door with the woman, at the address he'd just come from. There was amusement on the man's face.

'I think we spend our lives talking to those we cannot see, sometimes it's the only thing we have to connect us to those who have gone.'

Distancing himself from anything too personal, too raw, Cooper scratched his head, still aware of the strange tightness in his chest. 'Look, if you know something, I'm happy to pay you for any information. How is it you know him anyway?'

'How is it we know anybody?'

Cooper drove the butt end of his cigarette into the

crumbling wall, watching the red glow disappear. 'Listen, if you've got something to say, I'll be glad to hear it. If not, I'm out of here. Riddles have never been my thing.'

Cooper began to move.

Did the trick.

'Stop, wait! Emmanuel was a good man, but he was scared.'

'What of?'

The man stayed silent, and Cooper was annoyed with himself to hear the impatience coming into his voice. 'Look, like I say, if it's money you want, I can pay you. I just want to get some information about Emmanuel.'

'It's not about money.'

'Well it is for the bank who leant him the money for the plane. He either needs to start paying, or we need to take the plane back. So like I say, if you know anything I'd appreciate it, sir, if you could tell me. I'm not in the mood for games.'

The man looked at him coldly. 'This isn't a game.'

Then, sounding like the military man he'd once been, Cooper said, 'With respect, my only objective is the business I have with Emmanuel.'

'You have no business with Emmanuel. You only think you have. And whatever the reason you *think* you're here, it won't be the reason… Realize the truth, but to find it you need to look beyond. Look for the opposite of everything. The answers lie there.'

'Listen, why don't we go back to the house and talk?'

'I'm sorry. I've said enough already.'

Concern weaved with interest, Cooper said, 'Is he in trouble? Is that what you're trying to tell me?'

'Sometimes it takes a stranger to help.'

'Hey, Thomas. You there, boy?'

Rosedale's brash, booming voice carried through the rain and Cooper felt a sudden warmth return to his skin. The tightness of his chest disappeared. The headache subsided.

He turned his head towards the sound of Rosedale and stepped back out into the sludgy alleyway, to see Maddie and Rosedale walking towards him.

Even in the night sky, Cooper could see the concern on Maddie's face. He called out to her.

'You alright?'

Rosedale answered before Maddie had a chance to. 'I could ask you the same thing… If I gave a damn… Where the hell have you been? Don't start playing your Superman games here, Thomas. This isn't a one-man crusade. Whether you like it or not, sugar pie, whilst we're here, we're a team, which means it isn't okay to go out on one of your jaunts.'

Cooper bristled. Pissed with the way he was being spoken to. He tried to keep his anger hidden. It didn't work.

'What are you talking about now, Rosedale?'

Rosedale raised his voice. 'I'm talking about half an hour. Half a goddamn hour, Thomas. That's what you said. Even Miss Maddison here will agree with me on this one. When you say thirty minutes, mean thirty goddamn minutes. We've been looking for you for…' Rosedale paused to look at his very large and very gold and very garish watch. 'For the past ninety-six minutes. So by my reckoning you owe us both an apology… *and* an explanation.'

Shaking his head, Cooper stared at them both in bemusement. 'What?'

Rosedale stood, silhouetted in the alleyway as he lit his cigar. Reminded Cooper of the hard-boiled TV detective shows he'd watched as a kid.

'Where the hell were you, Thomas?'

Unwilling to engage any longer with Rosedale, Cooper turned to Maddie.

'Maddie, I'm sorry. But Jesus, there's no way I've been – what did you say – ninety minutes?'

Cooper looked at his watch. He could see the hands betraying him, supporting Rosedale's accusation. But he didn't believe it. There was no way he could've been gone that long. Hell, the address where the couple were staying was only ten minutes' walk away, at the most. And what else had he done? Nothing, besides having a cigarette. And a quick conversation.

Maddie said, 'What's going on, Tom? Are you okay?'

'Of course he's okay. Who wouldn't be if they had a pharmaceutical company in their back pocket?'

Cooper shrugged. He was on a hook and too tired to get into another something with Rosedale. He backed down. Tried the apologetic route.

'Sorry, I didn't think I was that long. I was talking to some guy about Emmanuel, he was really guarded. How did you get on by the way?'

Cooper walked back into the building with Maddie as they talked. 'Well it was obvious they were too frightened to say anything, though we did find out from the neighbor they're Emmanuel's aunt and uncle. In actual fact, Emmanuel and his family mainly come from a small village up in South Kivu, in the east of the country. Maybe he was just using their address. Who knows? But something is definitely going on here… What did your person say about Emmanuel?'

Cooper glanced around. Saw the crumbling building. The smashed row of windows and the broken door swinging from its hinges. And over in the far corner, there were piles of small empty cages, made from chicken wire, that he hadn't seen before. The building was somehow lighter now. Wondering what they were, absentmindedly he said, 'Oh nothing, nothing of interest, anyway. Just he knew Emmanuel, but that was it. Nothing to hold the front page.'

He gave a half smile. Wondered why he hadn't told Maddie the truth.

'What's that over there?'

Cooper walked across to the middle of the floor. Bent down to get a better look.

'I think it's the remains of a rat.' He looked closely at the little figure. 'Weird thing is, looks like it's been drained of all its blood. And look at the side of its body, all its fur's been shaved.'

Quickly. Too quickly, Maddie said, 'It's probably nothing. Come on, let's go back to the hotel now. I'm really beat. The sooner we find this plane the better.'

'Sure. Give me a sec.'

Cooper emptied the remaining cigarettes into his pocket, before ripping the packet open flat, enabling him to scrape up the rat before dropping it into one of the collecting bags he had in his jacket.

'What are you doing? Just leave it, Tom.'

Cooper raised his eyebrows, feeling puzzled himself. Shook his head. 'I'm not sure what I'm doing. I just think I need to look further.'

31

'Hey bud, how's it hanging?' Feeling the intense heat of the un-air conditioned room, and the effects of the pills, and unable to sleep, Cooper talked readily down the phone to Jackson.

'Hey Coop, good to hear from you... What's that noise?'

Cooper looked across the room to where Rosedale was deep in sleep. Snoring loudly.

'It's my roommate, don't even ask.'

Jackson's voice was full of hope. 'How's it going? Reckon you'll be back soon?'

'If it continues at this rate, I think we'll be home by the end of the week. We've just hit a wall. Maybe it's stupid we even came.'

'That's not the Coop I know. He wouldn't care jack-squat if he'd hit three hundred walls, there's no way he'd give up. What's got into you? You're the guy that drives people crazy always running after dead end leads... I'm sorry, I didn't mean that. Not like it sounded. Coop, you know I wasn't talking about Ellie, right?'

Cooper took a sharp in breath. It wasn't so much hearing the name of Ellie, though often that would do it. It was who had said it. He could count on one hand the amount of times Jackson had actually said it, since the accident. Of course he referred to her. Directly. Or indirectly. Never forgetting to send a note, a goofy card, or just a few words on a text each year on 12th July – the anniversary of the accident. But say her name? Rarely. Verging on never.

'I know you weren't, but you're right, sometimes it feels like all I did was run around after nothing but ghosts.'

Jackson stayed silent for a minute. 'I've never asked you this, but I was talking to Dad yesterday and he asked me a question I didn't know the answer to. He wanted to know if I thought you blamed me for the accident. Do you? Do you blame me, Coop?'

In the darkness of the room, Cooper smiled. But it felt like a sad one. 'Never.'

'You still miss her, don't you?'

'Always.'

Again there was silence until Jackson spoke, love and truth in his voice. 'I've always loved your attitude to life. To hell with what anyone has to say. Find the truth. Then look beyond.'

'That's funny.'

'What is?'

'Oh, just someone said that to me tonight.'

Jackson laughed. 'Well see, that proves it. Two people can't be wrong... But seriously, Coop, you're my hero. I'm so proud of you.'

Emotion caught in the back of Cooper's throat. 'Hey, embarrass a man, won't you?'

'It's true, Coop, you're the brother I never had.'

Cooper went rigid. His tone shifted. Strained surprise. 'Yeah?'

'Yeah.'

Cooper wanted to change the subject, but trying to think of what to say next suddenly became difficult. Finding it easier to cut the conversation short, Cooper yawned. Feigned tiredness. 'So listen, it's late here and I've got to be up early.'

'Okay, but it's true what I said, you are my hero. I've hidden myself away from the world whilst you're out there taking it on.'

'This is my version of hiding. What I do is hardly reality. I distance myself from that. Too difficult. Screws me up. You and I aren't that different in that respect.'

'Yes we are, Coop. Everything I do is out of fear. Everything you do is out of passion. Integrity. Justice… love. You loved her so much, didn't you?'

Rubbing his face, Cooper sighed loudly. 'Yeah I did. And I don't think I could love anyone else, not the way I loved her… Anyway, sleep well. I'll catch you soon.'

Cooper clicked off his phone and turned over on the uncomfortable sleeper.

Across the room on the double bed, next to the snoring form of Rosedale, Maddie lay rigid, awake, having heard every word.

32

In the shadow of the night, a truck pulled up to a grinding halt. The three men, armed with old Russian machine guns, taped and tied, waited patiently. Nodding a greeting to the driver they untied the blue tarpaulin sheet covering the load. Pulling it off to reveal a multitude of terrified, confused faces.

Undoing the bolts on the back of the truck, the men led their captives off. Pushing. Kicking. Forcing them into the middle of the red clay yard.

'Take all your clothes off… Do it.' The nervous, embarrassed, frightened glimpses of the old man, echoed in the thoughts of the others. A variety of ages, not knowing why they'd been chosen. Nor why they'd been taken.

'Now move it… Move.'

Walking naked with their arms raised high, heads bowed down, they moved in quiet unison towards the ice-cold showers, forced at gunpoint to walk and stand under the freezing water.

To an accompaniment of distant screams, which pierced the blanket of hush, the herded group were now taken down stairs into the enigma of deeper darkness. A long, low-roofed hallway led them to a metal door which opened and, once they were in, closed shut. Leaving them crammed tightly. Pushed up close to one another in a red, unplastered chamber of stifling heat.

33

'Can I have a word, Mr. President?'

'Sure.' John Woods sat in the Oval Office, finishing tying up his shoelaces before turning to look at Teddy. 'Is it me, or is it this sofa…? Can you feel it? It's like leaning on a goddamn corkscrew.'

'You often do that?'

'I do now.'

Teddy pressed the back cushion of the cream floral couch. 'Yeah, okay… I feel it. Think it's a spring. I'll get June to speak to maintenance.'

'Thanks… Anyway, what's up?'

'I know this is off schedule, but I need to run something by you.'

Naomi Tyler, an honours graduate of the University of Kentucky and a former communications director of the vice president, who'd been recently appointed as the newest of John Woods's senior advisors, clutched her mobile. 'Sorry, Teddy, you'll have to make this later. We've got a bi-partisan meeting on the Clean Power Plan, with only a five minute window before the Women in Science conference begins, plus we've then got an out of towner – West Virginia – regarding the epidemic of prescription drug abuse in America.'

'Remind me, why West Virginia?'

'Because it's the state that's home to the highest rate of overdose deaths in the nation… It's all in the speech, sir.

There's time to look over it on the way there, but bear in mind we've also got to facilitate your call to the president of Uruguay, which should've happened last week. We'll have approximately twenty-five minutes, but of course that's rounded off, which means...'

Teddy interrupted. 'Jesus, Naomi. By the time you've gone through the whole schedule, I could've had the conversation.'

'You can't do a walk and talk?'

Teddy Adleman stared in dismay. 'Naomi, if I'd wanted to do that, don't you think I would do...? Mr. President, help me out here.'

'Can't it wait?'

Teddy said, 'I don't think it should.'

'Okay... Naomi, give us a moment.'

'Mr. President, we really can't afford the time.'

Woods put his hand on Naomi's shoulder. 'Naomi, I tell you what, why don't you go get yourself a sandwich and whilst you're at it, try and relax.'

Naomi Tyler visibly jerked. Her smooth black skin beginning to patch from stress.

'Mr. President that just isn't possible. By the time I go and get it and then get back here, even if I ran, the schedule will be out by... at least eighteen minutes.'

'Naomi... Naomi. Breathe. Calm down. I was joking, okay. I know there's no time to go, I just love your reaction. Listen, wait outside the office. I'll be with you in a minute.'

Naomi gazed down at her phone. Then at Woods. 'Mr. President, would that be a literal minute, or...'

'Naomi, just go.'

*

Listening to Teddy, Woods gulped back his milky white nothing-fancy coffee.

'I've had a few interesting conversations with Donald Parker.'

'Recap.'

'He owns Nadbury Electronics.'

'Yeah, of course. At the fundraiser. Interesting guy.'

'More than that. He's a great supporter of yours, *and* the administration. I've spoken to a few people and he also had a good rep when it came to supporting Obama's administration. Fundraising and campaign donations. He's been around for quite a while and there's a lot of respect for him within the party. There are number of senators who owe their seat to him through his funding of their campaigns. And therefore he has a lot of favors he's able to pull in when it matters.'

As Woods listened, it struck him how Teddy had noticeably aged from when they first set out on the presidential trail a couple of years ago. His neat, relaxed, short hair, once a fine afro, had receded and thinned and grayed dramatically. Though in fairness to Teddy, he wasn't the only one. All of them, himself included, seemed to have been afflicted with the more-salt-than-pepper hair pandemic seemingly associated with the presidential office.

'I know it's not the usual way to do things, but I wouldn't suggest you speaking to him if I didn't think it might be of use to us. It seems he could really be helpful.'

'How so?'

'If you don't mind, I'd rather not brief you on what he's got to say.'

'You been drinking Teddy? Because, apart from Naomi, I don't know one other person who likes to brief as much as you do. Right down to the last semi-colon.'

Teddy smiled. Adjusted the buckle of his belt. 'I know, maybe I'm totally off-road here, but for some reason I really want you to hear what Donald Parker has to say first-hand. See what your initial reaction is.'

Woods swirled round his coffee, wanting to drink the last visible drops but at the same time wanting to avoid drawing up the skin of milk encircling the inside of the cup.

'Okay. Let's do it.'

Teddy pressed the intercom on the desk. 'Joan, get Mr. Parker on the line. It was the number I gave you when I came in this morning. Oh, and tell Naomi not to have a coronary. The president will be out in a couple of minutes. But, say to her, I can't guarantee them being literal ones.'

34

Woods said, 'Mr. Parker?'

'Mr. President, call me Donald.'

'It's good to speak to you again, Donald.'

'Well I'm honoured. And I realize we've only got a couple of minutes so I'll get straight to the point. As you know I own Nadbury, the twelfth largest American multinational technology company. Three years ago we were ranked as being one of the highest valued semiconductor chip makers. However, whilst other semiconductor companies have seen an average thirty-eight percent increase in chip sales, based on a seventy-three percent increase in the demand for smart cell unit sales, we've had to watch our sales drop by forty percent. As you can imagine these figures are significant, and as a result our company has taken a big knock when it comes to stock-performances on the Dow Jones. In short, we need to turn it round. But to turn it round we need something special to compete and not be undercut by larger corporations.'

'And based on the information you've just given me... '

Parker laughed. 'What exactly do I want?'

'Right.'

'Cutting right to the chase, Mr. President. I want you and your government to head our campaign. I want our products to be bought by every college kid. Every school. Every Ivy League graduate. We want to bring awareness and make the future of tomorrow a place where it isn't just a generation of what we can do for ourselves but a generation of what we can do for others. We are company with ethics right to the heart of who we are. We have mines in the Democratic Republic of the Congo, Mr. President. *Conflict free*. Which has been, to put it mildly, challenging. But it's integral to who Nadbury are. In essence this equates to all our products being *conflict free*, unlike most electronic companies. You could say we are the Fairtrade of electronics. I love my country but I understand more than ever there should be no borders on probity. How can I say I love my children if my company is part of hurting someone else's children? I don't want to pick up my cell phone or use a computer which has blood on it. However, I am a business man and my company has taken some pretty big hits of late. Taking an ethical stance means we have to charge more for our products whilst our competitors can be more cost effective and reap the profits by using minerals from mines where children are forced to work and violence is an everyday occurrence. To get back on top we need a campaign that will make a difference and get people to buy our products. Not just for the company, but for the good and wellbeing of others. I realize this is just a quick briefing and I'd like to explain in further detail when you have more time. Though I'm sure the question you want to ask now is, what I am going to do for you...'

There was a knock on the door. Naomi Tyler. 'Mr. President!'

Woods nodded. Waved away Naomi. 'Listen, Donald, I have to go before one of my staff combusts. We'll have to find a window to continue. I'll get Joan to liaise with my staff for an appropriate time. I want to hear more about this.'

'Mr. President, let me just tell you this. I have a lot of influence with senators up at Capitol Hill. If you help me with what I need, I *guarantee* you'll get the votes in Congress you need to pass your gun reforms.'

35

Cooper, Maddie and Rosedale sat in the white Toyota, watching whilst the heat of the morning steamed away the haze leaving an oppressive dampness. Rosedale sat behind the wheel with Cooper next to him whilst Maddie sat quietly at the back as the air conditioning blew out nothing but hot air, adding to the already stifling atmosphere.

Rosedale broke the silence. Sounded cheerful and unaffected by the heat. 'Guess what I saw running up the wall of the bathroom this morning?'

Maddie gave a sigh of resignation. 'Why don't you just tell us?'

'I'll think you'll like it.'

'I doubt it. You know what, on second thoughts, nobody cares.'

Rosedale glanced at Maddie in the driver's mirror. 'Speak for yourself, Maddison, I think Thomas here is gnashing at the teeth wanting to know, aren't you boy?'

With the discovery that the passenger window was jammed, Cooper now had to deal with the sunlight scorching onto the glass. He gave the same sigh of resignation Maddie had. 'What's with the *boy* thing, Rosedale? How about today, you give me and Maddie a break from anything which suggests it comes from the Rosedale school of behavior. What do you say?'

'I say, no-one's guessed what is was that I saw climbing up the bathroom wall.'

In an exaggerated manner, Cooper threw his arms wide open. 'You know we won't get a minute's peace till you tell us, will we? So fine. Fine, just tell us.'

Rosedale winked as he did a right turn on the Place de la Gare, near to the main railway station. 'Well if you insist. So when I went into the john...'

'Stop, there!'

Rosedale smirked. 'I've only just got going.'

'Shut up Rosedale,' said Cooper. 'Turn round the car if you can, I've just seen something.'

Without pausing to question, Rosedale spun the car round. Skidded it at speed whilst enjoying the cacophony of angry horns and the waving of fists and the mouthing of inaudible curse words by the other drivers.

Cooper kept an eye out for a safe place for Rosedale to pull over. He didn't want them to miss what he'd just seen. He pointed to the sidewalk. 'Here... Just park here. We'll be able to see it from there.'

Rosedale pulled on the handbrake. And Cooper, who'd been looking forward to stepping out into some fresh air, found himself jumping out quickly, only to be hit with the disappointment of the same cloying heat they'd suffered inside the car.

For all the military training he'd had, the heat was still the heat and he felt it like any other man. He tried to make his own breeze. Flapped his gray marl t-shirt at its hem. At the front. At the back. All it did was make him hotter. Irritated. And wondering again why the hell he'd been so eager to come.

He smiled at Maddie, who turned away, refusing to give

him eye contact. He lit a cigarette. He was on edge. And he needed something to bring him down.

'So what's with the eye spy, Thomas…? You look terrible, by the way. You should lay off those things.'

Not interested in what Rosedale had to say, Cooper pointed up to a massive billboard hauled high above the road. It showed a man. Arms crossed. Standing authoritatively in front of a whitewashed church with the words: *Be sober, be vigilant; because your adversary the devil, as a roaring lion, walks about, seeking whom he may devour*.

'What do you see?'

'I don't know. We give up, Thomas,'

'This might be a long shot but…'

Rosedale cut through his sentence. 'What the hell else have we to go on? A long shot. A blind shot. A shot in the dark. Who cares what kind of shot as long as it gives us something so I can get the hell out of here. Ain't that right, Miss Maddison?'

Maddie said nothing.

'Exactly,' said Cooper. 'So, here's the deal. The suit the guys wearing, it's the same suit the man was wearing at the fire at Emmanuel's aunt and uncle's house.'

Rosedale nodded. 'The one who warned us off?'

'Yeah.'

'Thomas, I know you don't want me to use the word boy, but *boy* I've got to use it for this one, sugar. That is one hell of a *long* shot. We're desperate, but if them using the same tailor is what we've got, let's give up and go home.'

Cooper scuffed his sand boot into a wet pool of stony gravel. Bit on his lip. And tried not to open up the box about the person who'd landed him with Rosedale. He was pissed.

But then he was always pissed with John. And as John wasn't here, he decided to be pissed with Rosedale instead.

'Have you finished now, Rosedale? Had your fun? Because I can wait, but whilst you're entertaining yourself maybe have a look at the guy's suit jacket. On the pocket. The initials, *NRC*, the same initials on the guy's jacket. And there at the bottom of the ad… Look there. *NRC – New Revivalist Church*. And contrary to it being a suit from…'

'Wal-Mart?'

Cooper gave Rosedale a dirty look. '…From the same tailor. It's clearly a regulation suit worn by the pastors of the New Revivalist Church. And if we want to speak to the guy about what the hell he was doing there and why was he trying to warn us off, I reckon it's a good bet we'll find him or at least find someone who knows him… And perhaps even knows Emmanuel.'

Rosedale began to clap slowly, grinning widely before taking his hat off to tip it. 'I got to give it to you… actually, no I don't.' He turned and walked away, calling back to Cooper. 'Come on, Thomas, we've got us some sins to go and repent.'

Not wanting to but needing to speak to Cooper, Maddie said, 'I don't know about this.'

'What do you mean?'

'Those churches. They're not always as they seem.'

'A church is a church… Come on, let's get back in the car.'

Maddie watched Cooper get back into the SUV, suddenly realizing she'd been holding her breath. Holding back her own fears.

36

'If anyone's interested it was a lizard.'

Cooper sat at the back of the New Revivalist church, staring at Rosedale as if he'd lost all sense. 'What?'

He whispered again to Maddie who sat tensely, eyes darting around.

'A lizard. In the bathroom this morning. It was a lizard.'

Fiddling with a pen and some leaflets he'd picked up at the entrance of the church, Cooper mouthed a silent, *what are you talking about?* before turning his attention back to the pastor on the stage.

The place was packed, and hot. Jammed to crushing point with the colorfully clad congregation, standing swaying as if they were flowers caught in a summer's breeze. A smell of sickly stale sweat rested in the air.

The building itself was a white block construction. High ceilings. Small windows. Flags and posters warned all those present of the dangers and temptations of Satan and near the front was a stage; on it, three dark wooden crosses as high and wide as any cross Cooper had ever seen. Twelve foot tall and looking like they'd come from a Klan rally. By the altar, there was a banner; it simply read:

Cast out the witches, we shall deliver and set them free

A loud voice boomed over the Tannoy. Wanting to see the

person who was speaking but unable to over the congregation, Cooper apologized and pushed past the row of people to make his way down to the end of the row.

Cooper stepped into the aisle. Nodded his head. Said a quiet 'Gotcha' to himself as he watched with interest the man they'd met at the fire, speaking with intimidating vigour whilst kneeling down in front of one of the crosses.

'You are the physician of my soul. You are the redemption of those who come to you. I ask you to make powerless, expel, and drive out every manifestation, every evil influence directed against us. Spirits of death and darkness, I renounce and admonish Satan and every evil power he has. I forsake any evil witchcraft practiced by the spirits around. I ask you to take me and burn my body with the fire of you. Let the holy spirits of your ancestors protect you.'

Maddie and Rosedale came to stand next to Cooper. She whispered in his ear urgently. 'Do you realize what's about to happen?'

About to reply, Cooper leant in to Maddie's ear, smelling the floral perfume she always wore. She smelled good. Fresh. Unlike Rosedale and himself, who hadn't stopped sweating since they arrived in the country. Suddenly a roar, a cheer as loud and intense as any Redskins match Cooper had ever been to, filled the building. Stopped him saying what he was about to. Cries of 'Amen' and 'Hallelujah' reverberated around the church. To the side of him, he could see people with their arms stretched up, visibly throwing themselves onto the floor as if they'd been hit by a charging fullback.

By now half of the church were lying down and Cooper could see the place was making Maddie feel more and more uncomfortable.

The cheer rose up again, only this time the lights of the

church dimmed and colorful spots whirled across the stage, like some kind of pop concert.

'Look.'

Cooper nodded his head to Maddie as he saw a man being led onto the stage. The hysteria began to grow, helped along by the sudden playing of a badly-recorded version of a Congolese hymn.

Fascinated by the man who'd been led on the stage, by both his long dazzling white Swarovski-adorned robe, and the fact he'd brought an almost reverent silence to the whole place, Cooper and Rosedale watched mesmerized.

'Je suis ici pour vous délivrer, pour vous débarrasser du mal. For those amongst you who don't know, who until now have been lost amongst the thorns of evil, and who sat at the table of the possessed, I am here to set you free. My name is Papa Bemba. Servant, slayer, washer of your sins, cleanser of your soul.'

It was only when Papa Bemba took off his dark shades that Cooper really noticed the guy had them on, but there was no escaping the angry, thick scar tissue which lay beneath, where his eyes should've been.

The three of them watched as Bemba took the cup which had just been handed to him, then a second later watched as he deliberately poured it over the front of his robe.

Cooper had no idea why, nor what his intention was, but as the red liquid soaked into his robe, the brilliance of the red in stark contrast to the brilliance of the white robe, the dramatic cry from Bemba chilled even him.

'I shall shed the blood. The blood of the witch. Come…! Come!'

Bemba raised his arms as three men, dressed in the regulation blue pinstripe suits, hurried onto stage a procession of children. Darting eyes. Scared faces. Fear staring out from the innocence of their youth.

'I gotta do something!' Maddie stepped forward but felt Rosedale's hand grabbing her arm. Pulling her back. 'Get the hell off me.'

Rosedale stared into her face. 'Whatever it is you're thinking you're going to do, I'm not going to let you. You hear me.'

Her face flushed with anger and pain and fear, and Maddie tried to shake Rosedale's grip off. 'I said get off me… I'm going to stop this and there's nothing you can do about it.'

With a mixture of surprise and shock, Rosedale saw Maddie go for the hidden .357 Smith & Wesson handgun they'd picked up from a contact when they'd arrived, and which she had hidden under her jacket. He hissed a warning. 'Put that away. Have you lost your goddamn mind? See those men over there dressed in suits? Standing against the wall just watching? Well I guarantee underneath those suits they're packing something which'll make that Magnum look like a toy gun.'

Blinking and refusing and fighting and battling the tears away, Maddie appealed, wanting to hear Rosedale say what she needed to hear. 'Please Rosedale, we can't just stand here and do nothing.'

'Maddie, I can't let you.'

'Do you know what they're about to do? Do you…? A deliverance. The so called cleansing of children. The purging of the Kindoki force.'

'I know.'

'Then get off me.'

'No… I'm sorry.'

'How dare you try to stop me… Go to hell, Rosedale.'

'I think we're already there… Look.'

Maddie didn't reply. Just watched. Felt sick. Her heart began to sink. Despair consuming her as she saw Papa Bemba walk with the help of one of his aides to the first child in the row. No older than five. Kneeling. Terrified. Shaking and crying.

She tried to run forward at the sight of Bemba pushing forcibly down on a little girl's head, but Rosedale's powerful grip held onto to her tightly.

'I deliver her! I baptize her in the spirit that is good and worthy. I throw the flames of your name to rid her of the evil.'

Another cup was given to Papa Bemba, only this time he gave it to the child to drink. Immediately she began to cough and the cry of 'Amen' catapulted once more around the church.

'Vomit up the devil. Vomir le diable.'

Maddie could hardly breathe as she continued to watch. She knew witchcraft was a system of belief, rooted in popular mentality from the uneducated right up to the high state officials. And she also knew traditional healing was nothing unusual where a medicine man, a *Nganga*, or a pastor helped and healed. But this form of belief in witchcraft, the deliverance, had been altered over the last decade. Twisting. Changing. Morphing into something dark. Something brutal where families and neighbors accused and cast out the children who were thought to be the possessed, and it had become common practice, and over the last few years the custom had grown.

Needing somebody to blame for a life of hardship and suffering and loss. Driven by Kinshasa and the rest of the country's economy and infrastructure collapsing, as well as the result of government corruption and war, the number of children accused of witchcraft exploded.

Thousands of innocent, traumatized children lived on the streets of Kinshasa. And their faces, bewildered and unknowing, haunted her and she couldn't help but think of Cora.

They were hunted down as witches by those who were supposed to protect them. Accused of using their supposed sorcery to bring harm to those around. Accused of causing illnesses. Loss of jobs. Loss of opportunity. Even the loss of items, sometimes as trivial as a mislaid ballpoint pen. Blamed for the difficulties of everyday life and powerless to defend themselves.

There'd always been the belief in spirits. She got it. Only too well. But what they were doing to the children was just plain wrong. And the rise of the revivalist church had exacerbated it, bringing about a rise in the business of witchcraft, making a business out of the deliverance of children – *the suffering of children.*

People were desperate for there to be a reason why pain and misery surrounded them, why the mouths they had to feed seemed as endless as the hunger pains. Human beings wanting answers, and believing all causation was spiritual.

So they turned to the church and the church pointed the blame at the young, promising to cleanse the child, driving out the evil spirit. But it didn't come free. The promise of a new life came with a fee. Desperate families gave money, jewellery, land, even properties to rid themselves of their curse. But the people who paid the real price, the highest price, were the kids. For the lucky ones, the fortunate few, the practice of exorcism would only consist of starving the Kindoki out.

A week.

A fortnight.

A month.

Until eventually they'd be taken back into the fold of the family. The others? Maddie knew were beaten.

Tortured.

Burnt.

Thrown out on the streets to die or, more likely, killed. Suffering was everywhere. And she hated the smell of it. And how could she love her daddy's country anymore – her country – when this was at the heart?

Maddie, her face strained, reflecting what Rosedale and Cooper were feeling, pushed Rosedale off.

'I've seen enough. I'm getting out of here.'

Both men nodded in agreement. Relieved they could walk away. Guilty the children couldn't.

Making their way out, none one of them looked back at the sound of the child screaming. They didn't want to know what caused such anguish within her cry.

A few feet before the exit, Cooper felt a hand on his shoulder. He turned, thinking it would be Rosedale, but faced two men. One he recognized. The guy from the fire.

'The Church of the New Revivalist turns no sinner away who wants to free his soul, but I fear that's not the purpose of your visit. I think it best we talk outside.' A moment later Cooper felt a gun in his side.

37

The exit took Cooper outside into an alleyway as long, and as mud-logged, as the one he'd been in last night. He could see Rosedale and Maddie standing by the wall with the men who'd escorted them out, but now a dozen more had joined them. Though these men were openly armed.

Cooper held Rosedale's gaze, but there was nothing there. No suggestion of him having a plan. It was clear the only thing they could do was try to talk themselves out of it. Anything else just wasn't an option. Basic rule of military training – know when you're out-gunned.

Cooper turned to the man. 'I didn't know it was crime to go to church.'

'Who said anything about it being a crime?'

Having been placed next to Rosedale and Maddie against the wall, Cooper stared directly into the man's face, who stared directly back. Hostility dripping from him like sweat.

'Then I'd appreciate it if you could let us leave now.'

'You'll leave. Make no mistake of that. But how you'll leave is a different matter. Tell me, why were you looking for Emmanuel? And don't bother denying it.'

Rosedale, sounding unlike the usual loud and booming Texan, said, 'We've just got some business with him, that's all, sir.'

The man turned to stare at Rosedale. Nodded his head.

Then brought back his fist. Hit him hard in the stomach. Caused Rosedale to bend up double.

And he brought his fist to Cooper, who refused to drop his stare, up to and during the powerful punch in his stomach.

Then to Maddie. But instead of a punch. A slap. A hard, stinging slap. A steely stare and she said, 'Go to hell.'

The man stepped in closer to her.

Cooper had been able to keep still till then. Hadn't flinched. But now. Oh God, now was different.

'No…! Leave it!'

The shout from Rosedale, telling him not to, was loud and cautionary. Telling him he had to keep it calm. To keep it down. Suck it up.

'I want you to get your things from the hotel and go back home. Tomorrow, I want you and your friends gone… Forget you even heard the name Emmanuel.'

The door was flung open and all heads turned. And there, like a vision, looking like he'd been in a mix of a car crash and an out-of-control frat party. Covered in blood. Covered in vomit. Papa Bemba

Bemba's frame was large and, although smaller than Cooper's, he was a formidable presence. The man from the fire spoke and, as he did, Bemba's mutilated face, which told a thousand stories, turned towards Cooper.

The man from the fire said, 'These are the people I was telling you about. The ones looking for Emmanuel.'

'Thank you, Lumumba.'

Papa Bemba felt his way along the wall, stopping as his hand brushed against Cooper. In his voice there was mockery, tied up with a bow of menace.

'I hope my men are treating you well.'

His hand felt Cooper's throat. Then his face. Pulling and

feeling his lips. His touch to Cooper felt as if a million tiny creatures were crawling over him.

Without a word, Bemba shuffled along to Maddie who stood motionlessly as his large imposing hands touched. Moved. Stroked… Caressed her body.

Rosedale's expression to Cooper served like a traffic stop. A warning not to do anything stupid.

And Maddie, although wanting to, refused to turn her head away as Papa Bemba seemed to stare at her. Moving closer, nearer. His lips almost touching her cheek as he said, 'Only those related to the possessed shall seek the possessed. Be warned.'

Then pulling away and moving off as quickly as he'd come, Bemba, led by Lumumba, headed towards the large waiting cavalcade, followed by his other men.

Rosedale and Cooper ran to the end of the alleyway watching the cars drive off at speed, mud and dirt flying everywhere.

Seeing them disappear into the distance, Rosedale ran back to Maddie, who lay her head back against the brick wall. He looked at her. Put his arm around her shoulder. Moved her away from the church. 'It's okay, Miss Maddison.'

She pulled away. 'You don't understand do you? It's not okay. You should've let me help those children when I had a chance.' She stared hard at him, spoke in a flat tone. 'And I don't think I'll ever be able to forgive you for that.'

38

Cooper watched Maddie sleep. 'You think she's alright?'

Rosedale took a moment to answer as they drove out and away from Kinshasa. Driving into the night, hoping to find a lead. Anything which would give them some answers.

'Maddison? I think she's stronger than the both of us. She can handle herself. Relax Thomas, she's fine.'

'What about what we're doing? Do you think that's fine? Are we doing the right thing?'

Rosedale changed gear. Swerved around the potholes. 'Probably not, but when have you ever worried about doing the right thing? There are four facts we got to keep in mind. Fact one, we've got nothing or as little as nothing to go on. Fact two, the *little as* we do have is that it's clear this Emmanuel guy seems to have pissed off Papa Bemba in some way, or at least he's involved in something which makes people want us to stop asking questions. Fact three, people wanting me to stop asking questions makes me want to ask them.'

'I don't know.'

Rosedale glanced at him sideward. 'Well I do and besides, we haven't got to my fact four yet. Fact four, as we saw when they sped away, the plates on the cars of Papa Bemba and his men are from the Buziba area of South Kivu, which, according to our hotelier is where the headquarters of the New Revivalist Church is. It's also where Emmanuel's aunt and uncle's neighbor said Emmanuel and his family came from. Which means if we want anything more than Granger being on our backs, about us not being able to do the job properly, then we need to get to Buziba and ask questions. Which is exactly why we're going there… Can I give you another fact?'

'No.'

'You know, you can be a real spoilsport, Thomas. Maybe if you lightened up a bit, you might have more luck with the ladies.'

Cooper stared at him with as much incredulity as he could muster. 'I do want to ask what the hell you're talking about, I really do, but you know something, Rosedale? I think I'm afraid of the answer.'

Rosedale laughed. Peered out from underneath his cowboy hat as the car headlights did an inadequate job of lighting up the road.

Cooper took a swig of water from the bottle in his bag.

'You taking them pills again?'

Cooper's tone was flat. 'I'm drinking water.'

'Don't try to deny it, Thomas. We both know in your bag in the side pocket, where the zipper could be stronger, you keep some of your pills, which are conveniently loose for moments just like these. We also both know that when you went in your bag to get the water you quickly slipped a couple in your hand. You've done it a thousand times before. Expertly done and put in your mouth without anybody noticing. Anybody apart from me, that is.'

'Leave me alone Rosedale, you're talking bull again.'

'Am I? Well how about this then? We both know when you swallow liquid your throat's relaxed, with complex volitional and reflex interactions. Yet your cricopharyngeus muscle pulled up harder on your anterior cricoid cartilage. Which means the difference although subtle, but obvious

199

to the trained eye, is that you, Thomas J. Cooper, have just swallowed something solid.'

Cooper didn't deny it. But he didn't admit it. Felt too much like a confessional. Instead he shook his head. 'Things just don't make sense anymore.'

'Why the sudden rush of doubt, boy? Is all this spiritual stuff taking over? Do Maddison and I need to start worrying?'

'No… it's…'

'It's just you've been listening to the likes of Granger, and all that stuff about you calming your ass down. But you haven't crossed any lines.'

'It's not that. It feels like something's not right here. Like I should be doing more. I've got a real sense of unease, Rosedale.'

'That's what I don't understand about you. Everything is always so personal. Like you're on some kind of quest. You look into things too deeply, Thomas. This is just a job. The job we were told to do and the job we get well paid for. That's it, honey. Nothing more. Track down Emmanuel and seize the plane. Fly it back to Nairobi. And that's exactly what we're trying to do. And if we don't, well, Granger will be bitching our ass off for a while because his recovery rate stats will drop. But that's all. It's a job. Stop trying to make everything your own private mission. Don't look beyond.'

Cooper stared out, unable to see anything in the pitch darkness. 'Maybe so.'

'I know so. It's not the job, it's you. Calm will never be inside of you, Thomas. Even if the accident never happened, I doubt you'd ever have peace. You'd always be looking for something which isn't there.'

Cooper's face twisted into a frown. His words followed suit. 'Thanks a lot, Rosedale. You certainly know how to make a guy feel good.'

'Like I say, Thomas, you need to lighten up. The American Indians used to talk about people like you. The people with restless souls who ran with the buffalo.'

Cooper tilted his head to one side, studying Rosedale. 'Have you been watching *Dances With Wolves* again?'

'So what if I have? There's not a film that comes close and I'm telling you, Thomas, Kevin Costner was robbed. He should've won the Oscar.'

'It won best picture, and he *did* get one for best director.'

Rosedale shook his head. 'But *not* best actor. You seriously going to sit here and tell me Jeremy Irons deserved it over Costner?'

Closing his eyes, Cooper couldn't help but smile. 'I liked that film… What was it? *Reversal of Fortune*?'

'Thomas, you know nothing, which is why you need to listen when I tell you to stop worrying. Stop medicating yourself before you get into real trouble again, like how it was before… By the way, did I ever tell you about the time I met Costner?'

39

Night turned inevitably into day, which turned into three more long days and nights on treacherous, unmarked roads, with no-one to keep Cooper sane in the heat apart from Rosedale which, on reflection was probably an unlikely source of sanity, and Maddie, who slept most of the time.

The vividly green countryside was abundant in its variety, and the beauty of the rainforests set against the mountains was breath-taking, with beautiful mud huts looking like dollhouses dotted in the distant picturesque villages.

But no matter how scenic the countryside was, it didn't distract Cooper from the bites on his legs, which were enough to play dot to dot, and he knew if he had to listen to Rosedale trying to sing 'The Trail of the Lonesome Pine' backwards once more, he was going to lose his mind.

The trip had been trying and the question, *what the hell was he thinking of, coming here?* had crossed his mind on a repeat loop.

On the first day they'd had to reroute and take a hundred-mile detour, as the tiny battered river ferry they'd been intending to sail on was stuck on the river banks waiting for an engine part to be delivered, having already waited three weeks for it.

On the second day they'd had torrential rain, but hadn't had the luxury of sitting in the car waiting for it to pass. Instead they'd suffered drenched clothing and blistered fingers whilst they'd dug the Toyota out from the rutted road, as muddy waters flooded into the car.

On the third day, with most bridges not inspiring the confidence to cross their contorted iron frames, they'd encountered four imprudent, unarmed men who'd blocked the road, bearing rocks in an attempt to get money. He'd allowed Rosedale the pleasure, and five minutes later they'd continued on their way.

And now, on the last day of the drive and nearing their destination of Buziba, he was in two minds whether or not to smash the passenger window. It was still stuck. Still driving him crazy, and once more the sun had risen, giving off its cruel, strangling heat, making the rays beating down through the window unbearable.

Maddie, whose window was able to open – something which Cooper and Rosedale looked on with envy throughout the trip – pointed to a large billboard on the side of the grassy bank. 'Look, guys. Over there.'

Peering across to where Maddie was pointing, Cooper could see a large advertisement for the New Revivalist Church, picturing Papa Bemba, minus his glasses, and with the words, *The Saviour*, blazoned across it.

Brown curls swaying in the breeze, which she was clearly enjoying, she said, 'You think he's talking about himself?'

Rosedale nodded. 'Probably. The guy's positively narcissistic.'

Cooper turned round to Maddie. 'What do you think happened to his eyes?'

'To me it looks like some sort of mutilation. Maiming. I don't know, perhaps it was something to do with the Hutu-Tutsi conflict. There was a hell of a lot of butchery, and this area was one of the worst for it. We're real close to the

Rwandan border and not too far from the Ugandan one, so right here would've been the hub for a lot of it. The genocide was like a hurricane.'

'Yeah and no-one was immune from the violence. Not even kids or babies.'

Cooper didn't reply. His mind was on Papa Bemba. It was clear he carried a lot of power and probably wealth as well. And the combination of the two, especially in a place like this, could be dangerous.

One of the things he couldn't stop thinking about was the young man he'd met the other night in the derelict building, and the words which he could still hear. *Whatever the reason you think you are here, it won't be the reason*.

He didn't know why he hadn't told Rosedale or Maddie the full extent of the conversation. But the sense of keeping it to himself for now was strong.

It had also struck him that Emmanuel wasn't the person he needed to find out about. Whether they found Emmanuel or not, the truth was, he couldn't care less. So the guy hadn't paid for a plane? Cooper didn't give a damn about the plane, nor the money owed. It felt nothing compared to the feelings he had about Bemba. And even though Emmanuel had been their reason to come, where he was and who he was, wasn't the point. For Cooper, the focus had changed to Papa Bemba, because whatever was happening here his instinct told him it was bigger. Much bigger than just a guy not having paid the loan back for his plane. Now all he had to do was look further.

Realize the truth, but to find it you need to look beyond.

40

'That looks interesting. What do you think it is?' Maddie called out from the back, breaking Cooper's chain of thought. Not that his chain of thoughts were beneficial to anyone else, given he was currently wondering if AJ's Fine Foods diner in Phoenix was going to carry any new flavors of iced tea this summer.

Across to the left, standing in a valley, were a handful of large industrial buildings. They looked very much out of place in the middle of the wild, provocative, paintbox-colored countryside, where fields and tracks slunk up the hills and mountains.

A large, pale yellow sign, with an embossed image of a drop of water with the word *Lemon*, in bold white writing, loomed by the side of the road.

A thought suddenly crossed Cooper's mind which he hoped was going to be more relevant than his previous ones. Sticking to the Toyota seat with sweat, he went into his jeans pocket. Pulled out the pen he'd picked up from the New Revivalist Church and passed it to Maddie.

'I don't know what it quite means, but here you go... The same logo's on the pen. What do you reckon, Rosedale? Worth taking a look?'

'Well, there's only one way to find out!' Rosedale shouted as if they weren't all sitting next to each other in the same car. He turned the Toyota round at speed. Veered off the dirt track road, to the rolling of eyes of Cooper and Maddie.

*

Parking up a few feet from a tall, solid black fence, topped off with razor-wire and a multitude of security cameras, Cooper jumped out of the car. Peeled off the sweat-drenched t-shirt that was stuck to his body. Wrung it out. Flung it on the floor of the car.

Throwing Cooper a dry t-shirt from the back, and breaking open a bottle of water which was supposed to be cold, Maddie offered it around.

'Anyone want some hot water? I have to warn you, the only thing it's got going for it, is it's wet.'

'Don't mind if I do.' Rosedale snatched the bottle as Maddie and Cooper walked ahead. They looked around, taking it all in.

The perfectly tarmacked road to the wrought iron gates was in absolute contrast to the roads they'd encountered on the journey. The ones outside Goma, which Rosedale had driven on a couple of hours back, had been the worst. Built-up craters of uneven tarmac encrusted with lava from the active volcano nearby had made it one hell of a precarious drive.

Almost at the gates, Cooper watched the cameras track their movement. An intercom system buzzed.

'Hello? Can I help you?'

Cooper looked at Maddie, whose expression reflected his surprise. The voice was American.

'Hi there!, Me and my friends were just driving past, saw the place and wondered what it was.'

'Well, it's great you've stopped by.'

The cheerful reply surprised them once more. And having been joined by a well-hydrated Rosedale, Cooper continued to chat to the intercom. 'It just seemed a bit out of place. A bit…'

The person on the other end laughed. 'New built? Listen, come in if you like. If you want to leave your car there that's fine, though it's a fairly long drive. Either way it won't be a problem. Just come up to the main building. Follow signs to the main lobby. I'll meet you there. The name's Charles by the way. See you in a minute.'

The intercom crackled before going silent. Maddie looked at Rosedale. 'What do you think?'

'Anchorage,' said Rosedale. 'I think that's an Anchorage accent.'

Cooper said, 'Maddie, I'm relying on you to keep me sane.'

41

The lobby, along with the building, was nothing like Cooper had expected to find in such a rural and out of the way place. It was of high spec. Expensive, state of the art security matched the expensive interior. Streamline smoked glass and chrome. Meticulous white marble flooring, topped off with a curving ornate stairwell going up to a glass-walled second floor. But he had to admit, as impressive as it all was, it was the high quality and high powered and no-expense-spared air conditioning system which really got him. Cool. Soothing. Luxurious. Something which seemed at that moment to have vice-like qualities.

'Anyone thinking the same thing as I am?' asked Cooper.

'This place needs a moose?'

'What…? What? What in all that is godly, Rosedale, are you talking about now?'

Rosedale stared at Cooper scornfully. 'You know nothing, Thomas. Every lobby needs a moose… Even the CIA had one in their headquarters in Langley.'

'No. No, they did not.'

With pride encasing his words, Rosedale said, 'Yes they did. In fact, part of the reason they had one was because of me. When Barack Obama nominated John Brennan for the second time to serve as Director of the Central Intelligence Agency, and he was successfully voted in, by way of a celebration, I suggested we get a moose.'

'Are you for real?'

As both Maddie and Cooper continued to shake their heads at Rosedale, a rotund man, ruddy- faced, with thinning remnants of brown hair, descended the stairs. His smile was warm and genuinely welcoming.

'Hi guys, I'm Charles. Charles Templin-Wright. Welcome to Lemon.' Charles stuck out his hand to shake Cooper's. He took it. Noticed and was surprised at the strength of the grip.

'Good to meet you, sir. I'm Thomas Cooper, this here is Austin Rosedale Young, and this is Maddie Coop...'

Cooper stopped not knowing quite how to introduce Maddie. She cut him a stare.

'Maddie Cooper, but not for long. I'm going back to my maiden name. Menga.'

Charles gave an awkward smile. 'Well it's good to meet you Maddie Menga. That's a Congolese surname isn't it?'

'It is. I've got family to the east of these parts.'

Templin-Wright nodded and then said, 'Drink?'

Cooper could almost taste it.

'Yeah, that would be great. Cold water if you have any.'

Charles laughed. 'Well you've come to the right place. In case you didn't guess, what you have here is a water treatment plant, providing the drinking water for public faucets around the local towns and villages. It's somewhat of a challenge, for a variety of reasons, but we're up to the job.'

He stopped to point to a large brown book sitting on the front desk. 'You wouldn't mind signing in the visitor's book, would you? It's crazy but even here, in the middle of nowhere, we seem to have all kinds of guidelines and regulations.'

Rosedale nodded, answering as pleasantly as the situation called for. 'Sure. No problem.'

'What brings you guys here anyway? I take it you're visiting family?'

With his back to Charles, Cooper signed in. He took the opportunity to, as discreetly as possible, look at the other couple of names written in the book. He frowned. A distant unformed thought beginning to play on his mind.

Suddenly, realizing nobody had answered Charles's question, he was about to apologize but Maddie got there first. 'Sorry, I'm a bit tired, not to mention hot... We're just touring the Congo before we move on to Rwanda. If we've got time we'll visit my family, but I don't think we will.'

'Well, I hope you manage to do what you have to do, but I'm delighted you stopped by... Come on.'

The three of them followed Charles into a board room. A fridge full of ice cold water took center space. To Cooper it was like some kind of mirage. A man could drown in such desire.

Talking as he handed the bottles out, Charles, affable in his manner, led them back into the lobby.

'We're a bit off the beaten track, really.'

'Yeah, it's quite a distance from any towns,' said Maddie. 'Didn't you want to go nearer?'

'Well Maddie... Sorry, it's alright if I call you Maddie?'

She nodded, smiling as Charles continued to talk, never having missed a beat. 'There were a few other places the plant could've been built, but this location had a lot of things going for it. Firstly, it's on high ground, as well as directly next to the river. Secondly, it makes it easier being away from the towns, less junk to clear out of the water. You go anywhere near the towns or villages and you're adding raw sewage, fertilizers, as well as the chemicals they use for mining – which is predominant in the area – to the water.

Makes purifying the water costlier. So right here was the sensible choice. Look, if you've got time I can show you around.'

Rosedale glanced at Cooper as he spoke to Charles. 'Appreciate the hospitality and all but it seems a bit unusual for us folk to wander off the street and you just show us round.'

Charles grinned, sliding open the glass door leading out to the smouldering heat.

'Actually Mr. Young.'

'Rosedale. Just Rosedale.'

'Actually, Rosedale, not so. This is both a water treatment plant *and* an educational facility. The powers that be back in the States thought it was important to show transparency and let the locals see what we were doing. So we do guided tours, as well as teaching an educational programme. It gets really busy. I think you must be the third or fourth lot of people in… oh, the past six months.'

'Who were the others?' asked Rosedale in good humor.

'I never took them round myself, so I don't know, I usually leave that pleasure to my assistants.'

Charles smiled, heading down to a grassy river bank as he began to explain the full scope of the water plant's work.

'So the river fills these sedimentation basins, the ones over there which look like giant swimming pools, and we get the dirt out which stops it from looking so cloudy, basically.'

Maddie, surprising both Rosedale and Cooper with what seemed to be a keen interest in water systems, asked, 'How?'

And although the simplest of questions and smallest of words, it seemed to make Charles Templin-Wright spring with animation.

'Good question, Maddie. Big bits of dust settle at the bottom and then we add chemicals that encourage any remaining, smaller particles to stick together in clumps, so they're easily filtered out when the water is pumped to the next stage. We also add chlorine to kill the bugs so it's drinkable – tastes like crap, but it won't kill you. This whole plant feeds faucets around the towns good, clean water, which is great. All the fighting in the area destroyed many things, whole villages were burnt down and people had to flee, but we're trying to rebuild and clean water is a great place to start. It's still a very precarious part of the DRC, of course. Hearing about militia raids and people being killed is, unfortunately, a weekly occurrence.'

'Though at least this water plant helps to cut down on disease.'

'It does, Maddie, but there are still a number of people round here, believe it or not, who won't use the faucets, they prefer to use rain water or water straight from river like their...' Charles paused, rolling his eyes to emphasize his point. 'Like their *ancestors* always did. They have some strong, traditional beliefs around here.'

Maddie gave Charles a piercing look. 'I take it you don't believe in spiritual traditions?'

'Look, I'm a scientist from Anchorage, Alaska.'

Rosedale nudged Maddie who scowled.

'Which is a long way from here. And whilst I respect everyone's right to freedom of belief, I put it down to a lot of mumbo jumbo.'

'Mumbo jumbo?'

'That's just my opinion. We're all entitled to one. Shall we...?'

With her mouth open to tell him exactly what she thought about his opinion, Rosedale touched Maddie's shoulder and shook his head. Oblivious, Charles pointed to a path leading towards the side of the main building.

Cooper watched Charles waddle away. The back of his bald head, round and flat, reminding him of the bulls-eye on an archery board. He felt irritated by the man. Maybe he was hungry. Maybe the trip was beginning to take its toll. Or maybe he just needed a bit of a fix. Whatever the reason, he couldn't stop himself wanting to pull Charles back. Shake him up a little. Make him see a little sense. But then he wasn't here to make a guy he didn't know see things the way they should be. So instead he inhaled. Deeply. Whispered '*Schmuck*,' under his breath, and said, 'What are those? It looks like you're going lobster fishing.'

Cooper gestured to piles of long, half-cylinder cages made out of chicken wire. The same kind he'd seen in the derelict building in Kinshasa.

Charles laughed. Irritating Cooper more.

'They do look like lobster cages don't they, now you come to mention it? Actually Mr. Cooper, they're rat traps. Very basic ones, but it's another project we do to help the community. We had a similar project in Kinshasa, where we were also based, but now it's only here. There are so many areas overrun with rats we decided we needed to come up with something. When Lemon first came into the DRC, especially this area, we saw kids turning rat-catching into a game. Heading out with bags and pointed sticks, challenging each other to see who could catch the most.'

'Sounds neat,' said Rosedale.

Templin-Wright said, 'I think so too. When I was a kid I did the same. It's a boy thing. But the difference is, when I was young, it didn't matter a jot if I actually caught one or not. Here, it's vital they do. Rats are very destructive, not to mention a source of disease. To find spaces to nest and breed in the over-crowded cities, they burrow underneath the buildings and destroy the foundations. They nibble through anything near the ground, and even bite sleeping children's fingers. Out here in the countryside the number of rats is overwhelming, and they grow to the size of cats.'

'You mean like that?'

Maddie pointed towards a man walking towards one of the far buildings. He was carrying a sealed clear plastic box. In it was a large rat.

For a moment Cooper thought Charles looked slightly ill at ease, but he turned back to Maddie and said, 'Exactly.'

'Why's it in a box like that?'

'No reason.'

'Can I see it?'

Again, Cooper noticed Charles's apprehension. But again, Charles pulled it back and smiled, calling out to the person.

'Obasi...! Obasi! Can you come here? I'd like to show our visitors your rat.'

The man duly walked towards them. Nodded and held up the box.

Maddie peered closely. Looking at the large black rat, her face changed from fascination to revulsion and back to fascination again. Reminded Cooper of Cora when he'd taken her to Washington Park Zoo.

'What are they?'

Charles answered indifferently, but neither Rosedale nor Cooper nor Maddie missed the quick glance Charles gave to his colleague.

'Just fleas I think. I guess all rats have them, but I couldn't be sure, they're not exactly my specialist area... Shall we?'

Charles continued along the path whilst Cooper talked.

'So what was the project you set up?'

'Sorry, yes. Well, we really took our lead from a charity which operates in South Africa, in the township of Alexandra. They're called Lifeline. And like here, Alexandra was overrun with rats. What they did was put a phone bounty on the vermin's head.'

'Say what?'

'Well they handed out the cages, similar to these, and said *Bring us sixty rats and we'll give you a cell phone.*'

Maddie laughed 'I love it.'

Flattered by Maddie's response, Charles carried on chatting with her as if the other two weren't there. 'Apparently some people frowned on it but it certainly helped to bring down the population of the rats.'

'And is that what you're doing?'

'Yes. Well, similar. We're giving people money instead. It isn't a great amount, and it's mainly kids who are rat-catching and although, like I say, the money isn't a lot, it could be a difference between eating and not eating that day or that week. And again, there's been a noticeable difference in the amount of rats... Anyway, come on, let me show you the rest of the place.'

Charles, walking side by side with the three of them, began to offer up more information.

'Unfortunately, a lot of people don't understand the health risks of dirty water. They just drink it without thinking. We put a lot of time and money into trying to keep the water clean from bacteria. There's a lot of disease here, and also a lot of toxic waste from some of the big companies. We here at Lemon care. We monitor the turbidity, pH and chlorine levels, twice a day in and outside the plant, and twice a week at the faucets around town. It's amazing the variation in levels we get, depending on recent rainfall, and sometimes the high levels of minerals getting into the water from mining just upstream. Pollution in sub-Saharan Africa is a real problem. Many rivers are now, and I don't want to be melodramatic here, but they're rivers of death. A lot of rivers are contaminated from spring to mouth. Did you know, every eight seconds, a child dies because of a disease transmitted through infected water? In developing countries, eighty per cent of the diseases are spread through the water.'

Scratching at another insect bite, Cooper stopped. 'They're some statistics, Charles.'

'They certainly are, Mr. Cooper. They certainly are.'

Charles continued on but Maddie stopped alongside Cooper to whisper in his ear. 'Have you seen his fingernails? Talk about yellow.'

Cooper scowled, on edge and annoyed and irritated as hell with her, but knowing it didn't take his shrink to tell him the issue wasn't really her. It was him. 'Leave the guy alone, Maddie. Jesus, he's hardly going to get a manicure around here, doing the job he's doing, is he?'

She looked hurt. But Cooper had to give it to her; she carried on talking without hesitation. She was a bigger man than him. 'I'm not saying he needs a manicure, I just think to have stained fingers like that, he must be smoking at least one hundred a day. Just a passing comment. An observation that's all.'

'Oh for God's sake, Maddie, have you heard yourself? Not everyone cares what they look like and I'm sure he doesn't need you judging him. You did enough of that with me.'

'Are you serious? How do you do it, Tom?'

'Do what?'

'Go from manicures to talking about you. I gotta give it

to you, you're good. And FYI, Tom. I didn't judge you. Not nearly enough, and maybe if I had we wouldn't be in this mess now, and I would've saved myself a hell of a lot of heartache… ' She trailed off and they stood in that awkward silence. The one where Cooper knew he should apologize for being a jackass. But couldn't… Wouldn't.

*

Charles waited with Rosedale by several large water tanks, looking at Cooper and Maddie who'd dropped quite far behind. He called over. 'Everything alright?'

Cooper gave a tight smile.

Maddie a tighter one.

Then in a unison born out of familiarity they said, 'Yeah, fine. Sorry. Please carry on.'

'Well these contain sand filter beds which catch most of the bits, and it's here where clean water is pumped out into the bottom and into a fresh water reservoir which supplies the town. Our pledge is to provide proper sanitation, so we test the water on its way out of the plant, taking samples and testing in the lab facility over there, making it easier to raise or lower the various chemicals needed for the best water we can supply.'

Cooper looked around and couldn't help but to be impressed by the set up. 'What's that building over there?'

'Oh, nothing interesting. Dry storage for chlorine but mainly a lot of spare parts for pumps. As you can imagine this whole place depends on pumps, which for some reason tend to go wrong all the time. I trained as a chemist but I seem to spend half my time dealing with pipework and pump machinery.' Charles stopped. Looked at his watch. 'I'm sorry to have to say this guys, but our tour has come to an end, and as I'm late for a conference call, I have to run. If you follow this path round, you'll get back to the lobby. And if you're ever in the area again, drop in… Oh, and make sure you sign out.' He winked adding, 'All comments are most welcome – as long as they're good!'

42

'What's on your mind, Thomas? It's unlike you not to be moaning like a girl about the heat.'

Cooper stayed silent, prompting Maddie to join in the conversation, making him feel worse than he did already about the way he'd behaved. Though that wasn't entirely the reason why he'd been quiet.

'You alright Tom? You haven't said anything since we left the plant… Tom?'

Without warning, Cooper pulled the Toyota up. Hard. He leant on the steering wheel before banging and shaking it and speaking out loud to himself. 'That's it.'

'What's *it*, Thomas?'

Turning to look at Rosedale but staring *through* him rather than *at* him, Cooper's thoughts stayed elsewhere. Without answering Rosedale's question he jumped out of the car. Raced round to the back to open the trunk.

He pulled out the heavy green canvas bag, stuffed with radio and phone equipment. Pulled out Maddie's suitcase as well as his own. He flicked the locks on the luggage. Opened hurriedly. Dragged out clothes to the sound of Maddie's exasperated proclamations.

'Tom, what the hell are you doing? Can you not throw my clean stuff on the ground… You've got mud all over my pants. Tom! Stop!'

Ignoring her plea, Cooper continued to rummage through

the case which was heaving to capacity. 'Jesus, who packed this?'

'You did…Tom, just tell me what you're looking for…? Tom!'

Giving up with a loud sigh, she stood back on the sludgy side of the road. Watching and glaring and staring with folded arms as Cooper hauled both clean and dirty clothes out of all their cases. Rosedale said nothing and Cooper suspected his curiosity was stronger than the want for laundered clothes.

*

A couple of silent minutes passed. Then a couple more. And having searched through the bags with passionate intensity, Cooper's words surfed off his wave of excitement, though it did nothing to alleviate the look on Maddie's face. 'Yes! Got them! Here… Guys, did you notice the names in the visitors' book?'

Maddie shook her head but Rosedale nodded. Lit a cigar as if he was standing in the Carnegie Club in New York. He looked at Cooper with interest. 'I did, and they were a whole heap of names I didn't recognize.'

'Exactly… But did you notice the last two people's names written in the book? The ones who came on the same day in May this year? *Edward Wynne* and *Phillip Holt*?'

'Okay.'

'It was obvious those two names were written by two different people.'

Rosedale squinted through the chamber of smoke around him. 'Yeah, so? That's what usually happens but go on.'

'Well the person who wrote the name *Edward Wynne* had identical handwriting to the previous visitor who came in

220

January, but back in *January* they'd used a different name, *Roger Stevenson*… People don't have the same handwriting, especially when it's so distinct. It's got to be the same person.'

Maddie shrugged. 'Maybe the receptionist signed them in and it's her writing. Anyway how can you be so sure it's the same? And what's the big deal anyway?'

'Look at this.'

He handed Maddie and Rosedale the documents he'd recovered from the luggage.

'They're Emmanuel's loan papers from the bank for the plane. Look at the writing…'

3mmanuel Mutombo

'…then look at the names in the visitor's book…'

Cooper paused for a moment, flicking out his phone. Showed her a photo of the handwriting in the visitors' book he'd taken when he'd signed out of Lemon water plant.

'Here… The writing's the same.'

Rosedale gave a surprised raise of his eyebrows whilst taking a deep, long drag on his cigar. 'How did you remember what his writing looked like?'

'I didn't. It wasn't the writing which struck me, it was the letter, E, and the way it's written. Remember the backwards E that Granger was bitching about? Moaning he couldn't read the signature, and I had to read it for him? Well there it is. The backward E on both the document and in the visitor's book…'

3dward Wynn3

… and

Rog3r St3v3nson.

Rosedale took the phone from Cooper. He nodded. Then nodded some more. Compared the writing and said, 'I'm impressed, I think you may be right. Though I must say I'm a bit disappointed, Thomas, I would've thought you'd have taken the photo with your hidden tie camera.'

Maddie laughed, turning her gaze away from the photo to look at Cooper. Her face was a picture of delight. He had to admit, she looked real pretty. 'A tie camera! As in a camera hidden in a tie? Tell me he's kidding.'

Cooper didn't know why the hell he blushed. He didn't even know he had it in him anymore *to* blush. But he did. One big red ass of a flaming blush. 'No… well, sort of. Granger gave Levi and I one, but you may as well have worn a sleuth sign round your neck.That would've been less obvious. I don't know what Granger was thinking. I should've brought it home. Cora would've loved it. It's hanging up in my closet at the ranch. I'll show it you next time you're over.'

'I'd like that.' Maddie's reply was warm and sensual. Like a static shock to Cooper, making him back off and refocus on the photo of the handwriting.

'So anyway, you can see for yourself the writing's identical.'

Maddie could feel Cooper's emotional retreat, and she answered coolly.

'Maybe. In fact, I don't think it looks the same at all.'

Cooper sighed. Making damn sure Maddie heard it. 'Okay, well for the time being let's just say it is Emmanuel's handwriting. So the question is why is Emmanuel visiting the water treatment plant using two different names? Both of which aren't his own.'

Rosedale sucked on the end of his cigar. 'I have no idea, but I do know that from what very little we know of Emmanuel, I have a strong suspicion he couldn't possibly afford to take out a loan on a plane by himself. So someone else was bankrolling him, allowing him to be able to get that kind of credit. But why? And it also makes me ask the question: why would a man need to give false names to visit a water company but have a plane registered in his own name?'

Maddie nodded. Smiled at Rosedale. Scowled at Cooper. 'Well Tom, what do you think? Because you seem to have all the answers.'

Kneeling down, and feeling it was best to ignore Maddie right now, Cooper somewhat obsessively begun to place various pieces of plants and tiny stones into one of his collecting bags. 'No Maddie, I think the one with all the answers is Papa Bemba. And that's who we need to go and find.'

43

'As we know Mr. President the Dodd-Frank Wall Street Reform and Consumer Protection Act was signed by Obama in response to the financial crisis and great recession of 2008 and it was also, as you know, one of the most significant changes to financial regulation since the Great Depression.'

John Woods sat in the winged armchair listening to Donald Parker whilst trying to stop himself fiddling and playing and pulling and tugging at the loose piece of cotton sticking out from the cushion next to him which Teddy was leaning on in between scribbling down numerous notes.

'… And amongst the many and varied provisions of Dodd-Frank, Mr. President, was section 1502, relating to conflict minerals.'

Woods's instinct was to stop Parker giving him a lecture on something he'd helped the Obama administration work on. But he guessed this was Parker's chance to put over to him what exactly he wanted. A sales pitch. A presentation. Call it what you will, the man had stated he'd help get the necessary votes for the gun reforms. And for that, he'd be willing to sit through anything. Even this. However, that didn't stop him hoping Parker would cut to the chase, or at least realize he didn't need to explain certain things because he damned near help write them.

'Human rights groups, Mr. President, have been campaigning for a long time to ensure mandatory labelling of conflict minerals which would then allow consumers as well as investors to avoid being part of funding these conflicts, through the buying of products. The 1502 section of the Dodd-Frank reform required the auditing of the minerals, with companies having to trace their supply chains. Then as you know they had to report back to the Securities and Exchanges Commission with their report on what due diligence they'd put in place to find out if their products were financing the conflict before publicly disclosing their findings. The SEC originally said in 2010 that the rules required any company for which conflict minerals were necessary, for the production of a product manufactured, or contracted to be manufactured, by that company, to disclose in its yearly report whether its conflict minerals originated in the Democratic Republic of the Congo or a bordering country.'

Parker handed Woods a piece of paper which he skim read. He hid his smile. He'd been at one of the meetings. 'You play golf?'

Puzzled, Parker said, 'A little bit. I think it's a prerequisite of being in Washington.'

'Come with me.'

Woods opened the glass Oval Office door and stepped out into the fresh air and onto a blended natural sandstone path which led past a number of Secret Service men and down to the White House's 2,000 square foot putting green which was under the shade of the Hoover oak tree.

Woods handed a Callaway putting iron to Parker from the small metal club stand. 'Coming out here helps me clear my head... You know a long time ago I played here with Clinton, he was the one who had the putting green moved to this location. He was on his second term and that day he had a lot on his mind. 11 February 1999. He didn't know it then but the next day he'd be acquitted by the Senate on both articles of impeachment. Though even with all the worry of not knowing what was going to happen, he still managed to put some excellent strokes in... Let's see what you've got.'

Focusing on the ball, bending his legs slightly before rocking himself into the golfer's stance, Parker gripped the club lightly in the palm and fingers of his hands. 'The extraction and sale of minerals from the DRC have always been hampered by chaotic and corrupt systems. We all know companies have been shipping minerals out of the country for years to other places, trying to dissociate the minerals from the DRC by pretending the place they shipped the minerals to, *is* the country of origin. Groups like Amnesty are forever trying to highlight the problems, but it's difficult with large companies who put smoke screens up so consumers don't know what they're buying. It becomes a minefield of corruption. And it's tragic and, quite frankly, I'm ashamed.'

Woods watched Parker's ball trickle past the hole. Lined his own club up. 'But that's why the conflict mineral section was created. That's why it was important to try to force the companies to do due diligence and publicly disclose.'

'*Try*, Mr. President. That's what you did. You *tried*, but it hasn't happened has it?'

'I admit, it's an ongoing struggle. Foreign policy is a complex beast... Dammit look at that. I hit it on the completely wrong angle.'

Parker looked at Woods with what he could only describe as scorn, which, the president had to admit, he didn't appreciate.

'Don't kid yourself. It's a stalemate. Since 2010 this section of the Dodd-Frank reform has been challenged and appealed on a repeat loop. Why? Because like always the companies felt like someone was squeezing their balls. And as a consequence claimed that the regulation violated their free speech rights under the first amendment by claiming they were essentially being forced to condemn their own products.'

Teddy Adleman, who'd just re-joined them, said, 'You don't think they had a point?'

'No,' said Parker. 'Do you? What makes it harder to swallow is the fact that we don't know exactly who these companies are. As usual the lawsuits were brought by a group of business lobby associations that include the US Chamber of Commerce and the National Association of Manufacturers. So, it makes it hard to pinpoint who's challenging the law. But by God, they're hiding, Mr. President. They're hiding. And it makes you think. Why?'

'I'm just playing devil's advocate here,' said Woods. 'But maybe they genuinely feel their rights are being violated.'

Donald Parker brushed back his head of full gray hair. 'You don't believe that any more than I do. Rather than face the challenges of trying to mine in an ethical way they brought legal procedures by talking about their rights, the constitution and the first amendment.'

Woods shook his head. Gave a wry smile. 'Amendment isn't my favorite word at the moment.'

'Right. Because the same is happening to you. People are saying you're challenging the amendment on the right to bear arms, instead of seeing it as you trying to change things. And that's what section 1502 was trying to do. Not stop people's freedom of speech, but stop *violence*, death, murder, rape and the use of children in the mines. Most mines are run by different militia groups and the people, including children, who work there do so under violence and sheer brutality. The decision for the reform was supposed to be about democracy and transparency. And what we have is clever attorneys turning the first amendment on its head, allowing multinationals to use it as something to undermine. The first amendment was supposed to protect the free speech rights of the American people, of individuals, and *not* giant companies. In the DRC there's no centralized taxation system, nothing to help the people who've seen and lived through decades of violence. And there's no-one to stop the armed groups making the Congolese miners do the hard labor and then making them surrender the minerals they've mined. The miners work under a reign of terror, and the militia give them nearly nothing, whilst they make a massive profit on the back of them. And all around the world consumers know very little or nothing about this.'

Woods nodded. 'It's a difficult situation. And my administration stands by the original 2010 reform.'

Donald Parker hit the golf ball with passion, sending it right off the green. 'It's no good you standing by it if it doesn't hold up in court. And for plaintiffs to argue that Congress had provided no evidence that public disclosures concerning whether a product is conflict free would lead to the advancement of amity in the DRC, well that's downright outrageous. If we don't try, nothing will change.'

John Woods found himself agreeing. 'It's the same with the gun reforms. People are saying there's no proof it'll make a difference. But I say, let's try first and then let's see.'

Parker became animated, waving his hands round and his hair falling once again over his eyes. 'Exactly. That's why I want to support you in this. We have the same vision. You'll have your reforms and I, Mr. President, can have peace of mind. Why wait for another court case, another appeal? When right here right now the consumer can have what they really want. Blood-free products. Everyone remembers the stuff about blood diamonds, but do they realize that their cell phones, laptops and motherboards could be and most likely are part of a bloody conflict? No, sir, I don't think they do. Tell me how many people, apart from those who watch C-Span, know what the companies are trying to do and withhold? There's going to be more appeals but this, as we both know, will go on for years, whilst innocent people are dying. My company, Nadbury, own mines in the DRC which are *not* controlled by armed groups. All the mines we own are conflict free. We've had the audits. We have the certificates. We don't need to argue that our first amendments are being violated. Do you know what one judge said regarding the freedom of speech in regards to this matter?'

'Remind me.'

Parker cleared his throat as he walked across to pick up his ball. 'The court of appeal basically determined that the regulations requiring public disclosure of the DRC conflict status of minerals did not qualify for rational basis review. I quote, *products and minerals do not fight conflicts. The label conflict free is a metaphor that conveys moral responsibility. By compelling an issuer to confess blood on his hands, the statute interferes with the exercise of the freedom of speech under the first amendment.*' Parker paused. 'Are you telling me this is right, Mr. President?'

'I'm just here to listen. Carry on…'

'I'm just angry that there's so much manipulation of something which is supposed to save lives and do so much good. The part of the reform where it states companies are required to do due diligence by sourcing their suppliers? Well that's a joke. Because what is due diligence? Who polices this? Who sets the bar? Companies just offer excuses that it's not possible to source. Deny all knowledge. Come on. There's a loophole there just for companies to jump through. This was supposed to encourage corporations, but instead it's got them hiding and shamefully they've spent millions trying to block these changes with challenges based on constitutional rights. But what about the rights of the people of the DRC, Mr. President?'

'You think it's that simple.'

'No, of course not. It would be stupid to oversimplify the conflict, but for companies to hide their sources and argue to the point of appeals and challenges and object to having to disclose when children are dying, well in my book that's not acceptable. This is about the consumers' right to know the truth, Mr. President. The American people are fed up with cover-ups. They want honesty and transparency from those in power. The DRC needs people who care. To foster reform, help stop corruption and most of all help create transparency. People here in the US need to know what they're buying.'

Woods looked at his watch. 'So what exactly do you want?'

'I want people to be able to switch on their cells and their laptops with the knowledge that none of the components have been made from conflict minerals. I don't want, when people call their friend, for them to have blood dripping down their hand.'

Woods glanced at Teddy who raised his eyebrows at the impassioned imagery.

'If the electronics industry wants to spend millions per month lobbying senate offices to try to relax the reforms, let them, because we at Nadbury will be the consumer's choice. Our supply chains for tin, tantalum, tungsten, and gold are conflict free, and we want the world to know that. But we can't do it without you, Mr. President. We need your voice.'

Woods heard slight scepticism in it as he sunk the putt. 'And this is the campaign you mentioned on the phone.'

'It is, and to me it's as important as the gun reforms. The next generation are becoming more aware. And maybe now more than ever people aren't thinking so much in term of *us* and *them*. I think social media has really connected the whole of the world.'

'And why can't you do this without us? If you've got the certificates, there shouldn't be a problem to do it without our help.'

'Come on Mr. President, you know as well as I do if we go it alone there won't be as much interest in it; people won't open their doors to it, schools will be sceptical to be associated with a profit-making company. And it certainly won't have kudos, and ultimately the success, if you weren't part of it. We need each other.'

'And of course if this administration gave you the support, this will make you and your company millions.'

'Yes. Millions and millions of dollars. But that's okay, because they'll be millions of *ethical* dollars.'

'Is there such a thing?'

'I don't apologize for being a businessman, but I won't be part of someone else's suffering. Stand by us, Mr. President. Head our campaign to encourage every kid, every American to know they're a part of changing the world. Part of making a painful part of history come to a full stop. America is a great nation but it'll be a greater one if it reaches out its hand to another and says to the world, no more.'

Teddy Adleman looked at his watch and took the putting iron from Parker. 'Mr. Parker, thank you for your time. We appreciate you coming today. Obviously there's a lot to think about. I'll escort you to security.'

Out of his pocket, Donald Parker passed Teddy an envelope. 'There's a list of senators' names in there. Call them, Mr. Adleman, and each one will tell you the same thing. They'll give their support to your gun reforms. You'll get your votes.'

'As long as the president supports your campaign.'

Parker smiled. Rubbed his front teeth with the tip of his tongue. 'Mr. Adleman, I'm a businessman, not a charity.'

44

'In the words of John McEnroe, you cannot be serious.'

'You're showing your age there, Maddison. The man retired in 1992, unless of course you're counting the ATP champions tour, then I...'

'Shut up, Rosedale. What is it with you, huh? When I want a lecture about the history of Grand Slams, I'll know who to come to.'

'I was just saying.'

'Well don't. Don't say anything else. All I want is to know why, Tom, you didn't listen to me when I told you we should've driven east towards the border, where we could've easily found a decent place to sleep. But you didn't, and now the rains have begun, and we're stuck here. Go figure. Seriously.'

Rosedale was not put off by Maddie's hostility. 'Oh I think he's serious alright, Maddison, see that twitch over his right eye? It always pulsates when he's saying something he means.'

Cooper snapped. 'Shut up, Rosedale,'–whilst at the same time trying to discreetly touch the point above his right eye to see if it was *actually* throbbing. 'Look, Maddie, I know you're right but now I've messed up I reckon this is the safest place to stay.'

Maddie gestured to where Cooper was standing. 'Okay

fine, let's do it, but we need to keep watch. We can rotate so at least we'll all get a couple of hours sleep.'

'You sleep first and Rosedale and I will do the first couple of hours then Rosedale can swap with you.'

'You sure?'

'I am.'

Trying to make peace, he offered her a piece of several-times-melted chocolate. She shook her head, which he had to admit was probably a wise decision.

45

'You sure? I am.'

Rosedale was in the full throes of imitating the conversation Maddie and Cooper had had earlier on in the night. Throwing a packet of potato chips at Cooper, he winked. 'That girl still loves you, Thomas, why don't you just put her out of her misery?'

Cooper drew deeply on his cigarette. He'd been doing okay. Well, with the cigarettes anyway, and that of course was if *doing okay* meant going a whole day without having a smoke. But today, day two, was different. Today had *not* been okay. Not even close. He could feel his patience at a dangerous low and his ability to stay calm was trickling away. And as well as that he'd had to compensate for the lack of nicotine with a couple of extra pills. Just to take the edge off.

With the smell of the wet forest around him, Cooper continued listening to Rosedale spouting bull. But then enough became enough. 'You gotta stop this.'

'Stop what, Thomas?'

He drove his cigarette into the wet undergrowth. 'Stop acting like a jackass. All this with Maddie… The only person you're hurting is her. Maddie and I, well… our marriage was over a long time ago. But it just took till now for both of us to realize it.'

'And you're cool with that.'

'No, of course not.'

'Well that's how it sounds. Like you're just throwing away a piece of trash in the garbage.'

'Shut up, Rosedale, my marriage was important to me. Maddie's important. But my point is maybe we shouldn't have happened in the first place. Not that I regret it. We had some good times, and of course we've got Cora.'

'Does she know that?'

Cooper pulled a face. Rosedale certainly knew how to get a guy wound up. 'Know what?'

'That it's over, Thomas. That there's no going back. You may be able to solve investigations – not that you're doing great on this one mind – but when it comes to women, to Maddie, you can't see what's in front of your cherry pickin' nose.'

'What are you talking about?'

'I think you need to look in those collecting bags of yours that you like to carry around, see if you've dropped all your sense in there... Don't you get it? Can't you see? She's holding out for you. She thinks it isn't over.'

Cooper shook his head, resigned to the fact he was already reaching for the next cigarette.

'You got it all wrong Rosedale. She was the one who left me.'

Rosedale pushed his hat to the back of his head. He whistled. 'Thomas, Thomas, Thomas. What are we going to do with you, sugar pie? Why do you think she left?'

'Because the marriage was over.'

Austin Rosedale Young looked at Cooper with rare compassion. 'Wrong. She left because she was drowning herself, but she also wanted you to realize you loved her. Not some ghost. Not some memories of the past. She needed you to want her, and stop your crazy ways. See what's important. What's real... Does she even know about Ellie's death certificate?'

Cooper bristled. 'You know?'

'It's my job to know.'

'It's no big deal.'

'But it is. Look at you, Thomas, it's sent you screwball again. Popping pills. Coming to Africa. We're all only here because of you. You think Maddie likes this job?'

'She loves her job and let's face it she's damn good at it.'

'Yes, but not this one. Haven't you noticed she's not herself? For some reason she doesn't want to be here in the heart of the DRC.'

'That's crap, she loves her country – albeit her country on her daddy's side. But nonetheless she feels a part of this place and rightly so… You're just talking bull.'

'No, sir, I am not and I'm telling you there's something wrong. She didn't want to come.'

'So why did she? To prove a point?'

'You're a fool sometimes, Thomas. She came here to look after you. To make sure she didn't lose you to a bullet or to a ghost. She put how she felt aside and is willing to put her life in danger all for you.'

Cooper stood up angrily. 'What the hell kind of crap are you talking?'

'Am I talking crap? Think about it, Thomas. Use that pretty little brain of yours for a moment. She goes on every job you go on, just to make sure you're okay. Hell, Thomas, she even risks her life to get you out of places like Eritrea with that klutz, Levi.'

'Leave him out of it.'

'But she does, and you accept her help like her life means nothing.'

Cooper glared at Rosedale, affronted he or anyone would think that. 'That's not true. I didn't even want her to come.'

237

'Oh it is though. It is true. You may not care about your life, but that doesn't mean you stop caring about the people around you, especially the people that love you. And she does.'

Cooper was angry now. Enraged at the man's accusations. His jaw clenched with his fist following in its wake. 'I don't have to listen to this.'

Spitting tobacco out of the side of his mouth, Rosedale looked on arrogantly at how far it'd gone. Gave Cooper a supercilious smile which ripped through him like a bush fire.

'You may not like what I'm saying Thomas, but it's the truth. I see it in her eyes every time she looks at you. *Let her go*. Set her free, Thomas, set her free. Let her have a life without you.'

Cooper bounded forward. Grabbed Rosedale's top. Rotated his body and brought back his fist. Palm up. Elbow in. Angle up. Relax fist. Tighten on impact. Knocks a man out before he knows what's hit him… That's what he was going to do. Until the fight drained out of him as quickly as it'd come. He left his hand hanging in the air. Then without looking directly at Rosedale, he asked, 'How do I do that? How do I set her free?'

'You'll find a way, but don't put it off. Don't hurt her any more than she's hurting already. You're lucky to have a woman like Maddison to love you. Real lucky. She's one special lady. Don't abuse that. There are a lot of people out there who'd give anything to feel that kind of love, even for just one day.'

Cooper didn't say anything for a while but looked at Rosedale with interest. 'Listen, why don't you get some sleep, I'll keep a watch… Go on… and Rosedale… Thanks.'

Even from where Cooper was sitting, with all the noise of an African forest resonating around the SUV, he had to smile to himself, acknowledging it was actually Rosedale's snoring which reverberated most loudly and echoed through the darkness of the storm-filled night.

He stood up. Stretched. Shook off the rain which trickled down his neck. Then walked towards the thick groves of the banana plants to take a leak. His mind on both Maddie and Ellie.

About to undo his buttons on his go-to faded jeans, his movements became slow and deliberate. He leant forward, listening to a new sound coming from far to the left of him. It was the sound of an engine. A truck, but an old one.

Unusually he was easily able to distinguish the make. He wasn't an expert on cars and trucks but he knew a few things. And he knew it was a British Commer. Nicknamed the Commer-knocker due to the distinctive noise it produced. The unmistakable sound of a two-stroke diesel three-cylinder horizontally opposed piston engine. One hell of a classic bit of engineering. Of course, distinguishing the make of a vehicle didn't explain why the hell a truck would be out here in the middle of the night, but then, like anything else, there was only one way to find out…

Cooper could just about hear his own breathing above the strange mating call of the reed frogs in the trees above him. He could feel the rain getting heavier and stronger, and it took all of his willpower to stay still despite the savage bites of the red army ants which seemed to be using his body as a bridge between one giant leafed plant and another.

He continued to crouch in the wet bushes, watching the Commer truck, driving rain making it difficult to see clearly. But he was just about able to make out the outlines of three people loading the truck. But with what? It was impossible for him to see unless he went further down the hill.

He felt for his gun. Edged along on the ground. Kept low. Pulled his body across the rutted and sodden and uneven earth, but even before he got halfway down the hill, he saw the men had pulled a large sheet of blue tarpaulin over the back load. Squinting. Annoyed with himself that he'd missed the chance to see what they were doing, he crept a fraction closer.

A bit further along from the truck, he could see another car. Though he couldn't decipher the make from where he was. But it was large. Black. Expensive. And taking into account where they were, he thought it was strange.

Just as he assumed both the car and the truck were going to drive off, the passenger door of the car opened. And there, in the rain, stood Papa Bemba.

Their gut feeling about coming to the area had been right. Instinct encouraged Cooper to get closer, to hear what Papa Bemba and the two other men – who'd also stepped out of the car – were saying. But then for no reason that Cooper could see, a tall, stocky man with tight plaits and a heavy jawline began to walk towards where he was hiding. And even though the man might've only wanted to take a leak, Cooper thought it was his cue to back away but not before seeing a man who was bound, gagged and blindfolded, being pulled out of the car.

Cooper stole silently into the night with the sounds of the forest surrounding him. A noise shot out of the darkness, making him stop, and then a snap behind him made him freeze. He reached for his gun. Scrutinized his surroundings quickly. Looked for hiding spots. Then felt a hand on his back.

Whipped round.

Gun drawn.

Leg taut out.

Ready to fight.

Bringing whoever it was, down.

'Jesus…! Jesus H. Christ…!' Cooper threw up his arms at Rosedale, before bringing them down to rest on his head. Gun in hand and breathing hard. 'Do you have to creep up on me like that? I could've blown your goddamn head off.'

Rosedale sniffed, speaking softly. 'Not a chance. You would've been toast, Thomas. Your last view would've been of that ants' nest over there.'

Crouching down again, Cooper wiped away the rain from his face, which bought him time to regain his composure.

'What the hell are you doing anyway, Rosedale? Sneaking up like that.'

'Babysitting you. That's why I'm here. You're lucky it

was me, because if it hadn't been, I reckon it would've been them… ' Rosedale, who was also now crouching in the wet, trailed off. Nodded towards some men who Cooper hadn't noticed – and who were fast approaching.

'What do you want to do? Stay still or shoot out? Your call, baby.'

Weighing up the situation, Cooper whispered back. 'I think stay still for now, the rain's heavy and it's doubtful they'll see us.'

Rosedale nodded. Winked. Whispered. 'So you haven't completely lost it and turned into Billy the Kid. I was worried for a while.'

For the next three minutes Rosedale and Cooper stayed still. Watching as the blindfolded man was pushed into the truck. Then they watched for another two as the Commer and the car drove off.

Moving away, heading back to the Toyota, Cooper said, 'I think tomorrow we need to go and speak to Bemba. Get him on his own somehow.'

'Don't know how easy that'll be, but when have you ever liked to do things the…'

'Maddie…? Maddie…? Maddison?'

Pulling out his 9mm Glock Gen 5 handgun from his concealed pistol holder, Cooper began to run, leaving Rosedale and the conversation behind as he spotted the doors of the Toyota were wide open.

Nearing the car, he could see it was empty. Alarmed, his eyes darted round in the darkness before settling on Rosedale. 'She's gone…! Maddie's gone!'

48

'Papa Bemba, thank you for coming.' The small woman greeted Bemba respectfully at the door, nodding her head to Lumumba and the other men who accompanied him.

Bemba's voice was gruff. 'Where is he?'

'Here. This way. He's bad. I haven't been able to control his fever.' She led the men, with Bemba being guided by Lumumba, to the tiny room at the back of the small brick hut.

In the darkness, a young boy no more than ten years old lay in the corner, his black skin marked by hard, painful, weeping lumps, split open and oozing yellow pus, which covered his neck, matching those which sat under his arms and between his legs.

His staggered breathing, loud and hoarse, was intermittently broken for large, red blood clots to be coughed and vomited up. The stench of his body filled the air with a repellent odour as he writhed in pain, muttering muted words. *Help. Please help me.*

The woman, wide eyed, stared at Bemba imploringly. 'Please, what can you do?'

Papa Bemba, guided to where the boy lay, sat down on the bed, his hands touching the sick child whilst addressing the woman.

'The Kindoki lives within him, I told you that before, but you didn't listen, Sister Zola. You refused to see, blinded by the sight of the possessed, yet you wish me to help you now. I fear it's too late. His mind is occupied with sorcery contaminating his body with witchcraft.' Papa Bemba stood up. He shook his head. 'There is nothing that can be done, Zola.'

The scream from Zola filled the small hut. She fell to her knees at the feet of Papa Bemba. Tears of grief and loss and pain spilled from her as she pulled at Bemba's clothes. Begging him. Pleading him. Needing him to help. 'S'il vous plaît prennez mon petit-fils. Please save him…deliver him.'

Papa Bemba put his hand on Zola's head. 'If I do, it still may be too late, especially if there are stronger, more powerful spirits working within him. But even to try to deliver him, there needs to be an exchange. The spirits as always will ask for that… The same exchange I told you of before.'

The woman, shaking, wiped her running nose on her sleeve. 'Mais oui… Yes, anything. Anything.'

Papa Bemba turned to Lumumba. 'Get the papers.'

Lumumba, took out an envelope from his jacket. Unfolded the papers. Passed them to Zola. His words matter-of-fact. 'Sign your name, and then it will be down to the spirits to see if they want to save him.'

Zola took the pen, signing her name at the bottom of the typed document.

49

'It's Granger!'

Cooper held the satellite phone away from him, looking to Rosedale who shrugged. He cut him a stare. Not appreciating being left to deal with the man.

'Cooper, goddammit, answer me!'

Hearing Granger loud and clear, Cooper said, 'I can't hear you Granger.'

'Don't be a jackass, I can hear you and I sure as hell have no doubt you can hear me.'

'You're cutting out, sorry Granger, I'll have to call you back.'

'Don't you dare put...'

Cooper switched off the phone. Closed his eyes. Caught his breath. The pressure he felt was intense. Almost physically so. Sweat was running down his face and down his neck and down his back and it was hot but he was shivering and it was like he'd just stepped into a goddamn cooler.

Sitting on the hood of the Toyota, he went into his pocket and pulled out some pills. He couldn't care less about being discreet. It took too much time. And time was something he didn't have. He threw them into his mouth. Swallowed. 'What are we going to do? What's the plan?'

'Well first, Thomas, you need to get off your sorry butt, and stop taking...'

Cooper bolted off the hood before Rosedale had finished.

Lunged. Sent him flying off balance and down into the muddy waters of the road. Leaning over him, Cooper grabbed hold of his shirt to the sound of ripping cotton. Dragged him up. Banged him. Snagged his back hard against the side of the car.

His eyes were bloodshot and his words were snarled as he panted hard into Rosedale's face. He pushed his weight against him. Keeping him up against the Toyota. 'I'm so tired, so sick of your jackass remarks, Rosedale. You gotta get off my case, you hear me. Get off my back because you're pushing me, man, and I don't need this crap now. We haven't got time. Each minute that passes is a minute more she's gone so what I need, *all* I need is for you to help me find her. Okay? You listening to me? I need you to help me find Ellie.'

'Maddie… You mean find Maddie?'

'Yeah, of course I mean Maddie.'

'You said…'

He stopped. 'What?… I said what? Don't play your games with me, what did I say?'

Rosedale looked at him with the same kind of pity he saw at funerals. Cooper wiped the dry spit from around his mouth. 'Look, I'm desperate here. I need you, okay. I need you to help me find her… *please*. I'm begging you Rosedale.'

'Thomas… I hear you. I'm going to help you. In fact I'm going to do more than that. I'm going to promise that we'll bring her back safely.'

'Yeah?'

'Yeah.'

Cooper's shoulders slumped. He had to dig deep to stop his feelings overwhelming him. He looked at Rosedale. Brushed down his ripped shirt. Tried to sound apologetic. 'Sorry, about that. I'll get you another one.'

'No need. Never liked it anyway.'

Cooper stared at Rosedale, or maybe it was Rosedale staring at him. He wasn't sure. But for a moment it felt like there was an understanding between them.

Getting into the car, Rosedale started the engine. 'We go down to the village. Speak to the locals. We can pay them to come and help search the area. It's light so it'll give us a great chance of finding her if she did wander off and get lost. Maddie isn't stupid. She's highly trained and knows exactly what she's doing. If she's hurt or lost she'll know what to do. If she's somewhere nearby, we'll find her.'

'And if she's been taken by some of the militia groups around here, which we know there are a whole heap of. What then?'

'Then, Thomas, we pray.'

50

'Naomi, if I ask you to find me ten minutes today to talk to Teddy, can you do that without making out we're in a state of Armageddon?… What do you reckon?'

Naomi Tyler went to say something but stopped. Felt a sharp pain in the corner of her mouth. She touched it gently. Felt the tiny open lesion from the beginnings of a cold sore. 'Actually, I can do more than that, Mr. President. I can give you fifteen minutes *and* you can have them now. We've got an unexpected window. The group who were coming to speak about combating wildlife trafficking, their flight's been delayed. They won't be able to have the meeting with you now and I don't think for the time being it's necessary to re-schedule. We can still find someone to speak to them, and I also thought we could give them a mini behind-the-scenes tour. Soften the blow.'

Woods, slightly distracted by Joan's copy of *National Geographic* sitting on his desk, said, 'Okay, sounds good. Oh, and Naomi, try some Zovirax on that, it looks sore. Too much stress.'

Naomi's fingers automatically went up to touch the corner of her mouth again. 'I usually use Fenistil, but I'll give it a go. My sister said to use orange balm.'

Teddy scratched his head, grateful most of the small burns on his scalp from the hair relaxing cream had finally gone. 'You don't want to use that. All that homemade remedy stuff, it's all a heap of junk. Only works if there's nothing wrong with you.'

Woods laughed and shook his head at his chief of staff. He winked at Naomi.

'Would you mind asking Joan to arrange a coffee for me in ten minutes…? You want one, Teddy?'

Teddy nodded.

'Make that two.'

With the door of the Oval Office now shut, Woods glanced at Teddy and said, 'What's the latest on Donald Parker?'

'All checks have come back clean. And his company, Nadbury electronics, are the same. His mines *are* conflict free. And unlike a lot of companies who mine in the DRC, he's put a lot back into the community.'

'That's pretty impressive.'

'I agree because although one of the stipulations for foreign companies to mine over there is that they invest correctly in communities and the environment, which companies are going to actually do it when there's no-one to check they're doing it properly?'

'I can't remember the name of them, but do you remember that American company a few years ago before I was in office that promised they'd build new hospitals and schools for the area if they were allowed to mine there? Well, they gave virtually nothing.'

'You mean the one who just gave crates of beer and a hundred dollars to the local church?'

Woods said, 'That's the one. And their company ended up earning millions and they would've earned more if the mines in that particular area hadn't been taken over by the local militia.'

'Tell me a mine in the DRC which hasn't.'

Woods flicked through the file Teddy had brought in on Nadbury Electronics. 'Well, clearly from reading this, not Donald Parker's mines. Conflict free. Militia free. That's some going. Maybe that's the key to it. Really invest into the community and you've got half a chance.'

'Or more likely he got lucky.'

Woods shook his head. 'There's no such thing as luck. The guy's clearly put his money where his mouth is and invested heavily in the area. But he knows it's worth it. The untapped resources around there are worth billions, and he can go in and reap millions and millions of dollars' profit, by putting in just a fraction of that to help rebuild the DRC with proper social investment. And because of that he can now offer clean minerals, which is an investment not only within the DRC but an investment for the future. We need to put our foot on the throat of other companies, but it's difficult with all the appeals, so I guess for now the real pressure will be from the consumers. Parker's right, the American people want to know they're helping, or at least not hurting others.'

'So you think this campaign with Nadbury is something you want to back?'

Woods stared out of the window at nothing particular. Yawned. Covered his mouth too late. 'I don't see why not. Obviously we'll speak to the others, but my feeling is this campaign with Nadbury can only spell good. Parker gets his products into schools and colleges and eventually his brand becomes the number one product, but not because of any manipulation or false advertising, or lobbying. But because people want to do what's right. And backing products which are conflict free is right. Period. And in return for this administration supporting the campaign, hey...'

'You get the votes you need for the gun reforms.'

'Whatever happened to the days of just doing things because it's morally right?'

'Was there such a day? Because if there was I can't remember. This is Washington, John. It's always been like this. You give something I want and then I give something you want back. It's like a giant game of Monopoly.'

Irritated, Woods clicked his fingers. 'Did you speak to the senators on the list by the way?'

'I did. And every single one of them will give their support.'

For the first time since the idea had been placed in front of him, Woods felt a rush of excitement. 'You think we can really do this Teddy? Pull it off?'

'I think so.'

'But the reforms are going on the floor in three weeks. Doesn't give us much time.'

'John, it only took twenty-eight days for us to go into Iraq after 9/11. I think between Parker and our team we can manage to rustle up a press package and a strategy campaign plan. He's not expecting us to be doing anything much before the vote. Only thing he wants is a press announcement in a couple of weeks, setting out our joint vision for both the national and international campaign. I'm quietly confident. I think it's a fantastic opportunity. You've put everything into these reforms. Let's make it happen.'

A smile slowly spread across Woods's face. 'Teddy, you really should go into politics.'

'Same couldn't be said about you.'

Woods winked and said, 'By the way, you didn't tell me exactly what Nadbury had done to invest into the community.'

'They built a water treatment plant. Supplies clean water for a large area in South Kivu, East of the DRC. It's called Lemon. Lemon Water plant.'

The trees and plants of the forest rioted upwards, shading the track from the river of sunlight as they twisted and bent and arched over the red mud road, creating a natural pergola. The air was heavy and oppressive and the stream of silence filled the car as Rosedale and Cooper drove towards the village.

An opening in the hillside allowed them to break from their thoughts, which neither of them wanted to share with each other.

Ahead they saw a small collection of huts, palm leafs and corrugated iron in the distance. Rosedale touched the brakes and they came to a stop on the brow of the hill.

'We take it easy okay? I know you're ready to bite, but we're in the middle of nowhere, and probably not more than a mile from a heavily armed militia group. So no accusations, no hostility. We just go in there and be polite. Ask questions, maybe even get their help. Remember who you are, Thomas, what you've been trained in. Separate emotion from action. Separate what our goal is with Maddie. From this moment on until we find her, we just think of her as our objective. You got that?'

Cooper nodded. At ease with Rosedale taking the lead.

'But more importantly, Thomas, and you need to hear me on this one… separate all this from Ellie.'

The criss-crossed dirt paths of the village were lined with people by the time Rosedale and Cooper had walked down the track. Impassable by car and only just manageable by foot. Curious, suspicious stares devoid of animosity, tracked their approach.

Rosedale tipped his hat. Smiled. Nodded respectfully. But Cooper had no doubt Rosedale was acutely aware of the time it would take him to draw on the two high capacity single action FN Five-seven MK handguns hidden beneath his clothing.

A man, wizened by age and the relentless Congolese sun, shuffled towards them. His greeting humble, but friendly. 'Can I help you?'

It was a straight, simple question, making it easy for Cooper to give a reply. He was wired; anything more, he would've struggled with. 'I hope so, we're looking for our friend. We were camped out in the forest last night, and we've lost her, we just hope nothing bad has happened.'

The man nodded as the onlookers moved in closer, forming a circle around them. 'Is she a good person?'

Without hesitation, Cooper said. 'She is. The best.'

'Then no doubt the spirits will keep her from harm.'

The old man turned to walk away, but stopped as Cooper struggled to heed Rosedale's words. 'Is that it?'

Surprised, the man answered, 'Yes.'

And that didn't sit well with Thomas J. Cooper. Not one little bit. He stepped forward. Shook Rosedale's hand off his arm. Raised his voice. 'I'm talking to you. Hey, I said I'm talking to you. And just so you know, that's not it. Not even close. You see usually when someone says a person's missing then the whole village, the whole town, the whole goddamn city does something about it.'

Rosedale tried to pull him away, but hadn't a hope. He had a dog in the fight.

And the distrust was beginning to appear on the faces of the men and women as the old man stared at Cooper intently before smiling.

'If she's meant to come back, she will. And if you say this friend of yours is a good person, then there's no need to worry… However, from your reaction I can see you're not a believer.'

Cooper started to grind his teeth in agitation. His jaw felt tight. Realized he was clenching it. 'A believer in what?'

In contrast, the man was calm. Warm. A hint of pity in his voice. 'In what you can't see. The souls, the spirits of those that have passed and now walk amongst us in the blanket of invisibility surrounding us. They're the ones who you need to ask, only they can find your friend.'

For some reason Cooper's vision began to blur in his left eye. He pushed his palm against it. Hollered after the man as he walked away. 'The hell you know what I believe in. The hell you do! You know nothing about me!'

The man threw his arms up in the air, not bothering turning back. 'Then wait, do nothing, let the spirits guide her back.' Then he stopped to swivel round, giving a large toothless grin to Cooper. 'Or if you wish, ask the members of the community to help you if it makes you feel better. I'm sure they'll be happy to.'

The cackle from the old man infuriated Cooper but he didn't have a chance to act on it with Rosedale whipping him round, jabbing and prodding and poking and pushing him angrily in the chest.

'What the hell's the matter with you, boy? What did I tell you? Keep it cool. Separate emotion. Think about our objective. And what do you go and goddamn do, hey?'

Cooper slammed back at Rosedale. Thumped him hard in the chest. 'Get the hell off me.'

'Look at you, you're a mess. You of all people, Thomas, should know better. Aren't you the one who's always telling us we need to look beyond the box? Yet here you are acting like a prize asshole with this guy. Sort yourself out or get off the job.'

'The hell I will.'

'I'll drag you off the job myself if I have to.'

'Just what is it you want from me?'

Rosedale raised his voice, not caring most of the villagers were standing around watching. 'I want you to decide right now if you're up to this, Lieutenant, because I don't think you are. I think you're a liability and as such you put the whole operation and us in danger.'

Cooper swiped his hand at the finger Rosedale was pointing at him. 'Where do you get off Rosedale? This isn't some military op we're on, and who do you think you are telling me I'm a liability? I've got your back; you know I have. Question is, have you got mine?'

Rosedale's cool was completely broken as he barked back angrily. 'Like a fool I have, like a goddamn fool. But you, Thomas, you continue putting us all at risk. Look at you, you're a junkie, a crazy-ass junkie. Whatever those pills are you take, they got you hooked and they're not going to let you go. They've addled your mind. But it's not them that's killing you. What's killing you is Ellie.'

Cooper struggled to speak. He felt like he couldn't breathe. 'Don't you say her name… Don't you say it.'

'Jesus Christ, Thomas, look at the state of you. Look at what you're doing. You've let it all fall through your hands.'

'You don't know anything.'

'Oh yes I do, because Granger told me you were doing okay last year, or as okay as you could ever be. But now, you're a mess. Back on the pills, or perhaps you were never off them. And the letters PTSD are written all over you like you're part of the Sesame Street alphabet song. Why don't you accept it and put everyone out of their misery, Thomas? Ellie isn't coming back. She's gone. Gone. Gone.'

The pain in Cooper's chest almost forced him to his knees as his voice lifted louder with blind grief. 'You don't know that! You don't know!'

'I know the death certificate says it. Her own father even says it. Everyone says it.'

'I don't care what anyone says. There were three skiffs!'

'Bullshit!'

Cooper whispered to himself and stared at Rosedale with coiled anger. 'So help me God, I'll kill you.'

'Come on Thomas, you must see that no-one believes it.'

A voice behind them: 'I believe it.'

Cooper and Rosedale span round to see Maddie standing behind them, seemingly unharmed. She gave a tiny smile to Cooper then turned a hard gaze on Rosedale. 'If Tom says there were three skiffs, then there were three skiffs. Why is it so hard for you to understand and just accept that, Rosedale?'

And with that, Maddie turned and walked away, towards the car of Charles Templin-Wright.

53

'So there she was.'

Charles Templin-Wright grinned as cheerfully as he had done the first time Cooper had met him, back at the water treatment plant. But it didn't stop him from thinking the man was a schmuck.

Noticing what looked like dermatitis on Charles's hands and wrists, Cooper tried to conjure up a smile for the man. Didn't work. 'Thank you. You can imagine how worried we were.'

Charles waved away the gratitude at the same time as basking in it. 'Oh, don't mention it, I'm just pleased it was me who found her. When I saw her hobbling along in the dark, I recognized her straight away from the other day.'

Cooper nodded. They stood a few feet away from where Maddie was standing with Rosedale. Charles continued. Milked out every bit of the story. Made him feel worse than he already did.

'As you can imagine, Tom, she was very worried. *Very*. But here's the thing, she wasn't worried about herself, she was worried about you. Can you imagine? Alone in the dark and all she was concerned about was how you'd be feeling. She was insistent about trying to get back to you but as the rain was so heavy, and had caused the mudslide, it was impossible. Still, she was in good hands.'

Cooper had heard enough. Didn't bother excusing himself

and walked across to Maddie. There was something about the man which irritated the hell out of him. He'd never enjoyed the company of someone as obsequious as Charles. They were the kind of guys who smiled at you before plunging a knife in your back. Though he guessed, whatever his feelings, it didn't deter or negate his thanks to him for looking after Maddie the way he had and bringing her back safely to him.

'I'm so sorry, Maddie.'

'Tom, I've told you it wasn't your fault. If it was anyone's, it was mine. When I woke up and neither of you was there, I should've just stayed put. I know the rules. But curiosity got the better of me. I thought I'd take a look round. See exactly where we were and try to work out some kind of plan.' She stopped and grinned sheepishly, adding, 'Though this wasn't quite what I imagined.'

'And Charles?'

Cooper stopped talking to regard Charles, who by now had wandered off to speak to one of the villagers.

'Actually, he was very sweet. I must've walked about a mile or so down the road. I was heading North East and planned to walk on no more than another half a mile. Then I made a total schoolgirl error. Tried to climb up one of the sliding banks to cut across a small stream. I slipped and twisted my ankle… I must be losing my touch. Anyway, Charles came by about an hour or so later. We tried to get back to you guys, but the road we were on totally collapsed from the heavy rain. So he brought me back here. I had my satellite phone on me and tried to call you from the top of the hill there, but for some reason couldn't get through, so that's why I called Granger, hoping he'd have more luck. Which I guess he did.'

Cooper groaned. Pictured Granger's face. Groaned some

more. 'Oh Christ. Tell me he doesn't know we lost you. Tell me anything but that.'

'Didn't you speak to him?'

Cooper blew out his cheeks. Felt light headed from the OxyContin and hoped Maddie wouldn't notice. 'No, not really. Bad connection… Really bad connection.'

Charles called across as he got back into the black car. 'Right, well I'll be off then. Good to see a happily ever after.'

As he pulled away, Cooper ran over. Flagging him down as he looked at the car's plates. Trying hard to push his lethargy away. Even to him, his speech sounded slightly slurred. 'I meant to ask you before. Do you happen to know a Papa Bemba?'

Charles frowned. Glanced at the steering wheel. Started nodding slowly. 'Yes, I've heard of him. I think you see the occasional poster around advertising his pastoral teachings. Any reason?'

Cooper shook his head, agitating his headache. Agitating the drugs in his system. 'No, just heard his church services are worth seeing. Anyway, thanks once again for everything you've done.'

Maddie and Cooper stood waving as he drove off. He turned to look at her. 'Tell me something, Maddison. How come Charles, who says he doesn't know Bemba, ends up driving his car?'

Before Maddie had time to answer, a piercing scream filled the air.

54

Maddie pointed. 'Rosedale! It came from over there.'

Cooper ran. Leading the trio. His hand wavering over where his gun sat in its holster.

They bolted forward to a tiny brick hut to see a woman staggering out covered in blood. Her arms open. Her face twisted in pain. She fell on the ground, her fingers scraping into the dirt as she cried out. 'Il est mort! Il est mort!'

Maddie, alarmed, stared. 'Who's dead? Madame, qui est mort?'

Cooper drew his gun. Pulled it close to his body as he nodded at Rosedale and Maddie to follow.

Cooper edged along the wall. Kicked open the door. Sidestepping into the candlelit hut. He nodded again to Rosedale, signalling he was going into the next room. Signalled to Maddie to go round the back.

With his weapon poised in the air, he swept forward. Rushed across. Pressed his body against the small bookshelf. Checking for signs of anybody there, Cooper crept forward. Slowly. Cautiously. Then he halted. Stopped dead in his tracks. 'Jesus Christ!'

Putting his Glock away, he took in the scene whilst quickly pulling up his t-shirt over his nose. Even though he was accustomed to seeing and being around dead bodies, the fetid stench of the body lying on the bed in front of him had him fighting the urge to gag. And the sorrow he felt overwhelmed.

In the oppressive heat the large black flies gorged on the bloated, putrefying corpse of the young boy. Mottled in color from the large gray seeping blisters and wounds. Blood drained out from the boy's mouth and nose. A multitude of large cuts wept with pus.

Rosedale came up by the side of Cooper. 'Oh Jesus, the poor kid. Christ, what the hell do you think happened?'

'Maybe bloodletting,' said Cooper, aware that his voice sounded shaken. 'But that's a guess.'

'Well that would account for the cuts but what about the rest?'

'Oh my God...!' Maddie stood behind the two men. 'He's just a kid.'

'Come on,' said Rosedale. 'Let's all get out of here.'

The trio walked out of the tiny brick hut. At which point Cooper promptly vomited. Inspired Maddie to do the same. With Rosedale only seconds behind.

55

Cooper and Maddie walked across to the small stream. He gave her the corner of his t-shirt to wipe her mouth on. She was tired and Rosedale was being a jerk and he himself was an out and out mess. 'This isn't okay, is it? None of it.'

Maddie looked at Cooper. A fresh spring of freckles covering her brown face.

'No, it's not.'

'That poor kid.'

'Any ideas what it was?'

'I know last year there was a number of cases of Ebola in this area and yes, you do get internal bleeding and yes, you also get blisters, but not like those. That was something different. I don't know what though.'

'I'm guessing it's not contagious either because the old woman doesn't look ill and neither does anybody else in the village.' She stopped. Sighed deeply. Looked across to the woman covered in blood, who was now sitting alone on the side of the track, crying quietly. More to herself she said, 'God, I never counted on this when I came here.'

'Counted on what?'

'Feeling so lost. I used to have such a connection with this place and now… Oh I don't know. Ignore me, I guess I'm just missing Cora. Leaving her never gets any easier. Look, you don't need to hear my problems… I'm sorry.'

'Maddison, you don't have to say sorry about anything.

If it wasn't for you, Rosedale and I would've probably killed each other by now and even after everything… Well let's just say I don't deserve you. Look, I know I've been acting like a jackass and I also know that nobody should have to put up with what you've put up with. It sounds hollow but I don't mean to treat you the way I do. I want to be the person you think I am and I'm sorry most of the time I'm not able to.'

Cooper held her stare as he pulled her in close. He traced her face with his eyes.

'Tom, I know…'

Quickly, gently, he put his finger over Maddie's lips. He didn't want her to talk. His head felt hazy. Everything around him didn't feel quite real. 'Sshhhh, don't say anything.'

Bending his face towards hers. He closed his eyes. Pushing his mind to imagine. His lips almost on hers… His lips on Ellie's.

'Thomas! Thomas! I need a word.'

Rosedale, cigar in mouth, boomed loudly. Real loud. He stood a few feet away from Cooper and Maddie.

'What is it Rosedale?'

'A word.'

Cooper shook his head but let go of Maddie and walked away towards Rosedale.

'What is it now?'

Rosedale, not moving his eyes away from Cooper, said, 'You may not be able to let Ellie go, but like I said before, you need to let Maddie go. Don't do this to her, Thomas. Unlike your emotions, hers are real. Don't cross me on this.'

Cooper bit down hard on his lip. It felt good. 'What the hell has it got to do with you? Who do you think you are? She's my wife.'

'No, she's not. Not anymore. Leave her alone.'

'Has it ever occurred to you that I may have feelings for her still? That I still love her.'

'Oh it's occurred to me alright, but that isn't the problem or the point. You're not good for her, Thomas, and as for making her happy? You will *never* be able to do that. Let her free. Do it now. I'm warning you, before it's too late.'

56

Rosedale had taken Maddie with him to bring the Toyota down to the village via a small track they'd missed earlier, and Cooper, trying not to feel too sorry for himself, made his way round the village.

He watched fascinated as a group of women finished off building a mud and stick wall for one of the huts, pressing and filling in wet mud balls between the horizontal poles which ran down from one side of the wooden frame to the other, giving the wall a solid appearance.

At that moment the place seemed so tranquil but Cooper knew only too well that weekly attacks including rape, looting and kidnapping were still part of the country's fabric. On the drive from Kinshasa they'd seen many villages burnt and empty and barely any evidence of civilian life was visible.

The village they were at was located near a high plateau of grassland which before the conflicts had held a wealth of grazing livestock. Now all that remained was a carpet of antipersonnel landmines. Ordinary life seemed impossible but he couldn't help, for all its troubles, still loving the country.

Moving away from the women, Cooper noticed the most notable feature about the small village were the rat cages outside the majority of huts. Some were crammed with large rodents, pushing and trying to claw their way out, whilst other cages were just being used to store various household objects.

He was hoping to speak to someone about the young boy, but so far he'd been unsuccessful. Each time he'd approached anyone they'd hurried away. Wary. At odds with how they'd been when he and Rosedale had first arrived in the village. Not that he blamed them. The argument he'd with Rosedale in public view certainly hadn't helped matters. And most certainly hadn't put the two of them in the best light.

He sighed. Pulled out the two Xanax and the one opioid he had hidden in his sock. Popped them, then slid a cigarette into his mouth. Decided not to light it quite yet and wanted his thoughts not to stray but to focus on the investigation and especially on Papa Bemba. The whereabouts of the plane. *Anything*, anything at all rather than think about how he was feeling. He was done with all that.

He followed the tiny stream running behind the small brick and mud huts, which from a distance looked like giant ant hills. Felt the nip of an insect on his neck. Slapped himself hard. Hoped to kill whatever it was which had bitten him. A moment later, he felt another bite on his leg. Bending down to scratch he noticed lots of dead tiny insects. The area seemed to be a breeding place for the things.

Knowing smoke was a great insect repellent, Cooper lit his cigarette. Dragged on it intensely. Was bitten a dozen times more.

He started to walk towards the hut of the dead child to speak to the woman he'd seen earlier. He knew it wasn't ideal to ask a grieving relative questions, though he had to admit, in the past amidst the intolerable pain of grief, in the immediate aftermath of death, the truth *did* prevail. Things which normally would be kept unspoken, were revealed.

He'd never been comfortable getting a lead that way. Intruding on a final goodbye. Infringing on a realization of never being able to hold or see a person again and somehow having to cope with being left in a life without them. He didn't want to encroach on that. That was *their* moment. One he didn't want to shatter or steal.

Continuing to walk as the sun began to set, giving way to the greed of the evening sky of blushing colors, Cooper stopped just behind the small brick hut, seeing something in the long grass.

He frowned. Bent down to take a closer look. It was charcoal. Perfectly piled. Built up like a pyramid with a circle of large black glossy berries around it. Exactly the same as he'd seen outside Emmanuel's aunt's house. Exactly like the charcoal and berries Marvin had talked about.

Taking out one of the semi-filled evidence bags, he dropped a piece of the coal in it, before letting his gaze wander around as he started to think. And then it suddenly hit him. Like a goddam steam train. And as it did, he began to run.

Chasing up and around and through and along and to the path and to the front of the hut and without knocking, Cooper barged inside.

A few of the old lady's clothes were scattered around and he hurriedly picked them up as he charged through to the next room, where the grief-stricken woman stood in the middle of the far doorway. Terror on her face. Fear in her eyes as she stared at Cooper.

'Laissez-moi tranquille! Get out!'

'It's okay… it's okay. Se il vous plaît, je suis là pour vous aider.'

The woman began to back away into the shadows of the room, next to where the reeking corpse of the child lay. And Cooper put his hand out to her, causing her to retreat further. And back towards the bed with the fly-covered body.

'Please, you've got to come with me. I'm here to help. Just trust me... You got to trust me.'

He left his hand stretched out, but the woman just continued to stare.

'Look... Jesus... It's not safe for you to be here. *Please*.'

Cooper's words implored. They didn't make a damn bit of difference. She was going nowhere fast. But he had to do something. He had to get her out. He thought about some of the things Maddie had explained to him and tried another tack. 'I've been sent here... by the spirits... By the spirits of the ancestors. They told me you were a good person. They know you are, so they sent me to keep you safe. Please come with me, you need to... I know it's their wish.'

Cooper was willing her to come but he decided not to say another word. He just watched without moving. She turned her head to the side looking like she was reviewing words. Then with the whispered agony of loss filtering into her voice, she said, 'What about my grandson? I can't leave him.'

Cooper glanced at the rotting body. At the child. Who seemed like he was almost moving from the sea of flies.

Maddie had told him about the strength of belief and importance of burial rites, but he also knew there was nothing he could do.

'Please.'

'I can't leave him. Non. C'est impossible.'

Cooper took the chance to step closer to her.

'You have to. I don't think we've got much time. I don't know if you want to take anything else, but here, I just grabbed these.'

He passed her the clothes he'd picked up from the room, which she took. Dropping them into the bag on the floor. Though uncertainty still remained.

From far in the distance Cooper heard noises. Voices. And with the front of the hut having no windows, he ran to the door, peering out to see a procession of people fronted by one of the men from the revivalist church back in Kinshasa, walking slowly up the hill towards them.

He turned to the woman. Gave a quick smile and said, 'I'm sorry, you've given me no other choice'

And without a moment of hesitation. He picked her up. Threw her gently over his shoulder before running out into the twilight.

57

Two hundred meters clear of the hut, hidden amongst the trees, Cooper put down the woman carefully, who'd surprised him by not objecting or hollering or fighting.

He spun round in time to watch the man from the church throw his burning torches on and into the hut. Turned it into a bonfire of orange and yellow flames.

The woman, scared and in shock seeing her house burning down, with the added knowledge her beloved grandson's body was inside, opened her mouth to scream. But Cooper, a step ahead, clapped his hand firmly across her mouth. Didn't even hesitate.

He shook his head, trying to reassure her as she stared with frog-wide eyes. His hand stayed tight across her face. Whispered. 'They'll hear you. I don't think it's a good idea for them to know you weren't inside, not for now at least.'

Slowly she nodded and for the first time he could feel the woman starting to accept the situation she found herself in. Gradually he took his hand away. Ready to slam it back if need be. 'They think I'm possessed.'

'Yes they do.'

'It was only my grandson who'd been possessed unless… unless…'

She stopped to let tears fall before continuing to talk with fearful conviction.

'I too am full of sorcery. Perhaps when I sleep the evil which lives within me leaves my body to harm those around.'

Cooper squeezed her hand and was pleased she didn't pull away. 'I don't think so…' Everything in him wanted to say her grandson wasn't possessed either. But he didn't.

The woman looked at him oddly and Cooper could see something which resembled hope in her eyes. 'How do you know? Have the spirits come to you?'

He hated having to mislead her. Hated it. But realizing and remembering everything Marvin had told them, and seeing for the time being it might be the only way, he nodded. Tried to convince himself his manipulation of her beliefs of the spirit world would be ultimately for her own good. 'Oui… yes. Yes, they have. That's exactly it. They know you're a good person, and I've been told to keep you safe.'

58

As they walked along the road together in the pitch of darkness, the woman told Cooper her name was Zola.

'Well it's good to meet you, Zola. It's a shame it's under these circumstances... And I'm so, so sorry for your loss.'

Zola said nothing. Her pace, much slower than he'd ideally have liked. He was hoping that any minute he'd see Rosedale and Maddie coming along the track in the Toyota, but so far all he'd heard was the calling of the monitor lizards.

Even though they'd been walking for the past half an hour they'd only managed to walk a short distance from the village due to Zola's bad legs. There was so much he wanted to ask her. But each time he'd questioned her, she'd moved even more slowly as she answered. So for now it all had to wait.

From behind him, Cooper heard an engine but straight away he knew it wasn't the Toyota. It was the Commer truck.

From the brow of the hill, he saw the lights of it approaching. Fast. He could also see the part of the dirt track they were on gave little place for them to hide. One side of the bank was steep. Dense. Wet. The other had large boulders and hunks of mud fallen from one of the numerous landslides which were commonplace due to the rains.

Whilst keeping his eye on the approaching truck, Cooper said, 'I'm sorry, I'm going to pick you up again.' Not waiting for any kind of reply, he lifted Zola up with ease onto his shoulder. Though this time he could feel her holding tightly. Firmly. Clinging onto the back of his top.

Deciding to take his chance with the mud side of the bank rather than the steep side, Cooper vaulted across the muddy earth. Scrambled across the boulders, being mindful of needing to hold his balance as he carried the old woman. And it was almost as if he could feel the heat of the lights speeding down the road, spotlighting their position. It struck him that he could still be seen by the truck if he continued to stand up. Twisting Zola off his shoulders and into his arms at rapid speed, Cooper flung himself down on the wet ground whilst holding her safe.

He was breathing hard and wild and he cursed to himself as the truck came to an absolute stop in front of them. He was certain they hadn't been seen. But how long that would last, he didn't know. But he was damned sure he wasn't going to wait around to find out.

He whispered to Zola, signalling with his hand. 'We've got to keep going.'

She nodded and Copper carefully got up.

Slowly.

Carefully.

Silently.

Backing away with Zola in his arms.

Hoping Maddie and Rosedale didn't come along any time soon. He didn't know who these people were, but they were trouble. Big trouble.

Minding his foot through the thick twisted vegetation of the forest as the rain began to pour down hitting them hard, Cooper glanced down at Zola as he carried her. She looked cold. But she smiled warmly. Croaked out her words. 'Over the river. There's a place we can shelter.'

He could see the small river was only few meters ahead. And he picked up his pace, wanting to take Zola as quickly as he could to the shelter. And from there he'd head back down to the village. All being well, meeting up again with Rosedale and Maddie.

*

By the time Cooper had waded through the fast flowing water, carried Zola up the wet and sludgy hill and along the high ground, avoided tripping over the labyrinth of buttress roots running along from the large trees which rose up like giant columns of a citadel, and almost twisted his right ankle, he could feel the tightening wheeze from his chest. The agitated come-down from the pills. The words of Zola, *'We're here,'* couldn't come soon enough.

He gazed round. Seeing a gap in the trees with three burnt-out derelict huts. He put Zola down, who nodded at him gratefully. In return he gave her a wink.

Cooper kicked at the dirt. Nothing but discarded, rusting household equipment. Broken bottles and cans. Picked up some of the things, dropping them as he always did into his collecting bag, knowing most, if not all the things he gathered, would turn out to be trash.

The shrink at the VA medical center had told him he collected items to seek some kind of comfort. That it acted as a coping mechanism for dealing with his anxiety and fear of losing control. Not that he'd taken much notice of what the Doc had had to say. He'd just looked at the clock and waited for his court ordered session to finish.

He'd first started collecting the bits and pieces he'd found when he'd searched for Ellie. To him, rather than it being a question of seeking comfort, it'd been a question of sheer desperation which had prompted it. It hadn't mattered what it was, he'd collected it. Just looked for anything, *anything* which would've given him a clue.

The thing was, he knew it'd become a habit. Another one to add to his list. Because even when he'd given up looking for Ellie, he'd continued to collect. Or, to use his doctor's words, *continued with his obsession*.

He'd drive himself crazy with his collecting and at the end of each trip, he'd throw everything from the bottle tops to the candy wraps, to the tiny shards glass, away. Convincing himself determinedly it'd be the last time, only for the damn thing to start all over again on his next trip. And like the pills, he found it hard to stop. Who was he kidding? *Couldn't.* Couldn't stop.

Cooper scratched his head. It felt heavy. Focused on something else and shone the florescent pink pen torch Maddie had given him. He knelt in the wet earth, seeing and picking up what looked like a piece of a broken glazed porcelain pot.

Turned it over and noted the inner part wasn't coated. Just an unfinished red matte clay with a pottery mark he couldn't quite read. There was also what looked like a piece of copper wire embedded into it. Puzzled, he slipped it into his bag.

With a sigh and a crick of his neck, he stood up. Brushing off the wet, Cooper caught sight of something else. It looked like the remains of a pile of charcoal. 'Are you sure it'll be safe here?'

Zola nodded, walking into one of the huts which, unlike the other two, still had part of its roof intact. 'No-one will come here.'

Following her in and clearing a spot for her to rest, Cooper said, 'Why? How can you be so sure?'

'They think it was the home of the possessed.'

Wanting to understand her better. 'Don't you?'

She shook her head emphatically. 'No. There's no evil here. I feel safe. This was the home of my friend, Emmanuel Mutombo… They say he walks amongst the dead trying to harm the living.'

Cooper stopped in his tracks. 'What did you say?'

A look of fear crossed Zola's face. She shook her head, reluctant to say anything more.

'Zola… *please*. Just repeat the name you said?'

Her eyes darted round nervously and it took a long moment but eventually and slowly she said, 'Emmanuel Mutombo. He was a good man, and I believe he's still alive.'

59

Cooper bounded back down the hillside without the weight of Zola. With the rain having subsided, the velvet night turned warm and clear, giving him a good view of the tiny village.

He slowed down by the track. Moved cautiously. Gun drawn. Looking. Listening. Stopped at every noise.

The quickest way back to the village was to hike along the road and although exposed, he didn't fancy his chances in the undergrowth with its hidden crevices and ditches and banks and the highly venomous black mamba snakes which hid and moved with swift deadly speed.

Pausing for a moment, he checked for lights. Not wanting to bring his presence to the attention of anyone, *especially* whoever it was driving the Commer truck. As certain as he could be that the coast was clear, he started to head as quickly as vigilance would allow. Back towards the village.

After ten minutes of watching his footing, avoiding the dips and hollows and holes and pits which would twist an ankle in a brutal second, Cooper saw headlights beginning to appear over the horizon. Lighting up the sky like an arc anti-aircraft searchlight.

He crouched down, noticing the headlights were lower and narrower than the Commer's. A blend of relief and exhaustion hit him as he realized they were the lights of the Toyota. He waved. Slowly at first then more frantically. Looked like the car wasn't going to slow down.

Hell, there was no way he was going to risk them not seeing him. The satellite phone he had was unreliable at the best of times, on top of which the battery for some reason was unable to keep its charge and was dangerously flat. Close to dying.

Deciding there was only one thing for it, Cooper leapt into the path of the oncoming car. An abrupt screech and squeal of the tires screamed out as the brakes locked and the car crunched into a stop.

He felt the heat from the Toyota's hood only inches away. And it was only when he opened his eyes did he notice he'd actually had them squeezed shut.

'What the hell do you think you're doing?'

Rosedale stretched out of the drivers' side window. His face as furious as it was shocked.

'I could've killed you... And whilst that would be no bad thing, perhaps now isn't the time. Anyway where've you been?'

Cooper glanced round, uneasy at us being in the middle of the road and knowing anything Rosedale had to say could wait.

Running round to the passenger side, Cooper jumped in. 'Come on, let's find somewhere to park the car, there was a clearing further up. I'll explain to you both on the way.'

60

Having concealed the Toyota thoroughly under the numerous large-leafed plants which grew and swelled in abundance, Cooper, Rosedale and Maddie dashed across the track, their guns drawn.

Cooper led the way. Tracking back through the river and up and beyond the bosongu trees to the clearing where Zola was waiting for them.

Just before they got to the three huts, Cooper stopped, not wanting Zola to hear what he had to say.

'Listen, we need to be real quiet. This woman, Zola, she's really jumpy. Understandably so. Obviously she's cut up over her grandson. But I think she knows some stuff which may be helpful to us.'

Maddie was curious. 'Like what?'

'Well she knows Emmanuel. And this place we're about to go to, the place she's hiding out, apparently was his home.'

Rosedale, who was usually indifferent to such pieces of information unless it came to some kind of fruition, looked suitably impressed. Which surprised Cooper after their showdown earlier.

'I'll give it to you Thomas, you pulled this one out of the bag.'

Giving Rosedale a wry smile, Cooper said, 'I found a pile of charcoal which makes me think it's the same kind of thing we saw back at Kinshasa and back down at the village. It's just like Marvin said and what you've explained, Maddie. The huts were torched as part of a deliverance to eradicate any witchcraft. I think that's the reason Emmanuel's aunt's house was burnt down. It looks like anyone who was part of his family are seen to be a threat to the community.'

'It's all part of the deliverance. Ridding the community of witchcraft.' Cooper, who was soaking wet and wishing he'd brought a change of clothes from the car, listened to what Maddie had to say whilst seeing the tension come over her.

Rosedale said, 'What about their friends? Their family. Don't they have anything to say about it?'

Sadly, Maddie replied, 'If you believe a person is possessed by bad spirits essentially that person's no longer the person you once knew. They've been taken over by a powerful force which is ultimately going to harm you. So it's not like you'd be actually hurting or performing a deliverance on your friend, who use to bake you the best pecan pie, you're getting rid of the witch who's taken over their body.'

'Thomas, do you think Zola will open up? Talk to us and tell us what she knows?'

Cooper shrugged at Rosedale. 'Maybe. I'm hoping so, it's the best lead we've got since we've arrived, but of course I don't want to panic her by putting too much pressure on… She's got a real belief in the spirt world. It seems to be her guide. She was worried to come with me and I feel terrible about this but when she thought I'd been asked by the spirits to help her, then she was more trusting. She's definitely scared. And we can't forget she's just lost her grandson.'

'Maybe Maddie should do most of the talking.'

Cooper nodded. 'Okay, sounds like a good idea. Come on, she's over here.'

61

'Zola…Zola. It's me, Tom.'

Not wanting to startle the old woman Cooper called out as he led the others into the derelict hut. He noticed she hadn't moved from where he'd left her. Not an inch. Not a foot. Not a yard. And from where he was standing, it looked to him as if she hadn't even moved her head.

He spoke warmly. The kind of warmth he knew he should've given Maddie. He pushed that thought away. 'Hey, Zola. Hey, how ya doing?'

She looked tired and anxious but she nodded.

'These are my friends. The ones I was telling you about. Remember they were down in the village with me earlier.'

Zola held her hand up, which displayed large purple veins pushing up from beneath her thinning black skin. She gave Maddie and Rosedale a small wave along with a small smile.

Cooper gave a quick glance to Rosedale before sitting down next to Zola. His patience was at an all-time low, almost as low as his supply of medication. So he was glad Maddie was taking the lead.

'You told Tom you knew Emmanuel. We're trying to find him. It's really important we do.'

'Emmanuel isn't here.'

'Where is he? Do you know?'

Zola was hesitant, which made Maddie want to blast

another question at her. She didn't. Just waited. Then waited some more.

'No, I don't, but I do know they say he walks amongst the dead. Though I feel he's still close. He was a good man. They say he was possessed by the Kindoki, but I don't know.'

'Who says, Zola?'

'Papa Bemba.'

Maddie didn't know if she sounded surprised or pleased but she glanced at Rosedale. 'You know him?'

'Of course. Everyone knows him.'

'And what did he say? What exactly happened with Emmanuel?'

'There was a deliverance. Here.' Zola gestured with her hand. 'But he fought it,' she added.

'The witchcraft?' Maddie said.

'No, he fought what Papa Bemba was saying for a long time, he refused to believe he was possessed. But eventually they went to find him.'

Cooper had agreed to keep silent, but he was curious. 'Okay, so you're saying Emmanuel didn't want to be delivered, but you're saying there are some people who actually agree to it? They volunteer themselves?'

Zola looked at him as if stupid. 'Mais oui…! Of course! No-one wants the spirit of the malevolent to live inside them. They ask for help. They ask to be delivered. And Papa Bemba helps.'

Maddie asked. 'And is that what Papa Bemba is? A healer?'

'Yes.'

'And would you say he was a good man, Zola?'

Zola's answer was reflective, as if she'd never asked herself the question before.

'Yes, he's a good man…He's helped a lot of people. He has also rid the community of witchcraft.'

'How? How, Zola?'

Zola looked at Maddie intently. 'By killing the Kindoki spirit in them… But it was too late for my grandson.'

Carefully, Maddie said, 'But why? Why was it too late for him?'

Her words sounded affronted. 'He came to warn us before, but I didn't believe my grandson was possessed and so refused Papa Bemba's help. My grandson behaved so normally. But that's how it is with the possessed, they'll say and act as if they have no evil in them, but often that's the Kindoki talking, trying to trick you.'

Cooper contemplated what Zola had said. It sounded like a hell of a catch-22. Admit you were a witch and you'd be delivered. Say you weren't, you'd be delivered anyway.

'When Bemba came to warn you, was your grandson ill?' Maddie asked.

'No, but Papa Bemba can see the spirit of the possessed before the sighted can. His darkness gives him the power of healing.'

'I'm sorry to go over this, Zola, but I just want to get this straight. Papa Bemba knew the so-called evil spirits were in your grandson *before* he was ill?'

'Oui.'

'Then when he *actually* gets ill, Papa Bemba says he'll heal him.'

Zola sounded slighted irritated by Maddie's questions. 'Yes.'

'But then when it comes down to it, he doesn't manage to save him because…'

Zola sighed, clearly disappointed by the lack of

understanding. 'Because it was *too late*. We'd angered the good spirits by not believing Papa Bemba when he came to warn us, and as a consequence, forces of evil began to grow inside and take over my grandson completely. It meant when I begged Papa Bemba to help us the Kindoki was too strong and therefore Bemba wasn't able to rid my grandson of them. It was evil which killed him.'

'And so this Bemba guy,' said Rosedale, also abandoning the plan of Maddie leading the questioning. 'He did all this for nothing? He does it just because he likes to go around healing? Caring about the community?'

Zola's eyes flashed furiously. 'No, for an exchange.'

Cooper touched Zola's hand, drawing her attention to him. And remembering what Maddie had explained about the different kind of ceremonies, he said, 'Where you give the spirits something in exchange for them doing something for you?'

'Yes.'

'But in this case it's Bemba who's reaping the reward,' said Rosedale. 'It's him you and other people are giving stuff to.'

Anger passed across Zola's face and travelled into her voice. 'No! Papa Bemba is the channel of the spirits. He's their vehicle. It is not for him. It is for them.'

Even Maddie, who understood and had been very much a part of the culture at one time, dug deep not to show her cynicism. 'So even though Bemba didn't cure your grandson from the Kindoki, there was still an exchange? You *still* paid him with something?'

'Of course.'

Already knowing she probably wasn't going to like what she was about to hear, Maddie had to ask. 'And what was the exchange? What did you give Papa Bemba, Zola?'

'My land. I gave him my land.'

'Your land?'

'Yes of course the evil was strong and therefore needed a just exchange... Children are often the hardest.'

Maddie stiffened with a scorn and a coldness in her eyes that Cooper rarely saw.

'What do you mean, hardest?'

'Hardest to rid of the sorcery. The evil takes over very quickly and they don't realize what's happening to them. So it is for the parents, grandparents and the community to make sure they're delivered.'

Knowing the answer but needing somehow to hear it, Maddie said, 'And if they refuse, come on Zola, tell me what you do?'

Picking up on her hostility, Rosedale tried to calm her. 'Maddie.'

'Oh no, I'm curious to hear what Zola has to say. Come on. Dîtes-moi.'

Zola stared Maddie straight in the eyes and spoke matter-of-factly. 'Hold them. Tie them down, or if the spirits really fight, you must beat them. Anything to stop the devil running away.'

'Jesus. They're children, Zola!'

'No. Not once they've been possessed. Only when they become free of the Kindoki do they become themselves again.'

'And is that what you did to your grandson? Is it? Did you tie him down, Zola?'

Rosedale raised his voice. 'What the hell are you doing, Maddie?'

With her eyes shining angrily, Maddie said, 'I just wanna know what she did to her own grandchild.'

Rosedale grabbed her arm. Shook it slightly. 'What is wrong with you?'

'Me? Nothing's wrong with me, Rosedale. And it seems clear there's nothing wrong with Zola because she doesn't think it's wrong, do you?'

The old lady, with just as much as fire in her belly as Maddie seemed to have, pointed her finger. 'Wrong? How can it be wrong to help rid them of bad spirits? To vomit up the devil and let them be free of the evil.'

'And what about them being frightened? Terrified? What about that, hey?'

'Their fear comes from the evil spirit inside. It knows it's going to be destroyed by the deliverance.'

'Non vous vous trompez! You're wrong! You're wrong. It's not the spirits, Zola, it's them. People like your grandson who are terrified. Being beaten. Starved. Thrown out onto the street because somebody needs somebody to blame. Children are dying because of this.'

'Maddie, enough!'

Angrily Zola said, 'If you die they'll exchange your life so you can be freed from the evil within, allowing you to be revered in death and walk once again amongst the good. It's the only way to atone for the harm your sorcery has done in *this* life.'

As Rosedale pulled her outside, Maddie shouted. 'Can you hear yourself Zola? These are children we're talking about. *Children.* Tu devrais avoir honte…! Tu m'entends? Tu devrais avoir honte!'

62

'What the hell do you thinking you're doing? Well go on, Maddison, tell me. Don't let the cat catch your tongue now, because hell, woman, you had enough to say to Zola.'

Not fully knowing if it was tears or the rain or both she felt running down her face, Maddie said, 'Just leave it Rosedale, okay.'

'Well that's not what I'm going to do. So why don't we make this easy on both of us and tell me what's going on'

Maddie shouted over the noise of the heavy rain. 'I would if there was anything to tell.'

'I know you Maddison, and okay I might not have known you long, but that wasn't you in there. The Maddison I know is one hell of a woman but she doesn't judge. Not like that. She understands her culture, proud of it like she should be. So unless this Kindoki is real and has taken you as well, then sugar, you need to start talking.'

'You think that's funny? To joke about Kindoki? Whether it's real or not and whether you believe it or not kids are being hurt because somehow it's okay to do that to them. How can it be okay, Rosedale? Did you see them in Kinshasa? Did you see how traumatized they were? They were babies, Rosedale. Six and seven years old. Some younger than that. UNICEF reported that there were over twenty thousand kids in Kinshasa alone accused of witchcraft. Twenty thousand, Rosedale. And nobody's helping. Not us, not anybody. They live on the streets with no food, no shelter. No-one to care for them because somebody somewhere didn't get that job or got sick and decided they were to blame. Innocent kids… So yes, I'm afraid it is me, Rosedale, who you saw in there. That's me. I am going to judge because I don't know how Zola can stand in there when her grandson's just died and talk about Kindoki and try telling me they don't feel fear when they're locked up in a dark room having the evil starved out of them. Can't she see her poor grandson had some sort of illness? It wasn't witchcraft.'

With the brim of his cowboy hat full of water and the sound of the tapping and patting of rain beating down on the large banana leaves, Rosedale said, 'What happened to you Maddie?'

'What?'

'You heard me. What happened to you, Maddison? Here. In the DRC. What happened to you? Is that why you haven't visited the country for years?'

'I don't know what you're talking about.'

'Yes you do… This happened to you didn't it…? Maddison. Talk to me.'

Maddison blinked, drew breath, and held her head high. She spoke with an equanimity Rosedale hadn't seen in her before.

'I was twelve years old and it was four years before the civil war broke out. I'd come to stay in a village not too far from here. They were close friends of my grandmother so I'd known them since as far back as I could remember. Every time I'd come to visit the country I pestered my grandparents to let me go and stay with them. Then one day after lots of persuasion, I was allowed to go. So you could imagine how excited I was. Daddy was in Kinshasa and my grandmother had taken the opportunity to go to a wedding over in Yangambi. And

I was delighted... Things were fine for the first few days. It was everything I thought it would be. We had fun. It was like staying with your favorite aunt and uncle at Christmas time.' She gave a melancholy smile. 'But then one night I was dragged out of bed and a hand put over my mouth. I was terrified. I tried to fight but it turned out there was more than one person. Holding my feet. Pulling my hands behind my back. I didn't know what was happening, I thought they were intruders but then I caught a glimpse of their faces. It was my so-called aunt and uncle. They looked at me with a mixture of revulsion and anger, and as I cried and begged them to stop there was no kind of empathy. They bound my legs and hands behind my back and they took me to the river. Tried to drown out the devil. Eventually I passed out and woke up in a small room. Still tied up but now there was not only my *aunt and uncle* but also a self-appointed pastor who force fed me a drink, just like we saw Bemba doing to those children back at the church. It made me vomit. I was so sick, Rosedale. I didn't think anybody could feel that sick. I was covered in it, but they didn't clean me up, they just bundled me in a large sack like a laundry bag. Tied the top of it and left me there. Locked up and terrified and every few hours they'd come in and beat me with belts through the bag. I was like that for two days in that sack but it felt like forever, Rosedale. No food. No water. And not being able to go to the bathroom. I sat in my own urine thinking I was going to die... So yeah, you were right, Rosedale, Tom's not the only one with ghosts.'

'Jesus, Maddie, I...'

'Don't know what to say? There isn't anything *to* say.'

'How did you get away?'

Maddie said, 'My grandmother came home. Simple as that. I know there was a huge argument but I was too traumatized to really know what went down. She took me back to Kinshasa and once I got checked out at the hospital I flew back home to the States with my daddy. And that was it. I've never been back. Until now. Daddy never spoke to his mom again. He blamed her and ironically she blamed the spirits. And you know what, Rosedale, the whole thing happened because my *uncle* had a bout of gastritis which made it impossible for him to go to work and he missed out on some opportunity.'

'What happened to them?'

Maddie shrugged. 'Nothing. That's just how it is. Something which happens. And it makes me so mad... So sad.'

'Honey, I'm so sorry. Does Thomas know this?'

Maddie shook her head. 'No and I don't want him to. Okay?'

'Whatever you say. Your call,' said Rosedale, then added: 'It doesn't take a shrink to know why you chose the job you did. You're kick ass, baby. Both in what you do and who you are. Don't you ever forget that, Miss Maddison.'

Maddie wiped away her tears along, pushing her memories away and smiled.

'I'm not sure if this place is good for any of us.'

'It's not the place. We take our baggage with us.'

'So what baggage are you carrying? Because I reckon there's one big suitcase.'

With the rain pouring down, Rosedale leant on the tree, picking out his cuticles with his thumb. 'Maddison, what the hell are you talking about?'

'I'm talking about you. The real you. You never tell me anything about your life.'

Rosedale shrugged. 'Nothing to say.'

'Don't give me that.'

'Okay. Lots to say. No-one to listen.'

'There must have been someone special at one time.'

'Imagined or real?'

Maddie said. 'What do you mean?'

'As you know I worked for the CIA Clan—'

She rolled her eyes then grinned and finished his sentence. 'Clandestine Service. Yes. Think we all do.'

He grinned. 'The point is you live a life where everything's pretend. A big ol' pretend world. Pretending to be somebody else. Pretending to be a guy with kids and a wife. Pretending to be love's young dream with some CIA operative who hates the sight of you and you hate the sight of them. And then what happens is because you submerge yourself in the make believe to do the job, you eventually end up believing it's real yourself. That you've got the wife. You've got the kids. You've got the house. And you've got the love. The American dream. Then one day, the mailman comes and delivers your pink slip and it all disappear in a cloud of smoke and you realize there's nobody there at all. Never was... And that's why I think he's a fool.'

'Who is?'

'Thomas.'

'Why?'

'For letting you go. If I'd been lucky enough to have someone like you, I would've never let you go.'

Maddie brushed the rain off the end of her nose. 'Rosedale. Thank you. That's the kindest thing someone has said about me in a very long time.'

Rosedale shuffled. Put his head down. 'I don't mean it to be kind, ma'am. It's the truth. I can't help the way I feel.'

'Rosedale, listen...'

'No.'

'Rosedale...'

'No, Miss Maddison. You want to know things about me. Well here are two things to know. I'm not real good at sentiment or disappointment, and I'm guessing what you're about to say is one of the two, so I think it's best we leave it there. But I will ask you this… What do you think of Kevin Costner?'

And in the middle of the dark, rain-soaked forest, Maddie stared at Rosedale.

'Seriously?'

'Seriously.'

A wide smile crossed Maddie's face. 'I think he was robbed.'

63

'Donald?'

'Speaking.'

'It's John Woods.'

Donald Parker used his tongue to push a piece of white bread to one side of his mouth. 'I have to admit this is an honour and a first, I don't usually get a call from the president of the United States when I'm tucking into a meatloaf sandwich. It's good you caught me, I'm due to fly out of town on some business this evening. Hence the rushed breakfast-cum-lunch-cum-dinner.'

Woods mouthed a silent *thank you* to Joan, as she placed a cup of coffee on his desk in front of him and he continued to fiddle with his red fountain pen, spinning it round between his fingers until it dropped on the floor. 'Well I hate to come between a man and his meatloaf, so I'll make this quick. I just wanted to call you personally to say this administration is excited to be part of such an innovative campaign. I know you've spoken to Teddy and my team since we made the decision, but I was going over some paperwork and what you've done in the DRC, well, it's really very impressive. Especially what you've done with Lemon water treatment. Exceptional, in fact. It shows such an altruistic responsibility. A real social conscience rather than just business acumen. Making a difference to the community is why I got into politics in the first place. You should be very proud of everything you've done and I look forward to being part of it.'

At which point Parker swallowed the piece of sandwich, and said, 'Thank you, Mr. President. I appreciate you taking time out of your schedule to make this call.'

'Well I feel it's important to support anything which puts us as a nation in the right direction. And clearly supporting conflict free products does just that.'

'As well as giving you your votes for the reforms.'

Woods wasn't quite sure why Parker's choice of words made him feel a little uneasy. A little like he was heading to sit in someone's pocket. But he carried on. 'And this administration appreciates your support. Anyhow, all the details, my team are working on at the moment and we should have a strategy put together pretty soon which, once you see it, I'm sure you'll approve of. Then as agreed we'll be making a press announcement.'

'Mr. President, I hope this doesn't sound too presumptuous. But I think you're doing the right thing.'

Woods bent down to pick up his red fountain pen. Took a sip of his coffee. 'You know something Parker, I think I am.'

64

With the morning sun rubbed out by the rain, the trio stood under the part of the hut's roof which still remained intact.

Maddie watched with some distaste as Rosedale enthusiastically poured some bottled water into a pouch of freeze-dried food to reconstitute the meal.

'You really like that stuff don't you? I hate it.'

With rain dripping off his cowboy hat, he grinned. 'It's not bad, you should eat yours up quick before Mr. Hungry Monster eats yours as well.'

She laughed. Scratched at the multitude of insect bites on her arm. 'You mean you? You're welcome to it. Here have it.'

'Nope, not me… look at Thomas, he's almost salivating for yours, ain't that right, boy?'

Cooper answered cordially but he was struggling. Struggling even to put one word in front of another. 'I'm with Maddie on this one. It's hardly Manny's Deli, is it?'

Maddie glanced at Rosedale who'd just finished sucking a large amount of the food pouch into his mouth. She reached out and tenderly wiped his face. 'You had some on your chin… What flavor's that anyway?'

Rosedale looked at her. Held her gentle stare before realising he'd held it too long and pulled away. Unused to the sense of fluster, he looked down at the nameless silver pouch which Granger sourced directly from one of his colleagues, a research scientist at NASA. He looked up and pretended what had just happened hadn't and as if judging a gourmet meal, he said, 'I'm not sure…I'm thinking beef lasagne but I'm tasting parsley.'

Cooper's thoughts were elsewhere, and he was aware his speech was slower than usual. 'Do you think this Bemba guy is for real? Do you think he believed her grandson had been possessed?'

Rosedale said, 'What do you think? The man's a charlatan if there ever was one. Praying on traditional beliefs for gain. Remember it was only after you'd told Zola that you'd been sent by the spirits to help her that she really began to trust you. So if *you* can manipulate her beliefs, think what a guy like Bemba can do to the whole community.'

'And just for greed?'

'I reckon. That's what makes the world go round.'

'And maybe for power as well,' suggested Maddie. 'Money and power. That reliable cliché.'

Cooper sighed. 'I can't believe she gave him her land for the exchange when a trip to hospital might've saved him.'

'Yeah but Tom, think about it. We're miles from anywhere and your core belief is the spirit world. And now it looks like your grandson is possessed by Kindoki and you think Bemba will free him of it and make him well again. Wouldn't you give him your land for that? I would. My land. My house. Anything to make it okay again.'

'You weren't this understanding last night.'

Maddie glanced at Rosedale who gave her a reassuring, encouraging smile. 'I'm not saying it's right. I'm saying that's what she believes. And it's complicated for me. In principal I respect and understand it but in actuality, I abhor it. Hate it. Especially how over the years it's morphed into a base for abuse and turned into some lucrative business. It's hard…'

Maddie trailed off as Cooper waved to greet Zola who'd been sleeping in the other hut.

'Hey! Good morning. I don't know if you're hungry, but we've got some freeze-dried food if you want. Sorry, it's not great but we didn't want to light a fire and cook anything in case the smoke attracted attention.'

Cooper passed Zola one of the pouches which she didn't even bother taking. Looked at it with as much disgust as Maddie had hers.

Not bothering to try to sell the idea of reconstituted food to Zola, Cooper told her their plans.

'We're going to leave you here for a while, and perhaps later you could show us where this land of yours is, would that be okay?'

She nodded without saying anything.

'We're not sure how long we'll be. We're going to go down to the water treatment plant which is about ten miles or so from here.'

Zola's face blanched. Didn't go unnoticed by any of them. A look of fear came into her eyes. And speaking quietly Cooper took hold of her hands which were shaking. 'Are you alright? What's going on, Zola?'

Zola glanced from Maddie, who didn't meet her gaze, to Rosedale, before leaning in to Cooper. Then speaking in a hush as if someone else was listening, she said, 'Emmanuel said it was a bad place.'

Cooper frowned. Saw how genuinely frightened she looked. 'Why?'

'They say the evil came from the sky. Black clouds of evil… And he saw *them*.'

'Who? Who did Emmanuel see?'

'He saw the undead.'

65

For most of the drive Cooper stayed silent. He was hoping that whatever it was he was missing would jump out at him. He could feel there was something else. Something far bigger which would help him make sense of it all. And he didn't know how he was supposed to go about *looking beyond,* when he didn't know what he was supposed to be seeing in the first place. It didn't help that his thoughts were foggy. He seemed to be spending his days looking out into some kind of blur. And as such he sighed. Real long. Real hard. Checked neither Rosedale nor Maddie was looking and took out a couple more pills to try to straighten himself out.

'A nickel for them.' It was Rosedale.

Cooper made an effort to sound cheerful. The last thing he needed was for Rosedale to be on his case again. 'Not even a dollar? Anyone tell you you're cheap, Rosedale?'

Rosedale, turning off down the now-familiar track towards the Lemon water treatment plant, winked. 'You're lucky it was even a nickel. I don't think your thoughts are worth more than that. Whatever goes on in that head of yours Thomas, it sure ain't worth a buck.'

Cooper rubbed his eyes. Tired from being awake most of the night. 'Let's see, shall we?'

'Go on, try me. I'll raise you five.'

Cooper gave Rosedale his best effort. Grinned at Maddie. 'Okay, what we've got is a plane registered to a guy,

Emmanuel. A plane we know he couldn't afford. Probably someone bankrolled his account so he could put it in his name. And now he seems to have disappeared off the face of the earth, although we *do* know he's been part of a deliverance. We know somehow Papa Bemba's involved. We also know Emmanuel has visited Lemon, twice, but both times under different names. But what we *don't* know is who the other person was who went with him. Then there's Zola, who lost her grandson, and although Bemba said he would heal him and couldn't or didn't, Bemba still did pretty damn well out of it. She seems to be terrified of Lemon which Emmanuel had warned her about, and then lastly there's good ol' Charles Templin-Wright, who says he only knows Bemba from the posters dotted around the area, *yet* he's driving his car around. The same car we saw the night in the forest with the Commer truck... Go figure.'

Cooper turned to Rosedale as they pulled up outside the large electric gates of Lemon. 'Now tell me *those* thoughts aren't worth a dollar.'

Rosedale nodded his head. Turned off the engine. Looked at Cooper. 'You're right, they aren't. Not even close, sugar... Come on, Maddison, let's go, unless of course you want to wait for boy wonder here.'

66

'Oh, okay, hold on.'

Charles Templin-Wright sounded surprised and a little ill at ease. The buzzer opened and the large electric gates opened gracefully. But this time, with the rain having ceased and wanting to get a different perspective on the place, Rosedale, Maddie and Cooper decided to walk down the long drive to the reception of the water treatment plant.

Two hundred yards or so from the large stone fountain, where a rainbow of colored flowers grew, a large Land Cruiser drove past at speed. And Cooper was able to get a quick glance.

The car was driven by a large, dark skinned black man, who appeared overheated, dressed in a full chauffeur's uniform that was a size too small. In the back was a leaner looking guy.

White.

Tanned.

Gray haired and well-dressed, in a weather cool expensive crisp white shirt.

Cooper made a mental note and waved a greeting to Charles who was already outside waiting for them. He waved back. Grinned widely. But unlike the first time they'd come, Cooper sensed Charles wasn't feeling quite as gregarious and quite as sociable as he was trying to make out.

'Can't stay away huh guys? Is my tour of the water plant so alluring you're coming back for more?'

Rosedale answered frostily. 'Yeah something like that.'

Charles attempted another wide smile but as it didn't hit his eyes, Cooper thought the result seemed manic.

Failing to get the response he wanted, Charles swivelled to a friendlier looking face than Rosedale's or Cooper's.

'Maddie, good to see you. You're looking so much better after your ordeal. I would've thought you guys would've been well on your way by now, get on the road again as it were. Not exactly Route 66, but we do our best.'

Maddie said nothing and Charles's laughter was a lone sound. Trickled off self-consciously. And Cooper wasn't interested in chit-chat. Not one bit. Not from this guy.

'Where's the best place to talk?'

Clapping his hands, which sounded muted due to his excessively sweating palms, Charles turned back towards reception. 'Okay, well… er, why don't we step inside? You can't beat a bit of air conditioning… and I must say I'm intrigued as to why you're here.'

Inside, the temperature was as refreshing as Cooper had remembered it. Reminding him of Joey's Ice Cream Parlour. A place he liked to visit with Cora if he was ever in Denver. It not only sold the best peanut butter ice cream, but when the scorching hot weather rose to one hundred degrees Fahrenheit, stepping inside the small establishment to be hit with a blast of cold relief was like meeting an old friend.

'Let me get straight to the point, Charles, I'm looking to find out about Papa Bemba.'

'Yes, you said.'

Cooper nodded. Rolled his tongue on his front teeth. His tone purposely condescending.

302

'Yes, *yes* I did, Charles, and I also remember what you said.'

Charles's small eyes narrowed even further. He glared at Cooper, taking exception as Cooper assumed he would to the tone he'd used.

'And I remember what I said too. Maybe you'd like me to repeat it. I told you that being in the area and seeing the billboards around which advertised his church made me aware of him.'

'That's right, so at least we're on agreement on something. What we're not in agreement on though, *Charles*, is you saying you don't know him.'

Charles's voice was tight. 'That's right, I don't.'

'Okay,' said Maddie. 'You see the thing is, this is where we have a problem or rather *you* have a problem. Because my friends and I want to know how it comes about that someone who doesn't know Bemba ends up driving his car?'

Charles's discomfort turned his face crimson. He dabbed it with the silk handkerchief he pulled out of his pocket. Then began to stutter, reminding Cooper of the cartoon character, Porky Pig.

'I... I... I don't... don't know. Let me think. The car I was driving, when?'

With exaggerated boredom, Cooper said, 'When we saw you in the village with Maddie.'

Charles became animated. 'Oh yes, sorry I forgot. That car was a...'

Cooper shook his head and interrupted. 'Rental? Nope. Don't say it. We both know you can't hire a car like that around here, and besides, the plates on the car were exactly the same as the car Bemba was in back in Kinshasa... So what do ya say? Shall we start again Mr. Templin-Wright?

How about I ask you the question again, *do you know Papa Bemba*, and then you start telling us the truth.'

Charles looked at the watch he wasn't wearing. 'Look, I've spent more time with you then I was supposed to. I've got an important meeting, so if you don't mind.'

Cooper took a step nearer to Charles. 'Not to be too much of a cliché, I do mind. I mind very much and I have a feeling that Maddie and Rosedale here, they mind too.'

Tipping his hat, Rosedale's gaze was hard and steely. 'You can bet your life I mind, *Charles*.'

'Hey Charles, and FYI, so do I,' added Maddie.

Bending to the pressure, Charles blustered. 'It was a friend's. Yes, I've just remembered, stupid me, maybe, perhaps, he borrowed it from this Bemba guy. I've no idea.'

Cooper scoffed. He'd been on edge but this felt like his perfect tonic. He poked Charles hard in the chest with two fingers. And hell, that was good. 'Now I'd say that was pretty convenient for you to suddenly have a friend who'd borrowed the car from Bemba. I don't suppose you could give me the name of this friend could you? Or has that slipped your memory?'

'I couldn't possibly just go around telling you the name of my friends.'

Cooper sneered. Bent down to his eye level. Winked. 'One last question, Charles. Who's Emmanuel Mutombo?'

'I don't know.'

Maddie said, 'You don't know or you won't say? What do you think, Tom?'

'I think that's all… For now. Thanks for your time.'

He paused, pointing at half a dozen large brown vases sitting upside down on the floor near the desk. 'Nice vases by the way.'

Charles's smile was tight. 'They're not actually vases. Just ornaments really. We commission local artisans to make things. It's better to support the community and buy things here rather than buy things in the States and get them shipped over. We've just had a bit of an overhaul. New décor, so why not have some new ornaments as well.'

Cooper stared at Charles coldly. 'Why not indeed.'

67

From the second floor window, Charles Templin-Wright watched Cooper, Maddie and Rosedale walk away. And picking up the phone on his desk, he dialled a number.

He said, 'It's me. We've got a problem.'

68

'What was that about the vases back there, Tom?' Maddie shouted from the back seat over the noisy engine of the white Toyota, which she'd become oddly fond of, as it picked up speed on a surprisingly accessible part of the road.

Cooper gazed out of the window, watching but not really seeing the passing countryside. He sighed. Yawned. Sighed some more. 'I don't know yet, though I…'

'Oh hell,' said Rosedale. 'Looks like we've got company… Look.'

Three cream Land Rovers were parked and spread across the entire width of the road. Cooper leant forward, staring intently at the men sitting in the vehicles. 'Holy crap, I think they're armed!'

Rosedale crunched the Toyota into reverse, spinning it round in a spray of mud as Cooper scrabbled over to the back passenger seat and Maddie rummaged in the bottom of one of the large canvas bags, pulling out two Colt M4 Carbines, one of which she passed to Cooper. The car weaved and snaked and threw them around and across the seat as it went at speed over the rough terrain.

Hammering the vehicle with his foot fully down on the gas, Rosedale yelled. 'How close Maddie?'

'Fifty foot and closing!'

A smell of burning tyres and engine fumes billowed into the open windows of the Toyota.

'Hold on, guys!' Rosedale span the wheel and a tight turn sent the car off the road, his expert driving crashing them through the thick vegetation. Careering and swaying and dipping and hurtling them along into the dense undergrowth.

Directly in front of them there was a line of trees and for a split second Cooper thought Rosedale was going to hit them straight on, but the brakes slammed, throwing Maddie to the floor.

She scrabbled back up as Rosedale wheelspun the Toyota and cranked it into a speeding reverse, sending mud flying everywhere. Covering the windows. Partially blocking the view.

Cooper shouted. 'They're shooting!'

Flicking the safety catch off the M4, Maddie ducked down as the back window exploded. Shattering and sending tiny fragments of glass ricocheting around the inside of the car. And the bullets continued to fly with Rosedale swerving along at speed. Faster and furious and driving through.

Leaning out of the window, hanging onto the grab handle, Maddie could see Rosedale was trying to head back to the road. She started to shoot. Felt the kickback from the gun pummelling her shoulder as Cooper fired shots out of the other window.

With no warning the Toyota violently jolted, nearly sending Cooper flying out of the window as the tyre struck something hard, making the SUV come to a stop.

With the tyre spinning round, Maddie and Cooper jumped out either side, shielding themselves with the doors.

Suddenly, Cooper shouted 'My gun's jammed…! Maddie!'

'Get back in the car, I'll cover you… Go!'

As Cooper raced for the car, Maddie continued to pump out bullets at the approaching cars, whilst Rosedale banged his foot on the gas, pushing the gears back and forth and willing the Toyota to move.

Covered and soaking wet from the shower of mud coming from the tyres, Maddie sprayed one of the oncoming Land Rovers with a round of bullets. The front tyres blew, sending it out of control. It veered off course and hit a low, twisted tree, which flung it high in the air where it twisted round and came down in an explosion of flames.

'Maddie! Get in…! Maddie!'

Rosedale leant out of the window, gesturing to her as the car became unstuck from the rocky hole.

And running backwards, Maddie fired at the other Land Rovers coming into view. She ran faster, shouting at Rosedale. 'Go! Go! Go!'

Maddie scrabbled and stumbled before jumping onto the car's running board and throwing herself in as Rosedale accelerated, driving through the twisted trunks of the banana trees to put them back onto the road.

Meanwhile Cooper had exchanged the jammed Colt for a Barrett 82A1 shoulder fired semi-automatic .50 calibre rifle, which he pointed out of the window, expecting any minute to see the Land Rovers coming into view. Holding tight. Holding tense. Scanning the bushes.

After a minute, he said, 'I guess we've lost them! Way to go, Rosedale… Way to go, Maddie. Sorry, guys, my gun totally screwed up… You okay, Maddie?'

Maddie sat clutching the top of her shoulder. Calmly she said, 'Yeah, I think I may have been hit.'

'Is she okay? Is she okay? Have a look… Thomas! Have a look!' Unusually, Rosedale sounded as if he'd lost his cool as he tried to drive and turn and look round.

'Okay, Rosedale! Keep your eyes on the road. I'm looking!'

Cooper quickly tore at the top of Maddie's shirt to get to the wound. Seeing that it was just a superficial one, he smiled. Surprised at how relived he felt. 'Yeah, she's okay. She'll live. It's not a bullet. It's from the back window.'

Very gently but firmly, Cooper pulled out a large splintered piece of glass which was deeply imbedded into Maddie's shoulder. She gritted her teeth and tried not to wince at the sharp pain and looked at him with a smile, wide eyed. Made him feel bad at the way he'd been treating her. He pushed that thought away.

'Who do you think they were? Local Militia?'

Cooper shook his head. 'No, they were definitely something to do with Bemba, I saw Lumumba.'

'Who?'

'The guy with the suit. The one from the church. He was in one of the Land Rovers. I also have a real hunch this was something to do with Charles.'

'You think so?'

'I know so. There's no way it's just a coincidence that on the day we go and put a little pressure on him, twenty minutes after we leave we have Bemba's men out in force.'

'Are you sure it was Lumumba? Because it's not altogether safe for travelers here. East DRC is pretty precarious. We've been lucky until now. But let's be honest, it isn't Santa Monica.'

'My aunt got mugged in Santa Monica. Walking on Ocean Avenue. Took everything, even her cat.'

'Her cat?'

'Yeah, she had it in her bag.'

'Shut up Rosedale,' snapped Maddie. 'You know what I mean.'

Rosedale looked at her in the driver's mirror. 'Just saying it can happen anywhere.'

'Being mugged?'

Rosedale looked at her solemnly. 'No, a cat in a bag.'

'Seriously. Shut up.'

'Whatever you say. Although I hate to admit it, Maddison, but on this, I reckon Thomas is finally talking sense. I also reckon our Mr. Templin-Wright is neck deep in whatever's going on.'

69

It was a couple of hours later. Cooper sat in the back of the Toyota with Zola. He wanted her to show him the stretch of land she'd signed over to Bemba.

He smiled at her. She looked nervous. They hadn't said much on the journey, they'd just sat listening to the clear plastic sheet which now sat in place of the rear windscreen, giving off a loud snapping sound as it billowed in the driving breeze.

'The only good thing about having no window is finally this piece of junk has some air conditioning... Are you okay, Zola?'

She nodded. Clasping her hands on her lap. And Cooper turned to watch out the window, noting in his head the landmarks Zola had described to help direct them.

The fallen eucalyptus tree at the bend of the river.

The burnt out car entwined with spider grass.

The large clearing by the white hut, giving a sight of the distant Rwandan mountains.

'I think this could be it Rosedale, but be careful. I'm not certain but I have a feeling we might've been followed.'

'By the red motorcycle?'

'Yeah, you saw it as well?'

'I was watching it for a while, but I think it might've been nothing.'

Cooper glanced round. 'Well, let's hope so.'

Rosedale put his foot on the brake. Slowed down and came to an eventual stop by the side of a dense forest. Zola nodded.

'Oui, nous sommes ici. It's through the other side.'

'Unless it's too difficult to walk, would you mind coming with us and showing us?' asked Rosedale.

Shaking her head emphatically, and with fear coming into her eyes once more, Zola whispered, 'This is not good land. It's where the souls of the dead used to walk and where evil rained down from the sky.'

'Is that why people don't come here?'

'Oui. That's why no-one lives here. The Kindoki here is too strong to expel it. No deliverance had the power to rid the place of it.'

'Does everyone believe that, Zola?'

'Of course, no-one wants to be here in case the Kindoki begins to live inside them.'

Wanting to have clarity, Cooper said, 'How does it? How does the Kindoki take over?'

'You saw my grandson.'

Cooper's mind began to tick over. 'And he was here? Is that where he got ill?'

'No, but it's where most of them got ill.'

Maddie, who hadn't spoken to Zola properly since her outburst, gently said, 'Can you tell me more, Zola, so I can understand properly… perhaps I'll be able to help you.'

Zola's lips pursed, her body becoming slightly more rigid. 'No, I've said too much already.'

*

Having left Zola with Maddie back in the car to keep a watch, Rosedale and Cooper made their way along a path

313

through the trees. Cooper didn't say anything. And neither did Rosedale. They were trying to reserve what little strength they had to tackle the humidity of the day along with the biting insects which attacked unforgivingly.

Lighting a cigarette, Cooper offered one to Rosedale who declined. 'You think you should be smoking that, Thomas? Smoke and the smell of tobacco, not exactly clandestine is it?'

Cooper knew Rosedale was right. He wasn't thinking. Not straight anyway. Put out his cigarette without resentment. Followed Rosedale into the vast open space just in front of them.

Heading up the steep grass, Rosedale – clad in a bright orange Tahitian shirt and blue jeans topped off with a Cowboy boots and hat, which Cooper thought was even less covert than his cigarette – called down to him as he got to the top.

'Looks like there's a whole heap of nothing here, Thomas. Grass, grass and hell, what d'ya know? More grass.'

Coming up alongside him, Cooper glanced around. Rosedale was right. There was nothing. Literally. Unless of course you counted the grass. He slapped his leg hard. 'Jeez, these damn insects are driving me crazy. Don't you get bitten, Rosedale?'

Rosedale spoke slowly, his drawl as always emphasizing his words. 'That I do, boy, my blood is just as sweet, if not sweeter than yours. Only difference here though is you complain like a billy goat who's lost their momma... Come on, don't look like there's a damn thing here.'

Bending down to pull up his jeans to scratch his leg, Cooper noticed a piece of porcelain pot. It was identical to the glazed piece he'd found back at the huts. It even had the same thin, tiny piece of copper wire embedded in it. Picked it up. Had a suspicion this might be different to the usual pieces of *nothing much* he collected. But then, he also had a suspicion that that was what he always thought.

70

'Where to, cowboy?' Cooper winked at Rosedale as they sat in the car.

'Well I reckon we should keep on driving along the road, see what's there. What do you say, Miss Maddison? Fancy a ride?'

'I'm good for it.'

'And you Miss Zola, are you okay?'

Zola looked at Rosedale. She didn't answer but gave a small smile.

To which Rosedale said, 'Alright-ee, let's go.'

Two miles down the road, Rosedale whistled as they passed a large rusting billboard of Bemba with the words, *Drive Them Out*, emblazed across the bottom of it. Maddie said, 'I have to give it to him, the man knows how to pull in the crowds. Hey, look over there.' She pointed to a low level fence which ran along a well-built track. It curved into a steep descent, prohibiting their view. 'Shall we?'

Rosedale turned the Toyota down the long red track.

The road was smooth and well fenced. Machinery, trucks and American haulage vehicles lined up against freshly excavated mounds of earth.

Rosedale drove the Toyota slowly along, driving up near the gates at the end which were manned with uniformed guards. Cooper instinctively reached for his gun from the side door compartment. 'What do you think? Shall we turn round?'

Rosedale, weighing up the situation, took a second to answer. 'No, they've seen us now, let's find out what's here but stay ready just in case. And Thomas. Keep that hidden.' He gestured to the hand gun. 'Oh, and this time, Thomas, try to keep your head.'

Maddie leant out of her window. 'Hi! I was wondering if you could help?'

A tall, light-skinned man who'd been overzealous on the aftershave walked up to the car. His face stern but not aggressive. With a curt British accent and holding a clipboard tightly to his body, he said, 'Look, we've already had our inspection.'

Cooper frowned, puzzled. Gave them one of his biggest smile. The kind he usually kept for his elderly neighbors back in Colorado. Then, noticing how much it ached the sides of his face, he toned it down a little. 'Excuse me?'

The over-perfumed man became irritated, blending typical British sarcasm into his words.

'Oh I'm sorry, I didn't know I was speaking quietly. Let me spell it out to you: maybe if your company was more organized, you wouldn't be troubled and I wouldn't be bothered by your pointless trip.'

Cooper thought he must have looked bemused; he certainly felt it. 'I can hear you real clearly, but I don't understand you.'

'I don't know how much more plain I can get,' said the man with the clipboard. 'We had our inspection about four months ago... I take it you're from the Bradadt Mining Inspection and Audit Company?'

Cooper nodded, letting the man continue to talk.

'Well then you, or whoever it is that's in charge, should've

317

known that your colleague, Dr. Foster, judged this mine and the other Condor Atlantic mine as being conflict free. We've got our certificate already. So this unscheduled visit is entirely inappropriate and you can tell your company from me that…'

Rosedale began to reverse. Left the man with the clip board to continue the conversation by himself.

Back on the main road, Rosedale said, 'The British are so uptight. Did you hear how that guy spoke? I thought he was going to have a coronary. *We've already had our inspection.*'

'That's such a bad attempt at a British accent,' said Maddie. 'You sound like Dick Van Dyke.'

'Let's hear you do better. Or better still, Thomas.'

Cooper wasn't sure why he felt better, but he did. Perhaps it was just a case of feeling less tired than he had done that morning. Or perhaps it was the couple of Xanax as well as the OxyContin he'd taken about twenty minutes ago. He cleared his throat. Felt pretty good. 'Okay, so here's how a British accent should sound… Fancy a cup o' tea? More milk, sir?'

Maddie and Rosedale both burst out laughing, but it was Rosedale who said, 'You sound like you've got something stuck up your ass, Thomas, leave the accents to those that know.'

'I take it you mean you.'

'If the cap fits.'

Maddie said, 'Well even if your British accents aren't up to scratch, at least we learnt a bit and got a name. What do you think? Maybe it'd be good to speak to this Dr. Foster if we could? Maybe I'll call Levi to do some digging. Who knows, maybe this doctor's seen or knows something?'

'Like what?' asked Rosedale.

'Well, if he's been around these parts inspecting the area, which he'd have to do to give certification for the mines to be conflict free, then maybe he's seen Bemba about, or perhaps seen more of this illness which Zola's grandson had. I don't know, it just seems like it may be good to talk to him.'

Cooper agreed. 'I second you on that. It's definitely worth a try. It was good to hear the mine was conflict free. But God knows how it is.'

Rosedale chipped in. 'You mean, God knows how the militia aren't crawling all over the mine. It's not the usual, is it? You'd expect the militia to be guarding the gate rather than some British guy… Look, guys, are you sure you're up for this? You know I'm all for doing what we have to do, but maybe we should start calling this a day. I mean our job from Onyx, from Granger was just *to find the plane*. We've tried, and we've tried hard. Nobody's going to lose out if we go back with empty hands. Emmanuel's bank loan can be written off against losses. I know it's not ideal, and we pride ourselves on doing the job, but let's face it, this isn't the job Granger sent us to do.'

'This is exactly it,' said Cooper.

'It doesn't have to be. Not every high asset recovery firm would go to this length. They'd take the easy option and get the banks to write it off on insurance or losses.'

'But that's why we're the best… You want out, Rosedale?'

'Not yet, I'm just making sure you know what you're doing, Thomas, because sometimes I wonder.'

'Pull over!' Cooper shouted, causing Rosedale to slam on the brakes.

'Back up a bit, Rosedale. I just saw something… Right there.'

Cooper peered across the road, seeing in the distance row upon row of white tents.

'What the hell's that?'

'The camp.'

Everyone turned to Zola who'd spoken quietly from the back.

Maddie said, 'Quel camp, Zola?'

'Ce est le camp de refugees.'

'A refugee camp?'

'Oui.'

They stared. Hearts all dropping as they looked at the sea of squalor. The desperate conditions the refugees were forced to live in. Even from a distance they could see the multiple piles of rubbish and raw filth piled high to rot in the scorching sun.

'Look!' Cooper nudged Rosedale. 'By the entrance. Coming up. It's the Commer truck we saw.'

'You want me to follow it?'

'Rosedale, I think you already know the answer to that one.'

71

'Well, would you look at that,' Rosedale commented as he watched the truck drive through the gates of the Lemon water treatment plant.

'This gets stranger.'

'It sure does, Maddison.'

Rosedale asked Cooper, 'You want to wait here and see where they go afterwards?'

'No, I think it's best we get back to the hideout. We all need to get some sleep, especially Zola. It's been a heavy day all round.'

'I think we should go back the long way though,' said Maddie. 'I know it'll add another forty minutes on our journey but I saw that motorcycle again. The red one.'

'You sure?'

'I think so, it may be nothing, but…'

Rosedale said, 'Better to be safe, hey?'

'Exactly.'

72

A couple of hours later, Cooper could once again hear the resounding snores of Rosedale. They'd decided to all sleep in the same hut, rather than scatter around. It was safer. Though it was a hell of a noise.

He stood in the darkness, looking up at the sky. Couldn't sleep, and not just because of Rosedale. He couldn't sleep because that was who he was. Or rather that was someone he'd become.

Insomnia was his bugbear. A bit like his Uncle Beau's sciatica was his. It wasn't just pharmaceutically led. It was the dreams. The flashbacks. The images which played in his head and kept him awake. And then in the morning the crippling tiredness which meant the exhaustion made it impossible to fight away thoughts. Bad memories he spent most of his life trying to avoid. Unless he had something to take away the edge, that was.

Quietly, he walked towards the trees. The area was inexplicably beautiful. In different circumstances there was something to be said about this true kind of isolation. The feel of the place was unique with the eerily primitive sounds of the forest and the almost prehistoric size of the trees and plants.

A noise made him break away from his thoughts and in a fluid unbroken movement, he pulled out his gun from his back holster and swivelled around to where the sound was coming from. 'Zola…! Jesus! You gave me a fright. You okay?'

'Yes, but your friend grunts loudly, though it gives me a chance to talk to my grandson. I can feel him here…' Her smile was radiant but her face turned suddenly serious. 'Why did you say I gave you a fright? Are you afraid the evil from the land we visited today has come here? To me?'

'No! Hell no… I thought you were someone else.'

'You didn't feel it was me?'

Cooper slipped his gun back, fascinated by the level of scrutiny Zola put on his words.

'No, I guess I didn't.'

She gave a half smile. 'You need to feel more, I think that's your problem, Thomas.'

Cooper couldn't help but laugh. It was the first time he'd heard Zola say his name, and the way she said it, with the drawl and emphasis on the *Tom*, it was clear she'd picked that up from Rosedale. 'I think I've done my fair share of feeling Zola, I'd rather give any more of that kind of stuff a miss.'

Zola scowled. 'Échapper à la vie?'

Cooper exhaled. 'Am I escaping life? Wow, you don't pull any punches do you?'

'Que voulez-vous dire?'

'What I mean is, I wasn't expecting you to be so straight. I guess I should've done, because it seems to be a *thing* with women to want to talk about feelings. Anytime. Anyplace. And hey, who am I to think standing in the middle of a Congolese forest, hiding from a variety of things, should be any different?'

Cooper winked as he pulled the shawl Maddie had given her around her shoulders.

Zola tilted her head to one side. 'You've lost someone too?'

It sounded like both a question and a statement. It also made Cooper feel uncomfortable.

He looked down at the ground. Kicked at nothing particular. Everything in him needed to avoid Zola's intense gaze because *now* he was beginning to feel. Feeling something he didn't want to. And there was nothing he could do to put the lid back on once it had been opened.

'I dunno... it's a long story, something I'd rather not get into.'

Cooper glanced up in time to see Zola give him a sad, almost pitiful look. 'You're already in it Thomas. You're running from yourself, but you can't. C'est impossible. You'll always be you. Tu ne peux pas t'en échapper.'

Cooper knew he sounded defensive. But she just needed to stop. Hell, this wasn't her concern.

'Look, Zola, I'm not running from myself. I'm just...'

'When did they die?'

It flicked a switch in him. He raised his voice. He didn't care. 'She isn't dead, okay! I just don't know where she is... not yet... I don't know... Maybe she is. That's what everyone thinks. Listen, Zola, I don't want to sound disrespectful especially after you've been so helpful, but I'm not real good at talking about her.'

'Why?'

He felt he should've said,

It's none of your business,

Get off my back.

Instead he said, 'It hurts.'

Zola nodded, looking like she understood. 'Have you seen her?'

'In what way?'

'Have you seen her walking with you since you lost her?'

It sounded crazy but he knew exactly what she meant. 'A long time ago when I was still searching for her. I used

324

to *think* I saw her. I saw her everywhere. In a bar. In a mall. At the movie-house. But not now.'

'Do you see her anywhere else?'

'My dreams. But I never see her face, not really, and the dreams aren't exactly great if you know what I mean. It's more like a constant reminder of what I did wrong.'

'Would you like to see her?'

'I don't even have the words for what I'd give for that, Zola. Just to see her again. Even once... I...' He stopped. Breathed deeply. Felt the emotion well up. Began to floor him.

'I can make you see her. I can help you do that.'

Cooper was stuck for words. But not for emotions. They came charging at him like a bull in a rodeo. Offended. Surprised. Angry. But most of all he was intrigued. 'See her how?'

'There's a root we eat. A root which allows us to see our ancestors and the ones lost to us.'

Cooper didn't say anything for a moment. He guessed she was talking about the Iboga root, which he knew was used in the DRC for visionary and hallucinogenic experiences. He'd heard it was often consumed in ceremonies for contacting the spirits of the ancestors, or providing a way to experience the journey to the other side. Giving the ability to communicate with the dead. The other thing he'd heard about the Iboga root was that it had a reputation of working on the specific. Almost individualized by the problems you had.

'I don't know.'

Zola tentatively took his hand. 'It will help you... Come on.'

Switching on the pocket torch, Cooper walked with Zola

along the path. Past the burnt out hut of Emmanuel's and along into the deep undergrowth.

'Have you a knife?'

Cooper pulled up the leg of his pants. Attached to his calf was a drop leg holster inside which was an Ontario ASEK survival knife He smiled to see Zola nodding in approval.

Then kneeling down next to several shrubs, with small green leaves and delicate white flowers, Zola began to pull at one of the plant's roots. Exerting so much strength, her face twisted with the effort.

'Let me do that.'

Cooper crouched down and with minimum struggle, pulled out the whole plant.

'Brush the earth off the root… Bon. Now you don't want the wood or the first layer of the bark, those parts you cannot eat. You need to use your knife to peel down to the second layer of the root… Oui, that's it… Not too deep. Scrape, not dig… Juste un peu. C'est tout.'

He used the side of the sharp blade. Followed her instructions carefully. Shaved off the bark to the wispy second layer which curled into strips and dropped into his lap.

Zola took the shaved root. Peering and examining them so closely he felt like he was in a high school woodwork exam.

'C'est ça. This will a good plant, and it'll be enough for you to see. Quel-est son prénom?'

'Ellie. Her name's Ellie.'

'Now you must go to her. It's time. Chew it. She's waiting for you.'

Cooper gazed into the old woman's large almond eyes, which seemed to hold a combination of wisdom and naivety.

'I'm not sure… I…'

'Are you scared?'

He ran his fingers through his mop of strawberry blond hair. Ill at ease. Jesus, he felt embarrassed. Scared wasn't a word he wanted to associate himself with.

'No, of course not, Zola, why would I be scared? I've been a military man, a Navy SEAL, served my country, been on the front line, flown planes, you name it, scared isn't in my vocabulary.'

'Those things are things that you *do*, they aren't who you are, not what you feel, here, inside.'

They both fell silent.

And Cooper ran his eyes around the darkness of the night. 'Okay, yeah… yeah I'm scared. I'm scared to see her. Maybe she'll hate me for what I did. I couldn't take that. Or maybe she'll not want to talk to me. I dunno, but… This is difficult to say, but the biggest thing I'm scared of, Zola, is tomorrow. When it's all over, when I have to let her go again. When I've lost her all over again… I don't know if I can do that.'

Once more, Zola took his hands. 'But you won't let her go, you've never let her go have you? She's with you all the time, but let her in properly or she'll keep on hurting you. Stop trying to keep her away. You won't even sleep in case she comes to you in your dreams. And she wants to. Crois-moi.'

Cooper buried his face in his hands, his body moving with silent racking sobs.

Zola stood up and waited patiently for him to calm down as he wiped his face on his sleeve. Smiling and taking the strips of root from Zola, he said, 'I'm ready.'

'Then I'll leave you on your own with her.'

She turned to walk away.

'Zola, stop! I never asked you your grandson's name.'

'Laurent. His name was Laurent and he was a good boy.'

'I'm sure he was, I have no doubt about it at all… and Zola, thank you.'

'Don't thank me, this is our exchange. Your ancestors helped to save me and now mine are helping to save you. It is the spirits we both should thank.'

Twenty-five minutes after Zola had gone, and having consumed the bitter tasting Iboga root, and having vomited twice, and wondering if he'd done the right thing, Cooper sat staring so intently at the tree, with his eyes stretched so open wide, they began to hurt.

He watched, certain a strong wind was getting up under the tree's branches but then, slowly, little by little, the bark of the tree started to change into a ripple of colors. Moving with grace along the ground.

Greens and blues. Visions spectacular. A fountain of pinks and gold, dancing round like magical raindrops falling from the moon which covered him with light. Grass growing so high he couldn't see where it ended, and water covering the floor which he didn't fall through.

He stretched out his arms straight in front of him. Felt the heavy weight of nothing. He looked along his arm and followed the dancing beams to his hands, and from his hands to the tips of his fingers. From the tips of his fingers he touched someone else's hand.

'Ellie?'

'Yes, Tom, it's me… I'm here. You've found me.'

Cooper managed to open his eyes on the third attempt. But hell did it hurt. He rolled his tongue round his mouth, wanting to conjure up enough saliva to alleviate the sticky dryness. It didn't work. His head pounded like he'd just banged it against a hard surface and his sinuses shot out hot pain, the kind which made it excruciating to even breathe.

His thoughts seemed hazy. Mind numb. Blank with tiredness. And even to try to contemplate reflecting on the experience he'd had, or how he felt, seemed impossible. Nothing seemed real. Not where he was. Not who he was. Like he was in a suspended state.

He pushed his back up against the tree trunk. Tried to slide up onto his feet. Got stuck half way. And though he aware of the scraping bark against his back, he wasn't quite sure if it hurt or not.

Blew out heavily. Hoped to steady himself as well as to avoid being sick. Didn't work.

'Come on, come on.'

He spoke out loud. Or he thought he did. And with huge exhaustive effort, he wiped the vomit off his chin and began to stagger back along the path, stopping occasionally to bend over and vomit and rest his hands on his legs.

'Where the hell have you been?'

Rosedale stood by one of the huts. Hands on hips. Towel draped over the back of his neck.

At first Cooper thought his words weren't going to come. He cleared his throat. A groggy croak followed. 'Not now Rosedale.'

'Listen, Thomas, I need to talk to you. It's important.'

'I said, not now!'

He staggered against a tree. The sound of his own voice making him wince and knocking him sideward.

Maddie said, 'Jesus, Tom, are you okay? You look really ill.'

He stared at Maddie. Memories from last night beginning to rush through his mind like a time-lapse video. 'What...? Yeah... I'm fine.'

She reached to touch him, but he pulled away. Rubbed his head and was barely able to stand. 'Look, I said I'm fine... Don't fuss.'

Rosedale roared. 'Of course he's fine. He's just a class-A mess. What did you do, hey, Thomas? Took too many of your candy pills? Or maybe this is the cold turkey talking? You run out of them, is that it? Talk to me, boy!'

Maddie's concern touched both her face and her voice. 'Shut up, Rosedale...! What is it, Tom? What's happened?'

Cold sweat was running down Cooper's face. He stared at her. Double vision. 'Look, just leave me alone, okay... I'll be back later... soon, whatever.'

Cooper staggered off to the sound of Maddie and Rosedale calling after him.

'Tom...! Tom!'

'Thomas, we need to talk!'

Cooper stumbled away into the forest. Headed for the river at the bottom of the hill. He needed to refresh. To cool. To think. He looked round, remembering it'd only been a couple of days ago since he'd been carrying Zola up the hill but now, hell, he was struggling even to walk. Leaning on every tree.

Having to rest to close his eyes, only to begin to fall into a light sleep before jolting himself awake on losing his balance.

And with all energy sapped and drained and drawn out of him, it seemed to take forever to get to the river. And by the time he did, a film of cold clammy sweat sat unwelcome beneath his clothes.

Managing a half run. He closed his eyes. Fell onto his knees as if he was beset by a religious epiphany.

And the cool water felt just like it should... God it felt good.

He leant further forwards, letting the river rush over his head before entirely submerging it. He came back up only to plunge his head back down towards the muted jingle of pebbles on the riverbed.

With his head under the water Cooper watched the bubbles aerate and sit round his nose. He left his eyes open, feeling the cool. Letting it soothe. Watched the swirl of the clear water. And then watched it change.

A channel of red streamed gently past him, flowing innocuously by, as if part of a summer's day.

He pulled quickly back up and felt the drag of the river weighing heavy. He looked around and wiped the water away and began to run and fought against the fatigue which was dragging him down.

He followed the trail of the blood upstream and on seeing something, he scrabbled down the bank and slipped and fell and tumbled into the water and waded across to the other side of the river, before he slowly realized what he was looking at.

'Zola...! Zola...! Zola!'

He reached. Hauling her towards him. Turning her over like he'd done to Jackson all those years ago. 'Zola!... Oh God, no!'

And he clasped her to him, lugging her out of the water

and up onto the bank. Then sat her up. Cradling her in his arms as he rocked her gently.

'Zola…' he whispered. 'Zola, it's me, Thomas… Answer me, Zola… réponds-moi… *please*, say something. Dis quelque chose.'

There was no response. Nothing. Nothing at all.

'Ne meure pas. Tu ne peux pas mourir… *S'il te plait*… ne meure pas.'

He felt a sudden wetness on his forearm. Then leaning Zola forward, he looked down in horror. The back of her skull had collapsed. Falling away. Leaving a gaping hole the size of his fist. Oozing fluid and oozing blood. Part of her brain falling out and onto his arm and dropping down to mix with the muddy, squelching ground.

He dropped her. His legs scrabbling underneath him faster than his body could move away. Staring at her lifeless body. Wondering if what he was seeing was real or not. Maybe this was part of the trip. The come down.

He touched her body gently with his boot to see if she was real… Yes. Oh my God. He looked her again. He thought she'd just fallen.

Slipped.

Hit her head.

Assumed she had. But there was no mistaking what'd happened.

Zola had been shot.

And Cooper, covered in blood, scooped her up, not hearing the sound of his own drawn out cry. And he struggled and tried to see through his tears as he walked along the road, carrying her body towards the village.

'Oh my God, Tom, what's happened? What have you done?'

333

It was Maddie coming up from behind him. But he didn't stop. Forced her to run in front of him with Rosedale blocking his way.

Rosedale stared. 'What the hell happened, Thomas? Tell me you haven't done this.'

'She's been shot.'

Rosedale paled. 'What?'

Cooper could hear his voice was strained. Pained. 'I think we were probably followed back here… That red motorcycle Maddie saw…' He trailed off. Couldn't focus, and he thought Rosedale was asking him questions, but his voice seemed too distant, too far away to hear.

'Thomas, do you think whoever did it was just after her, or us? Perhaps they saw her show us the land, and couldn't risk her talking. Or maybe it was a warning. But whatever way, I reckon this is Bemba's doing, I just know it. When did it happen…? Thomas! Thomas, I'm talking to you.'

'What…? What…? I don't know… I just found her.'

'What the hell do you mean, you don't know? I thought she was with you? You were supposed to be looking after her.'

His own thoughts confused him. 'She was, last night, then she left me and…'

'Left you, where? What the hell were you doing? Why weren't you keeping an eye on her?'

He tried to concentrate on Rosedale. He could see thoughts were playing out on his face. Angrily he spat out more words. 'Thomas, I reckon this has got something to do with the way you were behaving earlier… Well has it…? Answer me, boy!'

'Get out of my way.'

Rosedale shook his head. 'No, not until you tell me what's going on. That, and the fact we also need to move from here.

We can't afford to be seen, and carrying a dead body about, in my books, would make us look pretty suspicious.'

The anger rushed through Cooper. 'Everything's one big joke to you, Rosedale, isn't it?'

Rosedale leant in to Cooper as the rain began to pour down. 'You need to get a goddamn hold of yourself, Thomas. You're going to jeopardize everything here, probably even us, if you don't get off the road.'

'You can do what you like, Rosedale, but see right now, there are way more important things than Granger's freaking plane. Like this dead woman.'

Maddie tried to calm the situation. She glanced around, nervous for Cooper.

'Tom, please, Rosedale's right, we need to move. Whoever's done this to her, they might be still around. Come on... Now!'

Cooper turned on Maddie. 'What would you like me to do, Maddison? Leave her here? Just dump her on the road? That's what you want isn't it?'

Maddie reddened. 'No, God no, but you need to listen to me. We have to get out of here. Tom, look at me. Tom...'

'Leave it, Maddison, Thomas here doesn't want to listen, he's got that crazy look in his eyes. Unravelling right in front of us. But let me tell you something, boy. If you think you're going to do what you always do, go over the line, lose sight of the aim of the investigation, and the reason why we're here, then you've got another think coming. You are *not* going to put us in danger.'

Cooper felt a darkness descend on him. 'Like I said, get the hell out of my way.'

'No can do, Thomas. We, and that includes you, need to get off this road and fast.'

'I'm warning you.'

335

Rosedale tilted his head. His voice menacing. 'Is that a threat, Thomas? Are you threatening me?'

Maddie, pulled at Rosedale's arm. 'No, no, of course he's not saying that. Tell him, Tom, you're not threatening him, are you?'

'Yeah, Thomas, tell me…'

Rosedale waited for an answer from Cooper. And he got one.

Still holding Zola, he freed one of his hands to slip it to his back holster to draw out his gun. He saw only a flicker of emotion crossing Rosedale's face, unlike Maddie's who looked at him in alarm.

And even though Cooper held Zola in the crook of one arm, the gun, pointing at Rosedale, was precision steady. 'I'll ask you again, Rosedale… Move the hell out of my way.'

Rosedale pulled at the buttons on his shirt, exposing his chest. 'Be my guest, Thomas, but a word of advice… make sure you kill me.'

Cooper flicked off the safety catch with his thumb, drawing back the trigger on his Colt series 7. 'Your choice.'

'No! No! No!'

Maddie shouted as she jumped in front of Rosedale, who looked more shocked than he'd done when Cooper had pulled the gun on him. She cried as torrents of rainwater ran down her face. 'Put the gun down, Tom! Please, just put it down. We can work out whatever's going on. You don't need to do this…'

'Move out of the way, Maddie. This is between me and Rosedale.'

'No, I won't. I'm not moving. I'm going to stay right here. So if you want to shoot Rosedale, you'll have to shoot me, too. So come on, what's it going to be?'

Cooper gritted his teeth, this time able to feel the pulse throbbing above his eye. But he couldn't quite work out what he was feeling as he talked to her.

'You want to see if I'll shoot both of you? Is that what you want? Is that what you want to see? Why are you doing this, Maddie?'

Maddie didn't even bother trying to wipe away her tears. 'Me…? Why am *I* doing this? Look at yourself, Tom. You've lost it. You need to get help. I can't look after you anymore. I've tried, I really have but I can't do this. That's why I left, because I couldn't do it anymore and I didn't want Cora to see her daddy like this.'

'Leave her out of it.'

'No, you've got to listen. We're all here trying to help you.'

'I never asked you to come, Maddie, in fact I never wanted you to.'

'But I did, Tom, because I knew this was going to happen, like it used to when you were looking for *her*.'

The gun in Cooper's hand began to shake. 'I don't need you to look after me, but there you are. Hanging on, hanging around. When will it sink in, Maddie, I don't want you anywhere near me. Never have. Desperate isn't a good look.'

Rosedale intervened. 'Shut up, Thomas.'

'Shut up? Correct me if I'm wrong, Rosedale, but isn't it you who keeps on wanting me to speak to Maddie and tell her how it is? How I really feel about her. Well, that's exactly what I'm doing.'

There was the sound of another hammer cocking. This time it was Rosedale. He pointed his gun straight at Cooper. 'I said shut up, Thomas.'

As the Congolese rain thundered down, Cooper stood in the middle of the wide, red-mud road, pointing his weapon

337

at Rosedale, as he pointed one at him, with Maddie standing between them. But he wasn't backing down. Not one bit.

'Maddie, I don't love you. I never will, not even...'

Rosedale broke into his words. 'Shut up! Not unless you want me to blow you away, right now. Which is it going to be? Shut up or I'll do it for you, and you know I will, hell Thomas, you know it's true. Back when we worked together. Did I ever hesitate? Did I ever back down from killing a man? No, and I haven't changed.'

Cooper's lips moved to speak but it was Rosedale who got in first. 'Think about it real carefully before you say anything else, 'cos if you die, what's going to happen if she comes back?'

Cooper blinked. 'What?'

'What if Ellie is really alive and she comes looking for you? But it'll be no good if you're dead. What then? Haven't you already lost enough because of her? Your friends. Your family. Your kid. The chance of happiness, the chance of anything. Hell, if anyone's the living dead around here, it's you. Nothing else mattered apart from that search of yours, did it? How many years did you look? Travelling around and getting into trouble in the hope you'd find her. And every time, Maddie would come and find *you*. You should be ashamed, Thomas. But then everyone thought you'd come to your senses. Put it behind you. You got married, had a kid. And from the outside it looked so good. You and Maddie together. But up here. In your head. You never stopped searching, did you? Never really let her go. But you know what I think? I think it was never about Ellie. It was about you. The search was never about finding her, it was about finding yourself. You're lost Thomas, always have been, always will be. And the drugs have just finished you off. You've got nothing else, and this ghost of Ellie which haunts you is the only reason you've got to keep on living. Without it you're dead, but what you don't see Thomas, is *with it*, you're dead as well.'

And the only sound was the drone of the rain as Cooper lowered his gun. He walked round Maddie and Rosedale without saying anything else. In the distance he heard Rosedale talk with loving warmth. 'Maddison, listen to me, you know what…'

'Don't bother, Rosedale. I know what you're going to say, but both of us know full well he meant it. He meant every single word.'

75

The villagers stood back as Cooper laid Zola's body in front of them, watching on edge as he waved his gun. His top was covered in blood and he had no doubt his face was smeared red as well.

'I want you to bury her properly, you hear? This woman was a good woman. She had no evil in her, no Kindoki, nothing. The only thing she had inside her was love.'

He backed away from the sea of intrigued faces.

A black motorcycle, leaning up against the wall of one of the brick huts, grabbed his attention.

'Who owns this bike…? À qui appartient ce vélo?'

A young man, no older than twenty, stepped forward. 'I do.'

'Well I'm going to borrow it, but I'll bring it back, okay?'

With his eyes firmly fixed on Cooper's gun, the man nodded. Went into his pocket. Shakily handed him the keys. No doubt feeling it was a small price to pay.

76

Cooper had been waiting outside for the past eighty-six minutes. Not that he cared. He was happy to wait all day if he had to. Waiting was something he was good at. Something over the years he'd honed, especially when it meant seeing who he needed to see.

Thinking that he was going to be in for a long wait, but not particularly caring, he was happy to be proved wrong when the large gates suddenly glided open, letting out a nondescript car.

Taking advantage of the moment he'd been waiting for, Cooper slammed down hard on the kick-start. Sped the bike through the now open gates. Raced along the perfectly tarmacked road.

Jumping off the bike at the entrance, Cooper sent it spinning along the ground with the engine still revving. He ran into the main reception of the Lemon water treatment plant, calling out to the person he was wanting to see.

Wide eyed and wired and agitated, looking for someone to pay.

'Charles…! Charles…! Charles!'

He bellowed hard to the sheer terror of the woman working behind the desk, who stayed frozen at the sight of Cooper covered in blood.

'Where is he…? Where's Charles?'

Fear rendered the woman almost speechless. 'He's… he's…'

Cooper slammed on the desk. 'He's where? Upstairs? Is that where?'

The woman managed to nod. Managed to get out the words. 'Second floor... end of the hall.'

Cooper dashed up the stairs, calling out again. 'Charles...! Charles! Get the hell out here now, unless you want me to come and find you... Charles!'

A door opened at the end of the hall and there, standing nervously, was Charles Templin-Wright.

Before he had time to open his mouth, Cooper smashed his fist into Charles's face.

The blow split open his lip instantly.

But he hadn't finished. He slammed his forearm into Charles's throat to pin him against the wall, their noses nearly touching. 'She's dead, shot through the head, and unless I find out otherwise, I'm holding you responsible.'

'What... what are you talking about?'

'I'm talking about Zola, but you wouldn't have even bothered to know her name, would you?'

'I don't...'

'Know what I'm talking about...? Sure you don't.'

He kneed Charles in the stomach. Winded him. Caused his body to judder with pain as he kept him pinned against the wall.

'I'm going to find out, you hear me, Charles? And when I do, you'll wish your momma never gave birth to you. The thing is, I hate liars. I hate cowards. And you, Charles, are both... Don't bother trying to shake your head, because we both know that's true. Take the car I saw you in. Are you *still* going to tell me it was your friend not you who borrowed it off Bemba?'

He pushed harder on Charles's trachea. 'Well are you?'

With his face scarlet, Charles gave a tiny shake of his head and saliva spluttered out of his mouth as he scratched at Cooper's arm and desperately tried to pull it away from the choke-hold.

Cooper gave it another minute before releasing Charles, who fell forward and dropped on all fours and coughed violently. Not letting him off so easily, he joined him on his knees. He grabbed Charles's hair to lift his head up to look at him.

'Where's Bemba?'

'I... I don't know what you mean.'

The slap Cooper gave to the side of Charles's ear sounded along the hall. 'I think you know damn well what I mean. Don't waste my time Charles. I'm not in the mood to have it wasted.'

Charles stared. Looked terrified. 'Okay... okay, I know him... not well but...'

'Save the BS, Charles, just tell me where he is.'

'I don't know. I don't know that. His church in Buziba, maybe?'

Pulling Charles to a standing position by his thin, listless hair, Cooper was as red faced as Charles. 'Are you trying to play games with me, Charlie-boy? Because if you are, let me give you a word of advice: *never* take on a crazy man who's got nothing left to lose. And I haven't. I've got nothing left. So what's it going to be?'

Charles's face was a mixture of horror and panic and fear and dread. He shook violently as he spoke. 'I just don't know any more information than that. I swear.'

'You don't know where he lives?'

Charles shook his head as he gave his answer. 'No.'

Digesting the reply, Cooper let go of Charles's hair. 'Okay, this is how it's going to work. I'm leaving now, but I'm coming back for you. Understand? *I'm coming the hell back.'*

'Yes… okay…okay.'

'And when I do, you'll have found out where Bemba lives and what he does and where he goes.'

'But…'

Cooper put his finger on Charles's mouth, jamming it hard against the split lip which still seeped with blood. A tiny squeal of pain came from him.

'No buts, Charles, got that…? Because if you don't have the information by then, guess what?'

'I… I don't know.'

'Then I'm going to kill you… Real slow. Real painful… You got that, Charles?'

'Yes… yes.'

'Good… I'll see you soon.'

Turning and marching down the hallway, Cooper took the stairs at speed. Trailed his hand along the reception desk. Passed the frightened woman. Kicked at the brown ornaments he'd spoken with Charles about which sat on the floor.

They smashed, sending hundreds of fragmented pieces everywhere. With sarcasm rich in his voice he said, 'Oops, sorry about that.'

'It's… it's… it's fine. Really, don't worry.'

Striding to the door, he suddenly stopped dead in his tracks. And to the quiet consternation of the receptionist, he turned back. Bent down and picked up a piece of the clay ornament and then popped it into his pocket and turned and walked out into the Congolese rain.

In the second floor hallway, Charles Templin-Wright was attempting to recover from what he would describe later to one of his colleagues as a *terrible ordeal*.

The door of his office opened.

'You need to do better than that Charles. Much better.'

Papa Bemba spoke to Charles, the scars across his eye sockets looking red and raised, more sore than usual as the small razor cuts from his *spiritual* self-mutilation last week were beginning to become infected.

'I didn't tell him anything.'

The smile on Bemba's face was twisted and manic. 'He sees, Charles. He sees without words. The spirits for some reason are guiding, unlike the woman...'

'Maddie.'

'She is blind. Visionless. You should find her, Charles, and when you do, bring her here to me.'

Cooper wheel-slid the motorcycle in the thick mud, avoiding a head on collision with Rosedale, who sped directly towards him in the Toyota, sliding to a halt, blocking his way.

Rosedale opened the car door. Got out. Stood on the running board. 'I've been looking for you Thomas.'

'Well now you've found me, you can go right ahead and turn round.'

With the rain still hammering down, sounding like steel percussion on the bonnet of the SUV, Rosedale had to raise his voice over the noise. 'Thomas, listen, I have to talk to you.'

'Thing is, Rosedale, I've got nothing to say to you.'

'Thomas, come on. You're acting crazy.'

'I don't think I am. I know exactly what I'm doing.'

'You don't think dosing yourself up with all kinds of medication and carrying dead bodies around, pulling your gun on your team, is a little crazy? Not to mention this really wasn't the brief Granger gave us.'

'Rosedale, I know you. We go back a long way, and in that time, you must have pulled your gun on me at least a dozen times. And how come I didn't say that was crazy?'

A hint of amusement came into Rosedale's tone. 'It wasn't. I actually wanted to kill you.'

'Did you believe what you said back there about Ellie coming back to me?'

'No, Thomas, I didn't, and deep down I don't think you

believe it either. Guilt has a way of doing strange things to folk.'

'So why say it?'

'To make you shut up, and stop me having to put a bullet in you.'

Needing to use his whole arm to wipe away the rain from his face, Cooper said,

'Leave me alone Rosedale. Just go!'

'I wish I could but I made a promise, and I take my promises real seriously. Don't think for a moment it's got anything to do with me liking you.'

'Thought never crossed my mind...Where's Maddie, anyway? Is she in the back?'

'No, she's safe though, but she doesn't want to see you. She's going home, Thomas. I'm going to put her on a plane. She doesn't deserve what you did to her. She has her own stuff going on too, but you wouldn't know about that because you're too busy chasing your ass to care.'

'Does she know I didn't mean it? That I didn't mean a word. Does she know I love her? Always have. But I just don't know how to do it her way. How to be what I should be. To love the way other people do.'

'No, she doesn't, and I think it should stay like that. It hurts her now, but it'll be best for her in the long run. She'll finally be free.'

'I didn't just say it because you told me to, I wasn't going to do that. Well, not the way I did it. I was angry. Took it out on her. And I'm sorry, will you tell her that for me, Rosedale?'

'I will.'

'But as for you, Rosedale, you need to stay the hell out of my way.'

Rosedale climbed down from the Toyota to walk towards Cooper. 'I have something to tell you.'

And suddenly Cooper felt like a cornered animal. A deep agitation came into his manner. 'Don't come any closer, Rosedale, don't try anything stupid.'

'It's about Jackson.'

Cooper began to back away. Dragging the bike with him as Rosedale came closer. He pointed angrily. Emotion consuming him. 'Don't you mess with me, Rosedale! Don't you mess with my head. Not about Jackson. Not about him. You... you leave him alone.'

'I'm not, I wouldn't do that to you. There was a call. That fool, Levi, said Beau had been trying to contact you urgently. So I called Beau, and we spoke about Jackson.'

Cooper's gaze darted across Rosedale's face, seeing if there was any trace of lies. Of game playing. But all he could see was sincerity. Candid sincerity.

'You're being serious aren't you?'

'Yeah.'

Cooper almost couldn't stand to ask. His single word was breathless. 'Well?'

'Jackson's in hospital. He... there's no easy way to say it...'

'He took an overdose, didn't he?'

'Yes, he did.'

Despite anticipating the answer, it still stunned Cooper.

'And you know with Jackson, it's not even a cry for help. It's a cry to end it all.'

'I'm sorry.'

'He must've been in a dark place. And with him it comes from nowhere. We can be having a good time, doing a cook up, you know; ribs, steak, corn, like they do in Jerry's in Scottsdale, and everything seems to be fine. The next thing you know this dark cloud just descends. Weighs him down like nothing I've ever seen before. And that's it. I can't reach him. He's gone until that cloud lifts.'

'Sounds a bit like you, Thomas. There's a lot of pain about. A lot of people hurting, and there's a lot of healing still to do. A legacy from what happened.'

Bracing himself, Cooper asked, 'How bad is he?'

'Still unconscious. You need to go back home. I think we *all* need to go back. Kindoki force or not, this place is making us all crazy. Me, you and even Maddie. All of us are saying things we wouldn't normally say. This place has some kind of special... power.'

The stress Cooper felt was intense. 'No, no way. I can't leave here, not now, not with all this stuff going on. I'm not going to abandon it.'

Rosedale's shoulders slumped. His concern genuine. 'Listen to me, Thomas, I know you feel like you didn't save Ellie, that you could've done more, and if you had, she'd still be here. But that don't mean you have to make up for it by going around saving everyone else, even the ones who don't want to be saved. Don't make this a crusade, boy. You against the world. That's not how it works. Let it go.'

Cooper shook his head violently. His eyes wide open and deeply painful from the effects of the Iboga root. 'No... No... You see that, you see what you did, what you've just said. Well that's what they told me to do about Ellie. *Let her go*, and I did. Well, I tried to, but I'm not letting this go. I can't.'

'Thomas, you're worrying me. I gotta get you home. I heard what happened to you before. Maddie's right. You need to get help.'

'Why, because I want to find out the truth? The old woman, Zola, I'm not going to let her die for nothing... because of me.'

'It wasn't because of you.'

'But it was, I should've been watching her but I got a chance... A chance to see Ellie. She helped me see Ellie, Rosedale.'

Rosedale rubbed his chin as he stood in his soaking clothes. Shivered. Looked directly up to the sky and let the rain force him to squeeze his eyes shut. He spoke quietly.

'I get it now... Jesus, Thomas, is it that bad? Does it hurt so much you need to mess up your brain more than you do already with hallucinogenic crap? I've seen what that kind of thing can do to men's minds, *especially* if they're already out on that ledge. And you are, Thomas, you are... Look, you can't stay here, you need to go and see Jackson.'

'I don't know.'

'Okay, look. How about this? I'll stay here, Thomas. If it gets you to go back home, then alrighty. I don't know about Maddie, because I think she needs to go back, but I'll carry on. Find out what needs to be found out, and I'll keep you informed. When it's all settled with Jackson, and you've had a few days' break, then *maybe* you can come back. I'll keep Granger sweet, give him some bull. It works every time. The border of Rwanda isn't too far from here so you can fly almost directly from Kigali to DC. It'll take you less than twenty-four hours. What do you say, Thomas?'

The emotion cut at the back of Cooper's throat. He stared at the ground, not trusting himself not to cry. But eventually he spoke, looking directly at Rosedale. 'I say thank you, and yes... Yes.'

Rosedale chuckled. 'Oh don't thank me, boy, thank whatever strange and weird forces are at play here.'

79

Cooper stood looking out across the tree-lined neighborhood of Bethesda, Maryland, just northwest of the United States capital of Washington DC, in a private cubicle on the ICU, with the critical care monitors bleeping in the background.

The Walter Reed National Military Medical Center was the starkest of contrasts to where he'd just been. Since he'd landed at the international arrivals building of Dulles airport late last night, memories of the DRC seemed unreal now, reminiscent of half-forgotten dreams.

He turned to stare at Jackson in the hospital bed. He looked almost as white as the crisp cotton sheets he lay in. Wires and tubes trailed neatly to medical machines, and numerical read-outs constantly refreshed as various colored lines traced rhythmically and relentlessly across display screens. A blue plastic pipe held in Jackson's mouth was tied round his neck, held in place by white tapes. His chest lifted and fell. Lifted and fell. A respirator breathing into him. Breathing for him.

The nurse who'd been checking Jackson's obs was now facing Cooper, smiling. 'Hi, my name's Rosie. I'm Jackson's nurse today, if there's anything you want to ask, please feel free.'

Cooper said nothing. Barely gave a smile back. Slipped off his jacket. Sat down on the single hard seat and casually and vaguely patted down his blue jean pockets. Then, less casually and less vaguely, patted down his blue shirt pockets.

He flinched. Remembered where the strip of OxyContin hid, in the lining of his khaki jacket which hung in the wardrobe of the motel he'd checked into.

He exhaled. Tried not to feel anxious or agitated about the forgotten pills. 'How is he, Nurse? Is he going to make it?'

'The truth is it's hard to predict. As you know, he's had a previous brain trauma and during the overdose his breathing had almost stopped. The oxygen supply to his brain may have been compromised. His blood chemistry was badly affected and his organs – heart, liver, kidneys – they all took a hit.'

'But you can fix all that, right?'

'Well, of course we can support his organs, give them a chance to recover, but the main worry is whether his brain has been damaged by low oxygen levels, and whether any damage is permanent… and that's if he pulls through.'

The realization that this could be something he couldn't protect Jackson from, couldn't save him from, made Cooper want to run and keep on running. 'But what are the chances?'

'At the moment the machines are doing everything for him as we've put him in a medical coma. They're breathing for him. Pushing in the perfect amounts of oxygen into his blood. We're driving his blood pressure up with drugs to force that perfect oxygen level past any swelling in his brain, caused by the overdose. We're also trying to keep his brain tissue alive till the swelling goes down.'

'And then?'

'Then we turn the sedatives off, and we wait and we hope he wakes up.'

'And if he doesn't wake up?'

The nurse smiled warmly. 'We deal with that if it happens, but right now, his brain scans look okay. His other vital organs seem to be recovering so let's be positive. But there are no guarantees. Tomorrow or the day after we're going to turn off the sedatives to assess how well he breathes for himself, and look for signs he's waking up, signs that he is still able to hear us and respond to our voices.'

'And if he can?'

'Then we let him wake up completely, take out that breathing tube and the long, or hopefully short, recovery process begins.'

'What's the timeline?'

'I know I keep sounding vague but it may take time to find out how well he will recover. Some patients take weeks and months to slowly get back to full normal brain function, others seem to make rapid improvement in the early stages but never make a full recovery. And then there are some who wake up as if they've just had a nice long sleep and go home before the end of the week. That's what we're hoping for, but we really will have to wait and see.'

'Can I talk to him? Do you think he can hear me?'

'It's difficult to tell. Usually we like to think patients can hear us. They often seem to respond better to the comforting tones of familiar voices. But the drugs we put Jackson on are strong and they're designed to pretty much anaesthetize people, so they don't feel or remember anything at this stage. So it's very doubtful, in this case, that he'll able to hear you... Anyway, I'll leave you on your own with him. I'll just be right outside at my station if any of the alarms go off.'

'Appreciate that.'

With the nurse gone, Cooper slid his chair close up to the bed. Grasping hold of Jackson's hand. He squeezed and held on. Said, 'Hey, Jackson. It's me, Coop... Hey man, you should have called me. I would've come running, you know that, don't you? We were good weren't we? Jackson, you can't go and leave me like this. You gotta come back to me. You hear me? What am I going to do without you? I need you man. I can't do this life on my own. And what am I supposed to tell Cora...? Jesus, Jackson, did you think you had to hide this from me, the way you felt? You don't have to hide anything, not from me. That's what I do. Hide every goddamn thing there is. So many secrets. So many lies... I even lie to you, you know that? Been lying to you for years, but not anymore. On my way here I decided I'd tell you. Couldn't bear it if anything happened to you and I never told you the truth. But if I tell you, Jackson, you got to promise me you'll come back to me. Only this time I'm going to look after you like a brother should... That's right, Jackson,' said Cooper, 'I'm your brother. And I couldn't ask for a better one than you. I'm so sorry we didn't tell you before. We were going to just before the accident, but then after everything that happened, we thought it was best not to. We didn't want you to have to keep any more secrets. We were only trying to protect you, Jackson, and maybe we were wrong. But you were always so beautiful, so fragile, that we didn't want to burden you. Perhaps I should've told you myself when I found out that John was my father, but God knows it was complicated. My mom never told John she was pregnant, and he would've never known about me if she hadn't died. And after I went to live with Beau it was a while before he told John, then it was only when I was a teenager that I finally knew the truth and you, you were still too young, Jackson. Too innocent. Then time just seemed to pass, along with the rise of John's career and keeping the secret seemed the easiest thing to do. God, there are so many half-truths and half-lies but one thing that was never a lie is my love for you, Jackson. I cherish every moment we've shared, as kids and now. Remember the times when we played at the beach house? Those really were the best of times, dreaming of the future, playing soldiers when we always defeated the enemy. We were pure and strong back then, brave knights on a quest. And you haven't changed, but me? Look at me now, somehow I got lost along the way...'

Cooper stopped talking, but didn't turn as he felt the air kick slightly as the electric door seal hissed open then hissed shut. Locking out the rest of the world.

'Hello, Coop.'

Expecting the nurse and not the person who spoke, Cooper turned and with a flat, even tone said, 'Hello, John... Hey, Beau.'

'Thank you for coming back,' said Woods, with his eyes on Jackson.

'Why wouldn't I come back to see Jackson?'

Tired, Woods rubbed his head. 'Coop, I'm not looking for a fight.'

Beau, knowing now wasn't the time for tension and trouble said, 'I'm glad you came... How was the DRC?'

'Not good.'

'You don't look so good yourself,' said Beau. 'Want to talk about it?'

'Nope.'

'What about the investigation? How's that going? You collected anything interesting? Or is it just the usual crazy trash you like to pick up?'

Cooper refused to be offended. 'It depends if you call pieces of broken bits of pot and bottle tops interesting.'

Beau said, 'Anything I can help you with? Need a sounding board?'

'Maybe. I'll see.'

Beau nodded, moved to sit on the chair Cooper had vacated. He sat on the side of his buttock, something he often did to stop the sciatica taking a stronger hold. 'Well at least Rosedale did his job, got you back here in one piece.'

'Yeah, I guess so.'

'I've said it before,' said Beau. 'I'm not like you, John, I can't stand the man. Don't know many that do, but he's a good one to have on your side. The oddest ball out there, but he'd die along with you... How's Maddie?'

'Don't ask.'

Beau stared hard. 'Jesus, Coop, don't tell me you've been messing her about again. Last time this happened, I told you...'

Cooper snapped, not wanting to hear any more of the sentence. 'Why is it people love to tell me what Maddie and I should be doing?'

'Maybe it's because you don't know yourself. Look, nobody wants to see either of you hurt that's all. Oh, I spoke to Granger by the way. He's gunning for you big time.'

'When isn't he?'

Beau pulled a contemplative face. 'He's always been pig-headed... You want me to have a word?'

Cooper laughed, with an added sprinkling of bitterness. 'With Granger? Thanks for the offer Beau, but I think I'm old enough to handle things myself.'

'It hasn't always been that way.'

'No, and you haven't always offered.'

The men fell into tense silence.

Then, struggling to speak to Woods but pulling it out of the bag, Cooper said, 'How are you holding up?'

'Okay.'

'Don't listen to him, Coop,' said Beau. 'I'll tell you how he's doing. Not good. Isn't that right, John? Show me a man who's torn between country and family, and I'll show you this man here. It's tough because he's got to keep going.'

Woods said, 'Beau, seriously, it's cool.'

'Come off it. You work harder than anyone I know. Your workload's relentless at the best of times. What did you get last night, three, four hours sleep at the most? It's tough to watch, Coop. Though at least this hasn't got out. All the press know is that Jackson was unwell and taken in for tests. Usual line, and so far it seems to be yesterday's news, thanks to Senator Bowhurst. He got caught with his pants down with the family nanny. You got to love a cliché… Anyway, listen Coop, you need to make sure you don't bring any more trouble to an already overloaded pair of shoulders. You hear me? You really do look a mess by the way… You need to see your shrink? And I don't just mean the court appointed one.'

Snapping and not liking what Beau had just said, Cooper shook his head. 'Don't talk to me like I'm a kid okay? And don't tell me about bringing trouble to his front door, because I don't. And as for seeing a shrink? Why would I do that when I'm dealing with it myself?'

Woods looked at him sceptically. 'Coop, we just don't want what happened before to happen again. We're concerned.'

Cooper ran his tongue over his lips. Took a deep breath. Looked directly at Woods. 'Let's not go there, okay? Listen, I'm going to head out.' He stopped to pick up his bag. 'Oh, you might want to know that I've told him.'

Woods frowned. 'Who? Told who what?'

'I told Jackson… about us. I thought he should know. There are too many lies around here… Oh don't worry,

John, you don't have to look like that. He might not even wake up, so your secret will be safe.'

'Keep that kind of talk out of here. What the hell's the matter with you? This is not the time or the place.'

Woods said nothing and Cooper stepped closer and lowered his voice. 'I'm not going to go around calling you Dad, if that's what you're worried about.'

'You make it sound like it's a bad thing to be my son.'

Cooper's face flushed red. Scorn written over it. 'Don't play games, John. Have you lost your memory? Because if it's not such a bad thing to be your son, what's with the secret?'

'You know what, and you know why.'

Faces inches apart. 'Okay then, how about this one? How come you didn't let me call you Dad when I was a kid? *Before* it became a secret. How come you made me stay with Beau after you'd found out?'

'We've been over this.'

Cooper hissed. 'And I want to go over it again.'

'As you know my wife… '

Cooper cut in. 'Wouldn't have accepted me? It might've been difficult for you? Come on, it wasn't like you had an affair with my mom. You left her long before you met Jackson's mom.'

'I didn't leave your mom. We came to a decision. Well, she did. If it'd just been my choice we would've stayed together. And as for Jackson's mom, well…' He trailed off and Cooper, knowing the next words out of his mouth were going to be unfair, but knowing at that moment he didn't care, stared hard. 'You're a joke, John, you know that? You chose your new wife over me. The same wife who left you for your best friend. Was it worth it, John? Was it? Go figure.'

President Woods's infamous temper appeared and released. 'For God's sake it wasn't like that.'

'What I know is I was your kid.'

'Look, it wasn't that simple. My political career had already started then and it seemed sensible to keep it a secret. If you'd called me Dad, people would've found out… I get that it was the wrong decision. If I could I would do things differently. And I'm sorry you got hurt. I really am.'

'Oh, I never get hurt John. I just get angry.'

'Why won't you let me make it alright? Work things out?'

'Just like that, hey? Like the past never happened. I'd still be your secret though, wouldn't I?'

'Coop, come on, it's not like I wanted this. But if you need me to tell the world I'm your father then just say the word, and I'll do it.'

'You really think I want to carry any more guilt than I do already? Do ya? We both know if it got out now, along with all the other stuff, it would destroy you. Nobody wants a liar as their president. And I'm not going to be responsible for you having to step down. So guess what? You win.'

A flash of hurt passed through the president's eyes. 'Please Coop, don't be like this.'

Cooper shot Woods a stare. Refused to feed into the emotive reply. And all he wanted to do was get the hell out. 'Let's just let sleeping dogs lie, *John*.'

'Quit that, Coop.'

'For God's sake,' said Beau. 'We're in a hospital not a downtown bar.'

'Oh, don't worry, Beau. I'm going. Out of here. Gone.'

Woods grabbed Cooper's arm. 'Why do you have to resent me so much?'

Cooper gave a cold, tight smile. Grabbed his coat. 'Resent

you? Why would you think that, John? I mean look around. One of your sons is in an induced coma after overdosing, and your other son's one hell of a mess. How could I resent a great father like you?'

80

'Peace offering!'

Maddie ignored Cooper and his outstretched hand which held a bunch of yellow roses. She walked towards him, then around him, and threw the handmade Western saddle she was carrying expertly across the back of her favorite dappled gray mare, Arabella.

'Maddie, please… Talk to me.'

Tightening the girth before untying the reins from the paddock fence, Maddie led the mare slightly away before stepping up in the stirrup. Swung effortlessly into the saddle and, looking down at Cooper from her mount, she said, 'What are you doing here, Tom? What do you want?'

'I came to apologize.'

'And you thought a bunch of roses would do the trick? Way to go, Tom.' She turned away from him and lightly tapped Arabella with the heels of her cowboy boots.

'Walk on.'

'Wait, Maddie, please… We need to sort this out.'

Ignoring him she gently pulled on the left rein. Turned down a sandy path, which seemed to be Cooper's cue to dump the roses and follow.

Jogging behind her but not getting too close to Arabella's hind end, cautious of her *back off from me* kick, Cooper tried again. 'Maddie, stop! Wait… I'm sorry… Maddie…! I need to talk to you.'

'Oh, I think you've done enough of that. You certainly talked alright, and the message is loud, clear and very much received. But hey, at least I know you never loved me and maybe now I can let go of the idea that you ever did. Why don't we look at it as you've done me a favor and leave it at that... Make sure you close the gates on your way out.'

Sprinting round to get in front, as Maddie tapped into a trot, Cooper grabbed hold of Arabella's bridle, bringing her to a stop, much to her clear annoyance and stamping of hooves.

'Of course I loved you.'

'No you didn't, not really; I just happened to be there at the time you needed somebody, that's all.'

'You're wrong, Maddie, I know how I feel.'

Maddie laughed with hurt and scorn. 'You don't know how you feel. You don't even know who you are. The only thing you feel is with her, with your ghost, with Ellie. Anything else, especially love, you don't feel. You know sometimes I don't recognize who I've become. There were often days I'd wake up secretly wishing and praying that Ellie was really dead. That somehow I could prove it... I wanted her dead, Tom, so we could get on with our lives! Do you hear that? What kind of person does that make me?'

'Maddie...'

She shook her head and said, 'Just go home, Tom.'

'I know what I felt when I saw your face light up on the day Cora was born, and I know what I felt when it was you I woke up to in the morning, I know what I felt when I made love to you, Maddie. And I know I want to feel that again, but you're right; at the moment it feels like I'm empty. Numb. All regular emotions wiped away. But that doesn't mean I don't know I love you. It just makes me not be able to feel it, and be the person you deserve to be with. I wish

362

I could make you happy. Be together again. How it should be. How it was.'

'How it was? You're looking at our marriage through a rose-tinted lens. When I think about it, and look back, I don't know anything about you. What you think. What you feel. I don't really know your friends and I don't even know who your family are. You kept it all away from me. Everything's a secret and it always has been. Why, Tom? Even when we got married there was nobody there on your side, apart from our mutual friends.'

'There was Beau.'

'Beau. One person.'

'What do you want me to do? Conjure up people who aren't there? My mom died when I'd just turned nine and she had no family to speak of apart from Beau. And as for my daddy... well...' He trailed off for a moment, pictured John, refused to feel guilty, refused to acknowledge it as a lie for a lie's sake. 'Who knows where or who he is... So you see, Maddie, there isn't anybody else. Which means there aren't any secrets.'

'Who are you kidding? There are always secrets. Listen, Tom, I'm so tired, I just can't do this anymore, and I know we have to work together and co-parent and that's all fine but it's the *us* part of it I can't do anymore.'

'I know and I'm not asking you to, because I can see how much I'm hurting you.'

'It's not just me though is it? It's Cora as well.'

'Cora means everything to me.'

'No Tom, the *idea* of Cora means everything to you, but do you ever think about how *she* feels when you break promises to her? When she spends her birthday watching the door for you?'

'Come on Maddie, you know it's not that simple.'

'Oh but it is, it really is that simple and that's the point *and* the problem… Listen, I need to go.'

'Just give me another minute.'

'Why? So it's more difficult for me when I say goodbye? My heart's broken, Tom, and I'm not quite sure how to put it back together, and seeing you makes it a whole heap harder… You know every day I worry about you. Worry if you'll take one too many of those pills you tell me you don't take anymore. Worry if you'll fall off that edge you're always standing on, when I've taken my eyes off the ball. And I worry when you don't come home at night, or I don't hear from you, that you're lying somewhere with a bullet in your head. I don't think I'll ever stop worrying about you but I don't want to worry so much and so often. Not anymore. So I need you to let me go this time. And if you love me like you say you do, Tom, you'll do just that.'

81

In the lavish green countryside on the northern side of the river banks of Maryland, one mile from the great falls of the Potomac River, and only fourteen miles upstream from Washington DC, Cooper parked the hire car. Held hands with Cora and walked to the top of the gentle rolling knoll, part of the grounds of St. Francis's Monastery, home to two hundred Trappist monks.

'Hey, Beau!'

Beau Neill turned round from the oregano he was struggling to plant. Gave a huge smile, pushing himself to his feet as his sciatica forced him to perform the manoeuvre in three stages. He wiped his soil-covered hands on the black hooded sleeveless tunic he wore which draped over his long, coarse white robe. Pushed his hands into his spine. Arched his back. Then flinched with pain. *'For I reckon that the sufferings of this present time are not worthy to be compared with the glory which shall be revealed in us. Romans 8, Verse 18. Though I wish someone would tell my damn back that... Hey, Cora! I see you're wearing your birthday dress... It's good to see you Coop. After the other day, well it's not good to part like that. What's on your mind?'*

Cooper gave his Uncle Beau his arm to rest on. The once formidable captain. The man he'd once hated. The man he struggled at times to forgive.

'Why do you think I've got something on my mind?'

'Well haven't you? Most times you come to see me is when you've got something on your mind. I know what happened in the hospital with John must've brought up a lot of feelings for you. Come on, let's walk.'

Cooper sighed as Cora ran ahead, skipping and twirling and delighting in her own world. And Beau walked slowly. Linking arms with Cooper as they walked through the wood.

It was peaceful. Soothing and calming. And as much of a transition as it was for his Uncle Beau to go from captain to monk, Cooper could see why he'd chosen this life. And he envied it. 'Was I wrong?'

Beau Neill stopped. Pushed back his black tunic and put his hand into the large pocket on his robe. He pulled out a cigar. Lit it hungrily. Drew the smoke down into his lungs. He looked at Cooper. Then at his cigar. 'I'm still praying for guidance on this one… Yeah, I think you were.'

'I thought you'd say that.'

'But you still asked. Says something.'

'Not much.'

Beau snapped at Cooper. Reminiscent of the past. 'Grow the hell up, Coop, when did you become so childish? Why can't you just let him care? Be the father he wants to be?'

Cooper let him have that one. Didn't want to argue. Just wanted to sort it out. Leant back on the large white oak, feeling the bark scrape his skin through his top. 'You're kidding, right? He missed that boat a long time ago.'

Beau took another long drag of his cigar, clearly relishing every moment as he watched the tip burn. 'You sound like you did when you were fifteen, Coop. Let the man do what he needs to do.'

'That simple, hey?'

Beau said, 'Look at me. What is it you want him to do?

Because he wasn't kidding when he said he'll stand in front of the American people and announce your existence.'

Triggered by the smell of the cigar, Cooper lit his own cigarette. Enjoyed it in the same vein as Beau seemed to be enjoying his. 'You know, I don't want that. He's worked too hard.'

'Then let him do the small amount of things he can. He cares. I'm not going to talk about what happened over the last month and why, but no-one wants anything to happen to you. Look, if anyone's to blame, I am. When your mom was pregnant she told me she wasn't going to tell John about you. I wasn't sure she was doing the right thing, but she was adamant. And my sister was stubborn. A bit like you, Coop. And then when you were nine and your mom died, ten months later John came on a political rally to Hannibal.' Beau paused to sit down on the bench, carved out of a fallen tree. 'You know all this, I've already told you, but perhaps you need to hear it again... Where was I?'

Cooper answered dryly. 'At a political rally.'

'Yeah, right... so I told him about you, but it was *me*, Coop, who had to persuade him not to say who you are. Me not him. He wanted to shout it from the rooftops but by then he was doing well, making a name for himself. His political career was taking off and that's what your mom had always wanted for him. There was a hell of a lot to take into account. Apart from the party there was the fact he was married to Jackson's mother at the time, who I never cared for, and I don't think would've cared for you, but hey, she showed her true colors when she went off with John's best friend. Anyhow, I came to a compromise with John. I'd bring you up. But at the same time we both thought it was important for Jackson to get to know you, and you him, so we introduced you to each other just as play buddies, and even though you were seven years older than him, you got on just like what you were. Like brothers.'

'But Jackson's not the problem.'

'And neither is John. The reason why your mom didn't want to tell John in the first place was because she loved him. She always had, which meant she loved him enough to let him go. She knew John, and she knew he'd come running back to somewhere he'd spent his whole life trying to escape from. She didn't want that for him. She knew he wanted to make a difference, and no-one is sorrier than me that she's not here to see it. She would've been so proud of John. You're too hard on him... And I know I was hard on you when you were growing up, but I was a military man, I didn't know how to look after a kid.'

Cooper twisted his cigarette butt into the soft earth with his shoe. Wasn't comfortable with where the conversation was heading, so he did what he did best in these situations. He shrugged. 'Hey Beau, it was what it was.'

'Maybe... But at least now we're all older and wiser. Hopefully we've learnt from our mistakes. We've grown up. We've got our scars but we're managing. And I know you're finding it tough at the moment, Coop, but compared to your father, you've got it easy.'

'How so?'

'He's a torn man, Cooper. I've said it before but he's torn between his country and his sons. But like I say, one word is all it'll take and he'll be there for you. He'll throw everything away. All he believes in and everything he's work hard for. He'll be judged, not by one person but the whole world will look upon him like a fraud. All his good work will have a question mark over it. The vultures will circle, but he'll do it for you. I don't know many a man who'd do that. But that's love, Coop. That's a father's love. But the question is: what about a son's love? What will you do for him, Coop? He's one of the best presidents the country's seen in a long time. He's a man of truth. A man of honour, yet every day he carries secrets. You need to help him carry them. This is bigger than you or me now.'

'I don't know.'

'Well I do. You know, there was a time when I thought maybe you'd been robbed of a proper family life. But being here, I understand we're all supposed to take different paths, different journeys, and life isn't just made up of a simple equation. This is your journey, Coop, your equation, and I believe this is the way it's supposed to be. Accept it, and whatever you do, don't fight it. You're a good man, and so is your father. And as for Jackson, well he's always been different to you, Coop. I guess that's why we only told you and not him. Go and see John. Go and stay with him whilst Jackson's in hospital. I'm going to stay there tomorrow, but he needs you to go. I think you both do... You want to go and get a root beer? We made some last week. Best drink you'll ever taste.'

'Hey, Cora! Come on, we're going...! Cora!'

Cooper walked back with Beau towards the monastery in silence, reflecting on the last half hour. Eventually he broke the quiet. Tried to sound nonchalant. Fooled neither himself nor Beau.

'Did John tell you about Ellie's death certificate?'

'He did.'

'Well, when I was in the DRC, I got thinking. What if we're all wrong?'

'Coop...'

Cooper could hear the strain in his own voice. Threatening to push him over the edge. Allowing the monster to turn in on him. 'Don't do this to me, Beau. Not you.'

'Look, I'm a man who's lived and survived on his instinct, and I know yours says she didn't drown that day, but you were in shock. Traumatized. You weren't thinking straight.'

'Don't give me that.'

Beau stopped in the middle of the gravel pathway, turning to face Cooper straight on. 'But it's been seven years.'

'You don't need to tell me.'

'Make a choice, Coop. Lose everything, and I mean *everything*, including that little girl of yours, or let it go.'

'Now you're talking bull.'

'Coop. I can see it. Look at you. All reason and sanity is trickling through your fingers like grains in an hour glass. Stop, before it's too late. Hold on to the life you've built. I'm worried you're back on those pills. It's bad enough with Jackson, without you adding to it.'

'Hey, don't you worry about me.'

'It's hard not to... You just need to stop and let things go.'

The monastery's old tabby cat purred, wrapping its tail round Cooper's legs to get attention. It worked. He crouched down to stroke it. Gave him an excuse not to look at Beau when he said what he was about to.

'You were the one who taught me never to give up Beau. Those 5 a.m. runs you made me go on when I was barely thirteen through the Missouri snows. The cold river swims. The night treks without food or water when all my school buddies were tucked up asleep in bed. Never give up, Cooper, you said, and I didn't, but you want me to now.'

The box in Cooper's head, which he fought so hard to keep

closed, opened. And his anger allowed him to turn to stare up at Beau. Shame printed on his Uncle's face.

'I was tough on you, Coop, and I'm sorry. I'm not proud of that or what I did to you. I was wrong. Very. But all I'm saying now is to let it go and…'

Cooper stood up. Felt the rush of the OxyContin. 'You don't think I want to let it go? You don't think I don't want to just walk away like I wanted to when I was a kid? But like then I have nowhere else to go… Help me, Beau… *Please*.'

'Jesus, Coop. You need to get some help, but you also got to stop blaming yourself. You deserve to have a life. With Maddie. With Cora. They love you. And this death certificate, it just triggered you. You've got to see that, and I get it, it's bound to. But whatever you do don't start chasing after a ghost again. None of this was your fault, Coop.'

Bitterness tilted the balance of Cooper's voice. 'That's not what you said at the time, and you know what you said is as true today as it was back then. She was with me on the boat that *I* hired but *I* knew the dangers. Jackson, well he didn't know. I did, Beau. *I did*. She trusted me and I let her go. You talk about journeys? Well this is my journey. Don't ask me to stop feeling guilty, because I can't. More to the point, I don't know how to.'

82

Cooper's cell phone told him it was 3 a.m. It also told him Granger had called several times before leaving one hell of a terse message. But the last thing he wanted to do was have a conversation, which he knew would start off badly and end up worse.

Earlier he'd tried to call Rosedale, but it hadn't connected. Then he'd tried to get hold of Maddie, but Marvin had answered both the house phone and her cell, and the conversation and the phone had been put down by the time he'd said *hello*. Which left him with nothing else to do apart from some research on the computer. Though in truth, research had never been his strong point – neither had the patience to do it. Maddie had always been the one to do the ground work *especially* when it came to ground work on computers. He'd been the one who just went in and asked questions later.

However, sometimes there was nothing else for it. So he sat looking up information. About Lemon. About Charles. But so far, all he'd been able to find were smiling photographs and countless press releases singing the praises of both the man and Lemon. How they were an excellent example of social and humanitarian development in that particular area of the DRC.

'Want some company?'

President John Woods stood at the door of Jackson's room, dressed in silk spotty pyjamas and a thick, navy chenille robe.

Cooper grinned. 'Does America know you wear them?'

Woods kicked out his foot to the side, looking at the part of his pyjamas which was showing. 'Actually, they do. I did an interview with, I think it was *Good Morning America*, and the last question was, *what does the president wear in bed*?'

'And you told them?'

John grinned back. 'You're goddamn right I did. I'm proud of these… It's good to see you, Coop. Thanks for coming to stay.'

Woods went to give Cooper a hug but he backed away, putting out his hand instead. 'No problem, sir.'

Cooper heard John's sigh of quiet disappointment, but he pushed it aside, ignored it, as Woods pulled up the chair alongside him to see what he was looking at.

But his calm demeanour quickly changed. 'Coop, what the hell is this?'

Surprised at his tone, Cooper swivelled round to look at Woods, who was now holding Cooper's bag open, which held several unmarked bottles of pills.

Woods scooped his hand in. His face red and angry as he shook bottles which rattled like a baby's shaker. 'I'll ask you again. What the hell is this, Coop?'

Angry as hell, Cooper got up. Snatched at his bag, knocking it and the bottles out of Woods's hand. 'That must be record timing, John. How long have I been here? Six hours? Seven? And already you got a problem. Way to go, John. I should've listened to my gut and stayed away, but hey, we all learn by our mistakes.'

'Some of us clearly don't.'

'What's that supposed to mean?'

Woods stepped forward. 'You think you can bring that shit in here? Are you crazy? In case you've forgotten I'm the president of the United States and you happen to be in the White House, not on a street corner hustling pills. No way can you come in here with illegal drugs. I want you out of here. Gone. Take your stuff and go.'

Woods picked up the bag, stuffing the bottles back in. Zipped it up. Threw it at Cooper in a two hand shot. 'What happened to the clean living guy, hey, Coop? The one who hardly had a beer, let alone drugs?'

'You want me to give you a cliché? You want me to say he was left on that boat all those years ago?'

'I just want the truth.'

'You won't like the truth, because the truth is, John, it's just who I am. This is me, whether you like it or not.'

Woods shook his head. 'I'm so disappointed. I trusted you, and you do this. You said you were clean but now you're buying your shit off dealers.'

Cooper was angry, mad as hell and crazy like a rabid dog, and snarling just like one he said, 'Well thank you for trusting me, John. That makes me feel real good. I have done nothing but respect and protect your position as both the president and Jackson's father, and you know that. Yet knowing that, you still think I'd bring some stash in here, which I bought off the street, which would not only compromise myself but also you… Thank you for having such a high opinion of me. But hey, I'm going. No problem at all.'

Cooper headed for the door.

'Wait, goddamn it!'

'So you can tell me what a deadbeat I am? No thanks… Oh, and by the way, the pills, FYI, they're legit. Prescription. In fact, I think you'll find they were prescribed by the doctor

374

you recommend me last year, and the one Beau told me about.'

'Coop, you and I both know prescription drugs are just as dangerous as any other illegal drugs if they're misused. You're doctor shopping again, aren't you?'

'Leave it, John.'

'No, I won't. They might not be from some low-life, selling harm on the street, but there's a very fine line and I should know because like I told the good people of West Virginia recently, the Centres for Disease Control and Prevention have classified prescription drug abuse as an *epidemic* in this country and our administration will expand on the previous administration's 2011 Prescription Drug Abuse Prevention Plan.'

Cooper gave a half laugh. But it wasn't funny. Not one goddamn bit. 'Are you serious, John? You're really going to make this moment into some kind of campaign speech? A political rally?'

'No, of course not, I'm just saying... Look, I'm sorry for what I said about you bringing...'

Woods trailed off and Cooper thought he'd help him out. Hell, it was the least he could do. And laced with scorn he said, 'Street drugs in here? And how I was compromising your position? And you couldn't trust me?'

'Yeah, okay. It was stupid. I know you wouldn't do that. I'm just worried about you. We all are. What do you say about checking yourself into rehab? Just as a precaution. You've been bad on pills a few times before, and Granger said...'

Cooper put his hand up. 'Oh no. No way. I don't want to hear anything he has to say.'

'I just think you need to get some help again. Proper help.'

'Oh I did, John. And guess what? They gave me these.'

Cooper shook the bag he was holding, hearing the rattle of pills, and headed for the door.

Woods let out a sigh. The kind of sigh which usually had Cooper's name on it. 'Don't go, Coop. Stay. *Please*. Sit down.'

'Listen, I get that you're worried but there's nothing really to worry about. I got it. My back injury was playing up so I got some painkillers. And I had a bit of anxiety. It's no big deal. It's under control. Everything's cool now.'

Woods said nothing.

Cooper nodded.

Woods pulled out a piece of gum from his robe pocket, offered Cooper one, who refused with a wave of his hand. 'Truce?'

'Truce.'

'Room for one more? Couldn't sleep.' Beau appeared at the door, dressed in an identical robe to Woods's, only gray.

Cooper looked at both of them. 'What is it with you two and the robes?'

Beau winked. 'I actually got mine first.'

'That is so not true, Beau. That time you came to visit in early fall, correct me if I'm wrong here, you actually saw my robe and admired it.'

Beau sat on Jackson's bed, which looked out over the private rose garden of the White House. 'I can't remember that. In fact, I'll put it out there right now, that's a damn lie. Admit it, John, when you came to the Monastery last year, it was actually *you* who saw *my* robe.'

Woods looked at Beau and burst out laughing. 'I think I'm going to have to take the fifth on that. Not that amendments and I are the best of buddies right now.'

Cooper tuned out from John and Beau's conversation. He stared at the computer.

376

'Well, I'll be. Would you look at that?'

Woods turned with interest to see what Cooper was talking about. Mischief in his voice.

'I hope that's not some Playboy bunny website. There'll be no hiding it in this place, you know. Big Brother is certainly watching you.'

Cooper gave a side smile, keeping his eyes fixed on the large screen. 'Sorry to disappoint you John, only thing I'm looking at here is the man I've had dealings with in the DRC. I'm trying to find out who this other guy is. This one here. I saw him recently being chauffeured about in a car.'

Cooper pointed to the photo on the screen.

Woods put on his glasses. Leant slightly forward to get a better view. 'I can help you there. That's Donald Parker, head of Nadbury Electronics.'

'As in the multinational company, Nadbury?'

'Yeah. Parker's a great guy. Where did you see him?'

'Back in the DRC. At a water treatment plant.'

'Makes sense. He said he was flying out of town. The guy cares a lot about the place, and he's put a lot of money into it.'

'See the other guy in the photo he's with? That's Charles Templin-Wright, heads this water plant.'

'Yeah, Lemon.'

'You've heard of it?'

'Yeah, but only because I've been reading up on something about Nadbury Electronics… But *you've* actually seen Lemon? I knew you were in that area but it's fantastic you've actually seen it. I'd like to know what you think.'

Cooper looked at Woods and saw the genuine care in his eyes. He wasn't sure why John was asking. 'Well, Charles aside – because he's another story – the actual place itself is great. Real high tech stuff. Guaranteed clean water for the community. They also do some kind of education programme.'

Woods nodded approvingly. He grinned. 'I'm loving hearing that. You'll understand why soon.'

'But what's Nadbury to do with Lemon?'

'Well, they own it.'

Cooper was genuinely surprised. 'You're kidding? How come I didn't know?'

'Well it's out there in the public domain, but Nadbury, like a lot of businesses, own and have their fingers in lots of pies, so following the trail of who owns what and who's got shares in this or that, it's not always obvious. That guy, Donald Parker, what he's done for the community in the DRC reads exceptionally though. But he's pretty humble doesn't go round shouting about what he's done. And the fact you've said what a great place Lemon is, well let's just say that makes me really happy.'

'Want to share?'

'Wish I could, but what I will say is Parker has the same vision as my administration when it comes to Africa. A social conscience. A long term plan. The US really care about the place, and the DRC especially is somewhere which needs a lot of help, but to quote Obama…'

Beau raised his eyebrows. 'Really? Obama?'

'Yeah, I like the man. We've had some great conversations about Africa. Anyhow Coop, to quote Obama, he said, *We don't want to be a source of perpetual aid we want to be partners to make transformational change.* And that's the point and a great point. We want US companies who mine there to put something back into the country as well as trying to stop consumers having to be complicit with the mining of conflict minerals, because of the lack of transparency.'

Beau, eating on a bag of mixed nuts, wagged his finger at Woods. 'Wasn't it only a few years ago companies said that making a conflict-free product containing DRC minerals was impossible?'

'Yeah and Intel proved that to be wrong with a few of their microprocessors and chipsets. But Donald Parker, with Nadbury Electronics, went one step further. *All* their products are conflict free. And, like I say, I wish I could tell you more about how this administration is going to further that vision, but I'm afraid you'll have to wait. But trust me when I say there's going to be a very exciting announcement real soon, which will make a difference to a lot of people. This administration is about giving a voice and hope to the next generation.'

Beau responded slyly but with warmth. 'You've already got my vote, John, no need to milk it.'

Woods beamed playfully. 'You voted for me?'

'Yeah but maybe next time I won't. Not too keen on your ideas about reforms on gun law.'

Woods grinned. 'Shut up Beau, why does a monk need a gun?'

Beau joked along. 'You'd be surprised. Anyway, it's not about that, it's about the right to own them and all that entails.'

President Woods winked at Beau, but spoke to Cooper. 'Coop, ignore your uncle... You really won't vote for me again, Beau?'

'It'll all come down to the flick of a dime.'

And John laughed, looking grateful and relived to have his friend around, helping to take his mind off Jackson.

Still scrolling through the images on Google, but at the same time fascinated by the conversation, Cooper said, 'So really if the whole of the next generation decided to buy 100% conflict free, they could only buy them from Nadbury Electronics with maybe a few exceptions.'

'Exactly, so there's not only a moral gain but also a huge monetary gain to be made. We're talking billions of dollars.'

'But why do Nadbury bother owning and running Lemon? It must cost a hell of a lot.'

'Because unlike a lot of companies, Nadbury feel that commitment and investment is part of their social responsibility. And I guess when you own all the links in the chain, that's the way it should be done.'

'When you say links in the chain, what do you mean?'

'Well Nadbury Electronics actually own the mines where their minerals come from. Keeps the whole production tight, and it also allows for total transparency. There's no middlemen. No paying off corrupt owners and officials. They're able to know their miners are being paid and looked after decently, unlike in most mines where the average daily rate is a dollar a day. Off the top of my head. I think they're called Con...'

Cooper cut in. 'Condor Atlantic Mines.'

'Yeah, that's right... What's going on, Coop?'

'I haven't got it all clear yet, but I think the Lemon water treatment plant isn't all it seems to be. Which probably means, neither is Nadbury Electronics.'

83

'Holy crap.'

Woods leaned in to see what Cooper had found now, with Beau coming round the other side to see a faded image of a group of six people.

'What is it, Coop?'

Cooper pointed at the screen, going along the line. 'I've been searching for stuff on Charles Templin-Wright and this picture came up. Look. There's your Donald Parker. You can just make him out. That's Charles Templin-Wright, there, second row. You can't mistake him whatever the quality of the grain. And you see the sign behind them?'

Woods peered and nodded. 'Annual meeting for Partnership and Rights of America, 1994.'

'Right. And when I typed that into Google Images, more photos come up of the same meeting. But it's this one here I want to show you.'

Cooper flicked between windows from the photo of Donald Parker and Templin-Wright to another photo, complete with a list of names written underneath it.

'Here. It's that man there.' He pointed at the screen. 'That's Papa Bemba, but the Bemba of old. Because the guy I know, who we think's responsible for at the least gross manipulation, at the worst...' He stopped not wanting to divulge anything more, but added, 'Well, the Bemba I know has had some kind of accident, or maybe it was to do with the conflicts, who knows, but whatever's happened it's caused a serious facial disfigurement.'

Woods stared at Cooper. He was agitated. 'What are you talking about, Coop?'

'His eyes have been mutilated somehow. The only thing that's there is scar tissue which covers the sockets. He uses the disfigurement like it's part of his gig... But that's definitely him.'

'Are you sure that's him?' asked Woods.

'I'm positive, John. So that means Charles Templin-Wright and Papa Bemba are certainly well acquainted with your Donald Parker, which might mean whatever is going on there, Parker may be up to his neck in it too.'

Woods visually began to sweat. 'Up to his neck in what?' he snapped. 'What the hell are you talking about?'

'I don't know what, yet, that's the problem. I can't see what it is. But I know something's wrong. I can feel it. I just got to look beyond.'

'Jesus, Coop, listen to yourself. Look beyond what? This is what you always do. Jump five steps in the wrong direction. Just because someone was at a meeting once with someone else, a hell of a long time ago, it doesn't mean they know them. It's just a coincidence. And even if they do know each other. So what? Doesn't mean anything.'

'Oh come on, John. There isn't such a thing as a coincidence in business or politics.'

'Why not? You've been to the Lemon water plant, a place which is part of a project I'm interested in, and that's a coincidence, isn't it? Just stop looking for things which aren't there.'

Beau squinted. 'Lend me your glasses, John.'

Well-accustomed to this request, Woods passed Beau

his specs, who was then able to question Cooper about the photo. 'This guy?'

'Yeah.'

Beau looked along the names. 'But it says here his name is Simon Ballard.'

Not having bothered to look at the names, Cooper craned to see. 'It might say that, but that's not who he is.'

'Or it *is* Simon Ballard,' suggested Beau. 'And his name isn't really Bemba... What's up John? You okay?'

For the first time since the beginning of the conversation, Woods's anxiety showed through. He pulled at his bath robe. 'Just hot, that's all.'

'Maybe get some water,' said Cooper. 'Simon Ballard, why do I know that name, John?'

Woods shrugged and tried not to catch Cooper's eye. 'How should I know? Look, it's late. I think we all should get some rest.'

'Ballard... Ballard. That's it... Simon Ballard, was wanted by a whole heap of organizations, I'm sure he was. Before I left the Navy, remember when I advised on the US Special Warfare Command board? Well I'm certain his name was being bandied around. But we're going back a long time, mind, and it might not even be him. But I know he was Afro-American, and had some kind of links with Central Africa. I'll tell you the person who might know is my old buddy, Bill Travis. Remember Travis, Coop? Well you need to speak to him... Listen, John, I'll go and get you that water, you don't look good.'

Beau hurried out, leaving Woods with Cooper.

'This stuff about Ballard and Parker, it'll all turn out to be nothing.'

Cooper looked at Woods intrigued by his manner. 'Maybe.'

Woods's jaw clenched. His voice suddenly hostile. 'No *maybes* about it. Why is it that you can never let things go, Coop? You'll get some cookie idea in your head and you want everyone to believe it. Never mind Garp, it's the world according to Thomas.'

Cooper stared. Tilted his head to one side. 'What's with the attitude John? What's going on?'

'Nothing. I just think you're being paranoid. It's like conspiracy theories are an occupational hazard with you. And then you start sucking people in. I wouldn't mind so much if there was some basis too it… It's all that crap you're taking.'

Cooper stepped closer to Woods. He could smell the mint gum on his breath. 'I don't think it's me who's being paranoid, I think it's you. You're the one who seems to have the problem. It's not me who's getting upset.'

'Listen to me, Coop, and listen to me good, you need to leave all this nonsense alone. You've even got Beau wanting you to talk to Bill Travis.'

'Nonsense?'

'Yeah, nonsense, Coop. Trying to make out that good folk have things to hide. They're *your* issues.'

'Don't think I need to make that out, when I've got you standing here all jumpy. Never heard of a poker face, John?'

'I said, leave it. You hear me?'

'If there's something to find, I'm not going to leave anything.'

Cooper turned to walk out but he felt Woods grab him.

'Coop, I'm telling you, don't go stirring up trouble for Donald Parker. He's a good man. And whoever he does or doesn't know, just let sleeping dogs lie. Trust me, there's a lot I've got riding on him. And whether I love you or not, I'm not going to let you mess this up.'

84

It was 6 a.m. and Beau and Cooper were already on the road, driving through the heart of Northern Virginia with its beautiful small towns and vineyards and forests against the backdrop of the Blue Ridge Mountains. The place they were heading for was only an hour's drive from Washington DC.

'It's pretty out here. Maybe I should sell the ranch and settle down in a place like this.'

'Coop, I love you, but those are two things that both of us know will never happen.'

Cooper grinned and attempted to get the radio working on the hire car. He gave it a bang and gave it a thump and it worked straight away. He leant back in the white passenger car seat of the Audi sedan. 'Yeah, you're probably right. Still, it's a nice thought.'

Beau turned off the main highway which led on to Middleburg, indicating right into a large wine estate.

'This Travis guy, I don't know if you remember him from when you were little but he either likes you or he doesn't. He'll either help or he won't. You got the print out of the photo to show him?'

'Yeah, right here… Are you saying I shouldn't hold out much hope?'

'No, Coop, I'm saying it all depends how he got out of bed.'

Beau pulled up outside a large white brick house, trimmed

with lavender and ivy leaves, and set against a hill in the middle of the rolling vineyards.

'Come on, then, let's get on with this,' said Beau. 'We need to make sure we get back to the hospital by eleven. Though when John spoke to them this morning they assured him they wouldn't start to wake Jackson up until you get there.'

'Beau!'

A rotund woman, dyed blonde hair and large blue eyes, wearing too much make-up and an expensive dress a size too small, came running up to the car.

Although her eyes were youthful, Cooper guessed she was around sixty, and had treated herself to a hell of a lot of cosmetic surgery... A hell of a lot. She had a warm demeanour. Clearly happy to see Beau.

'Lucy, how are you? It's good to see you. This is my nephew, Thomas. Thomas this is Bill's wife, Lucy.'

She waved at Cooper across the roof of the sedan as he got out. Her Northern Virginian accent was velvety in tone. 'Nice to meet you, Thomas. Though I think I've met you before. Don't you remember, Beau, when we had that summer party outside? Years ago it was. But the whole thing was a disaster. The caterers didn't show up. The lobster was off. And then it rained buckets. We all thought Bill was going to pass out with rage. But I remember you had Thomas with you. I think you must've been about eight at the time. You were a sad little thing. Think it must have been just after your momma died. But look at you now. My, my, how you've grown.'

A glint came into Lucy's eyes as she licked her over-glossed lips and fluttered her thick, extended eyelashes at Cooper. 'If you're ever looking for a job, Thomas, there's always one here. Never a shortage of work for a big, tall, handsome, strong man like you. Haven't seen muscles like that for a long time.'

Lucy's trill laughter made Cooper look away. Could feel himself flush with embarrassment. As usual, he felt uncomfortable with any attention on him.

'Well I appreciate that, ma'am, thank you.'

Beau, who seemed to be amused at Cooper's, discomfort offered a suggestion. 'Perhaps you could invite Cooper to the party next month, Lucy. I'm sure he'd love to come.'

Lucy patted her coiffed hair. Pouted her lips provocatively, and actually purred.

'What a good idea, Beau. I most certainly will. Thomas, I'll let your uncle have all the details nearer the time… Now, if you two handsome gentlemen will excuse me, I've got an appointment to keep. And Thomas, I look forward to seeing you soon, it'll be nice to get a bit more… acquainted.'

Blowing a kiss, Lucy walked away, wiggling her hips in an exaggerated manner. Then as an afterthought she called back, 'Oh, sorry, I forgot to say, Bill's in the far field, by the large vineyard. But mind, he's in a foul mood.'

*

By the time Beau and Cooper had got to the far field, the sound of gunfire was loud and apparent.

'He'll be practising on his shooting range,' said Beau. 'The man loves his guns.'

'You've known him for a long time I take it.'

Beau smiled. 'Yeah, we go back years. Before you were born. I did my basic training with him and although we stayed friends, professionally we went our separate ways. He joined the CIA and went on to have a real successful career, and as

387

you know…' Beau stopped to look at Cooper to say the rest. A regretful look in his eye. 'And as you know all too well Coop, I stayed in the Navy… How come you're not smoking by the way? You quit?'

Cooper pulled up the sleeve of his sweater, revealing a large nicotine patch. 'I got this.'

'You got one on the other arm?'

'Yup, and on both my thighs.'

'And what about the pills? There's no patch for them.'

Cooper shook his head and tried not to let the agitation show in his voice. 'You been talking to John?'

'I don't need to. I can see it. Just like the last time.'

'Drop it, okay?'

'Beau! Beau! Goddamn it man, have you gone deaf?'

Bill Travis stood at the fence post of the far field, waving to Cooper and Beau. Like his wife, Lucy, Bill was small and rotund. But unlike his wife, the warmth was absent.

Beau picked up his pace slightly, talking as he walked. 'Bill, this is my nephew, Thomas, I was telling you about on the phone this morning.'

Travis sniffed, breaking open the barrel of the shotgun he was holding. He pushed back his surprisingly thick brown hair from his face.

'And that's what I don't understand. Why the hell you were telling me about him, when I already know all about him, already met him? We spoke last week about him, and the week before, and no doubt the week before that. Your uncle seems to be rather proud of you, Thomas, bores me senseless with all the stories. I've said it once and I'll say it again. That monastery isn't good for you, Beau. Not as sharp as you used to be because you've got nothing else to think about except Thomas and God. I bet the Goddamn place

388

doesn't even have a shooting range. A man has to let his frustrations out somehow.'

Beau shook his head, amused. 'That's what prayers are for, Bill. You've never heard of the power of prayer?'

'Hogwash, Beau. What will prayer do for you when there's a group of armed fanatics trying to gun down your front door?'

'That happens a lot here in Middleburg, Northern Virginia, does it?'

Bill peered at Beau from underneath his overgrown eyebrows. 'You being funny with me, Beau? I just don't see the point in this country having a constitution which says we have the right to bear arms but nobody owns a goddamn gun anymore.'

Beau laughed. 'Try telling that to the gun control groups.'

'And that's exactly my point… You own any guns, Thomas?'

Cooper nodded. 'I do sir. Thirty-six in total. Mainly high powered precision weapons. To name but a few I've got four or five auto-loading centerfire rifles, a couple of pump action shotguns – the Remington 870 wingmaster being my favorite. I've also got the Remington 1911 handgun, which I'm fond of as well. I've got a couple of Knight muzzle loaders, then there's the Colt M203 Grenade Launcher which is a lightweight, single-shot, breech-loaded 40mm weapon, and of course the Colt 9mm Submachine Gun, which every household should have.'

A silence fell until Bill Travis simply said, 'Right.'

*

They followed Bill down to the field where a couple of rifles and several rounds of ammunition sat on a small table.

Bill, picking up a Colt action rifle, passed it to Cooper.

He said, 'Let's see what you've got, Thomas.'

And without saying anything, Cooper took the safety glasses and ear protectors from the table. He put them on.

Glanced at the round red steel target around 300 yards away.

Looked round and saw the wind agitating the leaves on the tree.

Estimated the wind speed would be anywhere between 5 and 8 mph.

Took into account the wind direction.

Saw it was coming from twelve o'clock.

Knew he wouldn't have to compensate for any drift coming from the left or right.

And adjusting the safety glasses slightly he looked down the spotting scope.

Waited for the right moment.

Pulled the trigger…

… Hit and blew out the center of the target with a single bullet.

He placed the rifle along with the protectors and glasses back on the table. He looked at Bill. 'So, will you help me?'

Pulling out from his pocket the photo he'd printed from Google Images, Cooper passed it to Travis. 'Can you tell me if this is Simon Ballard?'

With only a hint of a pause, Bill said, 'That's him alright.'

'What do you know about him?'

'I guess Beau's told you that I worked in the CIA's counter-terrorism division for several years, mainly here in the states. Monitoring terror cells, making sure we were ready to act if need be. Before I retired we were watching a terror cell group who were in contact with, and helped to fund, a group in Nigeria which went on to officially become the Boko Haram in 2002. Anyhow, we suspected this cell group we were watching was being run by Simon Ballard, who was wanted for murder, as well as conspiracy to murder US nationals and US military personnel. Conspiracy to use weapons of mass destruction and providing material support to terrorist organizations. But believe me, Thomas, the list goes on. Ballard went underground for a while but then we got some HI on where Ballard was hiding out, and if I remember rightly, it was somewhere in Kentucky. Anyway, we were all set up to go, everything was ready down to the smallest detail. Everyone in our unit was eager to get Ballard. The stuff he did, which I can't go into, well the truth is, it was clear he enjoyed it. The man was a sadist. Nasty piece of work. Anyhow, right at the last minute, the raid was called off.'

'When was this?'

'September 11, 2001.'

Cooper nodded respectfully, not interrupting Bill.

'So because of the 9/11 attacks, we naturally concentrated on what was happening right there and then, and focused on searching out who was behind the atrocities. But when we did go back to monitor Ballard, we'd lost track of him. The only bit of information we had came from another division of intelligence, who told us he'd left the country. And there's been nothing more since. Not that I knew of anyway. But when Beau said you were driving up this morning, I did make a few calls to the guys I know who are still working in CT, and they said the same. No sign. No word. Nothing since 2001. Sorry if I couldn't be of any more help.'

Cooper breathed out heavily. Realized he'd been holding

391

his breath throughout most of Bill's conversation. 'No, sir, you've been amazingly helpful. Thank you.'

Travis nodded. 'Well, I'm pleased I could've been of assistance… It'd be nice to see you up here again, Thomas. Anytime. I like a man who knows his guns. It's been awhile since I've seen a man hit the target like that… though perhaps you just got lucky.' '

Cooper grinned. Modestly he said, 'Maybe I did, sir.'

Beau looked at his watch. 'Bill, listen, I owe you, but we've got to get back to DC as soon as possible. I'll call you later, fill you in.'

Cooper shook Bill's hand. Turned to go but stopped at the fence. 'Can I ask you something, Bill?'

Bill looked intrigued. 'Sure.'

'Do the CIA headquarters in Virginia have a moose in their reception?'

Travis stared at Cooper and then he smiled and laughed. 'I take it you're friends with Rosedale.'

85

Sitting two blocks away from the hospital, Cooper hung his arm out the open window, drumming his fingers on the outside of the door. His phone rang. It was the call he'd been waiting for. He stepped out of the car quickly, flicking the green button on his cell. 'Hey, Rosedale, what's happening?'

The line was bad and he found he had to put his finger in his ear to hear what was being said.

'Thomas, listen, I've found the plane.'

'That's great! I can't hear you real well, so save telling me everything until I see you. Look, if all goes well with Jackson I can get a flight out real soon. He managed to breathe on his own and now they're going to bring him round properly today. They weren't sure at first but all indications show it just might be alright.'

There was a pause. 'That's great Thomas, but what about you, are you okay?'

'The truth? I dunno.'

'I guess from you, Thomas, that's the best we can hope for... I spoke to Maddie, by the way, she said you'd been round.'

Shame swept over him. 'Yeah, though I think I've got a lot more work to do before I even come close to making it alright.'

'Just be careful with her Thomas. Understand?'

Too tired. Too high and with too many miles between them

to bother getting into a fight, Cooper ignored the comment. 'I hear you.'

'Okay. And Thomas, keep me posted when you're going to arrive... I've been fielding Granger's calls by the way.'

'Me too. I checked in with Levi quickly, all's okay back at the office but apparently he's steaming. Haven't even bothered listening to the voicemails he left this afternoon. I'm surprised my cell isn't in meltdown by now.'

'I think he enjoys the drama of it all,' said Rosedale. 'Anyway, you're breaking up. Have a good flight, and I'll see you on the other side.'

*

After Cooper had put down the phone to Rosedale, he decided to dial the office of Bradadt Mining Inspection Company based in Woodstown, a borough in Salem County, New Jersey. He wanted to speak to the person who audited Condor Atlantic Mines and certified them conflict free.

It took over twenty rings for the curt operator to answer the phone.

'Bradadt Mining, can I help you?'

'Hi, I was hoping you could put me through to Dr. Foster, or even to Dr. Foster's office if he's not about.'

The curt operator said, 'I'm sorry, sir, that won't be possible.'

'Has he left the company?'

There was a second's delay before she answered the question. 'I'm sorry sir, Dr. Foster died last month.'

86

'Hey Jackson, it's me… You gave me one hell of a fright back there. Stupid question, but how you feeling buddy?' Cooper sat on the hard hospital bed of the Walter Reed National Military Medical Center, smiling at Jackson who slowly opened his eyes.

Jackson glanced at Cooper. Moved his gaze to Beau and John, who stood by nervously. He brought his gaze back to Cooper and wiped his dry mouth sleepily, and even though the drugs inside his body still had a sedative effect, Jackson's face beamed. He spoke with a croak in his voice and a sore throat from the tube he'd had down it.

'Coop! Hey Coop, man, what you doing here?'

'Coming to see you, and find out what's going on.'

With great effort, Jackson squeezed Cooper's hand. 'You came the whole way back from the DRC to see me? You shouldn't have done, but I'm glad you did. I missed you man.'

Cooper stared at Jackson. Wished he could figure out what was going on in his mind. 'I missed you too, but next time if you want to see me, maybe just ask rather than go to this extent.'

Jackson laughed. Then coughed. 'You know you're not looking too good yourself, maybe it should be you instead of me who's lying here.'

'The way I feel right now, that doesn't seem like a bad idea.'

Jackson's forehead furrowed. 'Why, what's going on...? Oh wait, sorry Coop... Hey Dad, hey Beau.'

Jackson's greeting to Beau and Woods acted like a starter gun for them. Previously not moving and acting like they were fastened to the floor, the words catapulted them both forward to embrace Jackson.

Cooper watched Woods close his eyes as he held Jackson, looking like he was trying to steady himself from the overwhelming emotions he'd had to suppress over the past week or so.

Quietly Woods said, 'Jackson, if I'm doing something wrong, you gotta tell me. If I'm letting you down in anyway, let me know. If you need to spend more time with me, I can sort something out, shuffle things around. Hell, if you want me to walk away from my job, I will, if it means you staying with me. I can't lose you, Jackson. I love you. You hear that? I love you.'

Jackson gently pulled away from the embrace. 'Dad, please. It's not you and it's certainly nothing you've done. It just happens. The black dog just appears; a cloud comes over me. You know that.'

Woods's words were full of emotional anger. 'And I hate it. I hate that goddamn cloud which stops over your head. I just want it to keep on going, I don't understand why it has to be you. You don't deserve it.'

'And neither do you.'

'Is it so difficult to come and talk to me? Because even if you think I don't understand, at least I can get you help before it happens.'

'Dad it doesn't work that way, it kind of... locks me in. Before I realize the cloud has descended it's already there. And then even if I wanted to talk, I can't. But I'll try, Dad.

Next time I promise I'll try... Hi Beau. They let you out then?'

Beau chuckled. 'It's a monastery, not a prison... Good to see a smile on your face, Jackson. I knew Cooper here would be your tonic.'

Sleepily, Jackson smiled. 'It's good to see all of you... and I'm sorry, everyone.'

A round mix of:

You don't have to be sorry.

Don't even say that.

Sorry doesn't even come into it.

Cooper said, 'Would anyone mind if I had a word with Jackson on my own?'

John Woods pulled Beau's arm, who was wanting to sit down on the recliner chair in the corner. 'Come on, Beau, let's go and have our own chat, put the world to rights.'

'Not with your policies we won't.'

John rolled his eyes. A twitch of a smile on his lips. 'That's not funny, not even one little bit. But it was good... I like that.'

*

Cooper waited for Beau and John to leave before speaking to Jackson.

'Now, buddy, now we're on our own, I want to know if you're really okay. I'm supposed to be flying back to the DRC, but I won't if you need me.'

'No, Coop, there's no way you're going to stay around for me. Go.'

Cooper stretched across the bed, flicking through Jackson's notes. 'Why did you do it? What was it that made this time worse?'

Jackson touched the thick raised scar on his forehead. 'You don't make it easy for me do you, Coop? I don't want to sound like I'm feeling sorry for myself.'

'I won't think that. Say what you got to.'

'Okay, if you're sure. Mixed in with the depression... I don't really have a place... ah, you see, even I can hear my own self-pity.'

'Just go on, Jackson, I want to hear this.'

'Before the accident, everything was planned, laid out, I knew what I wanted to do.'

'An aerospace engineer. Even when you were a kid, I remembered you wanted to be that.'

'Exactly, but after what happened in Kenya, that all was cut dead, and with the combination of the partial paralysis and the effect the injury has on my memory, it wasn't even possible to get some sort of desk job at NASA. And that was a blow, I found it real tough. And with Dad going from strength to strength and then getting the number one job I felt even more displaced... and then of course there was you.'

Cooper was shocked. 'Me?'

'Yeah, Coop. You think I don't realize what I did to you? You took the rap, but you know it was me, we both do. There's no excuse. I was an arrogant jerk. A *drunk* arrogant jerk.'

Cooper looked down at the floor. 'No, you weren't, you just didn't...'

'I didn't know? Come off it.'

'My point is, it was my responsibility and mine alone.'

'No matter what you say, Coop, I know what I've done to you. Look at you. You're a mess.'

'Cheers, buddy! Any time!'

'I'm being serious. The accident damaged all of us, but you especially. You're killing yourself, Coop. I can see it, and so can everyone else. And that's what I've done. I killed Ellie and in the process, I killed you.'

The silence was overwhelming. Police sirens and a car alarm faded in and out in the distance, and the ticking of the clock on the wall sounded louder than it had done only a moment ago. Cooper could only manage a hoarse whisper.

'I never knew… Jesus, you've been carrying that round with you for all these years. Jackson, I'm sorry. I…'

'Stop, Coop, *please*. I don't want you to apologize. I just need you to understand where I'm coming from.'

Cooper tilted his head as was his habit and let the minutes tick by. 'Would it help if I tried to get myself clean? Get some real help? Sort things out with Maddie?'

'I'm not asking you to do that.'

'I'm not saying you are. But would it make a difference?'

Jackson studied Cooper's face. 'Yeah of course, because then I wouldn't have to watch you torturing and killing yourself slowly.'

They fell silent again.

Eventually – slowly, real slowly – Cooper said, 'Then I promise. That's what I'll do. I can't put you through this.'

'Coop, listen man, I wasn't trying to put pressure on you, I…'

Cooper snapped. 'I've made my decision, so let's leave it at that.'

Jackson, seeing Cooper wasn't willing to talk about it anymore, changed the subject. 'So tell me about the DRC.'

'There's nothing to tell really. Just bits and pieces that I can't figure out. Basically I've found out a whole heap of nothing, and collected a whole heap of nothing.'

'Come on Coop, I know you. It isn't ever nothing when it comes to you.'

Cooper raised his eyebrows. 'Oh yeah? Let me show you…'

He went across to his green canvas bag. Brought it back to the bed space. Pulled out three full-to-bursting evidence bags and threw them down next to Jackson. He grinned. 'There. Now try telling me you don't think it's a whole heap of nothing.'

Looking at the different objects through the transparent bag, Jackson said, 'A Coke top?'

Cooper shrugged sheepishly. 'I know. Go figure.'

'What you going to do with all this?'

'Nothing. Throw it all away, I guess. I haven't got time to go through anything, not that there's anything much to go through. I got to catch my flight.'

Jackson's smile hit his eyes. Lighting them up. Letting life back in. 'You want me to help you? I can go through them, it's not as if I've got anything else to do. What do you say?'

Cooper shrugged. 'Knock yourself out, but I'm telling you, it's junk.'

'I expect to be paid though.'

'I knew there'd be a catch. So what we talking? Breakfast at Jimmy T's place?'

'Nope, I'm looking for a steak from Sammy's, you know the place near your ranch? Well that's my price. No negotiation. T-bone, rare, with mustard and eggs over easy.'

Cooper shook his head. 'I dunno, you drive a hard bargain, Jackson… but I guess you're on.'

He tore a piece of paper from the notepad at the side, and quickly scribbled down a couple of names and handed it to Jackson.

'Seeing as you're now in my pocket, I'd like you to dig

up whatever you can about these people, especially this Dr. Foster. One minute the guy's in the DRC handing out certificates, next thing you know he's dead.'

'How?'

'I don't know. That's what I need you to find out.'

Jackson looked at the paper. 'Okay, I will. And I'll keep in touch, I'll get on to this right away. I won't let you down.'

Cooper winked. 'Jackson, you couldn't let me down if you tried.' He turned to go but then said, 'Can you remember anything?'

'What do you mean?'

'When you were knocked out. I kind of gave you my confessional.'

'Not a thing. Why have I missed something? Was it juicy?'

'Not really. Usual ramblings of a guilty man… Anyway, I love you, and I'll see you soon.'

Jackson said, 'I love you too, *bro*.'

87

'John, can I have a quick word?'

On his way out, Cooper looked at the Secret Service men a few yards away who were trained to watch and trained to be aware, as well as to listen acutely to what was going on around them. Feeling it would be prudent to move away a little bit more, Cooper stepped into the doorway of Jackson's hospital room.

He said, 'I don't know if Beau told you, but we managed to speak to Bill Travis.'

Woods checked and whispered and checked again no-one could hear him. 'I told you to leave it!'

'And I told you I wasn't going to... Anyway the point is that *was* Simon Ballard in the photo. AKA, Papa Bemba. I bet your life Charles and this Donald Parker probably know exactly who he is. But I'm flying back out there tonight, and you can be damn sure I'm going to find out.'

The president, digesting the information, stared coldly at Cooper. 'Look, Coop, you're putting me in a really difficult situation here.'

'Why?'

John's eyes flashed with anger. 'Because you're digging up stuff you shouldn't and you're trying to find some dirt on somebody because you have a *feeling* something's wrong. You're really going to cause a whole heap of problems over goddamn feelings?'

Cooper noticed some of Wood's staff glance over. 'I'd keep your voice down if I were you, John. I don't know what's going on with you and Donald Parker but I do know if there's anything going on at Lemon water treatment, you need to know about it.'

'I don't.'

Cooper looked bewildered. 'I don't get it, of course you do.'

Woods snarled and moved in real close. 'This is what I'm trying to tell you, Coop. I don't want to know, because if I do, then I might have to do something about it.'

88

John Woods sat in the Oval Office with his feet up on the desk. It was late – or rather it was very early – but either way, he couldn't sleep.

'Hey John, what's going on?'

Teddy Adleman walked in, wearing a striped red open neck shirt and blue pants. They were slightly creased and looking like he'd picked them up and pulled them on from where he'd thrown them the night before, but as usual his afro was military neat.

'Sorry to call you. Did I wake you?'

'John, it's in the middle of the night, of course you woke me.'

Woods knocked back the coffee he'd sent one of the Secret Service men out for. 'I need you to do a check on Donald Parker.'

Teddy looked puzzled. 'We already did. Came back clean.'

'I know but I need you to do another. Off record.'

Teddy slumped down on the sofa and realized he'd sat on the seat with the faulty spring. He made a mental note to personally follow up on maintenance and moved along to the next seat. 'Off record? I don't get it.'

'Just do it, Teddy. And I don't want anyone else seeing it apart from you and me. Got that?'

'Sure. Anything in particular you want me it to focus on? Because, like I say, the FBI check was clean.'

'I know. What I want is to find out is if there was ever a connection between Simon Ballard and Parker. If and how often they went to the same meeting. Hell, even if they ever frequented the same coffee house. I want to know.'

Teddy whistled. 'Simon Ballard as in…'

'Yeah, Teddy, *him*.'

89

Cooper was tired from the eighteen-hour flight followed by the long road journey from Rwanda. It was strange to be back in the DRC, in the same way being in Washington had been strange. And once more, where he'd just come from seemed like a movie he'd just watched. Only existing in the moment.

He'd travelled all over, but no other place had made him feel so on the edge. There was something claustrophobic about it. The intensity. The chaos. The overwhelming belief in the spirit world. Even the extreme weather appeared to be a powerful impacting entity in its own right. Triggering his darkest side.

The country had affected him more than he liked to admit. The negative outside influences saturated his whole being, reawakening the part of himself which he didn't like.

'I see your dress sense hasn't improved with your trip back to Washington.'

Rosedale sat in the Toyota wearing his favorite canary yellow suit whilst glancing disapprovingly at Cooper's go-to gray marl t-shirt and faded jeans.

With Rosedale's banter being the last thing Cooper was in the mood for, he stuck to talking about Maddie.

'I tried to persuade her to fly out here with me. I was hoping she would.'

Rosedale, checking the road for water-covered potholes in front of him, slowed down.

'I seriously worry about your state of mind. Don't you remember what happened? What you did? The way you behaved? Do you really think she'd want to come back to more of the same? And why the hell would you want her to anyway? She's better off without you.'

A flicker of hurt passed through Cooper. 'You think she'll ever forgive me? I mean properly forgive me?'

Trying to work out the way, Rosedale shrugged. 'Sadly, yes. That's the impression I got. Not that you deserve it.'

Cooper gave Rosedale a cutting stare. 'How many times have you spoken to her?'

'A few.'

'And you didn't think to say? I thought we were supposed to be a team.'

Not unkindly, Rosedale laughed. 'That's what I was saying to myself when I was looking down the barrel of your gun. Anyway, she's happy where she is. Probably knitting me a hat as we speak.'

Cooper knew he sounded amazed. That's because he was. 'Knitting you a hat?'

'Yeah, she told me she was going to knit me a hat. Is that so strange?'

'In a word, Rosedale, yes. I didn't even know she could knit.'

'Did you ask her?'

Cooper opened his arms in disbelief. 'Are you serious? Did I ask Maddie if she could knit? No, I did not. The thought never even entered my head. I never saw her once take out a pair of knitting needles when we were together. Anyway, did you?'

'Ask her? Of course. And that's why I'm getting a hat and you're not.'

Cooper fell silent. Stunned into it. He looked out of the window, trying to get some kind of sanity back. 'Tell me about the plane, Rosedale.'

'I will, but before I do, I want to say something… I know I may not be a person you think of when you need to talk to someone, but Thomas, at the moment, I'm all you've got. The stuff with your candy pills and especially the stuff with, well… that hallucinogenic trip you did. If you want to talk about it, about what you saw or if it's still messing with your head, I can listen.'

'I appreciate that but I'm not even going to think about it all. Not yet anyway. My head's a wreck and as for the trip I did, well, it wasn't good. Finding Zola when I was still coming down from the Iboga root was tough. I think half of me thought it was part of the trip. It messed me up more than I was already. Then seeing Ell… you know something, I can't do this. If you don't mind I'd rather not talk about it, but thanks anyway.'

'No problem… Anyhow, we'll be there in about ten minutes, not that there's much left of it. When you'd gone, there was a lot of activity with Bemba's people. I'm not sure if they were still looking for us, but they were certainly out in force. That's why I thought it was best to move camp fifty miles east from Zola's village. Not that I wasn't certain before, but it's clear it was Bemba's men who shot her and I did a lot of asking around in places. Paid a lot of people for a whole lot of nothing, but then I spoke to this woman who not only knew where the plane was, she saw what happened.'

'You think she's straight up?'

'Oh absolutely. I've seen the wreckage myself, and it was

exactly as she said, so there's no reason for the rest of it to be bull.'

'What did she say?'

'From what I can make out, it was pilot error... Come on. We're here. I'll show you.'

90

Cooper found himself with Rosedale in a small clearing, surrounded by trees. He could see the small pieces of wreckage from the plane scattered about the area.

'How far do you reckon the debris is spread out?'

Rosedale yawned. 'Not too far. The problem is getting to it. The main site will be over there. Across those trees. Most of what you see here is what I collected from nearer where the plane went down.'

'Do you think the crash was suspicious?'

'No, I doubt it. The larger parts of the wreckage which I managed to find, I've already examined them, and nothing leaps out to me. It's in line with a low flying crash. See the trees over there? Well apparently the plane was first skimming the tops of them, then apparently minutes later the woman who saw it said she remembered it actually hitting the trees. Kind of bouncing off them, she said.'

Cooper squinted. 'Which trees?'

'Those ones there. Told me it damaged the tail. She said something broke off. Which is consistent with this debris. Then... see over there, near the foot of those mountains? That's where she said it went down. The other thing she told me was the weather was bad. The fog gets pretty thick around here so I'm guessing our pilot wasn't experienced in instrument-only flying. Because what other reason is there for flying so low other than to have better visibility?

He couldn't have been preparing to land, because there *is* nowhere. Only trees, rivers and mountains. He hadn't run out of fuel, because the woman heard the engines. So it *has* to be a pilot error due to bad weather. That's what my money's on. But I guess we'll never know that, nor who was actually piloting the plane.'

'It's strange to be flying that low, though, to hit the trees.'

'Like I say, I reckon he came down because of the fog, but didn't realize how low he was until it was too late, or maybe he was already out of control by then.'

Cooper gazed out at the sea of trees. Tried to picture the scene. 'And you're certain we can't get over there to see it.'

'Not a hope in hell. Dense forest and mountains, no chance. I did have a look around, but just past those banana trees, there's a deep gorge. Impossible to go down, plus the further back the forest goes the more impenetrable it gets. It'd be crazy even to try. At least, though, we found it. Who bank-rolled the plane, we'll probably never find out. Where Emmanuel is, who knows?' Rosedale stopped and chuckled to himself. 'Apart from all those unanswered questions, Thomas. Job done.'

Cooper gave Rosedale a quick glance, but decided not to say anything about it. Not yet, anyway. 'We need to let Granger know, so he can inform the bank and deal with the paperwork, insurance, and all that admin stuff he loves to do.'

'I let Maddie know already,' said Rosedale, 'but I left her to deal with Granger. But now he knows he'll be wanting us to pull out. The plane was the main priority, not Emmanuel, so he'll see it as there's no reason for us to stay. And I second him on that.'

Cooper didn't look at Rosedale. 'I need a couple more days. Can you give me that?'

Rosedale pushed his cowboy hat off his forehead. Wiped the back of his neck with his hand. 'Why?'

'Don't ask me. I just want you to trust me on this.'

'I won't ask you, but as for trusting you? Thomas, that's a different ball game. But I'll give you two days… tops.'

Grateful, but not quite knowing how to say it, Cooper walked over to the trees. Called over his shoulder. 'Do you think there's a chance Emmanuel was piloting?'

Rosedale answered adamantly. 'No way. We obviously don't know where he is but both Zola and his aunt gave the impression he was safe. Go figure. But, if that writing is definitely Emmanuel's in the visitors' book in the Lemon water plant, then *factually* we can rule him out as being the pilot. The woman who told me about the plane said she was certain of the date of the crash. Apparently it was Liberation Day here in the DRC, which is May 17th. And the date Emmanuel visited was May 22nd.'

'And you don't think she could've got it wrong.'

'No, I don't. Because apart from it being Liberation Day, it's also a public holiday, and the woman spent part of the day with her family in Buziba. That's why she remembers it so well.'

Cooper pointed to some of the smaller debris. 'Is this what you collected?'

Rosedale, who was leaning against a tree and trying to get his cellphone to work, called back. 'No, that's from the tail of the plane.'

Continuing to inspect the ground, Cooper examined what seemed to be hundreds of tiny dead insects. 'Hey Rosedale, you got a collecting pot on you by any chance?'

Rosedale tried to be funny. He missed by a long shot. 'Oh,

don't tell me you haven't got one of your bags on you? I feel the world is less of a safe place now.'

Cooper snapped in irritation. 'Have you or not?'

And Rosedale pulled out his metal cigar tube. 'This any good to you?'

'Yeah, perfect.' Cooper took it and scooped up a sample of the insects. 'Okay, all done here. I'm ready to go.'

'Great. Actually, Thomas, before we decide anything else, I've got someone I'd like you to meet. His name's Father O'Malley. I think you'll be very interested to speak to him.'

91

Father O'Malley waved enthusiastically to Rosedale and Cooper.

'Hello! Hello…! Rosedale, I'm glad ye could come back. Ah, this must be Thomas, who you were telling me about. Spoke highly of ye. Fancy a cup of tea? It's one of the few luxuries I insist on having here.'

With his strong Irish accent as reassuring as it was welcoming, Cooper immediately warmed to Father O'Malley, a tall smooth skinned Afro-Irish man with hazel eyes and a smile which said it was okay.

Cooper followed him with interest into the small brick house which was tastefully yet simply decorated.

'Take a seat, Rosedale. Thomas, grab anything to sit on. There's no airs nor graces here.'

Cooper sat down on a small, hard square stool, topped off with a colorfully decorated cushion. 'Thank you, Father.'

Father O'Malley's rounded face shone brightly as he sat down himself. He smiled with delight as he slapped his hands into his lap. 'Well, this is nice… Thomas, tell me, have ye ever been to Ireland?'

'Yes, Father, once. About five years ago, I was lucky enough to go to County Kerry for a few days.'

'Oh, that's certainly some place to visit. Many a happy summer I spent there as a boy. What was it that took ye there, Thomas? Ye can't know what a delight it is for me to be able to talk about my homeland. As ye can imagine, I don't often get the pleasure to speak of such things.'

'I was assigned a job, many years ago, trying to find a racehorse. The owners had taken out a loan for it which they weren't paying back.'

Father O'Malley, tut-tutted. 'Who would do such a thing? Tell me, though, did you manage to find the horse?'

'I did Father, but it wasn't a particularly happy ending. The owners started a fire at their property, trying to make it look like an accident to claim on the insurance. Unfortunately, the fire got out of control and the stables caught alight, killing all the livestock.'

The priest who'd been leaning forward, and seemed to be hanging on Cooper's every word, drew physically back. Shock in his voice. 'Saints and mothers preserve us, what a wicked thing to do. Rosedale, have you ever heard such a thing?'

Rosedale grinned and said, 'No, father.'

'No indeed. Now let me make that tea, before we all die of thirst.'

*

Five minutes later, Father O'Malley was enjoying his cup of tea, explaining about the orphanage he ran.

'I was born here but grew up in Ireland, but I came back to help in 1997. But during the civil war, this place was briefly occupied by the armed forces, and we had to move to another area. But with the grace of God, we survived. It's a terrible thing but here, in the DRC, children are the most vulnerable and the recruitment of children for different militia groups is still happening. These children are trained to torture and kill. Never get to have a childhood. They come here disturbed and traumatized. So many of the children we care for have been subjected to forced labor in the mines and half the girls here have been forcibly prostituted. 'Tis an awful fact but thousands of women and girls in this country have been raped, and a lot of these children in this orphanage are the product of that crime or have simply been thrown out of their homes after being accused of witchcraft.'

Cooper put his tea down to the side, having surprisingly enjoyed the drink which he'd always equated with the British. 'You do an amazing job here, you should be proud of yourself.'

'To be sure, it's not me, it's the good Lord who drives me on. Filling me up with the spirit of Christ… I see you're smiling, Thomas, does that amuse you? I take it you're not a believer.'

'Oh, it's not that, Father, and please don't think for one minute I'm disrespecting you or your faith. You'd be surprised what I believe in. It's just what you said, I find ironic. You talk about the spirit of Christ, and no-one gives it a second thought, but when the people of the DRC talk about spirits, a lot of people look on them like they're crazy.'

''Tis true what you say Thomas, and another time, I'd be happy to talk to you about it, but sadly, I have to make my way to Kalundu, so I fear we're short of time, and Rosedale here tells me you want to know about the cursed land which the locals speak about.'

'I do, and if you know anything about Papa Bemba, I'd be grateful if you could tell me.'

Father O'Malley's face darkened. 'As a priest I have to look at everyone as a child of God. And at times, especially working here, in the DRC, that faith – that belief, Thomas – has surely been tested, but none more so than dealing with

416

that man, with Papa Bemba. It isn't often you come across true wickedness, even here. I believe there is redemption in everyone. I've met soldiers who've carried out the worst kind of atrocities known to man, but even in them I can usually see something inside. Some glimmer of hope that one day they'll ask for forgiveness and atone for their crimes. But with Bemba, I felt a chill, Thomas, so I did. A chill that I'm certain I would only feel if it was the devil himself.'

Cooper smiled, liking the priest more every minute. 'What can you tell me about the land?'

'As you know the belief in the spirit world is part of everyday life, but sadly this goes hand in hand with the darker side. The side which sees witchcraft, Kindoki, as a powerful force. And whether 'tis there or not, if you believe in it, then ultimately it will affect your life just the same. Now a couple of years ago, the land you're talking about was where people lived. But slowly over time a fear grew.'

Cooper asked. 'What kind of fear?'

'That the land was possessed.'

Rosedale, who'd been sitting quietly, said, 'Where did that idea come from?'

'Well, when things happen to people here, they want to know the reason for it… as we all do. But if there is no explanation, or perhaps if there is no explanation which they like, then it'll be put down to bad spirits. Witchcraft. People started to get ill, and sadly in this area, illness is very common. But when people started to get sick on the particular area of land you're talking about, a rumour spread that it was from a powerful Kindoki force.'

Cooper frowned. 'But if like you say disease is common-place why was it different this time?'

'Oh now, Thomas, don't get me wrong, all illness here is

put down to some kind of bad spirit, but the fear which this illness generated was something I hadn't seen in all my time. And the source, I believe, and it's only a guess, mind, was Bemba himself. Putting fear into the heart of people.'

'Why do you think he would do that?'

'I've given it a lot of thought over time, and I believe it was for power. I've always believed the greatest commodity for mankind is the grasp of power. The thought is, if you have power, then the spirit world will want to talk to you, and if the spirit world wants to talk to you that means the community will listen, and do what you ask of them. Because, Thomas, they don't want to make the spirits unhappy by not listening to who they see as the chosen one. It's something my parents believed, as does a lot of my family.'

'And you think that was all there was to it? Just for power?'

'It's difficult to say. The illness which went round, Bemba was always at the forefront of it, promising to heal the sick, even promising to keep them safe from being ill.'

Cooper said, 'Would that be for an exchange?'

'Yes, it was. And as people didn't have money, they gave him their land.'

'And nobody stopped him?'

'Who would stop him? There's no police around here. The only rule is from the spirit world or from a gun. And they have no reason to stop him, Thomas. You see, to a lot of people, Bemba was trying to help, guided by the spirits, and they saw it as only right to give the spirits something in return, even if they didn't get well... though a lot of them did.'

'They got better because of Bemba?'

'Well that's what they said, but who knows what this illness was. People get well all the time after being ill. Though, like I say, this illness was something I'd never seen before. But to my mind, Thomas, it was just a question of chance, who did or didn't get better. But either way, the family thanked Bemba, or the community did because he'd rid the neighborhood of witchcraft.'

'At one of the villages we were in, Father, a young boy died. And I was wondering if it was the same symptoms as the illness you describe… He had huge boils and sores as well as blisters all over him, which wept heavily with pus. I think he must've had a pretty painful death.'

Father O'Malley nodded. 'Aye, Thomas, that sounds like it.'

'Is the illness still widespread?'

'No, not really. Though there's a village further away from here. It's the village after the refugee camp, if you know where that is. But anyway, that seems to have had an outbreak recently. Though when I say outbreak, I don't think it's contagious meself.'

'How come?'

'Well, I've been around it several times, and I'm of the mindset, if the good Lord wants to take me, he will. But it seems he wants me to work hard for me place in heaven, because I haven't even had a sneeze in over two years. I was exposed to the illness on various occasions and so were some of the nuns who work here, and again, not even a cough. So I think it must be bacterial rather than viral, wouldn't you say? Problem is there's no aid or health care here, so as hard and unfair as it seems, if you're seriously ill, the odds are really against you.'

'And I guess that's where Bemba comes in. The idea of getting well would be worth paying out for, or in this case would be worth giving your land for. You've got nothing to lose, I guess. Those that get well put it down to Bemba, and those that didn't, well the community put it down to having the Kindoki force inside them.'

Father O'Malley nodded vigorously. 'Exactly.'

'And what about the land?' asked Cooper.

'What about it? The community no longer lived on it, they'd moved away. Fearful of the witchcraft living there. So giving it up as an exchange wasn't a problem. Even the militia are afraid of the land. Haven't you noticed in that area it's almost militia-free? Well, that's because of the fear of the power of Kindoki. The militia groups have stayed well away, so I suppose some good has come out of this.'

'And what's Bemba doing with the land?'

'I have me suspicions, but I'd rather not say. I hope you'll respect that. Life is difficult enough here without bringing the devil to the door.'

'Can I ask you one other thing though, Father? Have you ever heard of an Emmanuel Mutombo?'

Even though it was just the tiniest of movements, Cooper saw it.

The sudden jerk of the head.

The change in breathing; a reflex action from the change in heart rate and blood flow.

The shuffle of feet, telling him of Father O'Malley's discomfort and his unconscious desire to leave the situation.

And Cooper knew these things were all key ways to tell if someone was lying. And Father O'Malley was. Hell, wasn't he just. Question was, why?

'No… No… No, I've never heard of him.'

Cooper smiled. Knew another tell-tale sign was the repetition of words. 'Thanks anyway, Father.'

Father O'Malley clapped his hands and leapt up to his feet.

'Now, I hope ye can forgive me, but I really need to get on me way. Perhaps you'll come by another time, and I can show you round then, but if I don't see either of you again, look after yourselves and I'll be sure to say a prayer for both of ye.'

Cooper shook Father O'Malley's hand. 'I appreciate you giving us your time.'

'Not at all. But you could do me one thing though. Can I ask a favor?'

'Anything.'

A wistful look came into the priest's eyes. 'Well if ever ye find yourself back in the Emerald Isle again, Thomas, have a pint of Guinness for me. And then send it my love, for I doubt I'll ever set eyes on it again.'

92

In the early hours of the morning, Rosedale and Cooper sat in the Toyota, discussing Father O'Malley on their way to a tiny village, south of their base camp.

Cooper said. 'I liked him. There was something genuine about him.'

'Father O'Malley?'

'Yeah, where did you meet him?'

'In one of the villages, when I was asking round about the plane.'

'He seems a good guy. But…'

Rosedale turned left on the road. 'But you think he was lying about not knowing Emmanuel?'

'Don't you?'

'Oh yeah, hell yeah, without a doubt. Everyone in this place seems to have something to hide.'

Woods flashed into Cooper's mind. 'Believe me it's not just here people are hiding things… Anyhow, listen, before we go to the village, I'd like to go and see a mine.'

Rosedale looked puzzled. 'Which one? The Condor Atlantic mine? You thinking of going back there?'

'No, about twenty miles from here, there's another mine I looked up when I was back in DC.'

'What about it?'

'I'm just curious to see a *conflict* mine for myself, I guess. All this talk about the difference between conflict-free and conflict mines, and the stuff I told you about what Donald Parker and Nadbury Electronics are *supposed* to be doing with their mines and cell-phones and computer parts. Well, it makes me curious. So what do you say, Rosedale?'

Rosedale said, 'I say, which way?'

93

Cooper and Rosedale sat hidden halfway up a densely scrubbed green hillside, peering down at an excavated, exposed area of earth with a few dozen makeshift wooden structures covered in sheet plastic.

The hillside was a hive of activity as young men wearing rags hammered, dug, worked away.

Cooper estimated there were about a hundred people, walking single file in various lines which snaked around the undulating site where groups of tired-looking men with pickaxes stood in cloudy brown pools, hacking away at knee-high mud edges which dislodged and dropped down into the water at their feet.

Even from where Rosedale and Cooper sat they could hear the constant metallic percussion of pickaxes clinking against rocks. And Cooper watched men pulling basketball-sized chunks of wet earth from the water into flexible yellow buckets with handles on both sides. The weight of the buckets clearly making it necessary for two men to carry them, as they struggled up the winding track to higher ground and a waiting truck.

Rosedale handed Cooper his Steiner military binoculars, which he lifted to his eyes, following the line of yellow buckets. 'Jesus, Rosedale, some of them are just kids. The ones at the back can't be older than eight or nine.'

'I know, makes me want to go down there, Thomas.'

Continuing to watch, Cooper felt the rage begin to engulf him. He could see the children struggling to drag the heavy buckets along. He could also see the fearful expressions they held on their faces as the armed guards stood at vantage points around the whole operation. Chatting and smoking and laughing.

There was a sudden loud noise but Cooper couldn't make out what it was or where it was coming from. Then, without warning, the sound of clanking axes stopped. And he stared intently into the binoculars. Swept the whole site from left to right.

Rosedale said, 'Can you see what's happening?'

Over to the left by a mound of mud, Cooper saw one of the guards standing over a pair of children. One of them had collapsed. The other was struggling and terrified and trying quickly and desperately to shovel the heavy, soggy mud back into their upturned bucket. From the guards there were angry, threatening gestures whilst the children in another line backed away in fear.

A guard pointed his gun towards the collapsed boy.

And Cooper's stomach tightened. He was only yards away from being able to help, but all he could do was sit and watch. Sit and watch as the single bullet was fired at the boy's head. Blowing away half his skull. Blood mixing with the muddy earth.

The sound of the shot echoed through the trees and up around the natural basin of hills, causing hundreds of birds to take to the air, screeching and crying as if they were lamenting for the boy.

The noise of the birds masked the sound of the second shot which killed the other child as he struggled to drag the bucket alone. Trying to run. Trying to escape from somewhere inescapable.

And Rosedale put his hand over Cooper's mouth as he cried, curling up into a ball. He tried to fight Rosedale off as he went for his gun. But his arm was gripped and twisted by Rosedale until he dropped it.

'Leave it, Thomas, there's nothing you can do to save them. You *knew* this is what a conflict mine was like but *you* wanted to see it. Those two kids are dead already. If you go down there more people will get killed... I'm sorry but this is one of those times you have to let it go.'

94

'What difference does it make? So the guy knew Simon Ballard a long time ago.'

John Woods threw the file Teddy Adleman had given him on the small coffee table in front of him. He sat back and crossed his legs and then, agitated, uncrossed them and leant forward. He leant back again and said, 'It's more than just knowing him, Teddy. Jesus, turns out the guy was doing business with him.'

'So what? A lot of people probably did business with Ballard back then. *Innocently* doing business with him. Donald Parker would have had no more idea about Simon Ballard's fanatical ideology than his neighbor did or the mailman. Parker was a business man and so was Ballard. Let's be sensible, here. Look at it properly. They were in a couple of the same business and trade organizations, which means at times they went to the same meetings and conferences. If there had been something out of the ordinary, the intelligence services would've picked it up at the time. But he's clean, John. There's nothing on Parker apart from the fact that the man was unfortunate enough to cross paths *unintentionally* with Simon Ballard. It doesn't mean anything.'

Woods face twisted up in rage. 'How the hell can you say it doesn't mean anything?'

'Look, Ballard disappeared in 2001, and no-one knows where he is now. They've all but stopped looking for him.

Yes, he's still on the wanted list but that's just academic, isn't it? We don't even know if the guy's alive... Unless of course you're not telling me something I should know.'

Woods stared at Teddy. He'd battled with the question of whether he should divulge that Ballard was in fact very much alive. He wanted to tell himself the reason he hadn't was just a matter of not wanting to compromise Teddy at this moment in time... He wished it was. But he doubted it. He also wanted to tell himself that not picking up the phone to Central Intelligence was just him wanting to make sure the information about Ballard was correct. Again, he wished it was. But the truth? He needed time to work out the right thing to do... Bullshit. Who was he kidding? He knew what the right thing to do was. Tell Central Intelligence. Distance himself from Parker until an investigation, however long that would take, was done. Period. But the right thing to do wasn't always the right thing to do when there was so much resting on this one man.

'Look, what if it comes out and blows up in our face?'

'It's not going to though, is it? There's nothing to blow up. It's not like Parker knows him now. I just don't understand where this is coming from.'

'Maybe I should ask him.'

Teddy sounded mystified. 'Ask him what?'

'About his association with Ballard.'

Unusually for Teddy, he lost his cool. Slammed down his hands on the table. 'And risk him backing off? John, listen to me. I don't know why all of a sudden you wanted to dig around but you can't even *think* about asking him about it. The vote isn't far away. And you know how precarious it gets.'

'Truth is people don't back off when they've got nothing to hide.'

'Shall I tell you something, John? You want to know *my* truth? My truth is, I don't give a damn if he's got anything to hide. I say. Let it stay hidden… The gun reforms are coming up. That will change the course of history. The course of the next generation. It'll save lives. And you're going to mess it up by dragging up stuff from decades ago.'

Woods said, 'Try telling that to the people Ballard hurt.'

'No, John, I won't because they're not going to know. This is insane. Come on. I've known you a long time. And I'd put the primaries on the fact you're not telling me everything.'

Woods hesitated. Thought of Cooper. 'I just have a feeling about Parker.'

'A feeling. You kidding me? You're going to lose everything you worked so hard on, everything this administration has worked so hard on, because of a *feeling*?'

Woods sneered. 'Funny. I once told somebody just that.'

'Then maybe you should listen to your own advice.'

'All I'm saying is it suddenly hit me Donald Parker couldn't be that perfect. All this couldn't just be that easy. And look, hey what do you know, I'm right.'

'No kidding, John. He's a goddamn businessman, has senators in his pocket and you think he'll be Snow White.'

'No, of course not.'

'No, but *he* is going to be your fairy godmother. John, he's all you've got for the votes. You listen to me. Leave whatever it is that you think or you *know* alone. You're in the here and now. Sometimes you have to lose one thing to get another. Everything's an exchange, John, everything's an exchange.'

95

The morning brought a dank oppressive air. The village Father O'Malley had spoken about was a few miles past the refugee camp where Cooper had seen the Commer truck.

The position Rosedale had parked the Toyota in gave them a view of the tops of the brick huts, as well as the small roof of the chapel where Father O'Malley took his weekly services.

Without looking at Cooper, Rosedale said, 'What's the plan then? We just going to look around?'

'Yeah, I think so. I'd really like to go and see what's happening with this illness. O'Malley said there's been an outbreak in the village recently, it'd be good to see it close up. Because none of this feels right.'

You're okay about taking his word on it that it's not contagious?'

'I am, but I'm cool if you want to stay here.'

'And miss dying of a hideous disease, Thomas? Never.'

*

Walking down to the village along the familiar red mudded roads of the DRC, the rain began again in earnest. Soaked through Cooper's gray marl top.

As they neared the church, Rosedale pointed. 'Jesus, I think that's a person.'

They ran forward and Cooper, taking care not to slide on

the treacherous path, scrabbled down to the entrance of the church. Lying face down in the mud was the body of a man wearing just an old pair of shorts. Cooper didn't have to turn him over to know he was dead.

Huge swellings sat on the side of his neck and back. Tumours as large as apples, encrusted with blood. Purple spots disfiguring his arms and thighs. Black boils oozing pus.

'God, the poor guy. He must've collapsed. Are you certain we should be here, Thomas?'

'Look on the ground.'

Cooper pointed.

All around them were tiny dead insects. Hundreds, if not thousands. And Cooper couldn't be certain, but he thought they looked like the ones he'd taken samples of back at the crash site. He'd also seen the same type of thing when he'd been down by the river near Zola's hut.

'What the hell do you think they are?' said Rosedale. 'There was something similar near the water plant.'

'Why didn't you say anything?'

'I'm not sure, Thomas. Oh no, wait, you were trying to kill me.'

'You're not going to let that drop are you?'

'Nope.'

Before Cooper could answer, the sound of a familiar voice came from one of the huts.

'Quick!' said Rosedale. 'I think it's Bemba!' He gestured to Cooper to go round the other side of the church. Cooper quickly did but drew up when he saw two of Bemba's men holding military Colt 4 assault rifles, only meters in front of him.

Backing away he spotted Rosedale about to run across to hide amongst the huts near the river. Cooper yanked on

Rosedale's arm. Shook his head. Pulled him back. There were more of Bemba's men walking amongst the trees. The whole place was surrounded. *They were in trouble.*

Cooper nodded his head to Rosedale who ran, dipped his body down so he couldn't be seen, and sped to the end of the church wall. Sliding up next to him, Cooper spoke in the smallest of whispers. 'How many of them do you reckon there are?'

'More than a dozen, and every single one of them is armed.'

Quickly, Cooper put his head round, looking at the men. 'They're everywhere. And if we don't move, any minute now we're going to get busted.'

Rosedale looked around, spotted the glassless windows of the white, breezeblock church just above him. 'Thomas, in there!'

Cooper jumped at the window and managed easily to pull himself up on the ledge. He tucked his legs in through the window and vaulted down onto the floor below.

The roof dripped water onto the rows of mismatched plastic chairs. He pulled his hand gun from his back holster. And Rosedale did the same. Added a knife to the mix.

With caution, Cooper headed to the church door. It was slightly ajar. And not only was it thin, but also badly fitted. Bemba's voice was clear even in the heavy pouring rain.

Cooper was still. Frozen. He knew he couldn't make any mistakes. None of his movements could attract attention. And through the crack he could see Bemba, dressed in his usual white attire, as he talked to someone he couldn't see.

'I have no doubt your sister, Vanda, will be well in a few days. The spirits seem to be generous with their healing.'

'Are you sure they'll listen this time, Papa Bemba?'

Cooper heard the tone of derision in Bemba's voice.

'These doubts aren't the words of someone who believes. Do not allow the spirit of misgivings to enter your mind. The only way to rid your sister of the evil inside her is to respect the spirits' wishes, and in turn, they will help to exile the demons, to banish the witchcraft from the unclean.'

'And will they accept the exchange?'

'Now you've agreed to give them what was fitting, without insult, I am sure your sister will be well again. Come, there's something that you need to do.'

Cooper felt the warmth of his own breathing as he pressed his face against the door to watch the direction Bemba and some of his men walked towards. His view was cut off by the trees, with the voices disappearing, turning into a distant murmur. He glanced at Rosedale. 'There's probably some men still round the back of the church. Let's head to the hut where they came out from, go round the side...' Cooper mouthed the last words to him. 'You ready?' Rosedale nodded and drew his gun against his body.

Edging out of the door, Cooper winced at the sound of the creak. Craned round the corner, looked both ways. Pulled back. Retracted his whole body at the sight of Lumumba who was standing by the far trees, looking the other way.

Then he pointed at the hut. Signalled to Rosedale. Counted down with his fingers from five to one.

Sprinting across the small open area of grassland, Cooper slammed his body against the wall of the hut with Rosedale seconds behind.

Panting, he said, 'I think we're okay... Listen, Rosedale, I need you to cover me. I want to go and see what's going on inside.'

Rosedale's expression contorted into anger. 'What the hell

do you think you're playing at, Thomas? We're going to get out of here, *now*.'

Cooper's anger was just as forceful. He was hungry for this. And he wasn't about to walk away. 'Look, we're here now. And this is a chance to find out what's going on.'

Rosedale jabbed him hard in his chest. 'No way, you're crazy. You're going to get us killed. But then, sometimes I think that's what you want. I should've never trusted you. We should've flown back after I showed you the plane. I must be a fool to think you're anything but insane. You should be committed, Thomas.'

Cooper moved along the wall away from Rosedale, with the rain slashing into his face. He turned. He was ready for action. Ready and wired. And hell, it felt good.

'You going to cover me or not?'

And Rosedale felt he had no choice. He snarled at Cooper, keeping his voice low. 'After this, Thomas, after this you son of a bitch, believe me when I say you're on your own.'

96

Inside the hut, with his gun still drawn, Cooper snuck into the back room which was set up in the same way as Zola's hut had been. And freezing at every sound, he sidled into the bedroom. In front of him was a woman lying unconscious.

Putting his gun in his holster, Cooper recoiled at the strong aroma of gangrenous flesh.

Holding his breath he stepped towards her.

And although her condition looked bad – real bad – it was obvious to Cooper her body certainly hadn't broken down as much as Zola's grandson's had.

Her right leg was almost twice the size of her left one and swollen and mottled with stretched purple skin showing the beginning signs of necrosis. Leaning closer, he had to work hard not retch from the smell. Her whole body looked bloated, with her mouth slit with deep cracks, looking like she'd been deprived of fluids for a while.

And then, right there, Cooper noticed something.

Something which caught his eye.

He gently lifted up the woman's arm and carefully began to examine it in greater detail.

'Thomas! Move it…! Come on! Hurry up!'

Rosedale shouted urgent words and they were followed by the sound of gunshots. Immediately, Cooper bolted for the front door but on seeing three men racing down towards the hut, he backtracked, jumping through the open side window.

Machine gun fire came from the side, forcing him to roll behind the hut and to the right of him, he saw Rosedale, shooting and taking out one of the men, who fell. Dropped to the ground screaming in agony. His knee blown to pieces.

'Thomas, head to the river! Go! Go! Go!'

Whilst the gunfire continued, ricocheting around, Cooper turned his head to see one of Bemba's men charging up towards Rosedale from near the banks of the river, a Rimfire rifle in their hand.

'Rosedale! Six o clock!'

Rosedale, turned and aimed and fired but once again the gun jammed. For a split second Cooper saw the panic on his face but before Bemba's man had time to aim, and without a moment's hesitation, Rosedale grasped the tip of the six inch MK3 military knife he held, and expertly angled and threw it to flip with power in the air and hit home, puncturing deep into the man's chest.

Cooper fired in a 180-degree motion, throwing Rosedale his other handgun.

'Rosedale, I'll cover…! Go!'

Running backwards, Cooper continued to fire as he charged towards and into the river, which surged over his face. Deep and fast. Swollen from the heavy rain. And the bullets, unrelenting, blazed down, forcing both men to dive under the rushing brown waters where they headed upstream, fighting against the force of the river until they managed to clamber out onto the mud banks and charged up through the thick undergrowth back to the SUV. Skidding the white Toyota away.

97

Ten minutes later, and safely away from the village, Rosedale banged on the brakes. He pulled over. Turned to Cooper. Grabbed him by his top and slammed his fist into his face.

'Tell me why the hell I shouldn't kill you now?'

Cooper pushed him away and sucked on the blood from his lip. 'Because it was worth it, that's why.'

Rosedale was raging. 'Worth nearly getting us killed for?'

'Yes, it was. We're alive still aren't we? But I got what I wanted. Not that I knew what I was looking for before I saw it.'

'What the hell are you talking about? You're speaking in riddles.'

'I'm talking about the woman in the hut. I saw the track marks on her arm… Fresh injection sites.'

Rosedale reached across to grab Cooper again. 'Yeah, so? What the hell has that got to do with what happened just there?'

Cooper knocked his arm away. Pushing him back in his seat. 'Think about it! Someone's just given her an injection and we both know who that someone is.'

And Cooper could see Rosedale was too angry to think properly. He yelled at him. All control gone. 'I dunno Thomas, how the hell do I know? I'm guessing a doctor?'

'What doctor? Where? Remember what Father O'Malley said? There *is* no health care around here. The only thing around here is Bemba. And I bet my life on the fact, Bemba has just injected that woman with something.'

98

'I want you out of there, you hear me, Cooper? No bull, no excuses, just you and Rosedale's butt on a plane home, now!'

'Listen, Granger…'

Cooper gritted his teeth as Granger cut him off mid-sentence. Holding the cell slightly away from his ear, he listened to the rant. The guy drove him crazy.

'This is the last time, you understand me? You are *not* to be trusted… Just bring back the plane, just bring back the goddamn plane, that's what I said and that's all you needed to do, Cooper… But could you do that, could you? No, not you… You wanted to go and put the whole of the DRC to rights. You and Billy the Kid there. But *now*, now you have to listen to me, Cooper because I'm not warning you, oh no, I'm *promising* you that if you don't get back on a plane, *today*, then I'm going to make sure that your investigation license gets revoked.'

Even though they had a good few thousand miles between them, Cooper kicked the ground, angry at the way Granger spoke to him. 'Oh come on, Granger, you can't do that.'

'Oh yes I can. I can do what the hell I like, which seems to be what you're doing. Maddie has told me a bit about what happened out there. And she doesn't need to tell me much for me to guess the rest. You're a disgrace, Cooper, a mess, and I have to wonder if there's even going to be a job here when you get back. So I suggest if you *do* want to carry on working in this field, you get your sorry butts to Kigali and fly back home. Now!'

The line went dead with Rosedale staring hard at Cooper. He knew Rosedale was still pissed with him.

'Don't look back at me like that, Thomas. Granger's got a point. You need to go home to your shrink. You need to get off those pills and get your head sorted. Whatever's going on in there, only a doctor can help you. You've unravelled, Thomas, right in front of my goddamn eyes. I've seen crazy before, but you? You take crazy to a whole other level. You've lost the plot, baby. And I, for one, can't wait to get on that plane and see the back of this place.'

Cooper rubbed his face. 'Whatever you think of me, we've got a problem.'

'No, Thomas, *we* haven't. *You* have.'

Cooper was charged. Couldn't hold back. 'You know I'm not talking about me. I'm talking about what we saw. We're *this* close to solving what's going on. *This* close.'

'It's over. Our job was to find out about the plane. We have done and so it's time to go back. You asked me to give you two days, which I did, and hell, Thomas, those two days nearly cost me my life. But now, it's finished.'

Cooper felt a sudden adrenalin rush. A nervous energy. He couldn't keep still. And he was certain it wasn't just the pills. 'It's just begun, can't you see that, Rosedale? We're just beginning to get to the bottom of it.'

Rosedale shoved Cooper hard. Sent him backwards. 'Bottom of what, Thomas? There is no bottom to get to. That's not our job. Seriously, how much longer did you think you were planning to stay? A day? A week? A month? Can you see? There could be no end to this. And this place ain't good for you. This is exactly what Maddie meant about you getting lost in a place.'

'So you're telling me you don't want to find out what's really going on here? Even now with the injection marks… Bemba? Charles? Donald Parker? Doesn't the whole thing make you curious?'

'Yeah, I guess it does but then a lot of things make me curious, but here's the thing, *I don't go round trying to find the bottom of everything*, especially when it's nothing to do with me. If you did that with everything, you'd go crazy, and you're a case in fact.'

'But… '

Rosedale raised his voice. Real loud. 'No, Thomas. Stop trying to save the world, boy. You can't. You can't even save yourself, yet you want to try to solve the problems of the DRC. It's tough, real tough to know there are people who have no power, no control over their lives, but that's the way it is. We've done more than we were supposed to. Much more. And yeah, Bemba – or rather Simon Ballard – is as corrupt and dark as any man I know, and probably so is Charles and this Donald Parker. But there's only two of us. We can't do anything, even if we understood *exactly* what was going on. Look around you, Thomas, we're in the middle of *nobody cares*. There's no-one to help. This is the tragedy of this place. No police. No government to speak of. No real laws. So I'm telling you. Leave it, Thomas. Just know you tried, and no doubt tried harder than most people would ever do. But it's time to let it go.'

Cooper knew he sounded desperate. No doubt he looked it too. 'What about Emmanuel? Come on, Rosedale. You don't think it's strange he just disappeared? What about his family? Don't you think they want to know where he is? It's probably killing them not knowing. Every second of every day, just wondering what the hell happened.'

'Jesus, Thomas, this isn't about you.'

'I know that. Don't you think I know? But what about Zola? What about her grandson? You want me to walk away from that?'

'Listen to me carefully. We're going home, *today*, or at least I am, and that's all there is to it.'

99

Cooper's phone rang. He answered. Not caring how dull and listless he sounded. 'Yeah? What's up?'

It was Jackson.

'Hey Coop, listen I've got some news for you.'

'What are you talking about?'

'The collecting bags you gave me. I think I've found something.'

Looking out of the car window, Cooper couldn't keep the disappointment out of his voice.

'Jackson, it's over.'

'You're kidding me?'

'No, we pulled out, two days ago. I'm back in the States.'

'You should've called.'

'I know... sorry. The minute we landed I just took off. I haven't spoken to anyone since I got back. I needed to chill. I didn't want to deal with Granger or the situation with Maddie and I.'

'No, look, it's fine, but I still think you should come over and hear what I have to say. You at the ranch?'

'No, I'm in Western Maryland, I was just going to continue to disappear.'

'Then before you do, come over here and decide for yourself. I don't think you should throw the towel in so quickly.'

Remembering his promise to Jackson about getting clean, which he would, but not right now because now wasn't good,

Cooper swallowed the pills he had in his mouth. 'It's not as simple as that.'

'Coop, when I was in the hospital you told me how much you wanted to get a result from of all this. You believed in the cause. Remember? Now you're giving up? That just isn't you.'

Cooper gave a half smile. Grateful for Jackson's pep talk. It was good to hear his voice. Always was.

'No, it's just sometimes I have to learn to accept when over means over.'

'Oh come on, Coop. What harm can it do, hey?'

'I dunno.'

'Well I do. Look, you were right. Most of that stuff you collected was junk, but remember those three pieces of clay pot?'

Cooper scratched his head. Everything was becoming a blur. It was like he didn't know what was real anymore. 'Kind of.'

Jackson pressed on. 'Oh come on, you must remember. Two of the pieces had copper wire embedded in them, and the other piece was identical but without the wire. Remember now?'

'Yeah, I guess.'

'Well, I think you might be real interested in what I have to say. And besides, it'd be good to see you.'

Cooper didn't reply immediately. Just looked out across the rolling countryside, watching a mourning dove searching for seeds. 'Alright, but this is about seeing you, nothing else. I'll be with you in a couple of hours.'

100

It didn't matter how many times Cooper came to the White House, with its state rooms and officers, residency and bomb shelters, basketball courts and a basement with a life of its own where carpenters worked alongside a florist, a chocolate shop bustled and a dentist and doctor's office were on standby. The security checks were just as tight and as rigorous as ever. And today he could do without it. He could think of better ways to spend the next ten minutes or so than to stand and wait inside a state-of-the-art security check, prior to going through a metal and bomb detector, prior to going through another security check at the South Portico entrance, prior to having to put his admittance card under the ultraviolet scanner watched over by the Secret Service man who looked at him as if it was the first time they'd laid their eyes on him, before finally being allowed to get into the elevator which would take him up to the Executive Residence to see Jackson.

*

Sixteen minutes later, Jackson sat on his bed, with Cooper opting to sit on the floor as he listened to Jackson talk with enthusiastic animation.

'I've got a friend who did ceramics at collage, I think you met him once. Jerry Weiner. Anyway, I got in touch as I figured if anyone would know about the pieces of porcelain you gave me, he would. He's a member of the American Ceramic Society, so he knows his stuff.'

Cooper looked at Jackson. 'You went to that trouble for me?'

'Of course I did. Anyway, I gave him the pieces so he could analyze them. He got back to me yesterday. Jerry was pretty sure they're not your regular ornament from Macy's, and certainly not mass manufactured. More like a local craftsperson. It's quite basic.'

'Did your friend say whether he thought they were made at the same place?'

'Well he couldn't say for certain if they were made at the *same* place because there's nothing to identify it. The stamp on one of the pieces is apparently more likely to be the number of the mold rather than a manufacturer's mark. But he did say the composition of the porcelain was exactly the same. Apparently it can be highly variable depending on the mix, so it gives a good indication that it was made by the same person or company. And something else he did point out was the thickness of the pieces. He doubted anyone would use or want that kind of thickness for anything domestic, least of all vases or ornaments. But what I haven't told you, and this is really interesting; the pieces with the copper wire embedded in them...'

'Yeah, they're the ones I collected from outside.'

'Well, Jerry detected traces of the usual dust and dirt and insect residue *but*, and listen to this, the other thing he detected traces of was a nitroaromatic compound – more specifically, TNT – when he was doing a chemical profile to find out what, if anything, they'd used the pots for.'

Cooper was stunned. Of all the things he expected, this wasn't it. 'TNT? As in Trinitrotoluene?'

Jackson gave Cooper a bemused look. Good humor in his voice. 'Coop, remember who you're talking to. It's me. I'm just a civilian.'

It made Cooper laugh. It was good to be around Jackson. Really good. 'Sorry. I take it we're talking…'

Jackson leapt in. 'Dynamite, or similar to it. It's odd isn't it?'

Cooper nodded. 'What about the third piece? The one I picked up from the Lemon water treatment plant? Did that have any residue?'

'It had nothing on it. It pulled a blank. Here, take this, it's the print out of all the findings. You know, I didn't think people really used TNT so much now.'

'They do. It's a secondary explosive, meaning it requires a primary explosive to ignite it. Something like a detonator. Which might explain the embedded copper wire. The main things people use it for is stuff like mi…'

Cooper suddenly stopped, going into his own thoughts.

Jackson pushed him. 'Go on, Coop, what were you going to say?'

'Well I was going to say, mining. Though it doesn't quite add up… Anyway, I have to give it you, you've done great. You should get yourself a PI license.'

'Oh yeah, right, I think my cover would be blown straight away don't you?'

Cooper leant forward. Changed the subject. 'How did you get on with Dr. Foster, by the way? The guy from Bradadt Mining Inspection Company.'

'Turns out a probable suicide.'

'Jesus.'

'There wasn't a great deal written about it. A few articles saying how he owed money and was a heavy drinker. So the thinking is, it all got too much for him.'

Cooper was surprised. 'Really?'

'The way they've portrayed this Dr. Foster, they've made him sound like a real douchebag. According to the papers, the guy was, and I quote, *a difficult man*, who had a heavy gambling habit along with a massive debt. Apparently he was depressed about it all. Jumped off the balcony of his sixth floor apartment in Georgetown – though that wasn't his main residence. His main home was in Woodstown, Salem County.'

'Having an apartment in a nice part of DC as well as having another place in Woodstown doesn't really sound like someone with money problems.'

'I know.'

Picking up his well-worn suede fawn jacket, Cooper gave Jackson a hug.

'You know what, I think I need to go visit Dr. Foster's old office sometime soon.'

101

Cooper was on his way to see an old friend who worked off the Whitehurst Freeway, near Georgetown Waterfront Park, DC.

It was past six by the time he arrived and although most people looked like they'd gone home, he could see Eddie's yellow-and-black 1970 Buick.

About to park up, Cooper shouted out of the driver's window. 'Hey Eddie!'

A South-Asian man dressed in a raccoon outfit turned round. He grinned, waving back.

'Hey Coop! Good to see you. This is a surprise, I was just heading off.'

'Wasn't sure if it was you there, you Raccoons all look the same.'

'If you want, you can join me. I've got an identical costume upstairs in my office. Jennifer was supposed to be coming along to the party with me, but she's got a bad bout of morning sickness.'

Cooper said, 'Never understood the desire to dress up.'

'You're no fun, Coop, you need to get out more.'

'Not in that I don't. How's the children's party business going, anyway?'

'It's good, we're getting a lot of bookings.'

'So when are you going to give up the day job?'

'Well each time I think I will, Jenny gets pregnant again.'

'Just like that,' said Cooper.

Eddie laughed. 'Yeah, just like that… Hold on a minute, let me put this bag in the car.'

And as he watched Eddie jog across to the Buick, dressed in his Raccoon outfit complete with a three-foot-long stripy tail trailing behind him, Cooper laughed, which turned into a belly roar. Loud and raucous. Something it felt like he hadn't done in a while. And it was a feeling that Cooper wished he could've bottled.

Cooper had a lot of time for Eddie. Like Levi, he was one of the good guys. He ran the Forensic Laboratory of Entomology and Archaeology, which not only did the run-of-the-mill police forensic procedures, but also specialized in performing species identification, both at the morphological and molecular level, as well as insect work associated with archaeological human remains and post-mortems.

'So what can I do for you, buddy? Which reminds me, your god-daughters keep asking when they're going to see their Uncle Coop again. Apparently, nobody gives a piggy back like you. I can't live up to it, you've set the standards too high. The girls are always disappointed when I walk up the hill, rather than charging at full speed. I've sunk to a new low in their eyes. You've got a lot to answer for. Listen, why don't you spin by at the weekend? It'll be crazy busy as always, but it'd be great to catch up, and Jennifer would love to see you.'

Cooper had to push away the sense he was being forced into something. It was stupid, and it wasn't as if he wouldn't have loved to have gone. He would. But he had an over-whelming urge to run from anything which smelt like commitment. Or anything which would have people asking him if he was okay. 'Yeah, sure… soon. But I just have to sort some stuff out, that's why I'm here.'

450

'Go on.'

'I'd like you to tell me what these are.'

Cooper gave Eddie the cigar tin Rosedale had given him to scoop up the dead insects near the crash site.

Eddie opened the tin, smiling. 'What happened to your collecting bags?'

Cooper shrugged, slightly embarrassed by the idea of how synonymous he was with them.

'Thought it'd make a nice change.'

'Well, that's a good old collection you got there, Coop, where did they come from?'

'Eastern part of the DRC.'

'Any story I need to know behind it?'

'I'm just trying to put the pieces together. Only thing which really leaps to mind is that I saw these insects, or what looked like them, in various places. But each time they were dead. Hundreds of them just lying there, clustered together. I just thought it odd.'

Eddie nodded, causing the large nose of his Raccoon outfit to bob about. 'Okay, no problem. You need to know quickly?'

'Yeah, if you don't mind.'

'Sure, I'll work on it first thing tomorrow. Shall I call Onyx when I've got the results?'

'No, I'm not Granger's favorite person right now. Best if you just call me directly.'

Eddie raised his eyebrows, knowing the history between Cooper and Granger.

'Oh. Like that at the moment is it?'

'When isn't it?'

102

Cooper sat in the office of Bradadt Mining Inspection Company, in Woodstown, New Jersey. A secretary typed in the corner as he listened to Dr. Michaels, a bald-headed man verging on the obese, who'd been Dr. Foster's boss for the past two years.

The large wood and leather studded desk Dr. Michaels sat at was empty, apart from a salad and a family size packet of Oreos. Cooper sat trying to work out if Michaels had food inside his cheek, or if he was just afflicted with excess salvia, causing the bubbling build-up at one side of his mouth.

'It came as a shock to all of us but then, none of us knows what goes on behind closed doors, do they? You think you know your neighbor and what they're like, but then they turn out to be a mass murderer.'

Cooper raised his eyebrows and wondered if the man was talking from experience. Michaels, picking up on his curiosity was overly enthusiastic.

'You want to know if it's true or not, don't you? I can tell. You're sitting wondering if I lived next door to a killer aren't you?'

It'd been only a fleeting thought. And as such, he was only able to rouse a casual reply. Casual with zero enthusiasm. 'It crossed my mind.'

Sheer joy came into Dr. Michael's face. He clicked his large chubby fingers, pointing at Cooper. 'I knew it! I knew it! People always wonder. Well the answer is, yes. Yes! And now I bet you're wondering...'

Cooper cut in. Irritated to hell. And it showed. 'Actually, Dr. Michaels, I'm not wondering who it was, though of course I'm certainly relived that you escaped the clutches of a killer and lived to tell the tale. However, save the tale for somebody else. I'm not here for that. The reason, as I told you, is to talk about Dr. Foster. Whether you know how true, if at all, the reports in the papers were about him. Or if he spoke much about the DRC to you when he came back.'

Dr. Michaels's exuberance changed into sullenness. He scowled. Giving his best shot at disapproval. 'And where did you say you were from again?'

'I work as a high asset recovery investigator. For Onyx, they're based in Arizona. We're investigating a missing plane.'

'I don't know what that's got to do with Foster. The man was no pilot.'

Ignoring his comment, Cooper said, 'Did he say anything about his trip to the DRC?'

Michaels sneered. 'You mean did he have a good time?'

'Not quite.'

'Look, Mr. Cooper, Dr. Foster and I often didn't see eye to eye on a lot of matters. He and I were very different people. I run a company which works on profit and loss as well as time considerations.'

'And you're saying Foster wasn't interested in that?'

'What I'm saying is however noble Foster thought he was by wanting to save the world, it's actually very irritating if you've got a business to run. He should've been working for some sort of charity if you ask me.'

'What do you mean?'

'The man was always wanting to do some good.'

'And that's a bad thing?'

'It is if that's not your job. Foster was a mine inspector but he seemed intent on always sniffing out some worthy cause or trying to help the plight of some poverty stricken unfortunate.'

Cooper was lost for words. But Michaels was happy to carry on regardless.

'Look, it's clear the pressure of whatever he was doing caught up with him. By all reports he had turned to drink. Apparently he was a heavy drinker as well as a gambler. He was a difficult man.'

Cooper remembered the quote from the papers which Jackson had given him.

'Where did the papers get that information from, Dr. Michaels?'

'I have no idea.'

Cooper stared hard. The guy was a jerk. 'What? You didn't tell them that? You didn't say to them he was *a difficult man*?'

Foster shifted uncomfortably. 'Well, I… I… I might've said a bit. I don't know. Maybe when the local reporters asked me about him, I might've said that I thought he drank, and, perhaps, and this is only a guess, Mr. Cooper, maybe I said he was a difficult man. But I make no apologies for it, the man *was* a menace.'

'But you didn't know for sure if he drank.'

Foster snapped. 'No, but the man was very furtive, especially when he came back from the DRC. And I've read up on it, it's often a sign of a drinker, *and* he chose to take his own life. I think it kind of proves my point don't you?'

'I'd hardly say that.'

'I've done nothing wrong, Mr. Cooper, it was only my

opinion and whatever the papers choose or don't choose to write, that's down to them.'

Not for the first time, Cooper rubbed his head. 'Okay, look, is there anything you can tell me about his trip to the DRC? Did he mention anything about a man called Bemba? Or *anything* about the mines?'

Michaels, exaggerating his disinterest by looking at his cuticles, sniffed. 'No and no. Foster was supposed to write a report when he got back, for this company as well as for the International Conference on the Great Lakes Region.'

'Remind me, please.'

A long heavy sigh came from Michaels. 'They're an inter-governmental organization. They represent eleven countries including the DRC. They often subcontract mine certification to us. Anyhow, his report never saw the light of day, and let's face facts, it's not like I'm going to get it now, is it? So to answer your question, Mr. Cooper: I can't help you with anything.'

*

'Mr. Cooper…! Hold on…! Wait!'

Running across the carpark, a woman waved to Cooper. He allowed her to catch up with him and by the time she did, her face was red and patchy and she spoke breathlessly. 'Mr. Cooper, I saw you just now, I heard everything Dr. Michaels said to you.'

Cooper smiled, recognizing her as the typist who'd been in Michaels's office.

'It's about Dr. Foster. I was his personal secretary. All the things Dr. Michaels was saying about him are simply not true. He was a good man, Mr. Cooper. A conscientious one.

I'm not sure how much I can help you, but I can tell you all that I know. But not here. There's a coffee shop, Abbotts, it's two blocks down from here, I can meet you there in half an hour.'

103

Sitting at a table with a yellow plastic checked cloth, and the worst imitation flowers he had ever seen, Cooper hesitated to drink the tepid coffee in the chipped brown mug as he sat opposite Dr. Foster's secretary, Karen, listening to her talk.

She looked nervous and had a habit of pulling at her brown bobbed hair every couple of minutes. And although her face was young, her turtle neck and tweed skirt were better suited to a woman almost twice her age.

'Dr. Foster, he'd been shaken up pretty badly by the time he got back. I spoke to him a few times on the phone when he was in the DRC, and I saw him when he arrived at the airport, but only very briefly so he could give me something. We were supposed to meet the next day, but he didn't show.'

'Why didn't you meet, Karen?'

'I don't know, he just didn't show. Which is unlike him.'

'Where were you supposed to meet? At the office?'

Karen shook her head. 'Oh no, he didn't want anybody to know.'

Cooper looked puzzled. 'Know what?'

'That's the thing. I don't know. He didn't want to talk about it on the phone.'

'But what do you think it was?'

She shrugged, pulling on her hair and said, 'I wish I knew. But on the morning we were supposed to meet, he did call me. Not to cancel, but just to tell me...' Karen stopped. Looked around, chewing on her lip.

Cooper encouraged her. The woman was a nervous wreck. 'Go on, it's fine.'

'Well he thought he was being followed. He was frightened. Real frightened, Mr. Cooper.'

'Frightened of what?'

'I think of what he'd found out. Which, like I say, I don't know what it is.'

'Where was he when he called you?'

'I'm not sure because he called from his cell, but I do know he was going to see someone from Nadbury Electronics before he was supposed to meet me.'

'Did he say who? Do you know who he was going to visit?'

'A man called Parker. Donald Parker.'

'I don't suppose you know why he wanted to see him?'

'No. I'm sorry if I'm not being very helpful, but he really didn't tell me anything much. But, like I say, he was very frightened.'

'I appreciate you talking to me, it must be difficult.'

Karen's eyes filled with tears. 'It's terrible, Mr. Cooper. They said awful things about him in the papers. Dr. Michaels told them stuff which was untrue. He's a horrible man.'

'Did Dr. Foster say anything about feeling depressed or anything to do with money worries?'

Karen shook her head forlornly. 'No. And I realize you can't always tell, but he didn't seem depressed. I don't believe he took his own life.'

'Why do you say that?'

'Because he was planning to go back to the DRC.'

'When, and what for?'

Karen, seeing the waitress walk past, spoke quickly to her

before she went by. 'Excuse me, can I have another black coffee please?' She turned back to Cooper, looking apologetic for ordering in the middle of their talk. 'I think he wanted to go back as soon as possible. Once he had the evidence. Well, that's what he said.'

Slightly frustrated, Cooper tried to keep any hint of it out of his tone. 'Evidence of what?'

'I'm sorry, I don't know.'

'Did he mention anyone call Bemba? Or Ballard?'

Tugging at her hair again, Karen shook her head. Said nothing.

'What about the name Charles Templin-Wright? Does that mean anything to you, Karen?'

'No.'

'How about when he flew back to the States? Can you remember the date Foster arrived home?'

'Oh yes, because he was due back May 22nd but I had to change his ticket. I remember because they wanted to charge double for it if he flew back in June, so I booked him a flight for May 27th from Kigali.'

'Why was the date changed?'

'He said he had to go and see some place before he came home, and that's why I had to move it.'

'Is there anything else he said?'

'No, sorry. But when I met him at the airport, he gave me something to keep safe for him until we met the next day, but we never did… I've got it here.'

Karen went into her oversized gray handbag and pulled out a lipstick and an empty bottle of perfume and a couple of magazines and some old receipts and a hairbrush, before bringing out a small white padded envelope. 'This is what he gave me. I haven't opened it.'

She handed it to Cooper. It was cool to the touch. There was some handwriting on the front.

Karen Kirby, to be stored at 4°C

'Is that Dr. Foster's handwriting on the envelope?'

'Yes.'

Cooper didn't say anything. Just gathered his thoughts. Pulled out his phone in half the time it'd taken Karen to pull out the envelope, scrolled through some photos and zoomed in on the photo he'd taken of the names in Lemon's visitors' book.

'Is this Dr. Foster's writing as well?'

Karen studied it. 'The top one looks like his writing. But why did he write someone else's name?'

Cooper looked at the entry:

Phillip Holt.

'I don't know Karen, that's what I'm trying to find out. Can I ask why you didn't give this to the police? Why give it to me?'

'Mr. Cooper, I don't want any trouble. I look after my elderly parents. They live with me in a small apartment. They rely on me for everything. I can't afford to lose this job, and I know Dr. Michaels is always looking for an excuse to let me go. He's not interested in what did or didn't happen to Dr. Foster, he's just interested in me doing what I'm paid to do.'

'Sounds like somebody I know.'

'Jobs are hard to come by around here and, if I'm truthful, Dr. Foster sounded frightened the last time I spoke to him. I'm sorry but I've got to think of my parents. If anything happened to me… ' She stopped then added, 'You do understand?'

'Of course. But if you didn't want to get involved why give it to me?'

'It sounds silly but back in the office you sounded like you cared. That was like Dr. Foster, he always cared.'

'You sound like *you* cared about him.'

Karen's eyes filled up with tears, but she held his eye as she spoke. 'I did… I loved him, Mr. Cooper. He didn't know. I never told him, there wasn't any point. Like I say, I've got my elderly parents to think of.'

'I'm sorry, Karen… Do you mind if I open this?'

'Not at all. In fact, I'd rather you kept it. I haven't known what to do with it. I'm actually pleased I can give it to you.'

Cooper ripped it open. Inside was a small glass test tube full of blood. There was a label on the side of the test tube. *Emmanuel Mutombo.*

104

'Coop, it's me, Eddie, can you talk?' Eddie Cotton whispered down the phone.

'Yeah,' Cooper whispered back. 'Can you?'

'I'm doing that whispering thing again, aren't I?'

'Yes you are,' said Cooper. 'For a man with an IQ higher than Einstein's, I wonder how it is you still don't get that when you call *me*, asking if *I* can talk, *you* don't have to whisper.'

'That's what having too many kids does to you. Listen, are you still around? I got those results for you.'

'Okay, brilliant. I should be there in a couple of hours.'

'Mr. Cooper…? Mr. Cooper…!'

'Eddie, listen, I have to go, someone's calling me. I'll see you soon.'

Cooper clicked off his cell and turned to the large woman who sat at the desk summoning him in the kind of a tone he'd heard dog owners use in the park to call their canine friends.

'Sorry about that.'

The large woman with the dog owners' tone neglected to acknowledge Cooper's apology. 'Mr. Parker does not see visitors without an appointment. Imagine if everybody who wanted a word with Mr. Parker just turned up unannounced, where would we all be then? It would be chaos. Anarchy. Total pandemonium.'

'We wouldn't want that would we?' Cooper said flatly.

'No, indeed. Now if you want to make an appointment you need to go through his secretary, but that still won't guarantee you a meeting with him. Mr. Parker's a very busy man and if everybody tried to make an appointment with him, it would be…'

'Bedlam.'

The large woman looked puzzled. 'No, Mr. Cooper, it would be impractical.'

'Was this taken recently?'

Cooper nodded to a large color framed photograph on the reception desk.

'Yes, that's Mr. Parker accepting the North American Environmental Business Award last month. It's the second year the company's won it.'

Cooper studied the photo of Donald Parker smiling broadly as he held a seven-inch tall Silver Star trophy. 'Okay, well thank you for your time.'

105

Cooper walked into the research lab and looked at Eddie. 'I'm not even going to ask.'

'It's a theme party. The kid likes dinosaurs. What can I say?'

'But do you have to wear it at work?'

Eddie grinned. 'What do you take me for, Coop? I haven't worn it all day. Just thought I'd get ready whilst I was waiting for you.'

Cooper gave him a nudge. 'Hey, if that's the story you want to stick to, that's fine by me. What have you got anyway?'

Eddie flicked on a projector, which threw a huge black and white image onto the far wall.

'This is an X-ray of a flea. Your flea, actually.'

'I thought it was some kind of bug.'

'Nope. It's a Xenopsylla Cheopis flea, commonly known as an Oriental or tropical flea. It's mainly a parasite of rodents, but it can live off other animals as well. And see that dark part on the X-ray, right there? Well, that's a mass of bacteria in the insect's digestive system. If it were alive what would happen is that the mass would work like a blockage, stopping the flea ingesting a meal, which will make it real hungry. You see once they've swallowed the bacteria from the infected animal – say, a rat – the bacteria will multiply inside it. The hunger will make the flea go looking for a host to feed off, but because of the blockage, it can't eat properly, so it tries to regurgitate the bacteria back up, and this comes out in its bite, infecting the host with the flea's pathogen.'

'So what kind of disease are we talking about?'

'Primarily this sort of flea is a vector for *Yersinia Pestis*.'

Cooper looked at him as blankly as he could.

'The common name being the plague.'

'As in the bubonic plague?'

'That or the septicemic plague or the pneumonic plague.'

'Jesus. And that's the bacteria in my flea?'

Eddie shook his head, flipping off the projector. 'No, I thought at first it was, but although the initial tests show a lot of clinical similarities to the bacteria, it isn't it. Thing is, bacteria and disease do mutate, either naturally or from human intervention, but unless there's a lot of research done, it's hard to tell exactly what it is. But I have no doubt it's probably pretty nasty if you get bitten by it. You may even get similar symptoms to the plague. Say like swollen lymph glands, fever, bleeding, large boils, coughing up blood, black spots. But again, these are all on a maybe.'

'Do you think it's contagious?'

'I don't know, you'd have to do a lot more tests and observations before you could know how this bacteria works.'

Cooper tried to push him on it. 'What about giving me an educated guess?'

'I think it'd be wrong to do that because although the *actual* plague is an extremely virulent pathogen that's likely to cause severe illness and probably death if it isn't treated, it doesn't mean this pathogen does the same thing.'

'So what would you do to find out?'

'Sometimes the best thing to do is to go back to the source, as in the area it was found. In your case, if someone *were* to want to research this bacteria more, they'd go back to the area of the DRC where your flea came from. See if people there have been bitten by these fleas. Maybe they've fallen ill from the bites, maybe they haven't. If they have, then it's a question of finding out how it affects the individual. You also need to test the rats in the area, to see if they're carrying it, and, if not, why not. For all we know the people who live there may already know of the bacteria's existence in that area. If it's a remote place, there's no reason why we should know about it here in Washington, *especially* if it's never been reported or broken out into a massive epidemic like Ebola. It could just be isolated to that particular area.'

'Is that likely?'

'Well, the bacteria might've mutated in response to the area, like the environmental conditions. It could be a common problem there and it's been around for years. The local medics might not worry about it or call the World Health Authority in because they know that simple antibiotics will make it better. After all, it's simple antibiotics which cure the actual plague. So before you can even try to make an educated guess, you have a hell of a lot of questions to ask. You alright, Coop?'

'Yeah, just thinking.'

'You sure? You don't look so good… But this might put a smile on your face. Even though I can't tell you exactly what the bacteria is, I *can* tell you I've seen it once before. Here in DC in fact. Just recently.'

'What?'

Cooper leant on the side of the table.

'About a month ago, one of my colleagues was off sick from work, though in actual fact turns out he'd gone to Vegas and got busted by the cops with three joints of marijuana. Anyway, his work needed covering so I thought I might as well do it, even though it wasn't strictly my department.

466

There were some clothes to analyze. Really general stuff. The police weren't looking at anything in particular but there was a question mark around the circumstances. Anyway, I didn't find anything – apart from on the jacket, where I found a couple of fleas. It's not that unusual to find fleas. On the contrary, I often find them concealed in clothing fibers. It's quite common, really, people just don't know they're there. When I did some tests, the fleas were *Xenopsylla Cheopis*, tropical fleas, same as yours. And what I found that was really unusual was the bacteria inside them, which I hadn't come across before. Until now that is. That's crazy right?'

'Who was the person?'

'I can find out, hold on.' Eddie walked over to some files by the window. 'I do remember in the end they ruled it as a suicide. Here you go, his name was...'

'Foster. Dr. Foster.'

Eddie looked surprised. 'Yeah, Tim Foster. How did you know?'

'It's a long story, I'll tell you over a beer when I catch up with you properly. In the meantime, could you do me one other thing? Can you test some blood for me? I'd like you to test it for the same bacteria.'

'You want me to see if the blood has the same bacteria which is in the fleas?'

'Yeah, though I have a feeling I already know the answer.'

Cooper handed Eddie the test tube of blood. 'Thanks, I appreciate this, Ed.'

Eddie nodded, reading the label out loud.

'*Emmanuel Mutombo*... Listen, it's no problem. My pleasure. Give me a few hours to turn it round. I'll call you when I know.'

106

'Hey, Beau!'

Cooper walked up to his Uncle who was down on his hands and knees, weeding the flourishing green vegetable garden of the monastery.

Beau grinned widely. 'Right back at you, Coop… Give me a hand up, will you, damn sciatica is playing up again.'

Cooper stretched out his hand. Pulled up Beau with ease.

And using the bottom of the long cream robe he was wearing to wipe the soil from his hands, Beau eyed Cooper up and decided not to bother telling him how terrible he looked.

'What's on your mind? You've got that look in your eye you always had as a boy when something was troubling you.'

'I'm just stuck.'

'Aren't we all… Is this about Maddie? Cora? About your meds? Is there a problem? Please tell me this isn't about Ellie.'

That was a hell of a list, but for once it was none of those things.

'Nope, it isn't about her or her and no, there isn't a problem,' Cooper half joked. 'Well, there is and, as you point out, several of them, but that's not why I'm here.'

Beau winked. 'Go on.'

'I've got all these pieces of a jigsaw but I can't see how to put it together. I know the answer's there, but I'm missing something.'

'You wanna try me?'

'Well, you know most of it already. What you don't know is, Jackson found out…'

Beau interrupted sounding surprised to hear the name. 'Jackson?'

'I'll tell you about it later. Anyhow, Jackson found out that a couple of pieces of clay pot, which I collected in the DRC, had explosive residue on them. TNT as well as some kind of copper wire embedded in them. Then remember my friend Eddie?'

'The one who likes to dress up as a chicken?'

'Yeah, that and other things. Well, he did some tests on some bugs which I found at the crash site. Turned out to be fleas. Anyway, apparently they're carrying some crazy-ass disease he's never really seen before.'

Beau nodded, taking in the information. 'So you think the pieces of pot are significant? That they're relevant?'

'That's the thing I don't know. They might not be. But there was a third piece which I took from the water plant when I smashed the pots…'

'You smashed some pots? Any reason.'

'Let's just say I wasn't having the best of days. Anyway, that piece came up blank, but Jackson's friend seemed to think all three pieces were from the same kind of composition of porcelain. But then, all that could mean is that they were made by the same local craftsmen.'

'It's odd that TNT would be found on the pieces.'

'That's what I thought. I can't see a reason why there'd be explosive residue on something like a clay pot. It'd blow to pieces.'

Beau nodded in agreement. 'Nasty stuff, that TNT. Pretty toxic. I had a friend who use to work with it. Ended up with liver failure and damage to his spleen. There are stringent health and safety measures now, but during the First and Second World War they often called the munition workers who handled the chemical *canary girls*.'

'I don't understand.'

'Well, a canary is a bright yellow bird, and skin contact with TNT makes your skin turn yellow. Hence the nickname.'

'Say that again.'

'You going deaf, Coop, on top of everything else?'

Cooper snapped. 'Please, Beau, just tell me again.'

'Okay... It's one of the side effects of the chemical. Yellow skin as well as other skin irritations, like dermatitis... What's going on?'

'Charles, the guy in charge of Lemon, had really bad dermatitis on his hands and wrists, as well as really heavily stained yellow fingernails, which Maddie commented on. And get this: Donald Parker; I saw a recent photo of him, holding some award he'd won. I didn't think much of it at the time, but his hands were just like Charles's. Yellow staining and dermatitis.'

'So what does that prove?'

'It doesn't prove anything, but it points to them both handling TNT. Though that doesn't really help me, either. Can you can see why I'm stuck? All I've got are fleas, witchcraft, and a hell of a lot of pots.'

'What do you mean?'

'Charles had a vast collection of these pots. Didn't tell me why. He pretended it was to do with the new décor.'

'You don't believe him?'

Cooper scoffed. 'No, nothing spells liar like Charles Templin-Wright.'

Beau exhaled. 'I hate to say it, but I'm as stuck as you on

470

this. Can't see any connection. Did you tell me what happened to the plane? I can't remember.'

'At a guess, Rosedale thinks it was flying too low. Hit some trees, and went down. I reckon he's right.'

'To hit some trees. That's pretty low flying.'

Cooper said, 'Yeah, I know, but we think bad weather and bad piloting caused it. And that's it. Oh, and this… This is the printout of the findings from Jackson's friend. The ceramic guy.'

Cooper passed Beau the sheet of paper.

'Look at this, Coop. It says two of the pieces have insect residue on them.'

'So? I found them outside. Why wouldn't they have it? Place is crawling with bugs.'

'Exactly. Crawling with them. Insects walk over things they don't deposit themselves on stuff… Did your friend Eddie, give you a printout?'

'Yeah, here.'

Cooper pulled out another piece of paper from the inside of his jacket, being careful not to pull out the bottle of pills he had in there.

Beau took the printout. Read it and said, 'Hey, look, if you cross reference the insect residue on the two pieces of pot and this flea of yours, well the cell structures of the insects are all the same. Jesus, Cooper, think about this.'

'I am. And I'm getting nothing fast.'

Irritated, Beau said, 'It means that in all likelihood these fleas of yours were also the same kind of fleas on the two pieces of pot.'

Cooper stared on blankly.

'Just tell me what you're thinking.'

'No, Coop. This is what you were like as a kid. Always wanting to be spoon-fed. Think about it.'

Cooper rubbed the back of his neck. Took a deep breath. Then took another one. 'Beau, my childhood wasn't exactly *Mary Poppins*.'

'Coop, we're not going to go down this road again are we? You know what, I won't be drawn into a fight. Let's just stick to the reason why you're here. Remember the military history books I gave you as a kid?'

'Kind of. Hardly bedtime reading.'

Beau snapped. 'Maybe if you'd read them, Coop, then you'd know what I was getting at. What does this remind you of? The pots and the fleas and the TNT? Along with the plane and people getting ill? Come on, think about it.'

Cooper stared at his uncle. Trying to focus on what Beau was getting at rather than focus on his childhood. He said, 'You win, Beau, and before you say it, yes – I'm giving up, I don't know.'

'Well this reminds me – and it's the only thing that I know which ticks all these boxes – of General Ishii.'

'Who?'

'Jesus, Coop. Didn't you learn anything? No, don't answer that. Okay, in World War Two, the Japanese used insect warfare on a mass scale. General Ishii, well he used plague-infected fleas against the population of China, using flea-filled clay pots, dropped over the area in low flying planes. Think about it, Coop, it fits the profile. And this Simon Ballard, or Bemba as he calls himself now… well, from what Bill Travis said, he's as evil an individual as General Ishii ever was. Not to put too fine a point on it, I think what you're dealing with is some kind of entomological warfare.'

'What?'

'I might be so far out on this but my gut's saying different. I mean the concept of entomological warfare, that's been around for centuries. And what you've told me, I can't help thinking it's got all the hallmarks of it. Look, go and get some books from the library. Read it up. See what you think. The only thing I can't tell you is why it's happening. Maybe you just need to look further.'

107

Late into the night, Cooper sat up reading the books he'd picked up from the library. His mind was racing as he pored over the images and accounts. And for once he tried to fight against the urge to take the edge off... He lost that battle, but at least he was finally beginning to understand the part of the picture he hadn't been able to see before. He got it. And if it *was* what he was thinking, then the only thing he needed to work out was what he was going to do next.

Splashing water on his face, Cooper grabbed his pills, his wallet, and hoped he was about to grab the final piece of the jigsaw.

108

'Why, Thomas J. Cooper, I don't believe my eyes, what's it been, ten years or more?'

Janice Spencer-Wells, a proud Jewish New Yorker, gushed with warmth as she sat in her wheelchair behind the large desk at the Washington State University. Her green eyes twinkling with real surprise and delight.

'It's been more like thirteen, maybe fourteen.'

'Now this is the part where you're supposed to say to me that I don't look a day older.'

Cooper grinned. Gave a wink. 'Well you don't.'

She cackled and Cooper smiled. He'd forgotten how loud and infectious that cackle was.

'That's bull, and we both know it. I look in the mirror in the morning and it's not my mother I see, it's my grand-mother. But you, Thomas J., you look fine.'

'You're probably the only one who thinks so.'

'Oh no, I think age just seems to suit you. How old are you now? Forty? Forty-one? Thirty-nine? No, don't tell me, I just want to imagine you as perfect.'

There was the cackle again. Loud. Warm. Infectious. 'Come on then, Thomas J., what is it that you want?'

'Janice, I need a favor.'

She smiled playfully. 'Of course you do, and here's me thinking you were popping in for some action. So come on, what can I help you with?'

'I'm working on a case and I need to know about mining rights in Africa. The Democratic Republic of Congo, to be precise.'

'Well come on, pull up a chair, we can get cozy.'

Janice, an economics professor who Cooper had met through Beau, pushed the mouse on her computer, making it jump to life.

'Is that what you're working on?' He pointed to the Word document which was open.

'Yeah, I'm writing it for the *Post*. Funnily enough it's about African mineral reserves and various foreign billionaires that have been allowed to set up mines, and are shipping huge amounts of valuable ore out of poverty-stricken areas of Africa. It's tragic. A huge amount of people are just unaware of the great wealth which is basically beneath their feet, and they're certainly not seeing any of the profit generated. Problem is, a lot of people here think this is yesterday's news.'

Cooper read part of it aloud. *'The DRC has unexploited mineral reserves estimated at 24 billion US dollars, but without an effective army or police force to maintain law and order, armed militia groups control mining through force. In response, the DRC government encourages foreign investors to conduct private mining. Since 2002, the DRC Mining Code required foreign investors to surrender 5 per cent of company shares to the government and pay various taxes levied against profits. The industry has boomed in recent years, though lack of basic services like electricity and clean water have hindered progress, as have ongoing issues with armed militia groups. In February 2013, a draft bill proposed amendments to the 2002 mining code, including an increase from 5 to 35 per cent of foreign company shares to be given to the government, along with huge increases in taxes against mining profit, but in 2017...'*

Cooper stopped. 'I'd like to read this when you've finished, can you send me a copy?'

Janice laughed. 'Ay-yay-yay, buy the Post yourself, you cheapskate.'

Cooper roared with laughter. The second belly laugh in a week. That was some going.

'You're good for me, Janice, did I ever tell you that?'

'Yeah, you told me that the last time you saw me; thirteen years ago. It's becoming too much of a regular thing.'

Still chuckling, Cooper asked, 'How can I find out who's wanting to mine in a certain area?'

'Of the DRC? Well, mining rights and applications are granted on a first come first served basis. I can look up who's been granted a license if you like.'

Cooper watched Janice tap furiously on her computer. Logging into different websites and documents. 'It's a bit of a nightmare if you don't know how to find it, plus a lot of the information isn't always available to the public. But we're lucky at the University, we can usual get access to most records… like this… Okay, here it is, the DRC Ministry of Mines… if I click on *Contract-Natural-Resources*… and then again on *Mining Contracts*… there you go. It's the list of mining agreements between various companies and the DRC Government; take your pick, Thomas J.'

Skimming down the list Cooper was drawn to a group of five contracts awarded to Nadbury Electronics/Condor Atlantic Mines. A couple were dated as far back as two years ago, another one as recently as three months ago.

'Can you click on these for Nadbury Electronics and Condor Atlantic Mines, the ones there, in South Kivu…? Thanks.'

The first document opened up on the screen to reveal a

legible but poorly scanned copy of a lengthy legal contract written in French. In the bottom corner of each page there were two sets of hand-written initials and a government authentication stamp which read:

Republique Democratique du Congo L'office des mines d'or de sud Kivu.

'Can you click on the others, please Janice?'

Cooper read through them all. It was exactly what he'd thought.

'You see what you're looking for, Tom?'

'Too right I do. The companies I'm looking into, Nadbury Electronics and Condor Atlantic Mines, well it looks like they've been granted research permits for most of the land around Buziba, as well as some actual mining licenses. Do you know if there would be any restrictions on it?'

'On their mining? No, probably not. The only thing which is required is to commence testing the area within six months of getting the research permit, and once they've done their tests, to make sure the land is worth mining. Then they'd be free to apply for an actual mining license, which wouldn't be a problem to get, especially if they owned the land. And from there they could carry on mining for ten years before needing to renew it. At the moment companies only have to give 5 per cent of their company shares to the DRC Government, as the proposal for 35 per cent still hasn't been passed yet. But otherwise they're free to mine unrestricted. And in an area like that, the profits could run into hundreds of millions.'

'Janice, thanks, I owe you.'

Cooper got up to go.

'Oy vey. You don't get away that easily. I deserve a kiss for this. See that black mark on my face? That's where you kissed me last time, I've never washed there since.'

109

'Hey, Maddie.'

The next day, Cooper stood in the kitchen of Onyx feeling awkward and uncomfortable. He could think of a million places he'd rather be. Even though they'd had the conversation at her house, it still felt awkward. And he'd been trying to figure out what to say to Maddie for the past few minutes, but as he stirred his coffee, which didn't need stirring any more than it had done a minute ago, with Maddie staring and expecting him to talk, the only thing so far he'd managed to come up with was the greeting. And this time he knew she wasn't going to let him get away with a shrug.

In truth, he'd been hoping not to run into Maddie; she knew him too well and would know straight away something was going on. He'd also forgotten it was Granger's birthday, which meant everybody was around.

He wanted to make a quick exit and go find Rosedale, who he'd actually thought would be here. But with Maddie standing in the doorway, the quick exit he was planning on wasn't going to happen anytime soon.

Maddie's sharp voice crashed into the difficult silence.

'What's going on? How come all of a sudden you've got nothing to say?'

'Sorry, I just got stuff on my mind.'

'Like what? Tom, what are you hiding?'

Cooper held his hands up in the air. Felt an intense desire

to push past her and just get the hell out. His head was racing and he needed to get on with what he had to do.

'Maddie, listen. Can…'

'Oh don't tell me. Let me guess… *Can we do this another time*. That's what you were going to say wasn't it?'

Cooper knew he sounded breathless. Agitated by the adrenalin surging within him. 'Yeah. That's what I'd like. Please. I've got to go and find Rosedale.'

'Why?'

Cooper blinked several times. Gave a nervous laugh. Looked at her sideward.

'Why do I have to go and find Rosedale? Don't take this the wrong way, Maddie, and I don't mean to sound harsh, but your days of asking me where and why are over. You threw me out, remember?'

'Our truce didn't last long, did it? But don't kid yourself, Tom, my days were never there. You did what you liked when you liked.'

'I don't need to do this now.'

'No, you never do.'

Cooper looked down at nothing much. He could feel himself becoming jumpy. He felt cornered, and he needed to get out.

'Look, when I come back, I can give you all the time in the world. I'll sit down and I'll hear what you have to say and I'll tell you anything you wanna know, Maddie, and we can decide what to do from there. But right now, I gotta get out of here.'

She stepped in towards Cooper. Moved her head so she could look him right in the eye.

'Come back from where?'

'Jesus, Maddie. I dunno, come back from finding Rosedale.'

'No, that's not what you meant. Come back from *where*, Tom?'

Cooper closed his eyes. Opened them. She was still there staring. 'Why you doing this Maddie? I just want to go, okay?'

'I know you Tom, and I know when you're trying to avoid telling me something. You're doing that thing men do. Turn it round, make it look like *we're* doing something wrong, when all it is, is a simple question. Where will you be coming back from?'

They were interrupted, to Cooper's relief, by a little voice. 'Hey, Daddy!'

'Cora! Hey! Mommy didn't tell me you were here.'

'I didn't have the chance.'

Cooper gave a side glance to Maddie as he picked up Cora and gave her a big hug. 'I've missed you.'

'I missed you too, Daddy.'

'How's Mr. Crawley?'

'Dead.'

Cooper pulled a sad face. 'I'm sorry.'

'I woke up and he'd gone.'

'Doesn't mean he's dead just because he's gone missing.'

Cora's face lit up. 'You don't think so?'

'No, I don't, and don't let anyone tell you otherwise.'

Cooper put Cora down and watched her skip off happily along the hall.

'For God's sake, why did you go and say that? You know that caterpillar's been dead for about two months now. I threw the thing away a couple of days ago.'

'I just wanted to cheer her up.'

'Well you can cheer me up by telling me what's going on. What are you trying to keep from me?'

481

'I've told you, I'm not hiding anything, what do you take me for?'

'I don't know what I take you for, Tom, because you can't even answer a simple question. *Where will you be coming back from?*'

Cooper kicked the bottom of the cream kitchen cupboards. 'From the DRC. Happy now?'

'What do you mean?'

'I'm going back there tomorrow.'

'The hell you are!'

The roar of Granger's voice behind them was so loud both Maddie and Cooper jumped.

His face exploded with color. He ground his teeth as he snarled. His words almost lost in his yelling anger.

'What the hell game are you playing, Cooper? You've lost it this time. I told you. Didn't I tell you? What did I say? I said to get your ass back here or I revoke your license.'

'What's your problem, Granger? I came back, didn't I? We got the results, didn't we? The bank can claim back on insurance now. So what is it with you? You've got everything you wanted, Granger. This is my free time now. I can do as I please, but you still have to go there with me.'

'Got what I wanted? The hell I have, Cooper. The hell I have. What I wanted was a birthday card from my only child but I can't, can I? Because you made sure you took her away from me.'

'Is this it? Is this how it's going to be all the time? Because I've put up with it and I've put up with it from you. But you gotta stop now. You gotta stop doing this. Every time you're pissed, you bring up your daughter. But I'm trying, okay.'

Granger, although much smaller, leapt at Cooper. Grabbed onto his clothing. Slammed his fists into Cooper's chest.

'How dare you! You don't know what trying is. You cause pain wherever you go. To Maddie. To your friends. To me. Anybody who goes near you, you hurt because you're so lost. You've pushed everybody away. But you don't get it do you?'

'What don't I get?'

'You don't get that you and she were everything to me. The son I never had... The day of the accident, I lost both of you that day, because *you* never came back to me either. I loved you, Cooper. I needed you to share the pain with me, and the grief, as well as try to heal together. I never blamed you then, but by God I do now.'

Cooper's voice cracked. He pointed a finger to himself. 'And I loved you, Granger, but I'm still here.'

'Not to me you're not.'

Granger rummaged in his brown jacket pocket. Pulled out his wallet and took out a photo from it. 'See this. I carry this everywhere with me. It's the last photo I had of her. It was taken the day before you went out to Lamu... Look at it, Cooper... I said look at it!'

Cooper turned away. 'I can't.'

'Yes, you can. Look...! For God's sake, you son of a bitch, look!'

'Okay, okay.' Cooper turned and stared at the photo.

'You see that? You see the two of you looking so happy? So at peace? Well that's what you took away. You took away both of you and now, Cooper, I can't stand the sight of you.'

'You want me to quit? Is that it? Is that what you want? Fine. I'll quit this job then you won't have to see me again.'

Cooper went to walk out the door but Granger grabbed him by his arm.

'Oh no, no you don't. No way do you get off that lightly. You don't leave this job, Cooper. You're *never* going to get the luxury of not being reminded of the pain you've caused. Every day of your rotten, stinking life, I'm going to be right up your ass reminding you of what you did.'

Cooper held Granger's gaze, then turned and walked away.

110

'Coop!'

Levi Walker waved, running after Cooper's truck as he put it in gear. He slammed on the brakes, whirling gravel and dust into the air.

'Hey, Levi… Hey, man. It's good to see you. I could've done with seeing your face in there.'

Levi grinned. 'My face was hiding out in the other room, bro. I love you, but not that much. Granger's been like a lion looking for his prey. Man, I've never seen him so bad. I'm surprised he hasn't just gone right ahead and burst into flames, but he always gets like this round his birthday. He even slammed the phone down on Dorothy. She was ready to come over and give him a piece of her mind.'

Cooper laughed, picturing Dorothy, Levi's long-suffering wife, a short, stocky black woman who never wasted time on small-talk and didn't take fools lightly. He held her in the highest regard and always enjoyed her wise and kind company. 'How is Dorothy?'

'Bitching my butt off, that's how. She was born to moan. I said to her this morning, *Woman, the only time you'll stop moaning is when you're cold in your grave, and even then I have my doubts*… She was asking about you by the way.'

Grinning, Cooper shook his head. 'Levi, you'd be lost without her, Dorothy keeps you in line. Tell her I'll see her soon.'

'Well make sure you do. Otherwise, I've no doubt she'll call you up and give you a piece of her mind… Listen, is it true what I heard back there? You really going back?'

'Yeah, I've just got to go and find Rosedale, try to persuade him to come. I'll probably be flying out tomorrow.'

Levi whistled. 'Coop, I don't know what to say. I'm worried about you, man. Maddie told me what you were like over there. It don't sound good. And you look terrible. Nothing about it sounds good. I'm not going to ask you not to go, because I'll be wasting both our times. But I want you to think about the fact, this may be the last time I see you.'

Cooper turned away, looking across to the Granite Mountain in the distance. 'Levi, that's crazy talk. It sounds like something Mad…'

'I'd say?'

Maddie stood by the 1954 Chevrolet, her hands on her hips, but a softness in her voice.

'Yeah, I would say it, because after everything, we all still care, Tom. We love you. Levi, me, even Granger.'

Levi pursed his lips. 'Granger? Baby, I wouldn't go that far.'

Maddie cut her eye at Levi and carried on. 'He does, but he's hurt, like you're hurt. Tom, please, don't go. We all need you to stay. Cora needs her daddy.'

'Don't do that, Maddie. Don't bring her into it.'

'Why not? Because she's a part of it all, like we all are.'

'Look, I know you've heard it before, but this will be the last time. Okay? I'll rethink everything when I get back. I'll get myself cleaned up. But I gotta go, and Maddie, all those things I said back at the house I meant. I really did.'

'Then don't go. Stay here with us.'

Cooper shook his head. 'I can't.'

'But that's where you're wrong. You can. Of course you can. This is crazy.'

'Maddie, I'm sorry. For everything. I always have been.'

'Tom, you do realize you could be killed.'

Cooper reached out of the window to touch her hand. 'Let's just hope I'm not.'

'Tom…'

Cooper put the truck in gear and skidded away, speeding off down the cactus-lined dust road, leaving Maddie and Levi watching on.

She held Levi's hand. 'You think we'll see him again?'

'I don't know Maddie. I just don't know. All we can do is hope.'

Cooper had been driving around all the motels in the Scottsdale area where Rosedale had told him he occasionally stayed. He'd tried six so far, and each one had drawn a blank. But he doubted Rosedale had gone back to his place in Wimberley, Texas. It was clear to him that Rosedale and he were quite similar – though he knew Rosedale would never admit it.

The only thing either of them hadn't pushed away was their work, and without it they were both lost. Rosedale going back to Wimberley on his own accord was as likely as Cooper going back to the ranch.

His cell rang and vibrated on the dashboard. Reaching across, he switched it onto loud speaker. 'Cooper.'

'Hey, Coop, it's Eddie. And no, I'm not whispering.'

'Hey, Eddie, how's it going?'

'Good. Well, okay. Sorry I didn't call you yesterday, Jennifer had to go to the doctor's. This pregnancy has been a bit of a nightmare.'

'Eddie, I'm sorry. Is the baby okay?'

'Yeah, all fine, but she's under orders to take it easy.'

'Send her my love won't you.'

'Of course I will. So, listen, I've got the results of the blood. It was as you thought. The bacteria in Emmanuel's blood is exactly the same as the bacteria in the flea you brought in, and in the flea which was on Dr. Foster's clothes.'

'Rosedale? You in there?'

Cooper banged on room 16.

'Rosedale, if you didn't want anyone to know you were in there, perhaps next time try not leaving your cowboy boots outside.'

'If you have to come in, the door's open.'

Cooper walked into the motel room. Expected a plain room with drab, ugly furniture, practical yet functional. What he got was bright and cheerful, clean white wood with blinds to match.

'It's nice in here.'

Rosedale sat in a purple recliner, opposite the TV. 'Yep, it sure beats the floor of the jungle.'

Cooper perched on the end of the bed, looking at the movie Rosedale was watching.

'Is this the bit where the Sioux give Lieutenant John Dunbar his name, Dances With Wolves?'

Rosedale didn't say anything for a moment. He paused the DVD. Turned to Cooper, coldness in his eyes. 'What is it you want, Thomas?'

'I want to go back to the DRC, and I want you to come with me.'

'You crazy boy... Now, if you've got nothing more to say to me, close the door on the way out.'

'I'll leave, but only once I've told you what it is Templin-Wright and Bemba are doing out there.'

Rosedale tilted his head, putting an unlit cigar in his mouth. 'I'm listening.'

Cooper threw the books from the library on the bed, which Rosedale picked up with interest.

'*The Insect Army. The War of the Insects*. What is this, Thomas?'

'Well, I knew we had to look further. Emmanuel wasn't the problem, but I couldn't work out what was. But it only really started to come together for me when I saw the injection marks on that woman.'

'Like how?'

'Bemba, Charles and Donald Parker are the main players in this whole thing. And what they've done is use the people's strong spiritual belief to manipulate and defraud.'

Rosedale frowned. 'Go on.'

'With consumers beginning to demand conflict-free products the pressure on the American electronics companies is really on, but a lot of companies have realized how difficult it is due to the militias' presence and the constant violence, so they've either continued mining conflict minerals – although as we know there's legislation trying to stop that – or, like a lot of companies, they've upped and left the DRC, because unlike Nadbury Electronics, most of the other firms didn't own every link in the chain, and therefore didn't have a huge amount of investment.'

'You mean as in how Nadbury Electronics owns Condor Atlantic Mines.'

'Right. So what we have is Nadbury having spent a hell of a lot of money investing in these mines, so there's no way they want to pull out. Plus the fact they know there are millions and millions of dollars profit to be had in that area. They also see a huge opening in the market because of the demand for ethical mining, but only if they could prove to the world they were dealing with conflict-free minerals.'

Rosedale sighed. 'Yeah but what are you getting at?'

'Initially the militia were their main problem. That's what stood between them and the big profits. As we know the militia brought violence, extortion, protection taxes, interception of the minerals in transit. The list goes on. But get rid of the militia your problem goes away. Or rather, Nadbury Electronics's problem goes away. But the question is, how do they do it?'

'You're not making sense, Thomas. What has this got to do with the books?'

'Beau actually gave me the idea and showed me what I couldn't see. But once I read these books it all fell into place. Remember what Father O'Malley said to us about the militia not even wanting to go near what was seen as possessed land?'

'Yeah.'

'Well, this is where Bemba comes in. By using Bemba and getting him to work for them, Donald Parker and Charles were able to get Bemba to use the people's cultural beliefs to scare the militia off the land. But they *had* to make it look authentic. Make it look like there was another force at play. So what they did was use infected fleas to bite people and cause them to become ill. Making them think that *they* and their land were possessed. That's what the porcelain pots were about.'

Rosedale sat up in his chair.

Cooper continued. 'I think they've been constructing porcelain clay bombs filled with infected fleas and dropping them over the area. There are some photos in the books of the clay bombs that this Japanese General, Shirō Ishii, used to drop fleas to infect people. They're exactly the same as the pots we saw, or what I thought were pots, in the Lemon water plant… It's very basic, but clearly very effective.'

'You sure?'

'As sure as I can be. It all makes sense. They've been packaging the fleas inside the bomb and creating entomological warfare. That's why the plane was flying so low. According to the books, they could drop the bombs with a basic detonator on a five second timer from an aircraft at a height of 100-300 meters and they'd explode leaving almost no trace. In order to detonate TNT, it must be confined in a casing or shell, which makes the clay bomb perfect. I think Charles and Donald are in charge of, or are part of, the making of the bombs. They both have the tell-tale yellow staining on their skin from handling TNT.'

'You think someone like Donald Parker would get involved in the *actual* making of the things?'

'Normally, I'd say, no. But this isn't normal. No doubt they want as few as people knowing as possible. So if that means Parker has to do his share of things, then so be it. After all it was him I saw at Lemon only recently. And remember that rat we saw in the Perspex box on our first visit to Lemon water plant?'

'Yeah?'

'Well it was covered in fleas wasn't it? That's probably where they get the fleas from. They use the rats as a host.'

'That's a hell of a lot of rats they'd need to catch.'

'Which is why I think they got the kids in the area to collect the rats for money. So they have a constant supply of hosts for the fleas to breed and feed off, because otherwise if the fleas don't get enough blood it's impossible for the fleas to survive. In the books it talks about fleas having sturdy bodies, and being pretty hardy. So the packaging of the fleas, as well as the drop from the plane, doesn't have much of an effect on them. So once the porcelain bomb explodes, the fleas just jump out from the broken clay bombs without a problem. Obviously some will die, but they were probably the ones we saw in large clusters on the ground.'

'Jesus, Thomas. How come nobody noticed?'

'Like who? Who is it that cares? And the Lemon water plant is a perfect cover. They stay seemingly transparent, even doing educational tours. Plus, they're also involved in the community. So the whole place is something of an example for positive and social community projects.'

Rosedale was very interested by now. 'So maybe it was fleas Zola was talking about when she said people thought the witchcraft was coming from the skies. Perhaps there was a cloud of fleas.'

'I'm with you on that one.'

'But, wait a minute. If you think it was the militia they wanted off the land, why are the locals involved with it all?'

'This is a guess, okay, but I think the plan with the fleas probably worked so well with the militia, they started to use it to manipulate the locals off their land. After all, the whole area for miles and miles is prime mining land, worth millions, maybe billions of dollars in mineral reserves… It all started to make sense to me when I went to see a friend of mine who works at Washington University. She helped me check the mining licenses.'

'And?'

'And, Condor Atlantic Mines, owned as we know by Nadbury Electronics, applied for and was granted mining research permits, as well as mining licenses, for that same large area of land which the locals were afraid of.'

'Which happens to be the land Bemba got them to sign over in these so called exchanges.'

Cooper nodded. 'They've got it all locked down.'

'But Thomas, one thing I don't understand is, how come Bemba and Charles didn't get ill if they were around the fleas?'

'When I spoke to Eddie about the fleas he said not only does it depend on your immune system, there's a possibility that the disease the fleas are carrying is easily cured by basic antibiotics in the early stages. So if they ever *had* it, or showed any signs of getting it, they could just easily administer antibiotics on themselves. After that they'd be resistant to it. It's only when you allow the disease to the next stages there's no going back.'

'So perhaps whatever this disease is, it's the lack of knowledge which is the biggest danger.'

'Totally. A lot of the diseases in areas like the eastern part of the DRC, where there's poverty and lack of resources, wouldn't ever be a problem if the people had access to medicine and proper healthcare.'

'And I guess because they haven't got proper medical services there, what they've done is put all their trust in Bemba.'

'Right. Bemba's telling them that they're possessed, rather than the truth which is they're just ill. And he's done it by manipulating his position and status within the communities. I'm guessing he told people they were possessed, and so was the land, but for a price he would help rid them of the witchcraft, and knowing that as long as the disease hadn't progressed too much, the likelihood of the antibiotics working was pretty high. That's what I think the injection marks were on the woman's arm. The antibiotics. But I can't be a hundred percent sure. With people desperate to get well, and rid themselves of the Kindoki, they were willing to give an exchange to the spirit world via Bemba.'

'And Bemba insisted the exchange was their land.'

'Yeah, and even if, like Zola's grandson, it was too late for the antibiotics to work, it didn't matter to Bemba because in line with local beliefs, just trying to heal a person demands an exchange. And Bemba was the perfect person because I think not only was he violent and sadistic and power hungry, which we learnt he was from Bill Travis, I think he probably has some real belief in Kindoki himself. So the combination of his psychopathic ways along with his spiritual belief system equates to one hell of a twisted and dangerous mix.'

Rosedale lit his cigar. 'And Emmanuel?'

'What I think happened with Emmanuel is he found out something, and so did this Dr. Foster guy. They apparently visited the water treatment plant together before he flew home. I'm not sure why but it's obvious they both knew something. Emmanuel disappears, I suspect murdered, but all in the name of witchcraft. And if anyone did question or investigate, maybe like Emmanuel did, Bemba would turn the community against them, pronouncing them a witch. The sense of fear is huge, both from the spirit world *and* Bemba, who totally abused their beliefs and knew exactly how to.'

Rosedale said. 'What about this Dr. Foster?'

'Well they're saying he probably committed suicide, but I very much doubt that. I think it's got something to do with what he found out.'

'So you think he was murdered?'

'That's what my hunch is telling me. According to his secretary, Karen, he went to speak to Donald Parker at Nadbury. Maybe the guy realized Dr. Foster knew too much.'

'So he killed him and made it look like suicide.'

'Got it in one… So what do you reckon? It all makes sense, doesn't it? Can you see how it all fits into place?'

'Couple of questions, Thomas. You think the rats were diseased already?'

'Who knows? But all you need is one diseased rat, take the blood from it and inject it into a healthy rat. The process is effective but simple. But if they've been injecting the rats with the disease, or the rats were diseased already, the outcome is the same.'

'And the plane? What's your take on that?'

'I think it was registered to Emmanuel, not the Lemon water plant or Condor Atlantic Mines, to distance themselves completely from anything. And then like I say he probably found something out which he didn't like. Then they got rid of him, like they got rid of a lot of people.'

Rosedale gave Cooper a wry smile. 'Jesus, next time I think I'm just going to stick to Granger's orders. Just bring back the goddamn plane.'

'Look, I don't know how we're going to do it, but we've got to do something, Rosedale. I've found out that there's a connecting flight to Kigali tomorrow evening.'

Rosedale fell silent. He walked over to the small fridge in the corner, breaking open a bottle of beer. 'Is that everything?'

'Yeah, I think I covered everything. Can't think of anything else.'

Sitting down, Rosedale un-paused the movie. 'Well, if that's everything, then close the door on the way out. I'm just getting to the good bit.'

113

'You expect me to believe all this, Coop? Have you heard what you're saying?'

'Look, John. You don't think I know how crazy it sounds? But here's the thing: it's true.'

The two men stood in Woods's bedroom. A place which guaranteed privacy.

Woods said, 'I'm sorry. I can't take this seriously.'

'You mean you won't.'

'Coop, you're tired. There's a lot of things been happening, it's…'

'No, don't you do that. Don't you make it out that it's all in my head. Not on this.'

'Coop. Please.'

'Look at me, John. Look at me…! Do you really think there's nothing in what I've just told you?'

'That's right. I think you're so desperate to find the answers, you don't even look at the right sum.'

'Not on this.'

'It's just too crazy. Using insects as weapons? I know it happens but, come on Coop. You're talking about a water treatment plant, not Unit 731.'

'So, okay, okay. Forget about that at the moment. Donald Parker and Simon Ballard. You think there's nothing in that either?'

'It's the same thing,' said Woods, his patience running thin. 'You're looking for something which isn't there.'

'That's not true. Parker and Ballard are intrinsically linked. Why won't you open your goddamn eyes and see it?'

'Just because… forget it.'

Cooper strode up to Woods. Inches apart. He put his hand on John's chest. 'You already know something, don't you?'

'No.'

'You do. You're lying. I can always tell. Look at me.'

Woods pushed Cooper's hand off. 'Who the hell do you think you are?'

'Someone who knows the truth.'

Woods turned away but Cooper grabbed him, holding his arm tight. 'You know something don't you…? Don't you?'

'Look… Jesus, okay. Okay. I've done a bit of digging myself. And I know Donald Parker knew Simon Ballard a long time ago.'

'Bullshit, John! When did *today* suddenly become a long time ago?'

'Leave it, Coop. Why are you just pushing it? It's under control. It's okay. Now step off.'

Cooper shook his head. 'It's okay? What's okay? That Donald Parker and Simon Ballard are making people ill? That people are dying? That's okay, is it?'

'You don't know that!'

'Of course I do. It's there. Right in front of us.'

'No.'

'How the hell can you just say *no*?'

Woods raised his voice. 'I've told you before. I need you to leave it.'

'What? Why…? John, I don't get it. I brought you the evidence.'

'What evidence? There is none. This is just you.'

'It's not just me. Travis confirmed it was Ballard on the photo. He's out there with Templin-Wright and Parker. How much more evidence do you need?'

'It doesn't mean Parker's doing anything wrong.'

'Are you for real? Ballard's a wanted terrorist. And you're sitting on this like it's nothing. Why aren't you jumping at it?'

Woods paused. 'Because I can't... I've got everything riding on Parker. I need him.'

Cooper's voice turned into a whisper. 'What?'

'Oh, God, Coop. I'm breaking every rule in the book by telling you this, but the reforms...'

'Go on.'

'To get them through, I need Parker on side.'

Cooper stared at Woods then backed away, shaking his head. 'You're serious aren't you? Jesus. You son of a bitch. You goddamn son of a bitch. You know what I'm telling you is the truth, but you're not going to do anything about it because of some *reforms*?'

'Coop, listen...'

'Shut up! I can't believe what I'm hearing. You're going to allow Ballard to get away with what he's done *and* what's he doing. And Parker. You're going to allow people to die because of your *goddamn gun reforms*!'

Woods's voice cracked. 'You hold on a minute. It's your turn to shut up. People *here* will die if the reforms don't go through. Kids. Teenagers. Dying every day from guns, and I have to stop that, I have to. You have no idea what's it's like to see and meet the families who've lost loved ones because of a bullet. And they're looking at me to help them, to change things, to make sure that their son, their wife, their daughter, their husband didn't just die in vain. You gotta see that.'

'All I see is you exchanging one set of problems for another. I also see if you don't do something about it, John, you'll have a hell of a lot of people's blood on your hands. You may be able to live with that, but I can't.'

114

'Ladies and Gentleman, Welcome aboard flight 6531. Please pay attention to your flight attendants as we explain to you the emergency features of this aircraft. To fasten your seatbelt, place the metal tip into the buckle and tighten the strap. There are six emergency exits on board, two forward and two in the rear with two additional exits over the wing. In case of loss of cabin pressure…'

'Excuse me, sir?'

Cooper felt a tap on his shoulder as he sat listening to the air hostess. He turned round and immediately smiled, shaking his head. 'Rosedale!'

'Well what could I do, Thomas? There's only so many times a man can watch the same movie.'

115

With almost thirty hours of travelling behind them, Cooper and Rosedale finally found themselves on familiar territory. Verdant rolling hillsides, mud-red rivers, impassable roads and rain which felt it would never cease. But for Cooper, this was where he knew he needed to be. This was where he was going to finish what they'd started.

Pulling up on a mud verge with the windscreen wipers on full speed, Cooper was grateful to step out of the old green Land Rover Defender which they'd hired this time round. A leaking roof, and suspension which had all but disappeared, had made the journey from Kigali even more uncomfortable than usual. But that didn't matter. All that did was that they were here.

'You want to do the explaining, Thomas? The man seems to like you.'

Cooper was about to answer Rosedale, but the door to the brick hut opened and Father O'Malley stood in front of him, wearing a black sou'wester which perched on, rather than fitted over, his high afro. He wore a gray waterproof coat and a checked scarf and a look of shock on his face.

'Sorry, Father, we didn't mean to give you a fright. Can we have a word?'

'Thomas...! Er, it's good to see you, and Rosedale how are ye? I can't talk right now, I'm sorry. Just that I'm busy. I... I... I have to go and take a service.'

'At this time of night?'

Father O'Malley shrugged. 'What can I say? The Lord never sleeps.'

Cooper nodded, weighing up what the priest was saying. 'Right. Okay. I gotcha.'

O'Malley, who was clearly eager to get off, began to hurry away and waved his goodbyes.

'So it's good to see you both again. Cheerio!'

Cooper watched the priest head out into the rainy darkness. 'That man's one of the worst liars I've ever known.'

'Oh hell yeah. What he's hiding, I don't know, but come on before we lose him.'

*

Cooper and Rosedale followed and with curiosity watched Father O'Malley walk through the night. The lone shadowed figure of the priest in the darkness, silhouetted by the Congolese moon, stopping and watching and looking around at every sound.

Cooper whispered as the thick vegetation soaked and wrapped round his legs, as they headed down into the forest. 'Why do you think he's keeping off the main roads?'

'Seems to me our Father O'Malley is going to a lot of trouble not to be seen. And it's just like you said, Thomas, the man's certainly a liar. We passed the chapel he takes his services in about ten minutes ago.'

'Come on, I think he's heading for that clearing.'

Another three hundred yards further, Father O'Malley led them to a steep hill which took them down to a track.

'Look where we are.' He gestured his head towards the refugee camp, which was on the opposite side of the road.

'Jesus, Thomas, you don't think he's connected with Bemba, do you?'

Cooper didn't have time to answer before Father O'Malley disappeared behind a group of trees. Cooper followed and scrabbled down, not wanting to lose the trail of the priest. Feeling like a cobra stalking its prey he slunk along and kept his body low behind the sprawling rise of the banana plants, edging forward and past the side of a fallen tree, crawling on his hands and knees to see the priest come back into sight. He couldn't quite make out what O'Malley was doing but there was no way he wasn't going to find out.

Carefully, not wanting to alert the priest to their presence, Cooper crept even nearer. He was puzzled to see Father O'Malley glancing around anxiously as he approached the Commer truck, before lifting up the blue tarpaulin, looking in.

Turning to Rosedale, who was slightly behind him, Cooper nodded. Gave him the signal. 'Now! Go!'

Scrabbling to his feet, Cooper ran down the hill. Swivelling and turning as he drew his gun out at arm's length and charged towards the truck, throwing himself quietly against it.

Then still.

Frozen.

He listened.

Strained to hear anything other than the noise of the rain hitting down on the tarpaulin and the steel of the vehicle. He crouched down. Bent his head underneath the truck to see the priest's legs on the other side. Checking to see no-one else had joined him.

And giving Rosedale the thumbs up, he ran round the other side. At which point he took the priest by surprise. Grabbed him by the collar of his waterproof coat and pounded him up against the truck. Gripped O'Malley's arm and pulled it hard and twisted it behind his back, pressing him forward into the side of the truck.

He jammed his gun into the priest's cheek, whispering dangerously.

'Don't say a word Father, not a sound. I won't hesitate to pull the trigger if you try to alert anyone else.'

Father O'Malley's body was shaking. 'No, you don't understand, Thomas, there is no-one else. It's just me... it's just me on me own.'

'And I'm supposed to believe that, am I?'

'It's the truth. I swear on the good book.'

Cooper licked his lips, tasting the rain water on them. 'But the problem we've got here is you told me something before, told me you were off to take a service only it turned out to be a lie.'

'I'm sorry, I didn't know what else to say.'

Cooper pushed harder against the gun. 'Maybe the truth. That'd be a good place to start.'

'I can't... I can't.'

'I think that's where you and I will differ. I reckon you can, and once you hear the sound of the trigger on this gun being drawn back, maybe you'll realize how much and how quick you can.'

Rosedale leant in, pressing his face against the truck, to be in line with the priest's. 'I'd listen to him Father, Thomas here ain't one to say something he don't mean. And this boy's mad. He's mad as hell.'

Father O'Malley's eyes were wide with terror. 'Okay... okay, but please, Thomas, put that thing down.'

'I don't think so, Father, it serves as a nice reminder... So just tell me exactly what it is you're doing here, and why you told us you were on your way to a church when it's clear that's a downright lie.'

Father O'Malley blurted out the words. 'Bemba. It's Bemba.'

Cooper shook his head and looked at Rosedale. 'I knew it. But you know you had me taken in there. You had me thinking you were a good man when all along you've been in on Bemba and Lemon's sick games. Abusing the people's trust and faith. Shame on you, Father. Shame on you... So come on, O'Malley, what was in it for you?'

'No... no, you've got it wrong!'

'Have I? I don't think so. Tell me one good reason I shouldn't pull this trigger.'

'Because I'm telling the truth, and I can prove it.'

'How.'

'Just come with me, and let me show you.'

116

'Any luck?' Maddie stood behind Levi, hoping and waiting for him to get through to Cooper and Rosedale. She hadn't heard anything and even though she didn't want to – really didn't want to – she couldn't help but worry.

Levi shook his head. 'No, nothing. I'm pulling a blank on both their cells and GPS phones. But that will probably change in a day or so. The weather reports for East DRC are really bad. Heavy rain. So I guess once that's passed, it should be alright.'

'But when will that be?'

Levi himself trying but failing not to worry. 'I don't know.'

'Try again.'

Standing in the small communications room of Onyx, Levi said, 'I will but it's pointless. I've tried over twenty times today and yesterday... Why are you looking at me like that?'

Maddie said, 'I've got an idea,'

Levi recognized a familiar look coming into her eyes. 'Oh no. No. No way. If it's what I think you're thinking, you can count me out right now.'

117

The stench from the refugee camp was overpowering. Raw sewage and garbage and mud mixed together. A vast, sprawling sea of tents and tarpaulin with under-fed and under-nourished women, men and children looking out, desperate, displaced by conflicts of war and misrule.

Cooper glanced around, walking behind the priest. 'This better be good, Father. Don't forget, I'm still got my gun in my pocket. Make one move, and you won't have time to even say *Amen*.'

Having regained his composure slightly, Father O'Malley nodded. 'Don't worry. I won't be making any moves, Thomas, you can be assured of that. Come on, it's over here.'

O'Malley led Rosedale and Cooper across to a large white tent, set back away from the others.

And at the entrance, the priest drew back the thin piece of fabric which acted as the door. He stood for a moment. Looked solemn. 'Are you ready?'

'Is it in here?'

'It is, Thomas.'

'Then you go first, we'll follow… Oh, and Father, remember what I said.'

Without answering, the priest stepped inside.

It was spacious, but stifling, with pools of water from the dripping roof gathering on the floor.

Father O'Malley led the two men across to the far end,

where three people sat huddled in front of a thin, soiled mattress on the floor. On seeing the priest, they smiled in recognition. But a wary mistrust clouded their welcome when they saw Rosedale and Cooper come to stand by O'Malley's side.

The priest rubbed his hands anxiously. 'Thomas, I hope I'm right to trust you.'

'It's not us you need to worry about.'

Father O'Malley nodded to the three people. They moved aside, revealing a frail and sick man curled up under several layers of blankets.

'Thomas, I'd like you to meet Emmanuel Mutombo.'

118

'Why, this is another first. The president wanting to have late night chats with me.'

Woods got up and shook Parker's hand, who was let into the small office just off the West Wing reception room by one of Woods's junior advisors. 'Yeah, sorry about that. It's hard to get a window sometimes. And midnight chats is where it's at.'

Parker smoothed down his gray hair, sat down and moved his chair forward.

'I don't mean to be flippant, but I'm sure you haven't brought me here to chat about your schedule, or even about the planning strategy of our campaign. Though I must say, Mr. President, I'm certainly curious. Night meetings at the White House have the flavor of a TV drama, don't you think?'

Parker's manner made Woods uncomfortable. 'I wouldn't know, classic movies are more my thing… But you're right, I asked you in because I needed you to help me out on a couple of points.'

Parker shrugged. A supercilious smile spread across his face. 'Shoot.'

'Simon Ballard. Does the name mean anything to you?'

Parker's response came quickly, didn't disrupt his smile. 'No.'

'Are you sure?'

'Yeah. Totally.'

'You see, I actually know different. And that's where I start to have the problem. I know you're lying to me.'

Parker sniffed. 'Then, Mr. President, you know more than me. But then I'm guessing that's why you're president and I'm not.'

Woods had been trying to keep his anger under control. Failed. Slammed his fist on the desk. 'I know exactly what's been going on at the Lemon water plant.'

Parker pushed back his chair. Stood up. 'I don't know what's going on here. But I don't appreciate you accusing me of some unspecified *thing* that's been *going on*.'

'Why don't we cut the crap?

'Yours or mine?'

'Don't push me.'

Parker snorted his derision. 'I have no idea what you're talking about. Maybe my reference to a TV drama is more fitting than I'd thought. Now, if you've quite finished? It's late, and I'm up early tomorrow.'

If he'd been anyone else, anywhere else, John Woods knew he wouldn't have hesitated in punching Parker in the face. But as it was, he was the president of the United States of America, and so he took a calming breath. 'All that bull about caring? About conflict-free minerals. About the kids. About the atrocities. And all along you were playing a part in it… You son of a bitch, how could you? Why tell me you care?'

Parker pointed, his hand shaking. 'The thing is, Mr. President, I do care. I care very much. I've put a lot of investment into that country. I wasn't lying when I said my mines are conflict free. I've got no militia abusing and torturing kids, raping women. I've got men who are paid well. Who earn a decent living and can provide for their families. I have given men their dignity back. And I call that caring. I call that helping the people, don't you?'

Dangerously close, Woods took a step towards Parker. 'The only person you've helped is yourself.'

'This here, what you're doing right now, is madness. I don't know what the hell you're accusing me of but you're *way* off line. And you're wrong, I haven't just helped myself. I provide ethical products. Not ones with blood on them. The American people should be thanking me. Because nothing will be on their conscience.'

'Your products have more blood on them than the militia do.'

Parker raised his voice. 'Bullshit. Don't you understand? Without me, the people in that area of the DRC have nothing. They struggle to even provide for their own children, and that's not right. Think about that. Not being able to feed your own children. How must that feel? And then because of their cultural beliefs, when they look to find reasons why there's so much suffering, often it's the innocent who get the blame. The young. But I'm stopping that happening because people have jobs and money. They're not afraid to go to work in the morning. That's because of me. Me! Those people have a chance of a better life because of *me* and my vision. Not you. Not the rest of the goddamn world. But me! You've allowed companies to go into that country and take what they like without putting anything back in. So I'd say, *Mr. President*, you should be looking at yourself and those companies and asking them the questions.'

Woods slammed down his fists on the table before sweeping the decanter of water onto the floor, and with rage and wrath and fury he said, 'Stop playing your goddamn games

Parker, I know what you did. So stop the pretence. You bastard, you took their land away.'

'I haven't taken anything away. My understanding is they signed it over of their own free will. It was just an exchange for a better life.'

'A better life? You piece of scum. Just get out. Get out!'

With matching anger, Parker walked towards the door. 'It's a shame you're such a fool. You could've got what you wanted, you could've got your reforms, but instead you've just thrown all that away. Thrown the welfare of the people of America away. I would say it's you who's got blood on their hands, not me.'

Woods went to grab Parker but pulled himself back. Kicked a chair instead. 'I will bring you down. You hear me? No question. I will bring you down.'

119

'Just take your time, it's fine, and if it's too difficult to talk right now, that's okay. We can come back.' Cooper sat on the mattress next to Emmanuel, whose whole body was wrapped in stained bandages concealing his deep and painful burns. The smell was putrid. Sweet and sickly. Rotting flesh and wounds on his face which Cooper suspected would never heal.

Emmanuel's eyes were shrouded in a thick bloody gauze, covering the hideous injuries which Bemba had inflicted.

His voice rasped.

His breathing faltered.

'Je n'ai plus beaucoup de temps monsieur. I haven't much time left in this life, I want to tell you my story in case I am without my voice in the land of the dead.'

Cooper was worried. He gave a glance to Father O'Malley to say as much.

'Go ahead, Emmanuel… Thomas, this is something he needs to do. It'll give him peace.'

'Well, if you're sure.'

The priest nodded. 'I am… Go on, Emmanuel, Thomas and Rosedale are listening…'

There was a long pause. Then Emmanuel began to talk.

'I worked for Bemba. At first I thought it was a good job. A job which would enable me to feed my family. The *only* other way to get work and money was to join the rebels, which I didn't want to do. So I joined Bemba, though I didn't trust him.'

'Did he ever tell you about his past life?' asked Cooper. 'Does the name Simon Ballard mean anything to you?'

'No, he never said anything.'

'What work did you do for Bemba?'

'I was Bemba's sight. He took away his own eyes, believing that by doing so he'd be blessed with more power. So he needed a person he could trust to see for him.'

Cooper said, 'When you say *took away his eyes*, what do you mean, Emmanuel?'

'He'd gouged them out himself, just as he gouged out my eyes. The thing about it, monsieur, was part of him did truly believe he'd be able to see the spirits more clearly without the sight of the living, but the other part was driven on by power and greed. He used his beliefs and his own nature for wickedness.'

Cooper glanced at Rosedale, who looked as shocked as he felt. He'd thought the man had been injured in the conflicts somehow. But self-mutilation? Hell, it'd never even crossed his mind.

'And Bemba caused all your injuries?'

'Yes, but it certainly wasn't just me he hurt. As I continued to work for him the things I saw him do to people... I couldn't be a part of it. He enjoyed the violence and the cruelty. It gave him pleasure to hurt people. I kept quiet for a long time. I was frightened for the safety of my family. But eventually, even though I was scared, I started to ask questions. I saw how he was destroying the community I loved. Making the people fear themselves, believing they'd been cursed with Kindoki...'

Emmanuel stopped. Tried to catch his breath, exhausted by the conversation.

Rosedale said, 'Are you sure you want to go on? You can stop, we know a fair bit ourselves already.'

Desperation took over Emmanuel's voice. 'Laissez-moi finir s'il vous plaît.'

Cooper touched his hand. 'Okay, but just take your time.'

'In this country we have a strong belief in the spirits. We are guided by them, but what Bemba did was make people believe they were in disfavor, that they'd been cursed. Communities began to turn on each other, terrified their neighbor was filled with the spirit of the possessed. Parents threw out their children, accusing them of witchcraft as people became sick with his illness.'

'What do you mean by *his illness*?'

'Bemba was making people sick, but then he'd make them well again... the ones he chose to.'

'How did he make them better?'

'He would give them some medicine, but pretend it was the spirits vesting him with the power of healing. When I was sick, when I had the illness, I knew he would not give me the medicine, and no Nganga would come near me. Everything was done through Bemba.'

Rosedale, listening intently, said, '*Nganga*? I don't know what that is, Emmanuel.'

'Traditional healers, good people.'

'Tell me more about this illness, Emmanuel,' said Cooper.

'By making people ill and then promising to rid them of the Kindoki he was able to take away their land. They had nothing to give apart from that, and they believed the only way for the spirits to bless them with good health once more was to do what Papa Bemba said the spirits were asking for.'

Cooper probed. 'What else do you know about the land?'

'Bemba got the people to sign some documents just before

or after the exchange, so the land wouldn't be legally theirs anymore. Then Bemba gave the land to the people he was working for, in exchange for power and money. I tried to tell the people what Bemba was doing. People I had worked with and lived amongst. But no-one believed me, they thought I was possessed with evil to talk in such a way. And when I got ill, it confirmed their fears.'

'How did you get rid of your illness?'

Father O'Malley answered. 'The orphanage has very limited supplies of antibiotics and medicine, enough only for a few children a year. But when Emmanuel came here to the refugee camp, his injuries were so bad I gave him the antibiotics we had at the orphanage to stop his burns becoming infected, which as you see they aren't. But it also got rid of the illness.'

Cooper nodded, remembering what Eddie had said about simple antibiotics.

Emmanuel continued. 'When Bemba found out I was sick, he came to my house and made an exchange with the spirits for the healing of my soul. But it was all a show for the community, because he knew what the truth was and why I'd got ill. They locked me in my house for three weeks without food – something which is often done to starve the spirits out, though of course I knew it wasn't the spirits who'd done it to me. After three weeks they came back and I thought that was all Bemba was going to do to me, but...' Distraught, Emmanuel stopped.

Father O'Malley carried on in his place. 'Bemba did a deliverance. He tortured Emmanuel, I think probably to show what happened to people that questioned his authenticity. But that was also mixed in with Bemba's belief that Emmanuel *was* possessed. And of course he wanted to silence him.'

'How did he get here, Father?' asked Rosedale.

'I knew what was happening, I'd heard Bemba was going to do a deliverance, but there was nothing I could do on my own to help Emmanuel. As you know yourself there's nothing around here in the way of law and order. The only thing I could do therefore was wait and pray. Once the deliverance was over and everyone had gone, I went to the hut during the night, hoping he would be still alive, and I carried him out. I didn't know if it was too late, he was in such a bad way, and I didn't think he'd last till morning. But the good Lord was clearly looking over him. For the first few days, I had him back at the orphanage trying to give him whatever basic medical assistance I could, but I didn't think it was safe, so I moved him here. It isn't perfect but here in the refugee camp he's just another person amongst hundreds of others.'

'Monsieur…'

Cooper leant towards Emmanuel. 'Yes?'

'There was a man called Dr. Foster, do you know him?'

Cooper sounded surprised. 'Yeah. Well, I know *of* him.'

Even though Emmanuel's voice was weak, Cooper could still hear the sadness in it.

'He was a good man, he tried to help, but he promised he'd come back. He told me he was going to get some tests done so I waited for him, but he never returned. I think he forgot us.'

'Emmanuel, I'm sure Dr. Foster would've come back to you if he could, but he died over a month ago. I believe he was killed.'

'C'est vrai? …C'est tragique.'

'It is tragic and he didn't let you down, not in the slightest. He was doing everything he could to help, and that's part of the reason why I'm here now. Because of what he was trying to uncover. How did you get to know Foster?'

'He came from America, looking at the mines, but he also came to the village to ask questions about the land. But nobody would talk to him. I heard him speak to Bemba and from what he was asking, I could tell he didn't believe what he was being told. So I went to find him, and spoke of what I knew.'

Rosedale said, 'That was a big risk,'

'C'est vrai. But what else could I do? By this point I was desperate. I had nowhere to turn and knew something was going to happen to me, so I was willing to risk anything.'

'And he helped you?'

'He listened to what I had to say about the land and about the illness. I told him where it came from.'

'And where's that?'

'The water treatment plant; they call it the place of the undead.'

Cooper thought about what Zola had said. 'Is that why you took Dr. Foster there? You went with him, didn't you, as well as once on your own.'

'I was trying to find out what happened there. The first time, as you say, I went on my own, and the second time with Dr. Foster, but we used different names. I was too scared to use my own, even going there was a risk. But we didn't find out anything. You see, during the whole time I worked with Bemba, I was never allowed to go there. But it's where they take the truck.'

'The truck?'

'Yes, Bemba's men take people there in the truck.'

Cooper was puzzled. He said, 'What do you mean?'

'They pick up people. Anyone. Men, women, even children, and drive them there. But no-one ever sees them again.'

Cooper turned to Father O'Malley. 'Do you know anything about this?'

'I know about the truck driving round picking people up. That's why I was looking in it, I often do if I see it. Just in case I can rescue some poor soul. The truck often comes to this refugee camp, because it's the perfect place to take people from. Nobody misses them, nobody cares, Thomas, and there are no authorities to stop it.'

'Have you any idea why?'

'I wish I did. Maybe it's to make people forcibly join a militia group. That happens a lot, especially the children. They're often made to become child soldiers. Perhaps they're making them work in the mines. I don't know, and the worst thing is, there's nothing I can do. I just don't know where to turn.'

Father O'Malley paused, becoming visibly upset. 'Who is there to ask to investigate, and to help, Thomas? I'm powerless and all I could do is pray for them and for my country of birth. That's all I have and what use is that? And what use am I as a priest to these people if I can't do anything? Even though I have faith in the good Lord, I often feel this place and these people have been abandoned, forgotten by the rest of the world, forgotten by God.' He stopped to wipe away his tears. 'If there is anything, *anything* you can do, Thomas, I beg you: *help us*.'

120

'I owe you an apology.'

Cooper spoke as they stood outside Father O'Malley's brick hut.

'You need to do nothing of the sort.'

'No, I was wrong. I misjudged you. I'm sorry.'

The priest took hold of Cooper's hand and said, 'Thomas, you're a good man, and the only reason why you behaved as you did was because you thought I was betraying the people. Isn't that right, Rosedale?'

Rosedale leant on the wall under the roof which sheltered him from the rain. 'Our Thomas here, he likes to beat up on himself, feels like he owes the world. Feels like he's got a debt to pay back.'

Father O'Malley stared at Cooper with great concern, as if he were one of his parishioners.

'Is that right, Thomas? And why is that?'

Cooper gave a cold stare to Rosedale. He wasn't about to give a confession; he'd already done that with Jackson. 'It's a long story, Father, but I've got my reasons.'

'Then that's all that matters, Thomas. If you believe in something, never give up, no matter how great the challenge is. Everyone knows the story of David and Goliath. Do you remember? David didn't stop or even hesitate, no matter what other people around him said. Everyone else cowered and backed away in fear, but David ran and went forward into battle. He knew what needed to be done and he did the right thing in spite of dissuasion and threats.'

Cooper cocked the priest a half smile. He said, 'Thank you. I appreciate your words.'

As usual Cooper felt uncomfortable with the focus on him, so he changed the subject back to Emmanuel. 'So do you think he's going to make it?'

'No,' said O'Malley. 'No I don't. I'm surprised he lasted this long, but perhaps he knew he had to hold on because he knew you were coming.'

'It's a…'

Cooper stopped, hearing a noise coming from the other side of the hut. He signalled to Rosedale to go round the other way.

Slowly, Cooper moved along the wall. He could still hear the noise. His gun was at the ready and, squatting down, he surveyed the area but it was too dark to see anything. He could feel it, though. He knew there was somebody there.

Cautiously, he made his way across to the edge of the forest and the adrenalin rushed through his body as the rain pelted down, and he ran quickly across to one of the trees and pushed his body against it. Craning round, he saw a flicker of a shadow and watched intently and yes, it was there. He could see it. A tiny movement, followed by another.

Gradually he moved.

Sideward.

Wanting to get directly behind whoever it was.

He was meters away from the person now, but he waited for a moment before making his move.

Then he ran.

Dashed towards the tree and whirling his gun round from the side, he brought them down to the ground, jamming his knee into their back, gun pressed into their head as they lay face down.

'Ne bouge pas ou je te tue. You hear me? Don't move, otherwise I'll kill.'

'Get off me! Get off me!'

'Levi…? What the hell…? Jesus, Levi, I'm sorry, I had no idea. But more to the point, what the hell are you doing here?'

Quickly jumping off Levi Walker's back, Cooper pulled him up.

Annoyed, and brushing off the wet leaves and undergrowth which had stuck to him, Levi said, 'Oh I don't know, I did a wrong turn on Route 66, and found myself here…' He gave Cooper a hard shove, which he accepted, and then he added, 'What the hell do you think I'm doing, Coop? Making sure your sorry butt is okay, like all the other times. What were Maddie and I supposed to do? Just sit back and wait? *Hope* that you'd come back alive rather than in a body bag? As usual you gave us no choice. And as usual it was Maddie who led the way. She was worried when we couldn't get in contact with you, but once we got here and got through the worst of the weather we were able to find you via your GPS signal.'

Rosedale walked up behind them. He stretched out his hand. 'Levi, I never thought I'd say this, but it's good to see you.'

'Yeah, well, I was just saying to Coop here, he never gives us a choice.'

Cooper said, 'Where's Maddie?'

'Over there behind that outhouse. Come on. And let me give you an FYI: she's not best pleased.'

Rosedale and Cooper followed Levi across to the outhouse, oblivious and now accustomed to the heavy rain.

'Hey Maddie, we found them. Or rather, Coop found me… Maddie…? She was just here.'

A noise made them turn around. It was the Commer truck.

'Quick!' shouted Rosedale.

The men raced across the couple of meters to the road, and in the distance Cooper could see the rear flap of the blue tarpaulin cover being rolled and lowered down on the truck. But not before he saw Maddie bundled inside it.

121

'You can't do this. Jesus, John. Think about what you're saying. The gun reforms. We're this close... *This close*. And you want to throw it all away because of... something that hasn't been proved? It's crazy. There's no investigation. No federal charges. Nothing.'

'Teddy, listen to yourself. Morality doesn't always come into legal documents. Just because there's nothing official as of yet, it doesn't mean I should ignore it.'

'Why the hell not?'

'Are you for real?'

'You won't be the first president to cover up stuff. The word *Watergate* mean nothing to you?'

Woods threw a piece of gum in his mouth. Missed. And not bothering to pick it up from the floor, he said, 'For God's sake, what era are you living in? If I didn't think you were being serious, you'd be laughable, Teddy. And honestly, using a term which is basically a byword for corruption and scandal is hardly the way to convince me to see things your way.'

'I shouldn't have to convince you. The DRC... well, let's face it. It's not our business. Here. Now. *America's* our business, John. Making a change for the future.'

'At what cost, Teddy? How many lives have to suffer so we can get what we want?'

'It's not about *us*. It's about the American people.'

'Is it? Really? You sure about that?'

Teddy said, 'Damn sure.'

'So you really think the American people would want reforms pushed through on the back of people suffering? Children dying? Don't you think it's ironic that our reforms were about saving lives, and now it turns out that to get those reforms we'll be part of harming others.'

'Jesus, John. Every day that happens. This is politics for God's sake.'

Woods kicked one of the highly polished wooden chairs, as was his habit lately. It fell. Knocked into another one. 'Not the kind of politics I want to be involved in. Tell me something, Teddy. What about the people in the DRC? Who'll look out for them?'

'Like I said, it's not our problem. You need to forget about this and what you think you know and concentrate on what this administration has set out to do.'

Wood's anger filled the room along with the tears which filled his eyes. '*Bullshit!* I entered politics to help people. And that help doesn't have boundaries. Borders. Color. Culture or religion. I will *not* be part of the problem. I *refuse* to have blood on my hands.'

'Sorry to disappoint you, John, but that's *exactly* what you're going to have. Because no reforms mean no gun controls... Can't you just wait? Get the votes *then* do something if you have to.'

'Oh come on, that's not even an option. That's crazy talk. You think Parker wouldn't bring us down with him if we did that? You're not thinking straight.'

'Me? Me, John? Tell me something, how many presidents have tried and failed to get significant changes when it comes to gun control? You know how difficult it is. And you, John, have the chance to make a difference... Mr. President, I've been by your side since the beginning, both politically and as a friend, and throughout that time, I've admired and respected everything you've done and stood for in equal measure. But today, Mr. President. Today is a very dark day. Not only do you not have my support. You do not have my respect.'

Woods rubbed his face, taken aback by the wave of feeling. He swallowed hard, ignoring the cut of emotion at the back of his throat. Ignoring the tears which rolled down his face. 'Can't you see what you're asking me to do? You're asking me to let Parker do what he likes. You want me to exchange one lot of lives for another. Well I can't do it, Teddy… I can't, and it kills me that I can't because I know right now… and right now… and right now in this country, children and loved ones are being shot, and I was going to do something about it but that something has just slipped right through my fingers. You know how important these reforms were to me. What was it that Abraham Lincoln said when he spoke about the Emancipation Proclamation? *If ever my soul was in an act, it is this act*. Well that's exactly how I feel about the reforms, but I won't do it by causing someone else's suffering.'

'You'll regret this, John. Emotions are blinding you. And I'll tell you something else for nothing. I don't think the rest of the party is going to be too happy with you, do you?'

Woods walked up to Teddy, slowly. 'I don't give a damn what anybody thinks. Not you, or them. I won't be complicit to what Parker is doing, and if that means not getting the votes, that's the way it's got to be. I couldn't live with myself otherwise. How could I look myself in the mirror?'

Teddy scooped up the files from the table. He turned to Woods and said, 'John, if you wanted to look at yourself in the mirror, you should never have become president.'

122

Cooper slammed his fist hard on the bonnet of the Land Rover. The tyres had been slashed on every wheel. It was impossible to drive.

He was full of panic. Anger. But most of all, fear. 'What the hell are we going to do now?'

Father O'Malley pushed some keys into his hand. 'Take mine, come on, it's parked round the back.'

They raced across to the priest's battered old Subaru, jumping in, with Rosedale driving. Before the doors were even closed, he reversed out, sending mud and water up in sprays as he sped down the road.

Cooper glanced quickly at Rosedale. It was the first time he'd ever seen him look afraid.

The car dipped and juddered and the engine screamed as they drove at full speed. Rosedale kept his foot pressed down on the gas but the road was precarious. Thick red sludge caused by the heavy rain encased the wheels, slowing them down.

'There!' Cooper yelled. He could see the truck's lights in the distance as it made its way down the hill.

Rosedale cranked the car into fifth but the speed of the Subaru in the water-logged roads wasn't a match for the truck which hurtled along. Going faster. Skidding down towards the bottom.

'Look, it's turning off!'

The gap between the truck and the Subaru was getting wider, but it didn't matter because Cooper knew the road the Commer had just turned down led to only one place. The Lemon water plant.

They crawled along now, the tyres sunk, almost submerged in the mud, and Cooper turned to Rosedale. 'We going to go in?'

'That's crazy talk. We'll be totally outnumbered.'

Anger flared up inside Cooper. 'Then tell me exactly what we're going to do. Tell me how the hell we're going to get Maddie.'

Rosedale stared at Cooper. His eyes darting around. 'At this moment, Thomas, I have no idea. We go in, it'll be like a suicide mission. We might as well put a bullet to our heads now. They'll be waiting for us, and even if they're not, that place will be heavily guarded. There's only the three of us, four if we count Father O'Malley.'

'At least let us go in and try.'

'Can you hear yourself? Thomas, you aren't James Bond. We'll all be killed, which won't save Maddison.'

Blind rage struck Cooper. He grabbed Rosedale, yelling in his face. 'So we're just supposed to leave her in there? Is that what you're saying? Is it?'

'I'm not saying that, but what I am saying is if you want to stay alive and see Maddison again, going in *now* isn't the way to do it, and you know that. Separate your emotion, boy.'

'You bastard! You don't give a damn.'

Rosedale pushed Cooper off. 'That's where you're wrong. You have *no* idea how much I care but we have to be sensible about this.'

'And what if we wait, what happens if we leave it too late?

529

Because we've *only got one chance. One shot. One opportunity to get it right.'*

Father O'Malley leant forward, touching Cooper's shoulder gently.

Cooper wanted to push him away. Tell him to get the hell off. But there was something calming about the priest, which in turn impelled him to listen.

'Thomas, you need to listen to Rosedale. What he says makes sense.'

'Maybe it does, Father, but that don't mean it's going to keep Maddie alive.'

'Now listen to me, Thomas, I might have the answer. I may be able to help.'

123

Levi, Rosedale and Cooper stood in the middle of the refugee camp, listening to Father O'Malley speak to a large group of gathered men.

'These three people need our help, and in return we'll hopefully be able to help ourselves. It's an opportunity which I didn't think would come along. I know a lot of you have lived in fear, cast out by Bemba, or you've lost loved ones because of him. Some of you were displaced by the conflicts within the country, but when you tried to come back to your homes, return to your houses, you found you couldn't because of Bemba's reign of terror. A reign of terror which, as you know, was built on lies and the manipulation of your traditional beliefs. I love my country like you do, and we need to reclaim what we can of it. These men will pay you to help them, buy the arms we need, and as a consequence we will be able to take back our community and rid the place of the *real* evil. Nearly all of you have fought in wars, so you know what needs to be done. And whilst as a human being, and a man of God, I know violence is not the answer, sometimes it's the only solution.'

124

The sun rose, bursting out across the Congolese skies. Rosedale and Cooper lay on the top of the hill, looking down on the Lemon water treatment plant. The men who Father O'Malley had gathered from the refugee camp, one hundred and twelve in total, also lay hidden and armed, scattered over various vantage points around the plant.

The priest had confided in Cooper that the men had at one time or another been soldiers. Some child soldiers. Some forced into rebel groups to protect their land from other militia, or from the Congolese army. But the one thing they did have in common – no matter what their history – they all wanted the same thing: to claim back their lives and homes from Bemba.

All the men had readily agreed to join them, and in the early hours of the morning, directed by Father O'Malley, Rosedale, Levi and Cooper had gone to buy arms from one of the many dealers who flourished in the robust illegal arms trade, stealing, buying and selling from and to governments, armies and militia groups. With supply easy, due to a lack of government intervention and porous borders, and demand high due to the ongoing conflicts in sub-Saharan Africa, guns, grenades and rocket launchers brought in from neighboring countries were sold like apple pies in a bakery store.

AK-47s, AT4 shoulder-fired anti-tank missiles, SPG-9 Kopye 73-millimetre recoilless gun, , M72 light anti-armor weapons, along with a number of M249 Squad Automatic Weapons and a M240 Series medium machine gun, all paid for by Father O'Malley's church funds.

*

Cooper passed the binoculars back to Rosedale. 'So we know what the plan is, right?'

'Yeah, I'll take half of the men round to the south and west side, covering the whole of that area. We've got the stronghold, blocking road access to the area further down, and Levi is on his way to take the remainder of the men to cover the north and east side, both on the ground and the higher level. The good thing is, we won't have to worry about encountering any militia because of the fear they've got about the land. So it's just Bemba's men and us. Us against them. You sure you'll be alright?'

Not moving his gaze away from the water plant, Cooper said, 'Yeah, I think it's best this way. I'll take the river which runs along the side of the plant. We've got our watches synced so in twenty minutes exactly, you cause the distraction. Unleash everything we've got. Pound them with the fires from hell. They'll come out of the water plant, and when they do, I go in.'

'Okay, Thomas, if you're sure you'll be alright.'

'Oh I'm sure, alright. Maybe never been surer in my whole life. And I'll be fine, it's them who won't. I'm going to take those sons of bitches out.'

'Okay, you got it… And Lieutenant, good luck. Make sure you bring her back safe.'

125

Cooper charged down the hill towards the water plant, jumping over and crashing through the undergrowth. Over crevices and over streams. He could feel his body drenched with sweat but he pushed on harder and faster. Acutely aware of the time as he ran on. Knowing that Rosedale and Levi were going to detonate the first explosive in less than ten minutes.

He was making his way around to the far side so he could head up the river undetected. And in front of him he could see the river, flowing deep and fast, and he quickly glanced at his watch then dived in, swimming up against the current.

He'd wanted to swim beneath the water, making sure if Bemba's men were about he wouldn't be spotted, but the murky waters, swirling with mud churned up from the storms, made it impossible for him to see. Leaving him no other choice than to be exposed.

In front of him the buildings of the treatment plant came into view. He could feel the pull on his muscles as he fought against the river. But he knew he had to hold some reserve. He couldn't be exhausted. There was no way he was losing Maddie.

Checking his watch again, he saw the time.

Five minutes.

That was all he had. He picked up the pace and swam harder and felt the pressure, which drove his body forwards

Forcing it to the limit. Refusing anything less, knowing there was no way of delaying Rosedale or Levi.

As he neared the water plant, he chose to swim as low in the water as he could. From where he was he could see the main reception, but he figured he needed to head further up. Towards the buildings Charles hadn't shown them. His gut said that was where he needed to be.

Parallel to the back outhouses now, Cooper saw the Commer truck. Parked around one hundred yards away. Then real slowly, he pulled himself out of the river. The weight of it heavy on his clothes.

He lay on his stomach motionless.

Edged forward.

Gradually.

Carefully.

Looked at his watch.

One minute.

Breathed deeply.

Closed his eyes for a moment.

Readying himself.

Thirty seconds.

Calm.

Focused.

Twenty…

Ten…

Five…

And the explosion on the hillside tore through the air. Flames and black smoke filled the skies and flashes of gunfire shot out from the hillside and white light sparked, echoing around.

Cooper saw the door of the building flung open and six of Bemba's men ran out, armed with guns, and jumped into the truck. He rolled to the side behind a mound of sand, watching as the Commer and another car disappeared out of sight.

He waited a minute, checking to see if he had a clear run to the open door, then he ran. Bolting forward. Slipping himself into the darkness of the building.

The stairs led Cooper down into a maze of hallways which weaved along, forking into others. Large steel doors, chained and bolted, lined the walls, and the air was stifling. No windows and barely any light coming from the low voltage bulbs.

Cooper's breathing was hard and strained as he came to the end of the hall, where a large steel door blocked him from going any further. There was no way he was getting through quietly. After a quick glance round he aimed at the lock and fired. Deafening cracks echoed and reverberated round. But it was no good. The door stayed locked.

'Shit… Shit!'

Panic beginning to creep over him, he looked around and then his eyes caught an air vent, up in the ceiling. It was small. Maybe too small. But anything was worth a try.

Aiming up, he fired. Four corners. Four bolts. Four shots on target which sent the grate crashing down to the floor. He threw his gun up and inside. Took several steps back before he ran, leaping up and forcing his legs to pedal in the air and propelling himself forward towards the grate. His fingers brushed the edges of the ceiling, finding the ledge he needed.

But his hands began to slip.

'Come on… Come on.' He heard his voice echo along the dark maze of corridors as he cried out loud. He had to hang on. He tasted blood and he realized he was biting his tongue through his gritted teeth, as he tried to dig deeper and deeper finding the strength to pull himself up…

And slowly his body began to move, up towards the ceiling with his arms shaking and trembling as they took the strain.

It was a tight squeeze and he felt the jagged metal of the bullet-torn vent snag into his skin, tearing away his flesh whilst he pulled his entire body through.

The chamber he found himself in was hot and cramped, and he could only move inch by inch as he lay on his stomach. His whole body compressed. Didn't even have headroom to look up. But just a foot in front of him was another vent. This one was plastic, and quickly he used the butt of his gun to smash down on it, making it crack. Making it easy for him to break it apart. Just enough for him to get through.

The sweat dripped into his eyes as he hung upside down from the ceiling and, checking there was nobody coming, he pushed himself through the hole. A moment later, he was free-falling hard to the floor below. Hitting something solid as his body slammed down to the ground.

He was hurting now. Real bad. But he had to keep going… *had to.*

He felt along the floor for his gun before he slowly pulled himself up. And it took him a second for his eyes to adjust to the dim light… Then they did.

He was in some kind of lab and there were rats in cages, dead ones and live ones, rats that had been sewn together, and rats with electrodes covering their whole bodies as if in a sci-fi film.

Almost silently, he moved through the room, keeping still at every sound. He was on edge, and he didn't want to make any mistakes.

Over in the far corner, he could see five, maybe six rats, absolutely covered in fleas. Being eaten alive by a swarm of black, hungry creatures. The rats were frenzied, banging their bloodied bodies against the glass to escape the onslaught. Gnawing off their own legs in some kind of instinctual hope they'd get away.

Recoiling, he turned away, edging further down into the darkness of the lab, passing more cages full of fleas and rats.

A second later, he froze.

His stomach leapt. What he was looking at made him think he'd just stepped into hell.

All around were glass cages, and within them were people. Naked and strapped to the walls. Arms and legs spread out, looking like their whole faces and bodies were moving, as a dark, seething mass of fleas covered them, writhing and twisting.

Suddenly he understood. These were the hosts. These people. *Not* the rats he'd just seen. These were the people Emmanuel had spoken about. Taken and kidnapped as an instrument for Bemba's sick reign. Millions of fleas. Eating. Feeding. Surviving off the blood of the men and the women and the children.

Quickly he ran along the sealed tight cages, banging on each of them to see if anyone reacted, if anyone was still alive as the fleas continued to squirm and move and writhe. But there was nothing. Nothing at all. No signs. Only the movement from the insects. The adults, the children, all dead.

On the last cage, he banged hard. Angry, wanting revenge for these people.

And then he thought he saw something… There. A movement. Tiny at first but he could see the person was trying to raise their head. He looked again. Then with sinking, desperate horror, he saw it was Maddie.

She looked up at him, barely able to open her swollen, bitten eyes, and he cried out.

'Maddie…! Maddie…! Maddie!'

The movement of her head let him know she could hear him.

Then tapping the glass with the barrel of his gun, he began to examine it. It was toughened and he knew his bullet would shatter it, but he also knew there was a chance of the pieces ricocheting and flying into Maddie.

Quickly, he pressed the muzzle of his gun firmly against the corner of the main pane.

Turned his head.

Pulled the trigger.

And the glass became instantly opaque, as millions of tiny cracks shattered through the laminate. Whereupon Cooper raised the sole of his boot and kicked it through, stepping into the cage. A pain rushed through his legs as tiny fragments of glass embedded into his flesh.

Breathing out he rushed towards Maddie through the black cloud of fleas swarming.

'Maddie!' he called, regretting it immediately as he began to cough and choke and splutter and gag on the black cloud of insects as they filled up his nose and throat, making it difficult to breathe.

But without the slightest hesitation, he pulled at the straps Maddie was tied up with. Her body swollen and red. Dotted with thousands of pits of blood, marked raised bumps and blisters covering her. She was barely conscious.

With blood dripping down his leg, Cooper threw Maddie over his shoulder.

Then he began to run.

He ran back into the lab, towards a fire door he'd seen.

Knocking it open with his shoulder, he staggered to the side, trying to hold onto the walls whilst the blood from his leg continued to pour.

He could hear shots in the background, though he couldn't decipher if they were still coming from the hillside, or if they were getting nearer. But he had to get out. And fast.

The door he went through took him out into a hallway which took him back round into a stairwell. About to head up them, a shadow began to creep across the ceiling... Someone was coming.

Backing away into the shadows, Cooper stayed motionless then squatted down to set Maddie onto the floor, brushing away the last of the fleas that still clung to her. A thunder of boots followed as several of Bemba's men charged into the building and Cooper could see there were too many to take on by himself.

He crept further backwards, counting the men as they came. Seven... Eight... Nine. Running down with purpose. And the only thing he could do was hide... And wait.

Pulling Maddie into the darkness with him, Cooper's back banged into something hard. Turning round he expected to see a wall, but there, piled high to the ceiling were boxes marked: *DuPont Co. Explosive Nitrostarch.*

In the darkness Cooper waited for the sound of running feet to disappear, as the last of Bemba's men cleared the stairwell, the echoes of their urgent shouts disappearing down the hall.

Knowing this was his chance, he scooped up Maddie over his left shoulder, the pain from his legs surging through his body as he stooped down to grasp a case of explosives. Then with a deep driving force of breath, he ran up the stairs and out through the open doorway.

He stopped. Took a quick glance round. Placed the explosives by the door. Then charged across the grounds, sweating and desperate and hurrying and running to get to the relative safety of the trees, as quickly – and gently – as he could.

Cooper set an unconscious Maddie on the ground, covering her nakedness quickly with his jacket.

He turned. Faced the building and settled himself, forced his breathing to slow and steadied his grip on his gun, aimed at the explosives and waited for Bemba's men to reappear. And when they did, it'd be the final goodbye.

As the men came into sight, with the lightest of pressure and the most precise of aims, he pulled the trigger. Hitting and igniting the Nitrostarch, sending the whole building up into a spectacular fireball.

From the far side, Cooper saw Rosedale and Levi charging over to help.

He left Maddie on the ground. Something in the corner by the trees had caught his eye. Not for the first time that day, he began to run.

At the end of the low fence, he rounded the corner and stopped. And there, crawling on the ground, struggling, squirming and covered in the mud, was the pathetic figure of Papa Bemba.

Cooper walked up to him slowly. His desert boots stopping near Bemba's head, and he stood saying nothing as he saw Bemba sense that someone was there.

Bemba's hands reached out and touched his boots. Making their way up his shins, as he tried to work out who it was.

'Est-ce que vous Lumumba? Aidez moi. Aidez moi.'

Cooper crouched down, sticking his gun against Bemba's temple. 'No, it's not Lumumba. He's dead. But why ask my name? Don't you know? After all I thought you saw better than the ones that can see. But then, you don't need to worry about that no more, and the folk round here won't need to worry about you. And you know why? Because they're going to get peace, life without fear. But to get that for them, Bemba, I need one thing. You… That's right, you're going to be my exchange.'

'No, *please*…non, se il vous plaît ne pas.'

'Problem is if I let you go, we both know that you'll get away scot-free. You'll act with impunity as you always have.'

'Please, listen….'

'Save your words, Bemba… Simon. Hell, it doesn't matter now because you should've known… Never take on a crazy guy who's got nothing left to lose. This one's for Emmanuel.'

And without hesitation, Thomas J. Cooper pulled the trigger.

126

Rosedale and Cooper stood the next day with Father O'Malley, beside the repaired Land Rover. In the back, with his hands tied tightly behind him, was Charles Templin-Wright.

Levi had driven Maddie across the border to Rwanda straight after the explosion at the water plant, to get her checked over in hospital before they caught their flights back home.

The priest smiled. 'Thank you, gentlemen. It'll be a shame to see you go, but what you did will make a difference for generations to come.'

Rosedale tipped his hat. 'I'm glad we could help, and with Charles blabbing like a reporter on CNN, hopefully we'll be able to bring Donald Parker down. We're going to take Charles across the border, leave him at the US embassy. We can't really do anything more with him. I'll make a few calls to people I know. They're bound to detain him there, and hopefully send him straight back to the USA.'

Father O'Malley nodded. 'I hope so, and make sure you let me know. It's about time the people who lived in their ivory towers were brought to justice. There's been a lot of damage done here, by them, but I'm sure we'll heal. It'll take time but we'll get there. This community and this country is strong. It may have been damaged and wounded, but it's not broken. It's a shame Emmanuel didn't live to see it, but he's there, I'm sure of it, looking over us and blessing us all with his goodness.'

Rosedale got into the car, but as Cooper went to join him, Father O'Malley held his arm gently.

'Thomas, I wanted to say, your spirit has touched me. I'll never forget you. And whatever it is that troubles you. Whatever it is that keeps you awake at night, just know you're a good man. And one day whatever you're searching for, I believe in my heart you'll find it, and at last have the peace you deserve. Take care, Thomas... Take care.'

127

'This is so kind of you, Rosedale. But you know, I could've got to the airport myself. You didn't have to go to this trouble.'

Rosedale carried Maddie's bags to his car, where Cora was sitting patiently on the back seat talking to Mr. Crawley the Second. 'Well that just wouldn't feel right, Miss Maddison. Not after everything that's happened. And I know Thomas wanted to come and see you off. He told me to send his apologies but I don't think they'd take kindly to him missing another court-ordered session. So I'm here at your service. I want to make sure you get on that plane without any trouble.'

'Rosedale, I'm going to the Prescott Municipal Airport, I'm not sure much can happen.'

'Just like to be on the safe side. And whilst we're speaking our minds I just want to say, I'm not real happy about you checking yourself out of hospital.'

'I'm fine. I'm lucky. I lost a lot of blood, but I didn't contract anything, so really all I was going to do in the hospital was lie there and rest. So I figured I might as well lie on a beach and rest. It's more my head I need to get together, rather than my body. The bites will heal, but what happened over there is tougher to deal with. But I'll be okay.'

You can be one stubborn woman, Maddison, you know that? Have you got all your medication by the way? The antibiotics?'

'Yes and yes and yes. Now stop worrying.'

'Maddison?'

'Yes?'

Rosedale kicked at the gravel and looked up at the sky and pushed his cowboy hat down over his eyes. 'Maddison.'

'Yes?'

'Well… are you and Thomas still… are you…?'

'What?'

'I don't know.'

'Together?'

'Yeah…'

'Rosedale, I love Tom, but there is no him and me being together. He's got a lot of things to sort out. He's in love with Ellie and I'm not going to try to compete with a ghost any more, for my sake and for his. But mainly for Cora's.'

There was a pause, then Rosedale stopped to take his hat off. Pressing it against his chest he said, 'Can I ask you something else, then?'

'Yeah.'

'Well… '

Maddie looked at him curiously. 'Well what?'

'Miss Maddison, I was just wondering… when you come back from holiday… I was just wondering… well I was wondering, if you would do me the honour of letting me take you out to dinner.'

Maddie burst out into laughter. Looked at Rosedale and laughed harder.

'Rosedale, that's the craziest thing I've heard. You and me, going out to dinner?'

Rosedale bowed his head. 'Forget it. The DRC must've affected me more than I thought. You're right, it is crazy.'

'It is. It's so crazy. But you know something, Rosedale? After the past few weeks, I'm starting to like your kind of

546

crazy. I'm starting to like it a lot. So hell, why not. The answer is, yes. Yes, Mr. Austin Rosedale Young, I'd love to go out to dinner with you when I get back.'

128

Cooper sat with Rosedale underneath the large timber porch of his ranch, with their feet up on the carved wooden railings, sitting in identical rocking chairs looking out across the full bloom of the prairies. The smell of Rosedale's cigar smoke heavy in the air.

Cooper said, 'What's that on your head?'

'My hat?'

'That's a hat? It looks more like a tea cozy.'

'What the hell's a tea cozy?'

'It's what you've got on your head.'

'Admit it, you're just jealous of how fine it is, and of the fact that Miss Maddison knitted it for me and she didn't knit you one. And you can't stand that.'

Cooper looked at him incredulously. 'You kidding? Jealous of you? Listen, Maddie probably dislikes you more than she does me. And that's saying something, Rosedale.'

Rosedale's Texan accent was lilted with relaxation. 'Okay, Thomas, whatever you say…'

'What's that supposed to mean?'

'Nothing.'

Rosedale pulled hard on his cigar, letting the smoke circuit his lungs before blowing it out. Eventually he said, 'You fancy going fishing?'

'When?'

'Sometime.'

'Okay, sometime it is... Does that mean we're... *friends*?'

'Hell, no.' Rosedale paused, rocking a few times on the chair, then spoke thoughtfully. 'Would you ever go back to the DRC, Thomas?'

'I might. I know it sounds crazy, and the place had a lot of problems and pain, but there was something about it which made me love it. Perhaps it was the country itself, wild and unruly. Or maybe it was the spirit of the people. I dunno. All I know is it felt like a place which accepted me.'

'You ever going to tell me about what happened that night you saw Ellie?'

Cooper began to bristle. Then stopped himself. 'Maybe one day.'

'And what about you? Are you going to go and get yourself some help?'

Cooper paused. 'I want to say yes, but the truth is I don't know. I doubt it. Maybe I should? It feels so complicated... Maybe I'm just not ready.'

He fell silent, watching a white-tailed rabbit in the distance. He sighed but felt unusually at ease, the nearest he'd got to peace in a long time.

'Granger told me you were going to be staying around.'

'I might as well. Who else is going to look after you, Thomas?'

Cooper nodded, surprised how okay he was with Rosedale continuing to work for Onyx.

'Fair enough. Good idea.'

Rosedale laughed, flicking the ash from his cigar. 'So you're finally admitting that you need me to babysit you.'

'I never said that, I said *fair enough*, which isn't the same thing at all. Which reminds me, when I spoke to Bill Travis,

I asked him about the moose in the reception of the CIA headquarters.'

'And?'

'And there isn't one there. Not that I thought there was.'

Rosedale, yawned, pushing back on the cream rocking chair. 'What did he exactly say?'

'Well when I asked him about it, his reply was *You must be friends with Rosedale*.'

'You see what you've done? You've missed the point, Thomas, but that doesn't surprise me. You've been missing the point as long as I've known you… What I want to know is, did Bill Travis *actually* tell you there wasn't a moose?'

Cooper shook his head and smirked. 'I guess not.'

'You see, Thomas, that's why it's people like *me*, and not people like *you*, they have working in the CIA… Can I ask you something?'

'Go on.'

'Would you mind if Maddie stepped out with another man?'

'Where did that come from and what the hell is *stepped out*?'

'You know, went on the odd date. Would you mind?'

Cooper sat up straight. The thought had never occurred to him. 'It's not as if I don't love her, or I don't want to be with her, it's just I can't be who I need to be right now. But Maddie deserves every chance of happiness, and if someone else can make her happy, who am I to stop it…? But to answer your question – and call me old fashioned – I'd kill him. I'd kill any man that went near her.'

129

'**Y**ou staying about? I'm going downstairs to watch Dad's speech.'

Jackson spoke to Cooper as he stood in one of the hallways of the Executive Residence.

'Too damn right. Listen, you don't get away with beating me at Monopoly that easily. You're eleven to eight up, but I put it down to my mind being somewhere else.'

'Coop, you're tripping, man. I'm eleven up on this round alone. How many rounds have we played over the years? You've never managed to come better than third, and you only came third that time because Dad was attending the G8 summit.'

Cooper shook his head. 'No, that's not right. It was more than once. There was that other time last year. Remember?'

Jackson grinned. 'You're not serious? You have to be kidding me. You came third that time because Beau had an angina attack. *Literally*. When he was moving his piece around the board.'

'He rolled five. He would've landed on my property.'

'Well yeah, he would've done if he hadn't been rushed to hospital.'

'Do you know how much he would've had to pay? I had four houses on it. If you ask me, Beau rolled the five, saw the properties, and then decided to fake it. Don't you think it's funny how he had an angina attack seconds before he landed on my property?'

Jackson roared with laughter. It was so good to see.

'You need to step up those tactics of yours, Coop. You got it all wrong. Buying the expensive dark blue properties, Park Place and the Boardwalk is not the way to go. Buy the stations and then aim for the reds and yellows. They're the ones you gotta hit. Kentucky Avenue, Ventnor Avenue, those are the good ones. The hotels are cheap and the building costs are low.'

'Well let's bring it on. After you've come back from watching John's speech, let's see if you can put your money where your mouth is.'

Jackson went to walk away, but he stopped and turned to look at Cooper. 'Coop, I want to say thank you.'

'Thank you for what?'

'For sticking around. For the things you said at the hospital about getting some help. It means everything.'

130

'Coop, can I have a word with you?'

John Woods signalled to Teddy Adleman, letting him know he'd be with him in a minute.

'Sure. I thought you were about to do your speech.'

'I am, so I've only got a couple of minutes... Let's talk in here.'

John opened the door, leading him into the private West Sitting Hall.

'What's up, John?'

Woods sighed, looking not only apprehensive but also like he wasn't quite sure where to start.

'I know we spoke on the phone briefly, but I wanted to say it to you properly. I'm sorry. For the way I behaved. For the way I treated you. I lost sight of the truth. And I was wrong. I'm proud of you, Coop. Proud to be your... well, you know what I mean. I wish I had the integrity you have. Doesn't seem to matter what life throws at you. You just carry on and do what's right, rather than what's best for you. You'll be pleased to know the FBI are investigating the whole of Nadbury Electronics. They took Donald Parker into custody this morning. And as you know they've already got Charles Templin-Wright, who's apparently talking a lot. Think he's looking to get a deal on his sentence. But there's no doubt we'll get something to stick. And they'll both end up going away for a very long time. The other thing I'm sure you'll be pleased about is Dr. Foster. They're reopening the case. Look to see if it *was* a homicide. Hopefully, this Templin-Wright will have something to say on that as well. Anyhow, like I say. I'm proud of you. Real proud…'

Woods paused. Tried to say something, then stopped.

Cooper half-joked, picking up on the president's hesitation. 'Now *this* troubles me. You, stuck for words… What is it?'

Woods said, 'Did you ever tell anyone, *anyone* about the accident?'

It hit Cooper harder than any upper cut from Rosedale. 'What?'

'The accident. Did you ever tell anyone it was Jackson who sailed the boat that day?'

Cooper felt the energy beginning to drain out of him. 'Jesus, John, of all the things I thought you were going to say, this wasn't one of them.'

'I'm sorry, but I have to know.'

'Of course not, I'm surprised you even have to ask.'

'I had to ask because I got a letter. Well Beau got a letter, but it was addressed to me.'

Cooper instinctively pushed his hand against the large, white panelled door, making sure it was properly closed. 'And?'

'It basically said, they know it was Jackson who was sailing the boat that day.'

'That's impossible.'

Woods nodded in agreement. 'Well that's what I thought until I read the letters.'

'Letters?'

'Yeah, there's been two.'

Frustration rushed through Cooper. 'Why the hell didn't you tell me before?'

'Truthfully, I didn't want to admit it to myself. When the first one came, about three months ago, I just shredded it, and pushed any thoughts about it away. Then when Beau got the second one, last week, well, I can't ignore it anymore... As much as I'd like to.'

Cooper had to take a second to take it in. Then he said, 'What exactly does it say?'

Woods went into the inside pocket of his navy suit jacket, bringing out a typed letter. 'I've got it here, I only kept it to show you... it says...'

A knock on the door interrupted Woods. It was Naomi Tyler.

'Mr. President, they're waiting for you.'

The door handle turned but Cooper held the door shut, causing anxiety from Naomi on the other side.

'Mr. President? Mr. President are you alright, sir?'

Woods snapped. 'Yes, I'm fine, Naomi, Jesus, I just need a minute.'

There was a pause.

'Ok, if you're sure, sir. But we haven't much time.'

'I know, Naomi! I know! I'll be out in a minute...Thank you.'

Woods drew his attention back to Cooper.

'Sorry about that, Tom... anyway, let me read it... *'I understand that you're a busy man, so perhaps you didn't see my previous letter, but I feel I have no other choice than to write to you again. After all these years of wrestling with my conscience, and watching you I'm compelled to inform you that I know it was your son, Jackson Woods, who was in charge of the vessel that afternoon, contrary to the statement he made. I also feel it is your duty to make the appropriate steps to address this matter, and for there to be due process. If you do not act on this, you leave me no other option but to make this information public myself…* And it's signed, *Your supporter.'*

Cooper was shocked. 'Your supporter? Let me see it.'

Taking the letter, Cooper re-read it, while Woods contrived. 'I don't know what to do, Tom. I don't want this hanging over my head, and I don't want to lie. Maybe I should…'

Cooper scrunched up the letter angrily, putting it in his own pocket.

'Maybe you should what? Remember, you don't know anything. That conversation we had back on the boat? It never happened.'

'But…'

'*It never happened.* Okay? John, are you listening to me? As far as *you're* concerned I was sailing that day, and nobody is going to tell me any different.'

'Should we tell Jackson?'

'There isn't anything to tell. Whoever wrote those letters, they're just playing mind games. Didn't you tell me how opposing parties would try *anything* to start smear campaigns, or try to shake their opponent?'

'Yeah.'

'Well that's all this is. And by the looks of things it seems to be working. Look, every time there are talks about gun reforms… well, there are people out there who don't like it. They get upset. They do everything from threats to stuff like this. What else have you got in your past to bring up? There isn't anything to sling at you, John. So the only thing they have is the accident. They're just making a wild guess. Trying to see if there's anything there. The letter doesn't go into any details, no specifics, nothing. And you know why? Because they don't know anything. All they're doing is guessing. They're chancing it.'

'What if they're not? What if they do know something?'

Cooper leaned further into Woods, holding his gaze intently. 'John. There isn't anything to know. *I was sailing the yacht.*'

President Woods let out a long sigh. 'Okay… okay… You're not worried?'

'Not even a little bit. Let's see if another one comes. I doubt it will though; when they don't have a bite, there's nothing to reel in. Best thing you can do is forget about it.'

'Okay, thanks, Tom. I appreciate that… Listen, I gotta go. You hanging around up here to watch the speech on TV with Beau?'

'Absolutely.'

'Great, then we can see who really is the grand master of Monopoly. And Beau says he's going to cook, so we can make an evening of it.'

Cooper smiled, giving him a wink. 'I'd like that.'

He stepped away from the door, letting Woods open it. 'Oh, and John, this conversation never happened either.'

Once the door had shut, Cooper pulled out the letter from his pocket. He read it again, concern creeping all over him.

The ring from his cell made him jump, something he kept doing lately. Stuffing the letter back in his pocket, he popped a pill in his mouth from the blister strip he'd pulled out of his jacket. He answered, 'Cooper.'

131

Beau, walking into the West Sitting Hall carrying two cups of coffee, frowned at Cooper, gesturing towards the television.

He said, 'Turn it on, it's already started.' Then slammed down the drinks on the highly polished walnut table, eager to listen to John's speech, which was being broadcast live.

Cooper duly turned it on.

'...when businesses and companies fail in their social duty and are driven on by greed. When lies are in place of honesty, when deceit is above principle, we the American people...'

'Coop, where you going? I made you your drink.'

Beau broke away from the TV to look at Cooper as he picked up his wallet.

'Listen Beau, there's a job that's come up in Borno State, Nigeria. A few miles outside Maiduguri. I need to go and speak to Granger.'

'What the hell, Coop? That's the mainstay of the Boko Haram, are you looking for a death sentence?'

'No.'

Beau ground his teeth. Wiped his mouth, fury and hurt fusing his words. 'You listen to me, okay? You're not right. You need to go and get help. This is crazy, and I'll not let you go and do this.'

'You stopped being my captain a long time ago, Beau, so back off.'

He turned to go but Beau, consumed with rage, pulled him back.

'You promised Jackson. Remember? You told him you were going to stay about and get yourself clean. And now look at you, you're sneaking off without even giving him a goodbye. This is just so typical of you.'

Cooper stared at Beau. 'Is it, Beau?'

'You let everyone down. All the goddamn time. I've lost count the number of times you've done this. It's a good job Jackson doesn't know you're his brother. He's had a lucky escape.'

Moving his face nearer to Beau, Cooper stared at him, hissing a whisper. 'That's a low blow, and you know it.'

Beau, flushed red, grabbed hold of Cooper. 'It's the truth. You need to get your head out of your ass and see the day-light... What about John, hey? He's worried about you, and then there's all that stuff with the letter. You think he needs this right now? You running off? If it hasn't escaped your notice he's got a country to run.'

'Tell me something I don't know.'

'You're pathetic, Cooper. It's *here* you're needed. Here. Jackson needs you.'

Cooper shook off Beau's grip. 'I love Jackson, and I've never forgotten my responsibilities. Ever. I will always look out for him. Not because you say so, but because I want to.'

Beau pushed Cooper hard against the wall. 'What about Maddie? Cora?'

'Get the hell off me!'

'Not until you listen, and hear some sense.'

'Beau, get off me. Don't make me have to put my hands on you.'

'If it makes you feel better to hit me, then go ahead. Be my guest.'

Cooper shoved Beau hard away, causing him to stumble backwards towards the large velvet wingback chair. He reached out his hand to grab him, stopping Beau from falling, pulling him up, then using his grip to drag him close. Inches away.

'I wouldn't waste my time putting my hands on you.'

Beau's eyes darted around Cooper's face. 'I've never asked you anything before, but now I am. Don't do this. *Please*.'

And Cooper closed his eyes. Breathing. Stopping the pain from welling up. 'I once said exactly that to you. Seven years ago, to be precise. I asked you to help me. Begged you to and you know what you did, Beau? You know what you did? You walked away. You turned your back and you walked away. And now that's what I'm going to do now. I'm going to walk away through that door. But I'll level with you. I wasn't going to Africa. I was never going to go. Until now, that is. You just presumed… Granger's here in town, I was just going to meet him and tell him to find somebody else. Then you know what I was going to do? I was going to come straight back here, as I'd said I would. But hey thanks, Beau. Thanks for your vote of confidence. It's nice to know what you think of me.'

'Now listen, Coop—'

'And thanks for making it so easy to change my mind… And don't worry, I'll send you a postcard.'

132

Two hours later, Woods and Beau sat on the Truman Balcony overlooking the South Lawn.

'You tell him?'

Woods looked at Beau. 'Did I tell him about the letter? Yeah.'

'Not about the letter. About the report.'

Woods leant back on the white wicker chair. Adjusted the cushion behind his back. 'Why would I do that? I thought we decided it was best not to say anything.'

Beau nodded his head. 'I know. But I can't help thinking…'

'What? Don't go soft on me, Beau. We're doing the right thing. You need to forget about it. The only reason we know ourselves is because I got Teddy to get the accident reports, when I knew Granger was about to apply for Ellie's death certificate. I just didn't know what was in there. I was only making sure nothing could be dug up or said about Jackson in the documents when the authorities read them. Like I say, forget about it.'

'Does Granger know what was in there?'

Woods stretched his arms in front of him. 'No, I made sure that part of the document was pulled.'

'Jesus, John.'

Woods snapped. 'Beau, give me a break. It's an old report. It doesn't change a thing.'

'Apart from confirming what Tom's been saying all along.'

'Like I say, it doesn't make a difference. The accident happened. Period. The only thing different is that the helicopter pilot contradicted the original officer's statement. It means nothing.'

'No, John. It means everything. It means Tom was right all along. There were *three* skiffs. Not two. *Three*, John.'

Woods swivelled round in his chair to stare at Beau face on. 'How many more times? What difference does it make how many there were? Three, four, five, who cares?'

'Cooper cares, John. He thinks he's going crazy. It's torturing him.'

'You're wrong. What's driving him crazy is all that crap he takes.'

'You don't believe that,' said Beau. 'These past seven years he's been desperate for someone to believe him. Maybe it'd help him to find some kind of peace.'

'Help him? It would make him worse. You've seen what he's been like since the death certificate was granted. It's shaken him. Can you imagine what this would do to him? It'd send him over the edge, because he'd think he was right. And if he thinks he's right about the number of damn boats, he's going to think he's right about everything.'

'You sure?'

'Oh come on, Beau. Don't even go there with me. It was tragic, but Ellie died that day. And that's all there is to it. He doesn't need to know. It's the best thing for him.'

'What happened to the truth, John?'

'The truth? Sometimes the truth isn't all it's cut out to be.'

133

'Ladies and gentlemen, please fasten your seatbelts. We will soon be arriving in Lagos.'

Acknowledgements

I loved writing this book, it was so much fun and I met so many wonderful people during the writing of it but a big thanks especially must go to Dr. Mark Faulkner and Dr. Zoe Marriage from SOAS, University of London who gave up their free time to answer a thousand questions on the DRC. A shout out to Dr. Dale Mineshima who somehow made American realignment and the Presidential doctrines a huge amount of fun. A special thanks to the US veterans who sacrificed so much of their lives and their mental well being for their country. A huge thanks to everyone at the Darley Anderson agency and of course a massive thank you to Louise Page, who is just awesome. Thanks also goes to Sally Williamson, my editor and Lisa Milton, who encouraged me to put the kick ass into Maddie. And never ending love to my family, friends, horses and dogs. But most importantly of all to the thousands upon thousands of forgotten street children accused of witchcraft in the DRC who inspired this story – you are forever in my heart.

ONE PLACE. MANY STORIES

Bold, innovative and
empowering publishing.

FOLLOW US ON:

@HQStories